The Last
Changeling

F.R.MAHER

Published by The Art Clinic, Liverpool

Copyright © 2013 F.R.Maher

F.R.Maher has asserted her moral rights.

Extract from 'The Stolen Child' by W.B.Yeats

Extract from 'La Belle Dame Sans Merci' By John Keats

Extract from 'The Fairies' By William Allingham

First Edition

ISBN: 095623027X
ISBN-13: 978-0956230270

FOR PETER

ACKNOWLEDGMENTS

My thanks to Michelle Richards from The Art Clinic for her generous help in getting The Last Changeling to publication. Thanks also to Pauline Magee for all her hard work. For cheering me on when the going got tough, my special thanks go to Lynn Jarvis, who was the first person to meet D. I must acknowledge Liz D'Aste for her kind support and also Claire Milne for listening to the early drafts. Thank you, Stuart Sheldon, for your patience and kind help with everything 'webby.' Thanks also to Christian von Doneck for being an extra pair of eyes on the edit.
I am indebted to Greg Mallon for technical advice regarding the current and correct terminology regarding the London Underground and to Aled Jones and Andrea Perry-Jones for kindly sharing their knowledge of silver smithing.
Finally, I give my wholehearted thanks to Peter Stubbs for his unstinting encouragement.

'If you want your children to be intelligent, read them fairy tales. If you want them to be more intelligent read them *more* fairy tales.' ALBERT EINSTEIN

1

Just before midnight on a chilly north London street, a man was out walking. Strictly speaking D wasn't conventionally dressed for it.

His long dark coat billowed out behind him like a don's gown barely hiding his pyjamas, whilst his untied boots gaped revealing sockless feet.

He clutched a large envelope. He'd expended more time and emotion than he'd intended working on this wretched thing and he was, unusually for him, in a lather to get it posted.

He didn't let much get to him, but having to beg for what should rightfully be his *by royal decree*, always rankled. Habit, not necessity, made him pause to check his surroundings. He used the opportunity to tie his boots but he didn't look down. Through a wild corkscrew straggle of black hair he scanned the street, his mismatched green brown eyes taking in familiar and unfamiliar number plates, perfect snap shots of memory he could check through later.

Stooping there gangling and badly-built, his enormous hands pulling at his laces, he may have passed as an eccentric. Such a man in his pyjamas on a London street at what was still a fairly early hour might have attracted at least *some* interest, but this man did not. No one seemed to notice him.

Despite looking like he'd been painted by Edvard Munch on a sad day, he was good at *not* being noticed. In many ways it was what he did best.

As D set off again he glanced down at the large manilla envelope resting in his hands. Thick with hope it carried the many pages of justification he'd long laboured over and every last infuriating official hoop he'd unwillingly jumped through.

No Minister, even if they knew about D's secret

department, would ever willingly lay claim to D9. To D's everlasting chagrin not only did this official state of non-being fail to shield him from funding cuts, it made his particular line of work - and the money needed to do it - spectacularly difficult to justify.

His colleagues had often remarked that habitually using foolscap in an A4 world was indicative of his natural contrariness and that he only really did it to bait the bean counters. But if the money men had ever judged D by his stationery, it's a wonder they didn't ask if this odd-looking man wouldn't have felt more comfortable using a quill and sealing wax.

As he carried the envelope up the dark residential street, his peculiar loping stride became more exaggerated. Now as if by accident, his face was down or turned away from each hidden camera he passed.

D never used internal mail. He couldn't. D9 may have had a motto 'Video et Taceo,' *'I see and say nothing,'* but it existed without formal offices, secretaries, or indeed any of the common paraphernalia of government. Its scattered agents operated from private dwellings and left no electronic evidence - and scant paper trails - for the curious to follow. This manner of operating in a quasi-virtual world had always

7

made any accounting exquisitely more difficult, yet it had always been seen as a small price to pay for the benefits of extreme secrecy. Until now.

Long ago, D had decided never to trust texts or emails and although he was not completely off grid, use of either was rare, a last resort rather than a first. The majority of D9's written communication travelled back and forth via encoded notes in ever-changing drop boxes. The old-fashioned nature of written words pleased him on many levels. One of which was that it carried enough forensic information to reassure him of its genuine provenance.

As far as the cameras were concerned, D continued on up the street without breaking step. They failed to detect that he had posted his plea for further funding through a discreet letter box. D's stride returned to normal, but his extreme irritation with feckless government penny-pinching remained.

The sight of the two girls crashed his thoughts.

They sat on the club steps gasping down bottles of water. Once elaborate hairstyles had collapsed into wet, yellow-grey rats-tails and their faces showed pale under tangerine streaks of fake tan. Hunched in a tangle of skinny legs and elbows, their skimpy dresses greasy with sweat, they looked like they'd just run a marathon in their vertiginous heels. Even as D hurried across the road towards them, one started throwing up.

He looked up at the night sky and down at his watch and cursed. It was just gone midnight, and the moon was full.

Dipping down the steps, he entered the club unchallenged by the strangely passive, meaty guys in black. He pushed past hot bodies, analysing, targeting. Then the music morphed into something edgier. Figures disentangled from darkened booths and hurtled past him towards the dance floor in a frenzy of refreshed dance addiction. A plump bride-to-be adjusted her veil. Tugging her pelmet skirt down and her revealing neckline up, she tottered after her rabidly jerking hens.

D glanced up as he skirted the sound desk. A few inches above him the DJ moved as if spellbound. His unfocussed eyes moved sightlessly across his decks as his beefy, tattooed fingers twitched restlessly, coaxing even more entrancing sounds from his system to reel in the unwary. Fog-machines cloaked the dancers in swathes of unearthly green and magenta mist and the stabbing club lights flash-lit them in frozen attitudes of foot-stamping, arm-waving, wildest ecstasy.

A movement, something almost insect-like caught the corner of his eye. He knew that even he would find it difficult to see her reality face on. Glancing sideways, he took quick glimpses of his target.

The image she presented was one of breathtakingly fragile beauty, gamine and gorgeous. They always are D thought bitterly. Tall and slender as a young leaf, she had wound a slim arm around the neck of a helplessly fascinated young man. His hopeful, lost face shone in her reflected light. She turned away from him laughing, whilst her green-spangled dress trembled and threw arcs of fairy glamour. Tossing her long, artfully-tangled, blonde hair she entrapped her victim and drew him behind her in her wake. All the while the enchanted DJ ramped up the intoxicating music and the dance became wilder and more dangerous. D had to stop it before the inevitable happened.

The clubbers would be danced to death.

As in previous cases, a convenient fire would provide a literal smokescreen for the loss of life and the newspapers would castigate the club for an 'avoidable tragedy,' blaming the management for flaunting Health and Safety rules. Even without looking, he knew all the doors to the fire escapes would be locked by now.

Alarmingly, he felt his body begin to twitch in time to the sweating beat. Even he was not immune to the Dance of Death. He turned away from the bank of speakers, only to find himself entangled in a skein of frenzied dancers. In the pulsing half light, a wiry girl with red, witchy hair and melted makeup clutched at his arm dragging him towards the dance floor. He unclasped her hands from his coat and attempted to push her away. As soon as he unlocked each grasping finger, she simply changed hold, relocating her fierce grip on him.

From the corner of his eye, D could see the crowd part in a slow wave as the Wicked Fairy made her way towards him. He couldn't let her see him.

He deftly dropped, twisted and instead of pulling away, *pushed* violently towards the stage. It caught Velcro-girl off balance. She crashed backwards over a stool, and lay twitching to the beat like a broken robot.

In a flurry of black D spun on his heels and headed in the opposite direction. He spotted his goal - a matte-purple door marked *Staff Only*.

Although the thickest melee of the swirling dancers

lay between him and his goal, crowd-surfing wasn't an option. This mob didn't have the sense left to catch him. Unthinkingly they'd let him fall and blindly trample him to death. The addictive beat was burrowing deep into their brains, throbbing in their hearts, the driving bass thrumming through their ribs. Out of control, they were being helplessly compelled, propelled, impelled to *keep moving*.

He made his way slowly through the sweat-slick living tide, continually jostled and occasionally struck by flailing limbs. Shoving and pushing, he repelled over-heated bodies away from him spinning them into other clubbers, using their momentum to create fleeting gaps he could push forwards into. His tactic broke down when the mass became super-concentrated. In a heartbeat he was trapped between the wall and the press of bodies. A heavy arm crashed into his face and his nose gave a small but distinct pop. Involuntary tears sprang to his eyes and silvery stars wormed across his vision. Temporarily sightless, he crouched, dipping low towards the kicking, stamping feet. His probing fingers exploited tiny fragments of purchase offered by the rough wall and he painfully inched himself along, handhold over handhold, towards the door.

The horrifically irresistible music warped again. Without warning, his fingers responded to the beat and he lost his grip. Helpless, he was instantly sucked into the heart of the frenzied stampede. Somehow he caught his breath and his vision cleared. Immediately in front of him a heavy body collided with another and they both slammed into him, spinning him out of the maelstrom and smashing him into the door. Unable to recover his balance, he rebounded against a mass of bodies. The jostling press held him upright for a second whilst his feet scrambled for purchase, but he slipped and slid clumsily down between them.

The instant he hit the floor dancers began tripping over him. He couldn't even start to get to his feet. Multiple bodies were piling up on top of him. He filled his lungs, sucking in as much air as he could, but another dull impact knocked the breath from his body and then there was no space left for his ribs to expand into.

Fingers of strobing club-lights filtered down through a gap between tangled limbs. Quiet now, D gazed abstractedly up at them. The thumping music became blanketed and less distinct whilst inner sounds grew, until his circulation hissed in his ears like white noise. Then the dancing lights moved further away. Gathering speed, he retreated down the otherworldly rabbit-hole of tunnel-vision. The rushing hiss in his ears became the watery roar of a racing torrent as he was sucked down and swept along in subterranean caverns of blue. Currents dragged him further down as deeper vortices opened up to claim him. As he fell, D's brain calmly pointed out that he was dying, drowning under the crush and there was absolutely nothing he could do about it. Another part of his brain responded that it was a fascinating process and fervently hoped it would survive long enough to observe the event properly.

His lower brain responded by booting his fading senses back into action. It screamed at him to growl and roar and heave and struggle at the intense press of people lying on top of him. Beneath the human avalanche he felt rather than heard a series of uneven, popping cracks building into a rapid crescendo. Coolly observational once more, he queried the source. Were his ribs breaking? Surely they would be by now? With a cracking bang barely heard above the music, the door-frame finally gave way under the intense pressure. Ripped from its hinges the door crashed down like a felled tree into the corridor beyond.

Clubbers toppled and fell bewildered and unwilling into the newly created space. D gasped for air, rolled to one side and curled up, dodging the ejectees' feet as they fought like drowning rats to get back to the crushing music of the Death Dance.

Unseen, he crawled away from the felled door's enormous coffin-lid shape. He couldn't have stood up if he'd wanted to. He urgently needed to sit down and recover, but there wasn't time. He finally understood how much damage he'd sustained when it took him a full eight minutes to pick the primitive lock on the cellar door. It was a simple task that his practised fingers could normally accomplish in under a minute. He was acutely aware that this lost time might have cost lives.

The lock finally relented and he barged through the door. Staggering, he half rolled, half fell down a small flight of concrete steps and dragged himself painfully across the cellar floor. More precious moments were lost as he located the meter cupboards. Once found, he ripped open the doors and started flipping switches, cutting power to everything in the club. The pounding beat slewed drunkenly to a halt and D collapsed breathing heavily. He lay against the damp brickwork, listening. All was silent for a moment. Then, the faintest sounds of life gently floated down to him. Not an uproar, but more like an awakening.

D's analytical mind finally took a backseat and his primitive survival brain took over. He scrambled to his feet, turned and pulled the main breaker from the distribution panel to prevent the sound system being reinstated, then he cautiously crept back up the cellar steps.

He emerged to find clubbers already milling about the corridor. The creature that had sought so much destruction would be feeling robbed of an opportunity. It would be unfortunate if their paths were to cross.

A girl, dishevelled but otherwise unharmed, caught sight of his face and her hand shot to her mouth in shock. D raised his hand to his own face. He knew he must look a mess, but he wasn't expecting quite so much blood.

He looked down.

He'd forgotten he was still in his coat and pyjamas. He stood surrounded by strangers, knowing that there was absolutely nothing he could say to them that would make any sense whatsoever. Without missing a beat, he strode to the double fire doors and this time deftly picked the lock before a small audience of bewildered clubbers. Then with utmost composure D flung the doors wide open and vanished into the night.

2

'I saw that! You boy, there! What's your name? Carter? STOP PUSHING!'

They hadn't even boarded the coach yet and Mr. Butterworth had already lost it. Gnat chewed his lip and stared into space. Mr. Butterworth couldn't organise a... Gnat thought for a moment.... a sponsored silence in a Trappist monastery. Mmm, he liked that one. He whispered it to Matt, who giggled dutifully then asked, 'What's "Trappist" mean?'

Gnat sighed, 'Durr, it's like when monks take vows of silence?'

Matt nodded sagely, he got it now. He countered with, 'Mr. Butterworth couldn't organise a cake in a...'

Matt stretched for the right words, '...cake shop!'

Gnat shot him a sideways look. 'Dude, that needs a little work.'

Matt giggled at the word 'Dude' and ventured, 'Mr. Butterworth couldn't organise an orgy in Miss Stevenson's bedroom!'

Gnat gasped and his hand shot to his mouth masking a huge giggle. His eyes shone with suppressed mirth. He may not have been one hundred percent sure what an orgy was, but he knew it sounded dirty.

The more he tried not to laugh, the worse it got. Matt was laughing too. To a couple of fairly well brought up eleven year olds, the thought of any teacher being dirty was comedy gold of the purest alloy.

Gnat tried to be quiet but he just couldn't push down the rising bubbles of forbidden giggles. He pursed his lips but his mouth just wanted to spread into a big, fat grin. Gnat's shoulders shook with silent, helpless laughter and this set Matt off too. They were both laughing but Gnat was really losing it now. Matt kept nudging him suggestively until Gnat was completely overcome with the longest giggling fit he'd had in ages. He chewed his shirt collar and hid his face behind his hands, but he couldn't stop for his life. The forbidden laughter was just too sweet to resist and he had fallen completely under its spell. He was getting a stitch, it was beginning to hurt. Gnat dug deep and made a huge effort to regain control. Straightening his face he stamped, took a deep breath and reined in his giggles. He was making a valiant effort to calm down, but Matt shot a single, brilliantly timed, saucy sideways glance and Gnat collapsed into hysterical giggles again.

Every time he looked up Matt was mugging. Gnat's eyes swam. If he blinked all he could see was Matt being really naughty and every time he closed his eyes, all he could see was Mr. Butterworth with the school secretary, Miss Stevenson.

Gnat was gasping for breath now, it was simply the *funniest* thing he'd heard in his entire life. She was tragically old, *at least* twenty five!

Far too old for anyone to *really* fancy her!

'Do HURRY UP at the back there!' Mr. Butterworth barked. Gnat grabbed his rucksack and scrambled towards the coach with Matt hard on his heels. They were just scrabbling up the coach steps when Mr. Butterworth added, 'or I'll report you to Miss Stevenson for detention!'

Priceless! *He actually said Miss Stevenson*! Gnat gave a roar of laughter and his spindly legs buckled. Matt hoisted

Gnat by his rucksack straps and shoved hard at his limp, laughter-wracked body. Propelling Gnat up the coach's aisle in front of him, somehow Matt shepherded him towards the back. Butterworth was aghast.

'Is he having a fit?'

Matt shouted back over his shoulder, 'It's his condition, Sir. He'll be fine when he gets his breath back.'

At the idea of 'his condition,' Gnat took a fresh fit of extreme hilarity. He shrieked and Matt had to drag him onto a seat and sit on him.

'His *condition?* Why wasn't I told about this? Is *that* completely necessary?'

Matt was now flicking Gnat's nose in the hope that a bit of pain might shut him up. 'Yes, Sir, it is. You wasn't told because -'

'Weren't... "You *weren't* told." Not, "you *wasn't* told," ' Butterworth corrected.

Matt nodded gravely, 'Right, Sir, you weren't told -'

That seemed to be quite enough of an explanation for Butterworth, he merely shook his head and assuming his customary air of slight bewilderment went to sit in the seat behind the driver.

Matt was appalled at Butterworth's lack of interest. He'd just at that minute, on the spot, dreamed up a terrific story about Gnat having a rare form of giggling tourettes. Crestfallen, Matt dug deep and manfully accepted his improvised flash of brilliance would forever go unrecognised. Under Matt's weight, Gnat was recovering his composure. He shoved Matt off and sat up. His cheeks ached from grinning and his sides hurt, but the mood had passed and his attention was ready for something different. He struggled to get his rucksack off.

'What've you got?'

Matt meant food. It was his favourite hobby. He could work out all the permutations of any saver deals in any fast food outlet in town quicker than a server could pop a zit. Matt admitted he was crap at maths, but if any inspired teacher had ever just asked him to multiply or divide in burgers, then he'd have been an instant prodigy.

'Parrsnips!' someone shouted right from the back, in an attempt at a thick West Country burr. This was the new game, no rules - just this one word repeated until it got really, *really* funny.

'Parrsnips!' came a reply somewhere just behind Gnat.

'Parrsnips!' yelled Gnat. He was giggling, but not as madly as before.

'Parrsnips!' someone else shouted. The whole coach-load was going into hive-mind, morphing into a single unified organism with one precisely focussed goal. Year Seven was gearing itself up for a serious and sustained bout of extreme giggling.

The only people onboard who weren't part of the game - and thus didn't get the sheer rapturous joy of it - were the driver and Mr. Butterworth. Year Seven suspected they were both seriously fun-resistant anyway.

'Parrrrrrsnips!'

Beautifully rendered, this one was met by a hugely appreciative laugh. Mr. Butterworth was getting agitated. He took off his glasses to clean them. Gnat and Matt spotted this 'pre-kick-off' manoeuvre and turned their best 'shocked' faces to each other, posing like two old dears clutching handbags to their bosoms.

'Ooooo errr! Get her!' they softly cooed in unison.

'Parrrrrrrr…' someone began.

'WILL YOU BEHAVE!' Butterworth finally exploded. 'SHUT UP! OR WE'RE ALL GOING STRAIGHT BACK TO SCHOOL!'

He sat down to total silence. Gnat sighed and took out his sandwiches. Matt explored the depths of his bag and surfaced grinning. Slowly, suggestively, he unwrapped some foil and whispered in a breathy, girly voice, 'Oh my, Mr. Butterworth, whatever have you got there?'

With a rubbery spring action, Matt flipped a cold sausage so it stood erect right in front of Gnat's face.

Gnat gave an explosive guffaw, spraying half chewed sandwich clear across the seat-back directly in front of him. He only just managed to turn it into a coughing fit before Butterworth came to investigate.

Gnat spent the rest of the journey diligently staring out of the window, trying to avoid looking at Matt. Every time they went under a bridge or past something dark, Matt's reflection would do its utmost to make him laugh. Usually it succeeded.

After what had been for Gnat, a stomach-achingly funny journey the coach crunched on car park gravel and the doors sighed open. Coats fell in random flurries as they were dragged down from parcel racks and small arms punched out in all directions as the coats were pulled on.

A considerably older Mr. Butterworth disembarked from the coach than the one that had got on it. The day hadn't even started and Year Seven had wound him up with surgical precision to Defcon 1.

As the last child bounced down the steps and formed up dutifully beside Mr. Butterworth and his helpers, the driver slid from behind his wheel and sloped off gratefully for a sly ciggy and a trip to the nearest coffee shop. Hungry as he was, he couldn't face the soup of the day - spicy parsnip.

It may have stood for centuries, repelling many invaders and even making kings of men, but Mr. Butterworth wasn't sure if Warwick Castle was ready for its latest onslaught. As his party headed for the dungeons and torture chambers, he tried to keep any happy thoughts of vengeance well hidden from his face.

The afternoon passed remarkably without incident. Picnics had been eaten on Ethelfleda's mound, the unbelievably high and winding stairway of Guy's tower had been climbed and the state rooms viewed. Year Seven had loved the armour, the swords, the birds of prey, the cakes, the ice creams and the horrific instruments of torture. So far no one had been sick or fainted, or even dropped a water bomb from the ramparts onto the unsuspecting head of an elderly tourist.

All Butterworth had to do was get the little stinkers back to school and he was home and dry for another term. He lined them up again by the coach and repeated the head count. No, wrong number. He tried again.

'WILL YOU ALL KEEP STILL!'

Fidgeting children stopped playing with their souvenir trinkets and lined up sulkily. Butterworth counted again - fast. Heart sink. There was still one missing.

'You, boy!' He pointed accusingly at Matt. 'Where's your friend? The one with the "condition"?'

'Don't know, Sir.'

'When did you last see him?'

'Don't know, Sir.'

The coach driver shook his head and sighed, an already long day was just getting a whole lot longer.

Matt had been gorging on scones and clotted cream in the Orangery when Gnat had wandered off. He hadn't seen him for at least forty minutes.

'He might be in the... in the...' Matt chased the correct term, '...*bog*, Sir.'

Year Seven stifled giggles. Butterworth snorted.

'Then we're all just going to have to wait until...'

'He's finished, Sir?' Matt ventured brightly.

Butterworth turned away, cursing whatever spirits he'd unwittingly provoked to bring him to this pass.

Having left Matt to his troughing, Gnat had spotted Neave ducking under a roped off area and going into one of the smaller state rooms. Not quite knowing why, he had followed her.

There was something about Neave. She was the newest addition to Year Seven, she was quiet and she was very pretty. Gnat didn't really get on with girls, but he'd liked Neave at first sight. Most girls were far too bossy - and what was it with all that awful pink *and* fairies?

Gnat had watched the 'pinkerbelles' in his class catch pinkmania from one another, colluding to spread the vile hue like an unstoppable tide of strawberry custard until it encompassed bags, books, pens, pencil cases, phones and even umbrellas.

Neave was different and he appreciated her disdain for what the other girls were saying or doing. Not that Gnat would ever say. She was still a girl, after all.

Casting a sly glance back, Gnat saw the guide was busy with a fresh gaggle of kids from another school. He judged the right time to duck the crimson rope, then breathlessly crept towards the half open door Neave had vanished through.

This was exciting!

He emerged into a long, wide gallery but there was no longer any sign of Neave. With a sudden thrill, Gnat wondered if she had found a secret door in some panelling. No such luck. There was no secret door, just Neave's neat little footprints wandering off into the dusty distance. They went right up to a half open door that clearly led back to the main State Rooms. *Boring!* Gnat sighed and cast a glance around the forbidden room.

Floating ghostlike upon the dark oak floorboards, like a breaking ice shelf, floes of lumpy, angular furniture lurked under white sheets. Gnat lifted the corner of a dustsheet and saw an ornate bookcase. He flung himself down onto a deep, draped armchair and picked his nose thoroughly. It had been a good school trip, Matt was being dull and scoffing again, but there was the journey home and the inevitable winding-up of Mr. Butterworth to look forwards to.

He flicked a bogey and stretched his skinny legs, wiggling his toes, luxuriating in the new socks Dad had bought him. Gnat liked new socks. Once washed they were never the same. He yawned and glanced up, with a start he realised his last bogey was clinging to one of the pristine white sheets.

Gnat jumped up and delicately picked at the enormous white chalk face of the cloth. Without warning, the whole thing slid gracefully to the floor, revealing an enormous edifice. *Busted!* Gnat thought bitterly. There was no way he could reach up high enough to put the cloth back over such an enormous piece of furniture.

He could make a run for it, or...

Gnat stared through the glass door of the gigantic cupboard. It was stacked with shelves - shelves that held the weirdest array of objects Gnat had ever seen. There was a two-headed snake in a jar of crusted, yellowing liquid, a fossilised skull of something Gnat thought might be a small raptor and a coil of bleached golden hair labelled: *'Hair from an Angel. Naples 1768.'*

Now that he looked again, Gnat saw everything was labelled. From the *'Splinter of wood from the one true cross. Vatican 1766,'* *'A Chinese dragon's-claw. Venice 1790,'* *'The blood of St. Vitus. Berne 1763'* and *'The pickled eyes of a three headed dog. Montepellier 1741'* everything bore a description in the same ancient calligraphy.

Then, Gnat caught sight of something he recognised. His eyes grew huge as he stared up at it. This one was faded, its colours dulled by a yellowish cast, but it was still breathtakingly beautiful. The one he had hidden at home was probably a third bigger and far more vibrant.

This one was just over a metre long and took up nearly half a shelf, but Gnat knew it was as light as a feather - it was indeed a wing.

Looking as if it had belonged to the biggest dragonfly that ever lived, it was clear but veined with pale green and tinted with the faint iridescence of a fire-opal. It reminded him of a peacock's breast and butterfly wings and kingfishers' feathers. It looked like someone had captured a living rainbow in wafer-thin ice.

Gnat had found his wing two years ago. It had been hanging by a spider's thread outside his bedroom window. Dad hadn't wanted it in the house and that was when he had told the first lie Gnat had ever been aware of an adult telling him. His father had said that the beautiful insect wing was dangerous *and* poisonous and he had gone off to burn it. That had been the very same day Mrs. Green had bumped into the car and there had been a huge and prolonged row.

Gnat had never seen his father kick off at someone like that before. Whilst they were shouting – well, Dad had been shouting, Mrs. Green was mostly crying, Gnat had dutifully lit the dry bonfire and watched it go up like a rocket. He had been all of nine years old back then, and heady with the godlike power that only a box of matches can bring to a small boy.

When his father finally came back into the garden, Dad had been furious at that too. But not as mad as he would have been if he'd known that before setting the fire, Gnat had stolen back the unharmed wing and hidden it under the eaves in his attic bedroom. He had kept it there with all his other secret stuff, occasionally taking it out and marvelling at its sheen and sheer strange beauty. Staring at the iridescent pinky-green metallic residue on his fingers, that was how he had known his Dad had lied to him.

It wasn't poisonous.

Looking back, Gnat now realised it had done a lot to shape him - and his life, that strange wing. It had sparked his all encompassing interest in bugs and creepy crawly things and even changed 'Nat' to 'Gnat.' But try as he might, no matter how many books he scoured, or sites he Googled, he couldn't find anything out about the exotic creature that had shed it.

They had relocated twice since then and through both moves Gnat had faithfully kept his wing with him, using all his guile to smuggle it into each new place. Now here he was, breathlessly standing right in front of a nearly identical one. Beneath it, the ancient handwriting catalogued it as a:

Fairy wing. Found, Flintshire 1724

That was all. Gnat was bitterly disappointed, but he still stared.

'It's called "A Cabinet of Curiosities." '

Gnat jumped and spun around to see a stern, young woman marching towards him. Her sudden smile interrupted his instinct to turn on his heel and run.

She gathered up the puddled cloth and continued, 'People used to go on a special, long holiday called "*The Grand Tour.*" I suppose it would have been a bit like a gap year really. Anyway, as they went they'd collect things - the weirder the better, like holiday souvenirs. Then they'd bring them home and have a big cupboard built especially to house all the wonderful bits and pieces they'd collected. *Then* they'd throw a party and show off what they'd brought back to their friends... Beats a slide show of boring holiday photos any time!'

Gnat grabbed his chance. 'Do you know anything about this?'

Gnat pointed at the wing, suddenly unaccountably nervous about how important any answer was to him. He swallowed hard and waited for her reply. The guide was quietly surprised at his interest. This boy appeared to be hanging on her every word, best not to disappoint him.

'That's probably part of a *chimera.*'

She caught Gnat's puzzled look. 'In old times,

people used to stitch parts of different animals together to create fascinating monsters. Like the top-half of a stuffed dog or monkey stitched onto the bottom-half of a stuffed fish? Unscrupulous dealers used to create all sorts of clever things to part rich people from their money.'

Hope blazed in Gnat's chest. 'So this *is* some part of an animal?'

'Yes, intestines probably.'

'Guts?'

'Either guts or some other kind of membrane, varnished and stretched over a fine frame. It's very clever.'

'So, it's not real?'

'Obviously!'

'Couldn't it be from something they haven't discovered yet?' Gnat ventured hopefully.

'Seriously?' She eyed him quizzically, was this boy teasing her? No, he seemed genuine, if a little gullible.

'It's just a fake, like the angel-hair. That's from a horse's mane and the unicorn's horn is from a narwhal. Now, you know you shouldn't be in here, don't you?'

Her voice was kind and only slightly reproachful. Gnat nodded dumbly. He hung his head and the guide thought he looked very disappointed. Reaching under another cloth, she took out a pile of guide books and handed one to him.

'There's a shot of the cabinet in there, you can just about make out the fairy-wing.'

'Is there anywhere else I could find out about this stuff?' Gnat persisted.

'You could try the internet.'

Gnat knew when he was at another dead-end. Forcing a bright smile he thanked the woman for the booklet and left the room. Looking back from the door, he watched as she cast the dust sheet into the air like a fishing net, encompassing the enormous cabinet with one deft throw.

Gnat wandered unseen, past the fretting Butterworth's back and lined up with Matt. Head down, he was very thoughtful and missed Neave staring at him.

'You okay?' Matt whispered.

Gnat nodded.

'Look like you've seen a ghost.'

Gnat shrugged.

Butterworth turned and gave a start. Nathan Greville was standing in line. Joy of joys, the paedophiles hadn't got him, now it was possible to leave and go home before anything bad happened.

'All aboard!'

Butterworth bounded up the steps to the coach and joyfully threw himself down on his seat. Alleluia!

The prickle of thin glass came as a shock, but it wasn't until the overpowering stench overtook him, that he remembered the cluster of confiscated stink bombs nestling in his back pocket.

3

The parcel arrived directly at D's home via one of the BMXers he called 'The Street Biker Irregulars.' The deal was simple, they ran the odd errand and he turned a blind eye to them practising their stunts in the underground car park. It had been a heavy week, but he'd not expected the reaction he got when he opened his front door.

'Woo! Used yer 'ead to stop a lorry?'

D smiled ruefully, but offered no explanation.

'This was left at The White House.'

D nodded and took the small parcel. The White House was one of his many drop boxes. He reached behind the front door, brought out four cans from a stack and handed them to the boy.

'Rather have lager.'

D shrugged, 'A, you're underage and B, you don't even like the taste.'

The boy considered for a moment, 'Right on both counts.' He took the proffered cans and pedalled off, shouting over his shoulder, 'Still rather have lager!'

Smiling, D shut his front door and picked up the mail that had just arrived in the more usual manner. He groaned as he straightened up, rubbed his aching ribs and padded down the narrow hallway through to his kitchen.

Late morning sunlight filtered through the large

stained-glass windows casting multicoloured pools of light on the bleached floorboards. Magnus Magnificat was luxuriating in the warmth of one such sun-puddle. He purred and stretched out an overly large paw, then blinked a slow greeting with his huge Persian eyes.

D stepped over the cat and sat down at the kitchen table. He turned the small parcel over in his large hands. The neat lettering was identical to his own handwriting, but it wasn't his. He'd written it down for a non English-speaking, Japanese man and now this man had faithfully copied D's western script in order to send something D had long waited for.

The last time he had been in Japan, he had visited a small, nondescript office in Kyoto. The building belonged to one of the larger Japanese corporations, a name that was familiar all over the world. However, as far as anyone was concerned this single, small office appeared to be operating independently of its huge parent company.

The fact that it was an integral, if extraordinary, part of that company's research and development programme was known to less than a handful of people worldwide.

With most innovations there are often unexpected outcomes. Invention often begets additional creative usage unforeseen by the inventor. People naturally adapt stuff and use it in ways that it wasn't originally designed for. Then the genetics of invention naturally dictate that these adaptations should be fully exploited.

Early digital photography had revealed certain anomalies - things that weren't obvious to the naked eye. The phenomena of strange faces in the background of various photographs became a subject of interest and intense speculation. Websites were dedicated to the subject and a few of the most inexplicable were printed in newspapers. In time the technology improved and where earlier mass-produced digital cameras carried the ability to pick up non-human presences, all the later ones were digitally dampened – and so the stories faded. The Kyoto Office had helped by mopping up sites and burying as many of these reports as they could. Then they introduced a handy piece of geek-speak and dismissed the phenomena with the simple term '*artefacts.*' With just that one little label they pretty much killed any lingering sense of spookiness. However, yet again proving itself to be history's great magic eraser, it was zeitgeist's own short shelf-life that eventually saw the focus of the collective mentality move on.

In the meantime, it hadn't taken the Japanese technicians long to understand that their cameras really *were* seeing anomalies and that there was definitely something there in the photographs. What had begun as the desire to iron out any possible defects in their products had become, under the secret direction of their company chairman, a quest to uncover the truth.

These same techies had worked with D to perfect their understanding and develop the intriguing device that he now slid from its protective packaging.

D smiled - it felt lovely, as did all their products. It looked like a small, bronze-coloured digital camera. Far from being dampened, this one boasted radically enhanced detection facilities. There were no instructions, but he found the buttons were self-evident and it didn't take him long to figure out the basic functions.

All the careful watching, the scanning of peripheral vision, the hard fought for understanding of these creatures in and out of their places of natural habitation, indeed, everything that would take human eyes many years to develop could now be achieved by anyone *in moments* with such a device.

Magnus jumped up onto the table, stuck his head into the milk jug and began lapping noisily. When the cat had drunk his fill, he popped his head up again, his milk-laden face resembling the whiskers of some venerable Mandarin. D smiled, he didn't mind, he was looking forwards to testing this device against his own sharply-honed abilities. If it worked, D now knew he could arm his agents and win the clandestine war.

4

The fresh wind whipped the sawdust into soft swirling eddies. The Kew team stood back and watched the tall, well-built man working. In the centre of the dust storm, Phil Dunford chain-sawed a pin-sharp, conical piece of timber from the felled lime tree. He moved with the kind of graceful competence that only comes out of deep respect for a truly dangerous piece of kit. Whilst younger watchers were impressed that he could excise such an accurate shape using just a chainsaw, the older gardeners nodded, having seen it before, but all in silent accord that it was still good to watch Phil at work.

He'd previously carved a finely wrought mushroom from a piece of trunk to demonstrate the kind of precision that a seasoned chainsaw-user could achieve.

'Just take your time,' he advised, 'and take nothing for granted. There are no small accidents with one of these.'

He revved up his chainsaw for effect.

He surveyed his audience, hiding his sudden alarm. Had he seen it? Phil stood back and brushed the fine sawdust from his plastic visor. He'd caught sight of something out of the corner of his eye. That was invariably the way he'd seen them before. Yes. It was there, high up in one of the oaks, looking like a bundle of twigs. Only a trained eye like his could make out its lithe form hiding under the camouflage of leaves and branches.

It was a metahominid. From the Greek meaning *'other man,'* it was a life-form people traditionally called 'fairies.' Far from the pretty confections of hazy hippies, these were the malign entities spoken of in hushed whispers on stormy nights by country dwellers recalling forbidding tales from ancient folk lore. Metahominids were a dark secret of the countryside and had no place in a city like London. The wind was rising and it had settled itself to ride and break as many of the boughs as it could - boughs that were already bucking and diving like a lunging bronco.

'It's getting a bit breezy, if we stop for lunch now we can see what the weather's doing after.'

Phil stepped back from his handiwork to a round of applause. The small group broke up and he was anxious to get some space and decide what to do about the unwelcome visitor. He was waylaid by Tony, the man who'd booked him for the chainsaw masterclass. Smiling broadly, Tony shook his hand vigorously. Phil forced a smile back and suppressed his rising anxiety.

'Memorable as always, Phil.'

Tony's crinkly, bearded smile reminded Phil of a beneficent elf - if there ever could be such a thing.

'Can I take that for my daughter?'

Tony indicated the mushroom, Phil nodded, anxious not to be rude, but to bring this conversation to a rapid close.

'I don't like the look of this,' Tony's smiled faltered, as he gazed about him at the wind tossed branches, 'There'll be breakages.'

Whenever the wind got up, Tony couldn't help but think back to The Great Storm of 1987, the near hurricane that had decimated Kew's beautiful trees. He had been a very junior gardener back then, but he recalled the heartbreaking scenes to this day. The gardens had been rearranged overnight and entire vistas had changed. Every corner he turned revealed yet more victims uprooted, left lying like a mass stranding of whales across paths and lawns. Cutting up the corpses and dragging them away had left many workers at Kew in tears that day.

Tony shrugged and kept smiling, willing himself to stop fretting over his fragile trees, but he couldn't dismiss his anxiety. Tony cherished his trees every bit as much as he did his loved ones at home and Phil knew it. Yet whatever danger the trees might be in, Phil had seen at first hand how metahominids threatened far worse for any humans they encountered. He tapped his fingers against his belt, leaking anxiety, desperate for a moment alone. Still Tony lingered, appraising the weather whilst Phil's mind raced as to whether he should tackle the metahominid on his own, or get help. Neutralising that malicious creature sitting in the oak was of paramount importance, but he was wary of going up against it without back up.

That one should have found its way into central London was alarming, but if it was just one example from a multiple infestation, then Kew would be under even greater threat than it had ever been from the Great Storm.

'C'mon, let's go and eat,' Tony suggested and set off

towards his office. Phil hung back, trying to look casual, but his heart was pounding.

He'd spotted another one.

'Just got to make a call and I'll be with you.'

Phil swung his chainsaw onto the back of his pickup and jumped up into the cab. He accessed a number he had saved in his phone as 'DEE NINE' but hadn't used in almost five years. He was a little surprised when it was answered immediately.

'D.'

'D, it's Phil Dunford.'

'How is the Clocaenog Forest? All quiet now?'

'I'm not at home in Wales, I'm here in London. In Kew Gardens,' he could not suppress the rising alarm in his voice, 'D, they're here.'

The reply was calm, 'I'll be half an hour.'

A click and D was gone.

5

They met by the pagoda, smiling, keeping it light. Just like the two old acquaintances they were, meeting and catching up.

'Four o'clock high,' Phil muttered, being careful not to look up.

D's gaze casually swept the gardens. 'I see at least five,' he replied evenly, 'have a look through this,' he offered the detector to Phil.

'How's it work?' Phil asked, instinctively looking through the viewfinder. The detector's screen showed the gardens as a uniform grey field crossed with paths and dotted with ponds and pools. The landscape was blotted here and there with spots of movement.

'The red ones are human,' D explained.

'And the blue and green ones?'

'Aren't.'

D kept his tone level. He took the detector from Phil and adjusted the function. When Phil next scoped the scene, he saw the creatures in detail.

'Chunkheads, arboreals and greys.' Phil observed tersely, 'Excepting the aquids, they're all here. It's an infestation.'

'Looks that way.'

'Why here? Why now?'

D shrugged, the movement emphasising the awkwardness of his large, misshaped frame. Phil threw him a worried look, 'What if it's habitat destruction? What if they're moving in from the countryside… like urban foxes?'

Head turned away, D carefully scanned the trees from the corner of his eye, 'Unlikely. Government set-aside schemes protect their traditional haunts. No-one could possibly gain by disturbing them.'

'Another Operation Gawain then?' Phil suggested.

Operation Gawain had been the ill-fated capture and release programme, where D had first liaised with Phil. To their fury, subjects had been trapped and released into the depths of the Cloecaenog Forest in North Wales. It had met with some success, but following the death of one of D's more vulnerable colleagues at the hands of chunkheads, all such operations had been suspended.

D replied with ice in his voice, 'No. We are not dealing with a relocation issue. This could be a rising.' His tone softened, 'Thanks for calling me Phil, I appreciate your vigilance. I'll sort it from here.'

They shook hands and parted. Although Phil knew D was a formidable character, he couldn't shake off his sense of doom. On a sudden impulse he rang home.

'I'm just about to collect the girls from school.'

Karen sounded fine, but suddenly Phil found he needed to be completely sure.

'Everything okay there?' he asked breezily.

'Why wouldn't it be?' Karen asked warily.

'No reason.' Phil sounded extra-innocent.

'Now I know something's up!' she teased.

She was fine. Phil suppressed a sigh of relief.

'Just missing you all.'

'What have you bought now?' Karen laughed, mock-accusing.

'Nothing!' This, at least, was true.

'Yeah right. Gotta dash, speak later. Bye, Babe.'

Phil made up his mind to get home to the Clocaenog as quickly as he could – just as soon as he had bought something Karen didn't need, but would love just because he'd bought it.

6

It took the best part of two days for D's counter-metahominid department D9, to obtain all the necessary clearances and three nights before he found himself back in Kew Gardens. The public had gone home, the gardens had been locked and the 'finding of wartime munitions' was being used as the bottom half of a double-cover, with a 'top secret anti-terrorist operation,' above it being presented as the 'real' incident. These formed both an outer and a middle ring of security, designed to keep both staff and the necessary police presence, well clear.

Only D and his colleagues had access to the central arena of action.

The waning moon was hidden by cloud and a fine, drenching rain was falling by the time he carefully inserted a pair of exceptionally effective ear plugs, stepped under the incident tape and headed towards the designated meeting area. At his approach, three dark figures detached themselves from the shadows and emerged soundlessly. They followed him to a small rise overlooking a natural arena.

Without a word as one, they all lay on the bank and looked down into the clearing. In the misty rain shapes without shadows like clear flames seemed to move across the wide stretch of lawns. If any of the human observers cared to turn their gaze, they could catch a fleeting image of their enemy's dancing figures.

Faced with what would be a close-quarter fight, Jockey ignored the longbow on his back and hoisted his crossbow into position. Alongside the arrows fine, reed-like silver-tipped darts gleamed cruelly from his quiver.

Wordlessly D handed over the latest gift from the Japanese developers, a bronze coloured scope. With practised fingers, in the dark and in absolute silence, Jockey unscrewed the existing range finder from his crossbow and tried out the new one, sighting across the clearing and over to a stand of trees in the middle distance. Jockey, never a man of many words, smiled in admiration.

A discreet, clever young woman, Violet had first encountered chunkheads – or something very like them - on her second tour of duty in Afghanistan. Unlike her shocked, jabbering and ultimately discredited colleague, Violet had kept quiet. Her proximity to such non-human activity, combined with her discretion, had resulted in her being placed under surveillance by D. After losing her foot, Violet had been invalided out of the army and D hadn't hesitated in recruiting her.

She silently shed her backpack containing something the size of a shoebox and lay next to Jockey. Still and focussed, her thumb hovered over the box's power-on button. In the crook of her left arm she cradled the cold beauty everyone referred to as *Violet's Baby*. Precisely engineered, with just the perfect weight and balance, Violet's Baby was a solid twelve inches of heavily serrated survival knife. Violet had customised Baby by having had her laced with silver along each of her wicked blades, the best metal for the job.

The third operative was a slender young man with the memorable name of September Wright. He was particularly pained at the damp atmosphere. The rain threatened to jeopardise his contribution to the fight. He raised his hopeful face to the dark sky, as he could feel the rain thinning out and stopping, September breathed a quiet exhalation of relief. The moment it did stop, D touched his arm and September, a classically trained musician, lovingly unpacked his weapon of choice.

A Stradivarius violin.

Shrouded in soft black, September stood and began to play. Previous encounters had revealed that the enemy tended to respond best to Vaughan Williams. Under his expert fingers, September's violin spun notes of gold, magically transmuting the vibrations of wood, horsehair and strings into the finest filaments of pure music. Even Jockey caught his breath at the beauty and purity of the sound. The dizzying high-notes that announced 'The Lark Ascending' began rising high over the hushed, night-cloaked garden.

The spinning clear flames stopped their giddy dancing and drew nearer to the pure, liquid sound. They trembled and swayed gently as September's beguiling violin shed its notes like soft petals into the damp night air.

Now he had got their attention, D marvelled at how many of them pressed close into the arena. They were pouring down trees and crawling across the dewy lawns. All were drawn by the intoxicating music and their ears were fully open.

He tapped a silent count of ten on Violet's shoulder. On ten she pressed the button and deployed the infrasound generator. The enraptured creatures froze, temporarily paralysed by the hateful vibrational dissonance between the gently sighing violin and the bone-grinding subsonic bass.

Their enemy now effectively immobilised, Jockey and D opened fire in unison. D was armed with a small, handheld crossbow pistol which held four bolts on a revolve. Each projectile flew straight through one ethereal body to the next. Unhampered by anything as heavy as earthly flesh, bolts and darts scythed though the delicate flame beings, so that D accounted for at least eight kills with his first shot.

For a split second, on the point of death, the creatures revealed themselves. Slender green or grey bodies wracked in attitudes of pain and death, condensed into the visible spectrum, all wide-eyed, shocked, spinning, or flailing. As D9's silvered weapons hit their multiple marks,

Chunkheads - gnomes looking like old men, gaped sorrowfully as the fire left their wicked little eyes, beautiful arboreals became ugly, gash-mouthed demons and grey elves writhed and spat hatred.

Even before they hit the earth, every sub-physical body burst into a dewy haze, scattering falling droplets in sudden flurries into the grass. The only remains left were odd wings strewn across the clearing like oversized sycamore seeds.

D and Jockey pressed forwards down the slope, firing in a wide arc. Whilst September kept playing, Violet held back, watching. Although itching to join the fight, she kept up a continuous blanket of 'covering fire' by deploying the debilitating infrasound at regular intervals.

Outnumbered as they were, D's battle was becoming about as challenging as strimming an overgrown garden. As quickly as fresh creatures joined the fray, they were cut down. Within fifteen minutes, no new ones arrived and those already present started falling back.

Violet eventually judged it the right moment to hit the infrasound generator for the final time and join the operation to mop up any remaining stragglers. She scrambled down the slope and in moments, Baby had the chance to cut her teeth, slicing through the rapidly diminishing flames to D's right. That was when it all started going wrong.

To D's increasing alarm, Jockey was being drawn away. He was following the retreating flames to the edge of the clearing. D couldn't verbally warn him, but he knew he had to get Jockey back, to stop him being lured away into any unseen trap.

Then the gathering clouds abruptly unleashed another smattering of fine rain. September blinked and shook droplets from his lank fringe. His beloved violin was suffering. Notes were becoming a fraction sharper as the wood expanded imperceptibly. September despaired but he kept playing resolutely. The game was very nearly up though and he resigned himself to the fact that he couldn't hold any remaining creatures spellbound for much longer. Unable to alert the rest of the team, he stood his ground and bravely played on. He couldn't shout, as the whole operation still depended on unspoken communication. Surely D could detect the way his notes were beginning to slide off key? If he attempted to join D and the others, he might skid on the slope and even now, any movement that could potentially lift his bow from the strings for longer than the briefest moment would only invite disaster.

Violet sensed the sudden atmospheric change. She started falling back in an attempt to regain the infrasound generator. All around her, the clear flames were becoming more agitated as they regained control.

Then they vanished. She blinked in disbelief. She knew they could move with the speed of light when they had a mind to, but she had never seen them recover and run away so quickly before. Why had they scattered? What were they up to?

The answer came with the sound of a thousand tiny whips cracking through the air. It prompted D to hurl himself to the ground and drag Violet down after him. They frantically lowered their visors as tiny impacts pinged off their Kevlar body armour. They were under attack from elfshot. An agonised howl in the distance could only mean that Jockey had been hit. If they wanted to save him, there wasn't a moment to lose. Even now, tiny flint arrows would be working their way through his flesh. Like stony parasites, they would burrow in and squirm inexorably towards Jockey's heart.

D felt, rather than heard, the infrasound being deployed. Behind him, the rain had finally forced September to stop playing and he was now crouching over the machine.

The massed ranks of archers shivered under the sonic onslaught, but they kept firing at the humans. D unclipped his knife and crawling forwards, he swung it out before him in wide arcs. Scything through the ranks, he felled great swathes of the creatures.

Abruptly he sensed Jockey's presence. D could tell by the quick movements that Jockey was uninjured, his sense of relief was short lived though, Jockey was dragging something behind him. D risked a quick glimpse and saw it was the inert body of a young policeman.

The creatures were now swarming back again. Jockey dumped his cargo between them and he, D and Violet got to their feet. They stood back to back, dodging the deadly falling shards of elfshot and fighting solidly through the numbers pressing in on them.

The tiny chips of flint arrowheads clattered across D's visor, but he fought on, the creatures' death throes condensing out of seemingly thin air before his lethal blade. His fighting became almost a meditation, his thoughts clear against the windscreen-wiper action of his swinging knife. What was that idiot plod doing here? How had he penetrated the cordon?

Violet became aware of a sudden impact and a

constriction on her wrist. She looked away and half glanced back. In her peripheral vision, she saw a juvenile chunkhead was sitting on her arm, attempting to peel back her armoured gauntlet and pierce her flesh with a poisoned dagger. As Baby punched through his head, his form condensed and revealed him for a split second. His fierce grip grew faint, until he too fell away in a misty spray of non-being.

The rain stopped again, but September's violin was too affected to play properly. The fairy archers had been trying to target him as he repeatedly fired up the infrasound, but September was safe inside swathes of impenetrable black tweed spun with carbon-fibre.

Jockey knew it was only a matter of time before the young man he'd rescued would succumb to heart failure. Using his bow now, he redoubled his efforts, making every arrow count, causing as many multiple casualties as he could. There would be no survivors. Violet and Baby were following his deadly onslaught and despatching any injured. Sending them back to whatever twisted hell they might believe in.

The downfall of their arrows grew noticeably thinner and ragged, until like the last drops of a rainstorm, they petered out and stopped completely. The flickering clear flames no longer weaved around the clearing. Not fled but utterly destroyed.

Wearily Jockey straightened, it was over. An arc of silver whirled over his head and there was a heavy thud as Baby pinned something to a nearby tree. For a split second, the dying archer revealed itself. Giving a bitter grimace of pure evil, it dropped its slender bow and evaporated into nothing.

D swept the area for escapees with his detector. The only dots on the screen were red. All humans. The Battle of Kew had been won. D removed his ear plugs and signalled the all clear to September.

September shook the inert flints from his cloak and strode down the slope to join them. Violet crunched over shed wings as she crossed the battlefield to retrieve Baby. The fallen policeman gave a faint groan.

'He's still alive!' Aghast, ex-medic Jockey knelt but it was just too dark to ascertain the full extent of the man's injuries. Against his strongest instincts D announced, 'We'll take him to mine.'

He raced back to Jockey's 4x4, leaving Jockey to

keep watch over their injured intruder whilst the clean up began. Violet gathered up the discarded wings and September deployed a metal detector to find any recoverable spent bolts, darts and arrows. Still well inside the cordoned area, D quietly coasted the 4x4 back to the battlefield. He slid from behind the wheel and looked down at the young, pale face of the officer.

'Pulse shaky, temperature dropping, he's not got long.' Jockey reported without any noticeable emotion.

An abrupt squawk from the policeman's radio startled the quiet night. D switched it off. Then with Jockey's assistance, he heaved the unresponsive body onto the back seat. The sight made Violet uneasy.

'The last thing we need is a dead copper in the back.'

'Agreed,' said D, 'so let's keep him alive.'

September emerged from the bushes, smelling of metallic smoke. The fairy wings crackled and blazed drily behind him, whilst his arms were full of bolts and darts. He swiftly stowed them in the hidden ammo boxes in the 4x4's boot. Jockey squeezed himself into the back-seat, alongside the policeman, whilst Violet jumped into the front. D lowered the window, 'All housekeeping done?'

September nodded, 'Clean as a whistle.'

'Thank you. Give us time to get away and phone in the all-clear code.'

September stood by the side of the path and watched them go.

A lone figure clutching a violin case was now all that was left of The Great Battle of Kew, the biggest incident of malevolent fairy activity England had seen in over a thousand years.

September took out his mobile, punched in a number and quietly gave a code for the less specialised emergency services to stand down. Depending on their security clearance level, all were told that the 'wartime bomb'/'anti-terrorist' incident had been dealt with. Then he slipped away unseen.

Lost in the anonymity of London's rain slicked streets, September Wright returned to normality.

Back in his kitchen, D swept the kitchen table clear of papers and Jockey threw the policeman down across it. His skin was pale and clammy and his lips were going blue.

Whilst Jockey felt for the man's pulse, Violet and D started ripping off his jacket, looking for puncture marks. Like them, he was wearing body armour. They ripped away the Velcro straps, then lifted his limp body and pulled the vest off. Tiny chips of flint fell from it, but still they couldn't find any signs of injury.

Violet rattled the contents of the cutlery drawer and found a big pair of scissors. She frantically cut away at the man's trouser legs, 'There's nothing. Not a mark on him!'

'There! On his sleeve.'

Jockey had spotted the blue entry mark of elfshot. D grabbed the scissors from Violet and cut the sleeve away, revealing the man's shoulder and armpit. All of them could clearly trace the livid, blue-poisoned trail left by the arrowhead, as it made its way towards a vein. If it wasn't stopped, it would burrow in further, enter the vein and work its way towards his heart. The constricting armhole of the Kevlar vest was all that had saved him thus far, simply by holding up the elfshot's progress, but now they'd stripped it off, the lethal arrow head was free to move again.

'Just the one?' Jockey was already sterilising a blade from his leatherman on the gas flame of the cooker. D and Violet re-checked, but there were no further puncture marks, or blue trails, on the man.

'Looks like,' Violet confirmed.

'Lucky devil,' Jockey's blade glowed red. Unhesitatingly, he crossed back to the table and plunged the knife into the policeman's armpit. The flesh sizzled as the knife went in, but Violet and D watched without flinching.

They'd both seen far worse.

'That's one weird take on 'luck' you've got there Jockey,' Violet murmured as she watched him operate.

In a little under ten seconds, Jockey had found the vicious piece of flint. He flicked it out with the tip of his knife and it skittered onto the table.

Incorrigibly nosey, Magnus jumped up to investigate, hissed, batted it with his paw and jumped down straight away. They all laughed at his split second timing. After such a draining encounter, anything remotely normal felt very good indeed.

Relieved that the man's colour was returning and his breathing was becoming even again, D was acutely aware that the young policeman still had a full dose of fairy poison circulating in his system.

'He's not out of the woods yet,' he murmured sombrely.

'Tropical Medicine will sort him,' Violet sounded almost dismissive.

Grinning, Jockey was positively sunny. The end of a very long, but successful night was drawing near and Jockey was now about as cheerful as his dark Celtic heart would allow.

In the growing grey light of dawn, they redressed the policeman, whilst D took down a black box from a high shelf. It held a series of what looked like fine tweezers. He took out a pair labelled 'Steatoda Nobilis - False Widow' and pinched the policeman's arm. The resulting tiny puncture, surrounded by a livid red welt, looked very convincing.

'How do we explain this?' Violet indicated his ragged clothes.

Tired as he was, D answered carefully, 'You know nothing about any exotic spider bite. You found him like this. Victim of a prank. Someone taking the piss out of a collapsed copper. Whatever. He can make up his own theory when he's better.'

'And his cut arm?'

'You couldn't notice that. It's hidden under his jacket.'

Violet was dubious. D caught her look and smiled, 'Okay, tell them he was away with the fairies.'

'As if!'

'Anything he remembers,' D continued, 'Will be so fantastical, they'll put it down to a fever from his sting.'

'Aye, and if he persists, he'll lose all credibility, his job and his wife and kids, if he has any.' Jockey had returned to his customary dreich manner.

'Aww, Jockey,' Violet patted his back, 'Let's get Sleeping Beauty out of here.'

They hauled the young Constable back through D's hallway and got him into the car without being seen.

D stood outlined at his front door and waved them off. He'd gone beyond exhaustion. His handsome-ugly face was set, but his eyes were unnaturally bright from the numbing fatigue that comes in the aftermath of being stretched both physically and emotionally. He closed the door on the growing light and wandered back down the hallway. Then he sat on the stairs, reflecting on the night's events. After some inner argument, he decided he was just too tired to tackle anything else for now. He'd leave the necessary paperwork until the morning. It was easily shaping up to be the longest report he'd ever written. He dragged himself upstairs and fell asleep, still dressed in his Kevlar armour.

Back at Kew, Jockey and Violet carried the young policeman and gently laid him down outside one of the gates, then they called an ambulance and waited. They left alternative, perfectly traceable names with the crew, explained they were available to make statements should the need arise and quietly went home.

Neither they, nor D, suspected Constable Watkin had been occasionally awake through at least some of his ordeal and he had heard and seen far more than any of them had bargained for.

7

Extract from a letter sent by Sir Arthur Conan Doyle to Mr. Harry Houdini….

'I have something precious, two photos, one of a goblin, the other of four fairies in a Yorkshire wood. A fake! You will say. No, sir, I think not. In one there is a single goblin dancing. In the other four beautiful, luminous creatures. Yes it is a revelation.'

8

'Gnat ?'

Gnat flexed his beautiful wings and flew up into a corner of the room, marvelling at how quick and light he felt. Sitting up by the cornice, he shivered with delight and grinned at the answering husky, dry-quill clatter of his shimmering wings. Gnat was dizzy with pure glee. This must be how it felt to be a one of his very favourite flying bugs! Looking down at his thin arm, he could see the fine tracery of green veins through his semi opaque skin.

He flitted over his bed and perched on the top of the tall bookcase, looking down. It was his very own familiar room but from a completely *new* perspective. Then he attempted a complete circuit of the room but his wings were too large and he batted against the walls like an ungainly cranefly. He needed more space to - literally - spread his wings. He looked at the open window. It was tempting but he held back. What if he got lost in the dark? He drew the heavy curtains and hovered before the window looking out.

Like a lady emerging from a lake a pale, slender shadow floated up to him from the darkness. Gnat's eyes grew large as Neave reached her slender arms through the open bedroom window. Her tiny hands took his and she dragged him clear, freeing him from his imprisoning room, pulling him out into the cool night air. He was so grateful to see her, he was completely unfazed by the dizzying drop to the concrete street below them. Turning towards her, Gnat saw his own happy, smiling face reflected in Neave's huge eyes as she flew alongside him.

With a flick of their wings they changed direction and flitted lightly across the open fields and down towards the dark, enthralling woods.

Suddenly they were joined by thousands of fireflies – except these weren't flies, they were beings like him. They swooped and soared and swept under and over, between and around, racing through the fragrant woodland air, skimming lakes and flitting through the tracery of leaves and branches.

This was amazing! Gnat shot up through the canopy, up through straggling mist and stood on the moonlit edge of a cloudbank, gazing up at the twinkling stars. Their cold, serene light seemed to mean far more to him than it had ever done before. A profound sense of understanding permeated his every thought. Somehow everything had joined up, everything made sense and…

'Gnat!'

Gnat fell from the skies.

'Get out of that bed now!'

Gnat scrambled into yesterday's discarded school uniform. He knelt by the window and carefully prised open the loose panel of wainscoting. It came away soundlessly and he shone his torch into the void, peering in at his cache of secrets. The wing glinted, throwing faint rainbows back at him, Gnat couldn't resist reaching out to stroke it. He thrilled at the dry papery sound it made, *just* like the ones he'd had in his dream. He went to pull it out from its hiding place, but the old cigar box caught his gaze. On an impulse, he flipped open the lid and drew out the most precious thing he owned. A photograph. The image of his Mum smiled back at him. He held her picture in both hands and without a trace of bitterness, in a clear soft voice he sang:

All things bright and beautiful

All platelets great and small,

Cancer and leukaemia,

The lord God made them all.

Gnat sighed. He didn't remember the blonde lady who smiled out of the picture at him. She had 'gone away,' as Dad had put it, when Gnat was a baby and this was the very last picture anyone had of her.

After Gnat was born, Dad had digitised all the family snaps and uploaded them onto the computer. He hadn't backed them up on disc - as Dad had said, who did? Then the old photograph albums had been long lost during one of their many house moves. So, when the burglars came and stole Dad's phone and the pc, they took more than just replaceable electrical things, they effectively wiped out Gnat's entire past.

When he'd been little, whenever a pretty lady appeared on TV Gnat would always ask, 'Did Mummy look like that?'

None of them did, not Angelina, nor Kate, or Keira and Gnat could tell Dad was getting irritated at being asked all the time. With an understanding beyond his years, Gnat knew Mum was not a subject for casual discussion and that Dad still couldn't talk about her. Then one day, quite by accident, he had found this photograph tucked inside a dusty book of poetry. He'd known at that instant, with a certainty that penetrated to his very core that this was his Mum and someone had left that photo for him to find.

That had been the day he had stopped asking Dad what Mum looked like and he had read his father's unspoken relief as, 'Dad simply not noticing.'

Gnat ate his breakfast in silence. The dream still haunted him, it had felt so good, but somehow *forbidden*. He didn't know why, but he felt very guilty about having dreamt it. Like he'd done something really wrong.

'Got your homework?'

Gnat nodded. His Dad handed him a bottle of water and a plastic box with his packed-lunch in it. Gnat dutifully put it in his school bag. He could always throw it away later.

Miss Chadwick was not so much a teacher, as a living caricature. Like a time-travelled Bloomsbury Setter, this tiny, fervent spinster piled her black, steel-streaked hair high, wore diaphanous, unstructured drapes and weighted herself down with enormous pieces of dramatic 'art jewellery.' Despite her politely starched demeanour, no-one could murder a good poem quite like Miss Chadwick. She held the slender book of verse aloft and began declaiming in her broken falsetto. Today's innocent victim was W.B. Yeats and Chadwick's strangely elongated vowels and weird gutturals were busy strangling 'The Stolen Child.'

No-one was listening. Except Gnat. He fastened onto every word. The poem spoke of 'Sleuth Wood.' Did such a wonderful sounding place exist? Gnat fervently hoped it did. It sounded as wickedly forbidden as the woods he'd flown through with Neave, in his dream.

With an inappropriate flourish, Miss Chadwick's shrill voice climbed the heights of hysteria and dredged the depths of bathos to deliver the climactic final verse:

'Away with us he's going,

The solemn-eyed:

He'll hear no more the lowing

Of the calves on the warm hillside

Or the kettle on the hob

Sing peace into his breast,

Or see the brown mice bob

Round and round the oatmeal-chest.

For he comes, the human child,

To the waters and the wild

With a faery hand in hand,

From a world more full of weeping than he can understand…'

Miss Chadwick snapped her book shut for full effect and with shining eyes, surveyed the classroom. Her eager gaze faltered, met by a tableau that could well have been entitled '*Ennui - A Study in Boredom.*' Every child's spine appeared to have melted. They slumped in languid attitudes of disinterest. Liquid limbs dripped from chairs and desks into disinterested puddles.

All except Gnat. He sat bolt upright. Shocked,

Miss Chadwick scanned his shining, *alert* face. Hardly daring to hope, she asked hesitantly, 'Any questions?'

Gnat's hand shot up just as the dinner bell sounded. Jellified limbs set instantly and the class sprang up as one. Gnat's eager expression was momentarily wiped from Miss Chadwick's encouraged gaze by a moving screen of charging bodies. By the time they cleared, he was gone, swept up into the herd by Matt.

Disappointed, Miss Chadwick gathered up her books and thoughtfully placed them inside her outsized bag. Holding onto the image of Gnat's shining face, she brightened, *thrilling* with the spellbinding command she'd held over him. The more she thought about it, the better it got. Within moments, she was filled with the intoxicating sense of power she'd once felt long ago as a young teacher. She had awoken his enthusiasm - his *en theos* - the god within!

A revitalised Miss Chadwick almost skipped from the room. She *knew* she could open a wonderful world of strictly-selected *appropriate* literature to this thirsty young mind. He was gone for now, but there would be time.

There would always be time.

'Dude, that was *so* funny!' Matt guffawed into his rice pudding, revealing rather too much of it still in his mouth. 'You *totally* had her going!' He scooped up more of his pudding, 'What would you have said next?'

'Yes Gnat, what would you have said next... about the *fairies*?'

Surrounded by a gaggle of giggling girls, Neave looked down at Gnat, her huge eyes shining. Embarrassed Gnat shrugged. Without looking up and furiously stirring the remains of his pudding, Matt spoke for him.

'What's it to you, Weirdo?'

Looking straight through Matt, her perfect lips shaped into the coolest smile, Neave swept past and strode out of the canteen.

'*Matt!*' Gnat's voice was urgent, cautioning.

Matt raised a quizzical eyebrow, 'You scared of *that?*' Matt indicated Neave's retreating figure with his raised spoon. Gnat looked away.

Matt stirred a blob of strawberry jam into his pudding. 'Oooh, look at me, aren't I a pwetty liccul emo? An' no one knows where I come fwom, or where I live or what my daddy does, 'cos I like being stwange an' mysterious. An' all the girlies want to be me! Look how they copy me! Wiv my pwetty pwincess clothesies…'

Matt carried on mocking Neave, in a raspy, little-girl voice, but Gnat was no longer listening. Matt had unwittingly highlighted that when it came to Neave, no one actually knew much about her - including where she lived.

Gnat suddenly knew what he had to do. He resolved that the moment school finished he would secretly follow Neave home.

'Bet she lives in some trampy dump she's ashamed of!' Matt was triumphant, 'Let's find out! Let's follow her home!' Gnat shrugged, feeling thwarted, but not wanting to show it.

Abruptly Matt let out a huge, greasy burp. His face suddenly a sweaty, sickly grey. 'On second thoughts …'

He didn't finish. Scattering canteen chairs, Matt lurched out of the room and staggered to the toilets. A concerned dinner lady stopped clearing dishes, grabbed a mop and followed him. Gnat wrinkled his nose. He hated even the word *sick* let alone the action of actually being it. He plugged his ears in case Matt's barfing noises should, by chance, penetrate through several thicknesses of doors and walls. Secretly he was glad. It would be a lot easier to follow Neave home without Matt in tow.

9

Although the sun was beginning to warm his back, the early morning air still held a chill. Sitting on the park bench D huddled in his big, black coat and stifled a yawn. Unable to sleep, he'd spent most of the night wandering the streets on some kind of patrol. It had been more of an anxiety-limitation exercise than anything else. A scant week since the battle, sightings were coming in thick and fast and the more detectors he'd handed over to operatives, the more evidence was coming back. There certainly seemed to be some kind of massing of metahominids, but it was limited to just here in London. The rest of the UK and - as far as he could tell -the rest of Europe and the wider world remained unaffected. The last influx of Eastern European workers had brought the odd chunkhead with them - most immigrants did - but the evidence D was garnering pointed to *huge* numbers of indigenous creatures leaving every chase, moor and wilderness in the Home Counties and invading the City of London. Some unseen impetus was driving them to abandon their traditional haunts and inhabit the cityscape of artificially-created places mankind had made for itself.

There had been territorial disputes before, folk-tales record the turf-wars that had occasionally broken out between the races. Modern farming methods hadn't helped, placing stress on natural habitat. In order to ease the situation, certain disputed tracts of land had been discreetly included in the government's much vaunted 'Agricultural Set-Aside Schemes.' Whilst the public's attention was misdirected from querying the details by its fury at paying rich landowners subsidies for leaving fields fallow, these set-asides limited the potential for flare-ups and under their strict control such confrontations had, up until recently, all but died off.

Yet suddenly, all the old compromises appeared to be breaking down and yet there appeared to be no cause for such a long-rumbling, chronic problem to suddenly escalate into an acute and threatening one. Nothing seemed to correlate with the sudden uprising in such a relatively localised area and it irritated D that he couldn't find a cause.

He had come back to Kew to reassure himself that every last metahominid had been cleared from this site at least. To his vast relief, they had. Better yet, there was no sign of a fresh re-infestation. D exhaled and bent his big, misshapen head to the left until his ear touched his shoulder, enjoying the satisfying click of the bones in his neck. Then he bent to the right and spotted... Violet.

She was strolling along one of the wide gravel paths, apparently taking photographs with what looked like a small, bronze camera. She'd come to scope the place out and make sure too. D rang her. He watched her stop and retrieve her phone from her bag.

'Cat needs feeding,' he remarked lightly.

'Durr, silly me!' Violet replied pleasantly, 'Okay, I'll see to it.'

D's coded words alerted her to the fact that she was being followed. Her 'okay' meant she had covertly spotted her follower. Even before Violet saw that the man tailing her had his arm in a sling, she'd intuited it would be the same man they'd rescued from the midst of the battle.

D's photographic memory had faithfully recorded the policeman's number from his uniform. From there it had been a simple trace. D had pulled police records and with his customary thoroughness, checked the policeman's entire history. Young, keen, bit of a UFO nut, PC Watkin would be a persistent nuisance for a short time, but it was likely that he'd follow the usual pattern and soon grow tired of dead ends. Perhaps it was the tiredness, but D couldn't shift the sudden suspicion that Watkin might be harder to dislodge than most. He sat for a moment longer, then slowly rose, gave an enormous yawn and headed off to an area of the park that had become an unofficial skate park.

He was only gone for a matter of minutes. On his return, D scanned the immediate area, but Violet and Watkin were gone. The Street Biker Irregulars would deliver his hastily written note and a trusted operative would act upon his orders. There wasn't much more he could do, so D went home to bed.

Violet took two buses and doubled back on herself twice without shaking her ardent follower. This was just a bit of a warm-up really. She was going to enjoy this. Musing that she could almost pity poor Watkin, but not *that* much, she subjected him to the cruel and unusual torture commonly referred to as *a shopping trip*. Plunging into the hallowed halls of the biggest department store she could find, Violet unleashed her inner hedonist. She would amuse herself by subjecting Watkin to the full, soul-bruising, retail hell experience. Something, she understood, that the average man would find as enjoyable as a vasectomy undertaken without anaesthesia.

She pitifully pushed her victim to the limit as she browsed the lingerie department, endlessly discussing the finer points of intimate apparel with hopeful sales girls. Then she had her neglected fingernails subjected to a nourishing, *prolonged* treatment. Two hours down the line and still he stuck as close as a suckerfish on a pane of glass.

Violet approved, he would make someone a *wonderful* boyfriend. She moved onto phase two of her 'Dislodge the Plod,' campaign. She thought about the shoe department, but was loathe to reveal her disability to this prying man. Why? Violet stopped herself.

Vanity or fear?

Violet hated both, so she turned around and marched straight back into the shoe department. There she spent another wonderful hour or two, trying on fabulously-bejewelled creations in silks and finest leathers. She fell in love with a pair that were a restrained shade of amethyst and made from leather that was so soft, they felt like newly opened beech leaves. These she *had* to have. She would explain to D that they were a *necessary* part of the operation.

She mentally totted up what her expenses sheet might be looking like.

Not good.

Hey ho, but a girl has to do what a girl has to do. Anyway, she mentally justified, compared to the kind of budget usually expended to defend the realm, her *useful* and *beautiful* pair of shoes probably cost a lot less than a coat of paint on a missile.

Heartsink. Plod was persevering. Time for Phase Three.

This saw Violet having her eyebrows threaded and her lashes tinted. Rather disappointingly, the lady doing it was deft and very fast, so Violet shimmied into a paper thong and had a relaxing full-body massage. Then she had her teeth UV flashed unnaturally white and - why the hell not, this little lot was now *definitely* all going on expenses - her hair cut and coloured.

A mere three and a half hours later, Violet emerged, looking stunning and exactly like the actress she'd want to have play her in a film. Still her little playmate was shadowing her. In something approaching a state of bliss, she moved onto perfumes.

Poor suckerfish, she could keep this up *for days*.

'Mmm, I like the citrus notes, very fresh, but I'm more of a floral girl.'

'Then how about...' the sales girl turned away to find something more suitable. She came back smiling.

'How *utterly* romantic! Your boyfriend said he had to go, so he's left these for you.'

She handed Violet a bouquet of exquisite roses, deep and velvety and so red, they were shadowed almost black. A note nestled between the blooms. Violet unfolded it and read:

You win. Let's stop wasting both our times. D.W

P.S. Your hair looks nice x

'NICE?!' Exploded Violet, '*Nice?* What kind of a stupid word is that?'

Just a short time later, Dylan Watkin unwrapped the crunchy caramel biscuit and dunked it into his latte. He deserved it. He'd just surfaced from a half-lit underworld. A hellish temple dedicated to the dubious dark arts of the retail therapists, peopled by gurning, orange-faced harpies who'd repeatedly pounced on him from behind cosmetic counters, misreading his lurking as genuine interest in their exotic, if totally incomprehensible products.

He shuddered.

It confirmed one thing though - unless she was a genuine shopaholic and in serious debt, there was no way Ms. Sarah Deakin could afford to sate her eye-wateringly expensive tastes on an office workers' salary. He opened a non-police issue notebook and wrote:

Female. Additional notes: Missing her left foot.

Mid calf amputation. Clever, likeable …

He tapped his teeth with his pen for a moment and added …*but challenging.*

Watkin swilled his glass, watching as the swirling tide of coffee rinsed the foam from the sides. She'd spotted him with embarrassing haste. Either after all the spy books he'd read he wasn't as good at 'fieldcraft' as he'd hoped, or someone must have alerted her. Maybe it was one of the other members of her cell, or maybe he was just unlucky?

All Dylan Watkin could do for now was keep looking for the house he'd been taken to. The one that was half an hour from Kew.

D's urgent job request was swiftly responded to and at just about the same time Violet was perusing a tempting array of luscious nail colours, Jockey was busy letting himself into Watkin's flat. The door snicked closed behind him and satisfied he was alone, he set about finding out what the overly curious P.C. Watkin might know, or think he knew, about D9.

Watkin's flat was depressingly tidy. Books on physics and astronomy lined up with lurid covered tomes on alien abduction. Jockey opened Watkin's laptop and cracked open an array of hidden files.

He was mystified by the lack of porn. Watkin seemed a very earnest, clean-living boy indeed. The next task was to send a copy of all the files to D. Before leaving, Jockey removed the discreet, but still risky, hidden surveillance equipment he had installed the same night they had left Watkin lying outside the gates of Kew.

Jockey substituted the physical camera with a fugitive programme inside the laptop, one that would allow them the safer option of spying on Watkin via the integral camera in his own machine. It would limit their surveillance to the times Watkin was actually using it, but from the spying he'd already done on him, Jockey understood it was

Watkin's habitual home-companion and rarely off.

After a brief catnap, D showered, made himself a refreshing pot of tea and sat down to read the contents of Dylan Watkin's secret files. Cracking the simple cipher, he opened the one labelled, 'Top Secret M.I.B.' Smiling, he shook his head at the Men In Black reference and read on:

Attended Kew as part of the incident team. Left team to get closer look at wartime bomb, it seems to have been a cover story. Expecting spy/terrorist scenario, I ascertained that the cordoned off area held multiple examples of the aliens I'd seen as a kid. The aliens were visible to me when I turned my head and didn't look directly at them. Small unit engaged the aliens killing large numbers.

Unit comprised four people: a woman and three men.

First male: tall, white indeterminate age. Ungainly, perhaps dyspraxic. Seems to have the ability to avoid being seen. Weird, like your eyes slide off him. Anti-assassin response? Would be hard to shoot him - (with gun or camera). English accent. Above average vocabulary suggests good school, well educated.

Second male: average height, stockier build. Working class Scots accent. Possibly late thirties. Referred to by female as 'Jockey.' Medical training. Possibly ex-military.

Female: black, estuary accent. Possibly late twenties.

Likely to be ex-military. All wore specialised black armour.

Last man was less clear, sounds crazy but he played a fiddle and seemed to mesmerise the enemy. Originally thought this was part of the hallucinations after the fever, but I believe he was there too. No idea of age. Tall, skinny, wrapped in black cloth. Very posh accent.

I was hit by enemy fire. Removed from scene to a location approximately half an hour distance by car. Violin man no longer present. Operated upon. Unit removed alien technology from my shoulder and discussed cover up. They stung me with something. Removed from scene by female and second male. Second half hour journey back to Kew. Treated for spider-bite and released from hospital after three days.

"Witness names" check out. Gut instinct is they feel wrong. How easy to set up a couple of names? Check this out. Have I uncovered the real Men In Black? Will continue going back to Kew and see if I can see any of them again. Urgently need to find the place they took me. Couldn't keep track of all the turnings, but got the first few. It's just a matter of going through all the possible permutations until I find the house that's half an hour distance from Kew.

Secure in the knowledge that tens of thousands of properties stood within Watkin's search area, D took a gulp of coffee and murmured, 'Good luck with that.'

He pushed his chair away from his desk and shrugged the tension out of his shoulders. He was making his mind up about Watkin's notes. He passed over the reference to his ability to Hide in Plain Sight. D knew he was good at not being noticed. Big as he was, he could hide behind a clothes line. He pored over the document again, savouring every misdirected sentence. Watkin had made the common mistake of believing he was dealing with aliens. He wasn't the first and he wouldn't be the last. Modern tales of lost time and abduction were commonly attributed to alien activity. Excepting for a very few, the majority of people had simply forgotten the far older tradition of such acts being perpetrated, not by the alien 'greys,' but by the indigenous 'grey folk.'

D stopped reading and pondered. Whilst the word *'Ascertain'* was typical plodspeak, *'Dyspraxic'* was not.

He stared out of the window, the sun had gone down and it was 'the magic hour' between day and night. D had built a career on spotting the odd anomalous detail in the normal continuum and now one more cryptic clue in the gigantic cosmic crossword presented itself to be cracked.

Lured by the siren song of the atypical, D hung on that one word. Even though he'd summarily dismissed so

87

many previous snoopers over the years, from now on D knew he would make a point of looking out for Dylan Watkin.

10

On a brilliantly sunlit day in 1921, Sir Arthur Conan Doyle walked through the dappled gardens of Kensington, his mind occupied with many things, including his first contact with non-human creatures.

It was over twenty years since an extraordinary drama had played out in the leafy environs around the vicinities of Hindhead and Haselmere in Surrey. After the Hindhead air had been recommended as being particularly beneficial for his ailing wife's ill-health, he had carefully designed a house he'd called Undershaw – *'Under the Copse'* – up in the hills close to The Devils Punchbowl.

Undershaw was perfect in every sense and he had spent many happy hours exploring its magnificent setting, striding out every day with a sense of excited anticipation as to what he might find next.

Their new home had been constructed amidst a landscape of eerie beauty and stirring tales and he had researched a local grisly murder commemorated by the 'Sailors Stone' and become familiar with 'Gibbet Hill,' where the perpetrators had received their punishment.

With his wife, Touie confined to the house, Doyle had plenty of time for his solitary treks into the landscape and before long, he had become aware of the proximity of a fine estate called Lea Park.

Having familiarised himself with the immediate countryside around Undershaw, Doyle had found himself drawn by the strangely compelling spirit of the place. Just outside Lea Park, he had unexpectedly come across the bizarre apparition that was to shape his destiny. Following a narrow track that that cut through the scrubby heath-land, he had rounded the corner of a gorse bank and stopped dead. A terrible vision blocked his way.

He stared at it in fear and fascination. As the unearthly beast lifted its great head and gazed directly at him with flame-red eyes, the blood froze in Doyle's heart leaving him completely bereft of word or action. Apart from the unearthly glow emanating from its fur, it was the sheer size of the fey dog that had captured his imagination. Hardly daring to breathe, he stared in wonder. It gazed back at him levelly. Despite its ghastly appearance, nothing in the spectral hound's manner suggested aggression or malice. It turned its great head engagingly to one side, then turned and bounded away a few steps. If anything, the gigantic beast was playfully inviting rather than threatening.

Over the weeks it began to appear to him more regularly on his forays, but it never walked with him. Instead it always trotted slightly ahead and on more than one occasion, he had willingly allowed himself to be lured deep into the woods by the spirit-presence of the huge dog.

Whilst following this beast, Doyle had explored the extraordinary Lea Park, encountering other wonders on his way. In this manner, he had been introduced to a level of metaphysical reality he had only yet begun to hint at in his works.

Whitaker Wright was the creator of the wonderful park with its artificial lakes, sunken, subaquarean rooms and tunnels. He had constructed a breathtaking, glazed-dome chamber beneath the waters of a vast, artificial lake. Standing secure and dry within, his guests could look up and observe swimmers and fish alike through its thick glass panels. Under Wright's cunning misdirection, at least one medium had 'channelled' water spirits in the scintillating green light of that surreal room beneath the lake, unaware of their actual proximity.

As Doyle was soon to discover, Wright, a man who had become a millionaire from silver mining, had imprisoned metahominid water-spirits - the *aquids* - nixes, merrows, fossegrims and dryads in these waters, encircling and entrapping them in his man-made lakes with deadly cordons of solid silver.

Like an exquisite young woman oppressed by a degenerate old roué, that such a place of beauty should be blighted by the ownership of this man had struck Doyle as monstrous. When he had discovered how the bumptious, bullying Wright had been callously enslaving and mistreating the delicate, spectral creatures native to this place, he had been appalled.

One evening, Doyle had entered a strange, waking half-dream. Voices of such tender sweetness and heartbreaking sadness had floated to him, luring him far from his home, to wander on the brink of the very largest lake on Wright's land.

There, he had been granted the gift of seeing the water-spirits held captive by the evil Wright. They told him of their desolation, with singing words that appeared in his mind. Their siren songs told of their enemy, the human who had taken particular amusement in tormenting one of their kindred, an ethereal melusine.

Wright had cruelly separated her from her water-spirit lover by trapping her in a tank he'd had constructed within the underwater room. The tortured water-spirits had sung sadly of how the human derived much cruel pleasure from her anguish. A man of chivalry and action, Sir Arthur Conan Doyle had confronted Wright. Charging boldly past the housekeeper, he had swept through the house and finally found and cornered Wright in his own study. There, he had demanded the immediate release of *all* the pitifully trapped creatures, those within the lake - and the one *under* it.

Aghast that this intruder should be aware of so many of his hidden secrets, Wright had reacted with blind fury. Not one to be gainsaid or challenged, the clash had become even more dangerous when Wright had levelled a pistol at Doyle's head. That was the night Sherlock Holmes's creator might have died, but for one simple happenstance. Wright's gun had misfired.

In the thundering silence immediately following the impotent click of the misfired hammer, Wright had gathered his scattered senses. Collapsing into an armchair, he had half-swooned, then apologised with many tears and much hand-wringing.

Despite this extraordinary performance, there still remained such a cowardly air of cunning and deeply sly malice about the man that Doyle had fled. Living in continuing fear for his life, he had risked madness by shutting his ears to the pleading songs of the water-spirits, but he had never returned to Lea Park.

Not long afterwards, Wright had killed himself. Doyle was apprised of certain details that never reached the public, by a good and trusted friend closer to the matter than he. Even now, he still derived great satisfaction in the thought that Wright's death had been an act of vengeance, enacted upon their tormentor by the water people. Their pleading songs had certainly ceased on the very day of Wright's death.

Without that extraordinary encounter with the strange beings in Surrey, he may never have written 'The Hound of the Baskervilles'... Or have championed the cause of Elsie and Frances.

These two little girls had been wont to play by a shallow tree-lined beck, just outside the Yorkshire village of

Cottingley. In this beautiful, sylvan setting they had been befriended by similar metaphysical creatures to the ones Doyle had encountered - and more magical yet - these little girls had actually managed to *photograph* them! The sensation their pictures had caused had been just three years ago. Now he intuited that those same photographs - being the basis of his latest book, 'The Coming of The Fairies' - were to form the crux of this afternoon's coming interview with Jim Barrie.

Amidst the riotous wind-cuffed blossoms of Kensington Gardens, Doyle approached the lonely figure of his old friend, nodded grimly and sat down beside him. He understood the raw, unhealing wound of deep grief having lost his own beloved son Raymond in the Great War. Thus he could only express wonder that this particular spot had been chosen for their meeting. Barely two months since his drowning at Sandford weir, Kensington Gardens held a very poignant reminder of Barrie's own stepson, Michael Llewellyn Davies. Now here they were sitting right by it, the statue of Peter Pan.

Doyle couldn't resist looking at it. The base of the statue was surrounded by ethereal fairies. Fairies that looked so very like the ones that had danced for the girls at Cottingley. James Barrie followed his gaze. He'd known and respected Arthur for many years, but he had summoned him here for the telling of a few painful home-truths. His apprehension at having to speak unkindly, but wisely, to his old friend - who was fast becoming a laughing-stock - had left Barrie cross and out of sorts.

'Can't stand the thing!' He barked, 'That Frampton! Call himself a sculptor? That mimsy little character, look at it! It doesn't even approach what it could be. It completely fails to show the devil in Peter!'

'And why should you wish to see the devil inhabiting such a free spirit?' asked Arthur, dismayed.

'Because he's wicked! *They all are!*' James practically spat the words.

'They *all* are?' Conan Doyle studied the statue of Peter thoughtfully, 'Do you mean children? Or fairies?'

Barrie didn't reply.

Doyle persisted, 'Then at least you admit that you believe there is a glamour and mystery to life?'

Still Barrie didn't make any answer. Doyle couldn't resist giving him a wicked wink, 'Come now, if you say you don't believe in fairies, Tinkerbell will be inordinately disappointed! Giving Barrie a gentle prod with his elbow, he chuckled, 'Surely, she will *die*?'

Barrie snapped, 'You cannot see what they're doing to you with this latest business!'

'Meaning?' Doyle feigned being mystified, although he knew exactly what Barrie was driving at.

Barrie grumbled, 'They are playing with you, man, and you can't see it. This business will *ruin* you!'

Doyle straightened his back and sat full-square to the statue, keeping his breathing even, quelling his rising annoyance. James was bereft, he had lost his adopted son. He must be allowed some leeway to vent his grief, however provoking. Doyle fell to musing about the paranormal affair of what had become universally known as 'The Cottingley Fairies.' Following on from his Christmas essay in *The Strand*, he had recently submitted a series of higher resolution photographs to promote his latest book, 'The Coming of the Fairies.'

The photographs *plainly* showed fairies frolicking in the leafy glades around Cottingley Beck. He had been careful to protect the identity of Elsie and Frances, the two girls who had taken these remarkable pictures, by calling them 'Alice' and 'Iris,' but had blithely risked his own entire reputation by promoting their photographs. Even with his prominence, his stature as a 'great man,' Doyle had found that the logic-bound, die-hards refused to be swayed. It had stung him bitterly when his compelling article had been met with bemusement - and even ridicule.

This, despite the fact that the girls were two children of the artisan class and such photographic trickery would be entirely beyond them. Furthermore, the negatives had been submitted to not one, but *two* photographic experts, one in London and one in Leeds and had been declared to be genuine.

Now it would seem even his old friend and cricketing comrade, Jim Barrie, was doubting too. Conan Doyle shook his head in disbelief. Of all people!

Surely, Jim Barrie was the one man in the whole of London who could be credited with some apprehension of these psychical beings?

Sir Arthur quietly employed the same precision of thought he'd imbued his greatest creation with, and asked gently again, 'Are you saying those little girls with their photographs are wicked? Or that *the fairies* are wicked?'

'Both.'

'Then at least you admit that you believe in these beings?'

'I am certain one of them killed Michael!'

Barrie let the words sink in, then drove home his argument. 'Far from giving you the concrete evidence you crave, these malicious creatures will destroy your credibility.'

'How do you propose they will do that?'

'Think about it! You have been unerringly faithful to the notion that these creatures, however strange, are a reality…'

Doyle opened his mouth to interject, but Barrie quickly silenced him with, '…*and I agree!* But now those very fairies will influence you, work through you and, using your own enthusiasm, two malleable girls and their *bogus* photographs, will turn the very things you see as *evidence* into irrefutable proof that *you have been fooled!*'

Doyle sat back shocked, as Barrie concluded.

'In short these malign entities will use you, your name and your greatness, to prove, once and for all, that they *simply don't exist!*'

'I can assure you, there is absolutely no danger of that!'

'Really?'

Doyle had no answer. For the first time he fully understood the depth of Barrie's enmity towards these creatures - and that because of it, he and his old friend were now seemingly on implacably opposing sides.

Barrie continued softly, 'Would you deny that your long association with these things hasn't affected the direction of your thoughts?'

Doyle frowned, but Barrie persisted, 'Surrendering yourself to these creatures, has rendered you willing prey to all sorts of fakery!'

Doyle snorted. If Barrie was daring to question his views on mediumship, he was going too far. As for the fairies, he stated his case simply but forcibly.

'There is simply too much evidence building up. All of it supporting my - and many other peoples' - views. Remember this and mark it well!' He eyed Barrie fiercely, 'Once you have removed the impossible, whatever remains, however improbable, *has* to be the truth!'

Barrie crossed his arms, 'Do not quote your fiction at me, Sir!'

Stalemate. The two men lapsed into a dignified, if uneasy, silence. Unable to argue any further, Sir Arthur rose, doffed his hat and made his way home.

Barrie watched him go. He had obeyed D9's instructions, yet Doyle was not to be dissuaded. The section head, someone traditionally referred to only as 'D,' would have to deal with the matter personally.

Barrie stayed seated until twilight came and the attendants ushered all the remaining visitors out. He took one look back at the statue of Peter, half expecting it to be surrounded by hovering fireflies that weren't fireflies. The small figure stood untroubled and Barrie sagged with unexpected disappointment. There were no dashing shadows or distant, chilling laughter though he longed to see and hear them again. With a start, Barrie realised he was at the sharp end of an addiction. This was how these creatures operated upon a man's mind. Once detected, these supernatural beings infested a man until all he could think about was glimpsing them once again. It had happened to Conan Doyle and now suddenly, Jim Barrie finally understood how deep his own enchantment went.

Far from saving Doyle from folly, all he had done was to entrench the man further in his stubborn persistence. Worse yet, he had revealed that his own misadventure had been just as disastrous.

Chastened, Barrie scurried home.

11

'There comes a point at every festival when it just starts getting a bit... Breughelesque, yeah?'

Diamond didn't look directly at her silent visitor, instead she deftly ripped up a small piece of card and rolled it into a tiny tube. She carefully placed it beside the prepared cigarette papers and began assembling a joint. Her once beautiful, now ragged and worn fingers peeped out of her mittens, like dirty toes poking through holey socks. They were heavy with silver rings and deeply ingrained with dirt.

Diamond continued in her little London-street-urchin voice, 'Like a Breughel painting, yeah? All the people, they all start looking extra weird - I mean they *do* anyway, right?' she laughed, '*every* festival, I *always* say, "*Where* do all these amazing looking, *beautiful* people come from?" I always say that. I mean it's not like you ever see them on the streets is it? Look at 'em! Their clothes! I swear, they are walking works of art!'

Now and again, usually to emphasise some half-thought-out notion, she'd stop and make a strange gesture, wriggling her once-lovely fingers as if she was playing an invisible piano mid-air. Every time she gesticulated close to her listener he recoiled, as if her rings promised the kiss of a knuckle-duster. Or as if he didn't like silver.

Diamond turned back to the task at hand. Her robust, grubby nails crumbled the burnt slate and she delicately sprinkled it like fine seasoning over the ragged tobacco.

'S'obviously down to what yer on… But it's like when you're tripping, yeah? Like you just *know*, out of the whole lot of them, who's tripping with you. Like yeah, you're trippin', an' you, an' you.'

Her forefinger jabbed the air, pointing out her fellow acid-travellers, invisible faces in a crowd that wasn't there. Her silent visitor smiled enigmatically. Diamond didn't care if he was following her or not, she just wanted him to stay. She'd gone to a lot of trouble to get him here. She had layered on a costume of delicate white lace rags, anointed her body with earthy patchouli and tinted her hair and painted her skin with henna. The candles sparked whorls of red from her luxuriant halo of corkscrew curls.

'Di?'

A sleepy child of about nine emerged from the back of the chaotic living wagon. He was skinny, with long matted dreadlocks of white-blonde hair. Like a tiny pirate, he held on to the waistband of some black and white stripy trousers that were several sizes too big for him.

'I'm hungry, what've you got?'

Diamond pulled him onto her lap, 'There's an apple.'

'Get lost.'

'Then you ain't hungry.'

'I am. I'm starving. I want toast. And jam.'

'You'll have bread and like it.'

Diamond ripped a hunk of bread off the loaf she'd baked yesterday. The boy snatched it, jumped down and bounced back down the length of the wagon to his sleeping platform. Holding the chunk of bread between his teeth, Rhys drew back the Indian bedspread hangings and climbed up into his nest. Once there, he wriggled until he was almost comfortable, then he got up again and punched at his hard block of a pillow. Sighing, Rhys lay on his belly on his lumpy futon and chewed at the hard corners of the bread. He pulled a silk scarf drape back and peered out of the square window. When Rhys had been really little, one of Diamond's exes had installed it into the side of her living wagon. He loved this window. It was from a *real* house, not a converted removals lorry painted red and green like the one he had lived in all his short life. This window was 'proper' and it had bits of stained-glass in it and it distorted the view outside.

Standing out against the darkness, bright yellow-orange lights swooped and danced nearby and he could hear the rushing sounds as the fire-jugglers spun their ignited sticks and clubs. Rhys loved this festival, there were no smoky generators rattling away, they weren't allowed. Everything was sun, or wind, or people powered, from the screen at The Groovy Movie to the Rinkydink.

The Rinkydink was a snakelike creature, formed from a dozen or so childrens' pushbikes, all of different shapes and sizes. They were tethered two abreast by a complicated variety of free-moving, universal joints. This meant the bike-train could twist and turn as its mini-operatives dictated, like a kid-driven wonky strand of pure-fun DNA.

Halfway along the Rinkydink bike-train sat an inflatable octopus on top of a sound-system. The harder the motley crew of different sized kids on their mismatched bikes pedalled, the louder the music got. Chocked, Rinkydink made an impromptu dance stage for the adults. Unchecked, it flew at breakneck speed between the tents and stalls, traceable anywhere on the festival-field by the boom and slump of its approaching or retreating sound-system. Rhys had put in many an hour pedalling like fury and he'd heard one bloke say it was the best use of small children since child-labour had been abolished in the UK.

It was after dark that the ban on fossil fuel energy came into its own. Without the backdrop of the fug and asthmatic chug of the generators, the festival reclaimed its true voice. Rhys loved this special non-quiet. All night long, all he could hear was distant chanting and music - and of course drumming. Good drumming, the kind you could go to sleep to, not the epileptic-dog-having-a-fit-in-a-skip row that the stupid townie drum-workshoppers made when they came.

His reverie was interrupted by his mother's cackle. Diamond was on one tonight. It worried Rhys, but she'd be straight again in a few days and they'd move on to the next place and nothing would be said about 'the visitor.' For now, he knew it was best that he kept out of the way. He'd tried to tell her once that nobody was there and that she was talking to thin air, but he'd just got a crack around the ear for that comment. Nowadays, he just let her get on with it and tried to ignore her one-way conversations with no-one.

Rhys crammed more of the hard bread into his mouth. Organic? Spelt? Whatever, it was gritty and it tasted like a brown cardboard box he'd once sucked on when he'd got so hungry his belly had ached. One day he'd get away from this and get a *real* house, with proper windows and electricity and a television and maybe even a *toaster* too! Bliss out! He'd have a kid, a son and he would *never* go hungry, he'd see to that. His kid would be the best looked after kid in the whole, wide world *ever*. He'd go to proper school and Diamond wouldn't ever be allowed to see him. No way. *Not ever.*

Now, twenty years later, Rhys ripped up the unopened letter from his mother. Somehow she'd found him again and there was only one thing for it. He sighed and looked round the little home he'd made for his son. It would all have to be packed up and moved somewhere else now. Somewhere safer. Rhys peered out of the window and tried not to worry.

Gnat was late home.

12

It was a perfect day in 1921. The cloudless sky was the deep, un-English blue of a Mediterranean painting and people were already saying that this summer was promising to be the best they'd seen in the three years since the end of the Great War.

It was unseasonably hot for May and Michael had been finding it hard to work. His stuffy rooms were suddenly no longer a place of refuge and it hadn't taken much persuasion for him to abandon his studies and escape Oxford for the day.

Waiting by the bridge, he swept his dark, sweat-streaked curls back from his forehead. Fatigue seeped into his bones and hollow-eyed melancholy gnawed at his thoughts. Even the bright, burning sunlight couldn't dispel his lingering pain. He'd been sacrificing his body for peace of mind. Three nights without sleep had allowed Michael a little respite, but his night terrors were becoming increasingly violent.

He despaired of ever finding escape, let alone true peace. From the corner of his eye, he detected a familiar figure. The breath fluttering in his throat, he leaned forwards, shading his eyes to watch...

Rupert, striding through mists of purple-spotted orchids, making his way across the riverside meadow, Rupert, dashing cascading plumes of thistledown from last years' ragged weeds as he went.

Even through his exhaustion, Michael smiled at this arresting vision of perfect youth. Immaculate in cricket whites, with the late May sun striking gold from his thick blonde hair, Rupert caught Michael's gaze, laughed and posed good-humouredly for his spectator. Rupert could be so many things at one and the same time, immaculate and casual, arch and relaxed. All this might be considered posturing in someone else, but not in him. Everything he did was hallmarked by the same unaffected, easy grace. Son of Sir Thomas Fowell Victor Buxton, 4th Baronet, the Right Honourable Rupert Buxton, was the flower of so many hopes and the white knight come to rescue Michael from his dark despondency.

Michael sighed and turned away. He suddenly felt out of sorts, self-conscious and over dressed in his blazer and bags. As Rupert approached, Michael inwardly scolded himself. He mustn't let his tiredness spoil their long planned day. With customary grace, Rupert vaulted the wall, landing as light as a kitten beside him.

'Old Potts done us proud, has he?' Rupert queried mock-serious as he lifted the check cloth to peruse the contents of the picnic basket. Michael rapidly listed the comestibles he'd gathered, suddenly anxious that his friend should find them pleasing.

'Eggs, cold cuts, stilton, chutneys, a *good* white loaf, butter, *decent* mustard, salad stuff, including Potts *very best* toms, one of Mrs. P's Victoria sponges and…. Damn! I forgot the bottled beer!'

'Good!' remarked Rupert pleasantly and leapt back over the wall, deftly swinging the picnic basket Michael had long laboured over.

'I've got a perfectly lovely Pouilly-Fumé chilling in the pool. Beer's for horrid, dirty workmen!'

Rupert routinely insulted all classes equally and without hint of any genuine malice. Michael wanly and without demur, roused himself to follow. With the picnic-basket balanced elegantly on his head, Rupert glided through the tall grasses, towards Sandford Pool.

As Michael trailed forlornly in his wake, Rupert called out, cheerfully, 'Oh what can ail thee knight at arms? Alone and palely loitering?' Another stride and he added, 'have to say you look hellish, Old Boy!'

If anyone held him in thrall it was Rupert. Brightening a little, Michael hurried to catch him up.

They emerged onto short, rabbit-cropped turf, where the riverbank swelled into a natural landing stage. A couple of beached skiffs reminded Michael of slender, landed fish, even down to their smoked-herring coloured mid-ribs.

A few feet away, the lithe green torso of the sinuous river shattered into plashy shards of churning, sunlit crystal. All was reflected light and movement as the captive Thames water frothed and splashed over the honey-coloured

Cotswold stones of Sandford Weir.

Rupert, his perfect face dancing with dappled reflections, turned and grinned in gleeful anticipation. Tiredness forgotten, Michael realised that this was the happiest he'd ever been, or could be.

The sweeping, protective arm of the weir and the cool, rippling depths of Sandford pool lay just the other side of a narrow spine of treacherous, moss slick stones.

Michael, never a good swimmer, quelled his customary pang at the sight of the deep pool. He lifted his chin defiantly and made to manfully step forwards, but before he had a chance to mask his anxiety - or even make a complete fool of himself - Rupert squeezed his arm. Just the lightest touch, but firm enough to reassure and steady him. It was a typical Rupert gesture and it thrilled Michael to the core. Thoroughly emboldened, he headed confidently along the narrow ledge to the rocks that overhung the very deepest water.

Even as they ate, Michael knew they were laying down a precious memory, as good as any fine wine. Perhaps on a day yet to be, when he was a very old man, he'd pull the cork and savour every golden drop of the long-hoarded contents. He'd remember how the setting had been idyllic, the weather glorious and the company perfect.

Basket and bottle emptied, Michael and Rupert lay companionably close, stretched out like basking seals, on the big stones by the weir, being particularly careful not to touch. They had often referred to Sandford Pool as their secret place. Though it was hardly crowded, on a lovely day like this, they were far from alone.

Rupert drew from his pocket a small, exquisitely bound book of Keats' poetry and began reading. Smiling blissfully, Michael lay back and let the sounds of the gentle, chuckling water and Rupert's mellifluous tones wash over him as he read:

'Oh what can ail thee, knight-at-arms,

Alone and palely loitering?

The sedge has withered from the lake,

And no birds sing.

I see a lily on thy brow,

With anguish moist and fever-dew,

And on thy cheeks a fading rose

Fast withereth too.

I met a lady in the meads,

Full beautiful - a faery's child,

112

Her hair was long her foot was light,

And her eyes were wild.

And there she lulled me asleep

And there I dreamed - Ah! woe betide!

The latest dream I ever dreamt

On the cold hill side.

I saw pale kings and princes too,

Pale warriors, death-pale were they all;

They cried – 'La Belle Dame sans Merci

Hath thee in thrall!'

I saw their starved lips in the gloam,

With horrid warning gaped wide,

And I awoke and found me here,

On the cold hill's side.

And this is why I sojourn here

Alone and palely loitering,

Though the sedge is withered from the lake,

And no birds sing.'

As the last syllables of the final verse floated away on the warm breeze, Michael's heavy eyes succumbed to sleep. Twitching like a puppy, he gave a yelp and slid from his rock. In a flash Rupert leapt up, catching him before he hit the water.

He didn't have to ask. Rupert knew all about Michael's nightmares.

'Off to Neverland again Peter Pan?'

Rupert's shining eyes were gently mocking. Suddenly, Michael found himself thinking about 'Uncle Jim.' Jim Barrie, *confident*, step-father and storyteller extraordinaire.

With a stab of regret, Michael realised he hadn't replied to Uncle Jim's last letter. He lay back on his rock and stared up into the dizzying, cloudless depths above him. There was time. There would always be time, after all Michael reflected, he *was* The Boy Who Wouldn't Grow Up.

He lay listening to the liquid grace of the waters lost in a timeless daze on that hot, drowsy May afternoon in 1921, blithely unaware of the approaching darkness.

When he had been very little, Nana Evie had told Michael about the wicked fairies who stole children and left horrid creatures called *changelings* in their places. He recalled how Nana had been dismissed for filling his head with such stories. Ironic then that he, Michael, should have become the model for Peter Pan, one of the most famous stories ever told. Michael closed his eyes and turned his face to the sun that burned orange through his closed lids.

He licked his lips where Rupert's smoky wine lingered at the corners. Deep water and high places all held their own special, secret magnetism and Michael imagined giving himself up as a willing victim to the thrillingly dangerous pull of Sandford Pool. A delicious shiver ran through him. As he lay listening to the throaty roar of the weir, something disgorged from the depths of Michael's memory and floated free. A ragged remembrance scratched at the back of his brain like a dog whining to be let in.

Hadn't there had been a tug of war between Nana Evie and himself…? No, that wasn't right. He had been *the rope*… the tug of war had been *over him*… it had been between Nana Evie and… who?

Who did those other hands belong to? Those *unseen* hands? Those hands that had clutched and tickled and all but pulled him from his cot? From the darkest, most suppressed regions of his mind, a latent memory coalesced into a scene of startling clarity.

Reality snapped as inexorable truth slammed Michael square on. With a crashing jolt he suddenly understood what monsters lay in the fathomless deeps and emerged every night in his tormented dreams. Stunned, Michael slowly sat up.

Without knowing how he had ever forgotten now, for the first time in his life, he remembered. Everything.

He had been a very small boy and Nana was battling valiantly to stop him being stolen away. He clearly remembered laughing, *giggling*, through the entire abduction attempt and how Nana Evie had howled and struggled so hard to keep hold of him. But he had giggled hysterically.

He couldn't help it, he had been so little. So terrified. Terrified by the laughing, huge-eyed fairies trying so very hard to drag him away. Though all he wanted to do was scream, he was compelled to keep giggling, held under a dreadful spell by their manic chuckles, drowning in his own mirthless laughter.

When it was all over, Nana had drunk brandy. Then she was crying on the back step. Then she had left. What had George said about it? Michael wished he'd listened more to what his older brother George had said. It was too late now. George had become yet another lost boy, sleeping under the mud of Flanders.

116

So, Nana's stories had been more than just stories. Poor, sacked Nana Evie really had been locked in some fearful battle for Michael's mortal soul. A thought hit him like a leaden blow. Had his nightmares been stolen away by Uncle Jim Barrie and transmuted into 'Peter Pan?'

Conclusions started dropping like pennies from hell. How many little ones hadn't had a safe pair of hands like Nana Evie's to drag them back and save them? How many had been lost forever?

Michael shivered in the bright sunshine, what would a changeling look like? He cast a wary eye over the scant gatherings of students and visitors.

Slender sylphs of girls in white summer muslin, gathered swanlike at the glistening waters edge. Fey young men with suffering faces glanced up from their reflections and regarded him with solemn eyes. How many? Some of them? *All of them?* Dazed, Michael jumped up and looked for safety, for Rupert.

Rupert was now sitting like a beautiful merman on a rock, right in the centre of the weir. Michael knew, with a certainty beyond all logic, that he was in extreme danger and that, bad swimmer or no, he simply had to get to Rupert.

The cold shock of the water took his breath the moment he plunged into the deep pool. Michael gasped and struck out towards the weir, but something was entangling his legs, anchoring him to the spot.

He kicked to free himself of what he thought must be weed, but it felt like grasping arms were pulling him under. He kicked again and broke the surface only to be dragged back down in a tussle suddenly far more terrifying than the remembered tug of war.

The sky was reflected weirdly in the underside of the mirrored surface of the pool, as Michael strained to push his face up through it. Flailing wildly, he surfaced and managed one last, gasping howl before the unseen arms claimed him.

At the subsequent coroner's inquest into the deaths, it was reported that the water in Sandford Pool was twenty to thirty feet deep and calm. That Rupert Buxton was a good swimmer, but that Michael Llewelyn Davies had a fear of water and could not swim 'effectively.' A witness reported that one man was swimming to join the other who was sitting on a stone on the weir, but that he experienced *difficulties* and the other dived in to reach him. However, the witness also reported that when he saw their heads together in the water, they did not appear to be struggling. Their bodies were recovered 'clasped' together the next day.

Despite much fevered speculation that these two young men had entered into a suicide pact, the coroner's conclusion was that Davies had drowned accidentally and that Buxton had drowned trying to save him.

13

'Are you following me?' Neave's gaze was level, challenging, but not unfriendly. Busted, Gnat didn't know how to reply.

'It's okay,' Neave's sudden smile was like the sun coming out from behind a cloud. Gnat bathed in its sudden, unexpected warmth.

'I…' Still he couldn't speak, he looked down at his shoes, dumbstruck.

'Nice socks,' Neave observed.

Suddenly, Gnat found his voice, 'Dad got them for me.'

'Not your Mum?' Neave asked innocently.

'She…' Gnat struggled.

'Went away?' Neave ventured.

Gnat nodded, 'Something like that.'

'I live over there,' Neave pointed to the green hill beyond the village.

'I didn't know there were any houses there,' Gnat said uncertainly. Was she teasing him? He *knew* there weren't any houses there.

'Well, there's *one*!' Neave giggled and linked her slender arm through his. Normally Gnat would have drawn away, embarrassed. But this felt right. No, better than that. This felt *good*.

They headed up Church Lane. As they passed the ancient stones of the church boundary wall, Neave's face grew dark. Gnat looked over the wall. The sandstone glowed in the warm afternoon light, the mismatched stones dating the many restorations of the old church through the ages. Dark, diamond panes of stained glass hinted at the glowing colours that could only be seen from the inside.

A single Scots Pine had stood as a lone sentinel by

the bell tower for the last century at least and clipped yews lined the long avenue to the big, wooden doors. They formed a guard of honour that had greeted countless new brides over many, many centuries. To Gnat's eyes it was beautiful. A wonderful place to hunt bugs and butterflies. Bright spots of orange lichen dotted the older gravestones, whilst the newer headstones proudly sported lovingly left offerings of fresh flowers.

'I *hate* going past that place,' Neave grumbled.

'They can't hurt you, they're all dead.'

Neave shrugged, but still she looked uneasy.

'When I was little, I told Dad I was scared of going past the graveyard near where we lived back then… and you know what he said?'

Neave turned huge, questioning eyes towards him and shook her head. Gnat continued, 'Dad said, "it's the living you have to be careful of!" '

Neave giggled, 'He's right. People can be very scary.'

Gnat felt he ought to apologise for what Matt had said, but he didn't want the memory of it to spoil such a lovely afternoon.

They wandered on and Gnat told her all about his life constantly on the move with Dad. He really wanted to tell her about the wing, but he held back. He had never told anyone about it. Even Dad had never mentioned it since the bonfire.

They followed the footpath to the old wooden stile and scrambling over, dropped into the cool, deep green of the field beyond. With exaggerated strides, they waded through the lush meadow-grass.

Gnat was transported with delight. He'd never seen so many butterflies in all his life. Mentally he counted them off, naming as many of them as he could. Skippers, hairstreaks, fritillaries, tortoiseshells. This was the nearest thing to heaven he had ever encountered. Wrapt, he plunged deeper into a living dream.

'Don't move!' he whispered. A rare Adonis Blue had settled on Neave's blonde hair. Like a living jewel of purest azure, it blinked its scintillating wings and trembled in the light meadow airs. Gnat stood over Neave, peering in wonder at it the creature's fragile loveliness. Neave caught his look and giggled, 'That's nothing, watch this!'

Before he could stop her, Neave sprang away. Disappointed, Gnat watched the beautiful butterfly take flight. Neave ran to a small rise. Standing knee deep in a drift of meadow flowers and smiling brightly, she flung her arms wide.

Breathless, Gnat watched as rainbow shards took flight from every part of the meadow. Hundreds of butterflies, of every size and hue, skipped and danced towards Neave as if she was some kind of irresistible flower. Within seconds, she was enveloped in a cloud of thousands of bright wings. Hundreds of them settled upon her, until she was clothed in a moving coat of vibrant colours.

Dumbly Gnat approached her, seeing, but not believing. Neave stood smiling proudly, turning to display her living adornments. As she turned, the glowing aura of rainbow-light wings shimmered. Fluttering flakes of pure colour.

Gnat trembled with awe. Overwhelmed by the vision, he was barely aware of the beguiling music that had begun floating towards him on the warm breeze. Spellbound, he sank to the grass. Kneeling there, he looked and looked, hungrily filling his eyes and ears with every last detail of the scene. From Neave's liquid laugh, to the way the delicate creatures lifted and resettled every time she made a movement. Gnat was dazed. It was the loveliest thing he'd ever seen in his whole life.

Occasionally, a butterfly would detach and fly to him. He felt the faintest draft on his cheek as it dusted him with colour, but what would have normally sent him giddy with delight barely registered, compared to the enthralling sight of Neave, dancing gracefully with the butterflies.

'Welcome to our home,' the lilting words hung gently on the air and Gnat turned to the speaker. A pale, slender woman looked down at him. Behind her he felt, rather than saw, that there were many more present.

'You look like your Mother.'

Stunned, Gnat rose to his feet, 'How do you know…?' he began, but the woman continued, 'she misses you!'

'In heaven?'

The woman laughed. The musical lightness of it was just like Neave's.

'She's not in heaven!'

Mystified, Gnat looked back at Neave. She had

124

shaken off the multicoloured insects and now joined her mother.

'Shall we go inside, Mama? Gnat's hungry.'

He hadn't been aware of it, but now that she mentioned it, Gnat found he was suddenly ravenous. He nodded in eager agreement and they linked their slender arms with his and led him away. Gnat gazed back at the meadow. The butterflies danced about the flowers like butterflies usually did, as if they had quite forgotten all about dancing with Neave.

Still he couldn't see any house, just the green hill, topped with the grassy mounds of its Iron-Age earthworks looming above them. He looked questioningly at Neave's Mum, but she just smiled back encouragingly.

'Mama makes the sweetest cakes you've ever eaten!' Neave remarked brightly. Gnat stared at her, Neave had never looked so beautiful, so grown up. She looked like a magical princess in some old story.

Wait 'til he told Matt. Gnat faltered. How could he possibly explain all this to Matt? Thoughts of home flooded his mind and suddenly, unaccountably, Gnat found himself filled with instant longing and regret.

He missed his Dad.

As if in answer, Neave's grip tightened on his arm. Her Mum's arm lightly slipped up and around his shoulders as she gently propelled him forwards. He could see they were walking towards the grassy, green wall of the mound, but there was no obvious way up - or in.

Before he could gather his thoughts any further, the barely perceptible music swelled, releasing Gnat from all his anxieties. He was *so* tired and hungry. He would rest, then drink and eat his fill and then dance and dance and dance with Neave and her people. He'd never wanted to move his body as much as he did now.

Enraptured, he sailed towards the foot of the grassy slope, borne on a current of pure, joyous sound. Neave smiled. From the depths of this wonderful waking dream, Gnat smiled back blissfully. He could see that both Neave and her Mum now bore something like arcs of light behind them. As if it was the most natural thing in the world, he saw that they were wings, far bigger than the butterflies. So beautiful, so like the wings he'd had in his dream. Like the one he had at home.

Gnat missed his dream wings. He wanted to fly again. To feel the rapturous, dizzying...

Noise hit him, like a punch in the head. A hateful, crashing din smashed the idyll breaking all enchantment. A screeching, dissonant, man-made alarm screamed its foul note across the cosmos. Gnat surfaced from the spell and was amazed to find the ear-shattering row was nothing more than his mobile going off.

'Where on earth have you got to?' Dad demanded.

Gnat blinked. Neave and her Mum were nowhere to be seen. Suddenly he was quite alone on the cold hillside.

Shivering, he mumbled, 'Lost track of time.'

'I was worried. Your tea's getting cold.'

'Coming now.' Gnat shoved his phone in his pocket and stumbled away from the hill. Terrified, he pelted through the enchanted meadow. The long grass whipped against his legs and he scattered butterflies as he ran.

He was back home within twenty minutes. Dad didn't remark on his pale and sweaty face. He was too busy opening a fresh roll of parcel tape. Everything was packed in bin bags and boxes. Gnat didn't have to ask. Perching on a camp chair, he ate his tea in silence.

They were on the move again.

14

Almost weightless, D turned flipped and kicked. His feet pushed hard against the tiles and he flew beneath the surface of the water. Like an aquatic creature away from the land, all his clumsiness had vanished and he demonstrated the authentic grace of a being in its true element.

Sharklike, his hands finned elegantly as he cut through the pool with speed and precision. His movements were so natural to him that he no longer had to concentrate on correct form and remembering to breathe.

Grasping great armfuls of water, he cast them away behind him without thought and the rhythm of his strokes became a backbeat to his meditation. Propelling himself through the swimming pool, D mentally prepared for the coming mission. In a little under two hours he would rendezvous at the Wiltshire site with the team from the children's hospital. Then he would liaise with the archaeologist and they would enter a place that was D's idea of hell on earth. Or rather *under* it.

D dried himself off and quickly dressed. His clothes were quiet but exuded the quality of being carefully tailored – they had to be, to fit his odd shape. He shook his shaggy black hair like a dog. He might require fine fabrics for his sensitive skin, but he was naturally low maintenance.

Just before 5 a.m. he turned his battered old Saab onto the M5. Dawn was already streaking the sky and the traffic was light at such an early hour. He made good progress and although there was nothing obvious to hold him up, D instinctively slowed down at one particular spot close to the Frankwell services.

Two lines of geopathic stress cross the M5, both have earned the reputation of being notorious accident black spots and this was one of them. D didn't ever use the term *ley lines* and still questioned the exact nature of these ancient energy trackways, but it was matter of record that apart from the above average incidence of collisions occurring here, such crossings were centres of fairy activity. He checked that his remedy was still in place. It was.

A stake of iron, disguised to resemble an innocent-looking mile marker, pierced the earth and continued to divert the negative stream. To the common eye it was just another clunky piece of metal adorning the roadside. If this job had taught D one thing, it was that the majority of people failed to see - let alone question - much of anything that went on around them. Every day, motorists drove safely by this and similar iron guardians, blithely unaware of their existence, let alone their otherworldly function.

The iron stake had fallen once, victim to an overzealous road repair crew. Within hours there had been a multiple pile up. After that, D had seen to it that all the stakes he'd had placed around the roads of Britain now had their own watchers.

D reached the site just before sunrise and found the archaeologist, Claire, slowly limping up the lane away from the dig. Her face was pale and feverish in the early light and all trace of her customary grin and good humour had gone. He stopped the car, reached across and opened the door.

Claire flopped onto the passenger seat pushing damp corkscrew tendrils of hair away from her glistening forehead. Despite the coolness of the morning, she shrugged off her heavy, hooded sweatshirt. Then she pulled out an inhaler from a pocket in her combats and sucked in her medication. D slowly drove down the lane giving her time to recover.

'Activity?' he whispered.

In a soft Merseyside accent, Claire answered quietly.

'They nearly danced me to death.'

'No hostilities? No attacks?'

'*Excuse me?*' Claire hissed, her green eyes wide with indignation, 'since when was trying to kill me *not* counted as hostile?'

D grinned.

'No,' she conceded in a whisper, 'Other than trying to murder me, they were sweetness and light. They didn't even try to shoot me. But by the third hour of all that stupid jigging about, I sincerely wished they would.'

D suppressed a chuckle and whispered back, 'Nothing like a bit of exercise. Good for the soul.'

'If the sun hadn't come up and they hadn't skedaddled back inside to sleep, my poor blessed soul would have departed for good!'

D raised his forefinger and Claire fell quiet, they were now inside the silent zone. He cut the engine and they coasted to a halt. Claire stayed in the car, grateful for the rest, whilst D got out, gently closing the door behind him.

He took a few light steps and stood by the old stile, scenting the air like a hound, filling his senses with faint traces of the enemy. D's mismatched eyes could differentiate between fairy tracks and those of the sheep. He read the infested landscape and saw the broken stems where the clumsier chunkheads preferred to pass. He spotted where they had all danced and recently eaten. Luckily for Claire, she had neither been offered food nor drink, or she would not have escaped so easily. D traced where the enemy's faint trails led homewards through the dew. Two sentries stood nearby. Chunkheads. One disguised as the broken trunk of an old oak and the other as a single mossy dolmen. Both appeared to be dozing. D was about to turn back to the car when he noticed a mass of movement in a nearby thicket of hawthorn. Clear flames passed between the tangled undergrowth, stragglers, out late after their revelry. There were dozens of them. He froze and without lifting a foot, tilted his body back by degrees so most of his bulk was now masked by the broad, silvern trunk of a beech tree.

Beguiling, musical laughter rang out against the gentle thrum of insectlike chatter, as the faery troop made their way home. They passed close by, but D didn't peek. He didn't need to. He knew there would be light and colour and beauty enough to fill up any human heart so it burst with delight. Sights so beguiling, they would reach out slender filaments of fairy glamour to encircle the mind and trap the unwary into their clan forever. In centuries gone by, many a naïve farmhand had been caught thus - simply by looking.

Closing his eyes, D steadied his heart like a sniper preparing to fire. He began his inner mantra *'Don't see me, don't see me,'* and listened as the fairy procession passed right by him just the other side of the hedge, making their way homewards to the barrow. He heard the swish and click of wings, the improbably light steps of the greys and arboreals, the heavier stamp of chunkheads, their music, chatter and mirth.

The sounds receded and D slowly opened his eyes and froze. A creature had broken away from the throng and it was staring directly at him, sniffing the air. Smaller than usual, its huge head weaved from side to side, like a snake mesmerising its prey, its ugly gash of a mouth showed pointed teeth.

D saw it lift its face to scan… nothing. The eyes were milky. Although indeed, it hadn't seen him, his 'don't see me' mantra had been made redundant by those pale and blighted eyes. This creature was all but blind.

A chunkhead detached from the troop and came to

collect the wanderer. He slapped the blind youngster heavily on one of its delicate ears and it yelped and gave a long whine like a beaten puppy. To D's alarm, the coarse and heavy-handed chunkhead abruptly stiffened. Straightening its bent back, it peered hard in his direction and took a step towards D's hiding place. It came so close, he could smell its mossy, rotten-wood breath hanging in the cold morning air. He caught his own breathing, deliberately dropped his heart rate even further, and practised perfect stillness. Long moments later, the chunkhead gave a grunt and moved off, propelling the still whining youngster homewards with a great kick.

D remained cocooned in absolute silence and stillness. His back muscles were beginning to complain, but he held his position, suspended in silence, hanging on the slender thread of hope that he hadn't been spotted.

The rendezvous point was just outside the silent zone, in a discreet layby a couple of hundred yards up the tree-shaded lane. Jockey jumped out of the back of the armoured Land-Rover. Inside it a dog-cage held a snarling something.

'Nasty wee scumbag,' Jockey observed lightly.

The doctor, Prateeka, peered in at her charge. The

creature was furious but increasingly sleepy. It blinked milky, weeping eyes at an unseen world.

'What is that? Myxi?' Jockey took a cautious step closer to the cage

'Myxomatosis? Yes,' she nodded in confirmation, 'They catch it off the young hares they torment.'

'Then why don't we just spray the barrows?'

Prateeka shrugged, 'I am told they tried that in the fifties. They claimed it was all being done to keep down the wild rabbit population. I believe it caused universal uproar.'

'Aye, but what's a few bunnies compared to these?'

The creature was shaking with the effort to raise itself up, fighting the sedative. Prateeka had dosed it as much as she dared, if she overdid it and it died, they could never recover its human counterpart.

D had maintained his awkward, leaning pose for a full twenty minutes before even daring to shift his weight. His back muscles were screaming and he was beginning to shake. Suppressing a groan, he leaned against the beech's silky trunk. Judging enough time had elapsed to risk moving, with utmost relief he stretched his knotted neck, touching his left ear to his left shoulder. Breathing softly with each gentle click, he turned to the right. Cold metal stung his exposed neck.

In plain light, fully visible, a haughty, aristocratic-looking arboreal held him at sword point whilst three grey archers targeted him with their bows.

The regal looking creature with the sword fixed D with huge glittering eyes. D stood poised, but his enemy made no move to kill. They were weighing him up and seemed content to detain him there. D could only hope they didn't recognise him as the one who had harried them through all the long years.

If they did, he didn't want to start wondering what special treatment they might have ready for him. Cornered and outnumbered, D contemplated. His knife would be no match for the reach of the sword. He'd be impaled before he could strike at the creature behind it. Any attempt at a throw would invite attack even before he could fully draw his arm back. Even if he managed it, he could only hit one of them.

His mind next fixed upon the tiny canister nestling in his pocket. His best chance lay with its payload of lethal spray. He tried a basic feint, a classic misdirection move, but the creature didn't follow. It wouldn't look away. It never broke its penetrating gaze. It wasn't a chunkhead and it couldn't be fooled so easily.

Violet's crashing fall through the bracken proved a much more effective distraction. As the creatures turned, D sprayed the silver dust in a huge arc. Lethal droplets of atomised silver solution hit the sword wielder directly in the face. It barely had time to register shock before it fell as rain. The archers dropped silently even before Violet regained her footing and Baby came out to play.

'You okay?' she whispered.

'Yeah, think so.'

Violet was not convinced. D seemed to be in pain.

'Did they get you?'

'I got me,' D grimaced. Violet raised her eyebrows, as he murmured, 'laugh it up, I stuck myself with my own weapon.'

'Sir, with respect, you're a dickhead.'

From being comfortably curled-up in D's passenger seat, Claire had roused herself groggily from a deep sleep. Her leg muscles burned and it took her a lot of effort just to get out of the car. As she made her way back up the lane, she'd already mentally phoned in a sickie to the dig director and decided on a hot bath before bed. She approached Jockey and the others.

'All done?' she yawned. Her face fell as she spotted the occupant in the cage, 'you haven't even started? Where's D? He's been ages.'

Jockey took sudden alarm and sprinted down the lane. He met Violet and D on their way back up. The look on Violet's face was enough.

'Trouble?'

'Fairy liquid.' Violet stated flatly.

'Great. Are they all riled up now? Waiting for us?'

'All quiet,' D countered tersely.

Claire was still recovering, except now she was in the Land Rover's passenger seat, so D sat on the step to begin the briefing. With Claire tucked in behind him, Violet and Jockey stood looking down at him.

'Sedation working?' D looked questioningly at the crash team.

Even Jockey winced as the male medic, Paddy stretched his arm through the bars and stroked the creature's instep. It was totally unresponsive. Paddy nodded, the sedation was working. He removed his arm from the cage and Jockey breathed again. The two had been comrades in Bosnia and Jockey knew Paddy could take insane risks.

D dragged a rucksack from the foot-well by Claire's feet and pulled out some slender boxes.

'New toys, kids.' He handed over the bronze night-vision goggles. 'Calibrated to detect the enemy. Claire!'

D's bark cut through Claire's nap. She roused herself and slid out of her seat. Digging into one of the many pockets in her combat trousers, she pulled out a crumpled piece of paper and unfolded it. It was a crude map of the interior of the barrow. Prateeka and Paddy drew nearer to see it, and Claire began explaining what the entire team had come to call *Clairoglyphs*.

'It's a little more elaborate than the last one. There's the usual central chamber here, but there's a side gallery here and a couple of ante-chambers leading off here.'

Her finger traced the lines she'd made. 'I've removed the boards from the entrance and it dips a few inches, but then the floor gets really uneven about ten feet in, so watch your footing. They prefer to sleep in the long gallery rather than the central chamber, but I guess that's because of the disturbance from the current dig.'

'And the target?' Jockey asked.

'I couldn't see anything definite, sorry.'

Violet peered at Claire's map. 'He'll be tucked away on a high shelf, I shouldn't wonder.'

'Sorry to disappoint, but there aren't any niches in this set up.'

'Then he's been Hidden in Plain Sight,' Jockey suggested, 'or maybe holed up in a closed chamber?'

D continued, 'So this one isn't going to be straightforward. When we've located the target, Vi, you follow me in for the extraction. Paddy, once she's clear, you drop the replacement, exactly as directed. Jockey, you're on watch inside. Prateeka, you're on watch outside, but keep close to the entrance. Usual drill with the extractee. Got that?'

They all nodded.

'For now, there are two chunkheads out front to be

dealt with. Cheers Claire, you can stand down.'

'Can I grab a kip in the Landy 'til you all get back?'

D nodded, checked his watch and addressed Violet and Jockey, 'If you two go now, we'll follow in ten.'

Jockey pursed his lips but said nothing.

'I know you can sort the chunkies in five, Jockey. We'll follow in ten,' D repeated firmly, 'that'll give you time to check the barrow really is as quiet as I hope it is.'

The pair of them headed back down the lane, but just outside the silent zone, Violet pulled Jockey aside.

'They didn't kill him. Jockey, he was alone, up against four of them, they had him - and they *hesitated*.'

'Their mistake.'

Whilst Jockey and Violet were busy turning the sentries to morning dew in the grass, D motioned to Prateeka. She left Paddy checking the caged creature and approached D. He revealed his right forefinger, the skin on the fingertip was grey, burned and raw as if he'd been hit with acid.

'Nasty.'

'And embarrassing. I can't tell my patrol I'm sensitive to silver spray!'

Prateeka smiled grimly, 'Your secret is safe with me. I can wash it out with saline, but it might need further attention.' Grabbing a small, plastic bottle, she squirted enough liquid to drench the ragged flesh, 'silver's a natural antiseptic. Too much and it's a poison. You've got some argyria discoloration there already - that didn't just happen today.'

She carefully bound D's finger in light gauze and watched as he gingerly tucked his hands into gloves.

'Acute exposure to this stuff doesn't do us much good either. Have you *seen* the pictures of colloidal silver victims on the 'net? You should have taken the time to put gloves on in the first place.'

D nodded ruefully, thinking *as if I'd had time,* whilst saying, 'Thanks. *Really* got to go.'

D and Paddy dragged the cage from the back of the Land Rover, slipped long poles through the top-rings and hoisted it to shoulder height. The sleeping creature inside was light, but the cage was necessarily strong and heavy. Once detected, changelings could turn extremely nasty.

Prateeka let them move off and then followed, carrying a light stretcher under her arm.

She and Paddy were part of an elite group of medics. Known to the few as 'The Aranars,' their name originated from their original job description of 'Rescue and Restore.' Their illustrious history showed as much courage and valour as any regiment in the British army, yet few people were aware of the existence of this highly specialised force.

Founded in the late eighteenth century, The Aranars inception had been every bit as secret as when Queen Elizabeth I had consulted with Dr. John Dee and created the Commission for Metaphysic - D's D9.

Some, like Paddy, had been honoured for spectacular acts of bravery during brief secondments into the regular forces, yet not one Aranar had ever been decorated specifically for the work they actually did.

Aranar deeds were unspoken. Unlike D's D9 with its 'Video et Taceo,' they had no motto. They wore no cap badges or regimental ties and rarely met, except on active service. Seeded throughout society, one Aranar might pass by another without ever knowing they were part of the same unit. By comparison, they made the SAS look positively chatty.

The need for Aranars had been established when the largest and oldest children's hospital in London first opened. It had started out, not as a Foundlings Hospital as is commonly thought, but as a *Changelings* Hospital. Informed by long tradition and folklore, earlier generations were more attuned to the possibility of substitutes, quickly abandoning any children they couldn't accept as their own. Thus, The London Hospital for Changelings was established to meet the growing need for exchange.

By necessity, a group of medically trained men - and it was always men back in the early days - had been formed to repatriate the changelings, to take them back to their own kind and when possible, retrieve the children they had replaced.

It was extremely dangerous work, a lot of fatal and near fatal mistakes had been made and many good people had been lost forever, but those who had survived learnt quickly and a huge body of knowledge about the metahominids had been built up.

Prateeka grudgingly admired these creatures for their sheer tenacity and their exceptional adaptation skills. Like cuckoos matching their egg shells to blend in with the eggs of the unwitting host birds, these creatures aped the features of the living children they replaced. Now, once again, as she turned her back on the bright morning sunshine, she braced herself for the strangeness of the otherworld she was about to enter.

Violet and Jockey stood at the entrance to the barrow. The dolmen and oak stump had both vanished. The chunkheads had been dealt with. Soundlessly D and Paddy lowered the cage. Paddy unlocked it and pulled the still-sleeping creature into a thick, canvas sack, which he carefully drew over his shoulder. Prateeka placed the evac-stretcher on the ground and the team stood to attention, signalling their readiness.

Silently, D dipped into the barrow. He switched on his goggles and cautiously moved forwards, whilst the others edged in behind him.

Like a miser's dream, the chamber was filled with enchanted treasure and amidst it all lay the forms of sleeping figures. High status arboreals slumbered like knights in armour, spectral hounds and horses sleeping with them, all in readiness for the Wild Hunt. That was when they would charge through the lands at night, sweeping all living creatures before them and villagers would turn their faces away, in fear of catching a glimpse of them and being lost in their thrall.

Violet scanned the chamber and her heart ached with the beauty of it, but she was experienced enough to know that the trappings were all part of the trap. She steeled herself to resist the sights she was seeing, yet she couldn't deny she was stirred by the cruel beauty of these creatures. That a sight so noble could be so vicious brought to mind Wagner's soaring *Der Ring des Nibelungen* played amidst the grotesque grandeur of a Nazi rally. Violet dug deep and caught a tight grip on her wandering thoughts. Sleeping though they may be, these creatures could still play with human minds.

Jockey quelled his immediate impulse to liberally spray the room with silver. He knew that to do so would only get everyone killed and lose the target, but he could not stop the hatred rising like a bitter taste on the back of his tongue.

These vile beings had cost him everything.

Tight lipped, Paddy quickly took stock of the sleeping battalions. He was cut with biting disappointment, but registered nothing. Perhaps one day he would find the lost wife he never spoke about. But she wasn't here, so it would not be today.

D stalked his enemy's lair, exuding cold fury.

He'd long ago stopped asking why they insisted on giving up their own in exchange for human offspring. In his early days with D9 he had used to wonder if it was because they loved human children more than their own, or even if they loved their offspring enough to willingly give them up, in the hope of a better life for them with the humans. Over time, he'd come to see that love played no part in this malevolent exchange. Subjecting both child and changeling to a half-life entrapped in worlds to which they simply did not belong was the highest cruelty to both, a despicably spiteful act that spread lasting misery for generations.

Only Prateeka remained unmoved, viewing her surroundings and the sleeping subjects with the keen, detached interest of a scientist. She'd seen similar sights before, but this encounter appeared to offer a richness of body-types not usually found in a single barrow. She noted the variations in shapes and sizes of skull, the likeness of the grey elves to the classic, grey alien form and how some of them were all but indistinguishable from human children, afflicted with the premature ageing disease *progeria*.

The cultural artefacts were exceptionally well-wrought and even the creatures clothing appeared to demonstrate a degree of innovation.

Whilst the knights were clad in traditional cloaks and armour and chunkheads stuck to their common uniforms of red and green, non combatants, particularly the arboreals had adopted a more subtle approach to dress. Still favouring the broad tradition of long, floating garments, Prateeka realised, with fascinated alarm that they would not have been out of place in any modern city.

D raised his hand and his unit stopped at the entrance to the long gallery. Claire had considered this to be the place full of sleepers, believing the central chamber to be empty. If she had only detected a percentage of the occupants, then it was likely to be a real crush in the gallery.

Still unable to locate his target, D signalled Violet to come with him whilst the others stayed back as ordered.

Re-gathering her scattered thoughts, Violet stepped through into the gallery. She couldn't read the floor surface with her left 'foot,' a carbon fibre prosthetic, so she was forced to repeatedly scan the floor and constantly check for trip-hazards, be they the out thrust limbs of the sleepers, their clothing and artefacts, or the trailing tails of fairy hounds. Every time she looked down, Violet had to quickly dart a glance back up, lest she walk straight into something unseen at head height. Consequently, she found herself taking in more detail than her fogging brain could handle. And it was fogging. They couldn't stay down here much longer, or they too would succumb to the long sleep of the fairies. Some people took a hundred years to awaken. Most never did.

As they moved through the gallery, carefully threading their way through the massed, sleeping forms, something like a storm was erupting in D's head. He was being battered by a blizzard of living light breathed out from these creatures of the deep. Everywhere he turned, flashes of blue astral light exploded in the subterranean cavern. The dazzling bio-luminescence pounded his retinas, leaving black blobs of unresponsive vision in their wake, inviting him to stumble. Every sleeper's dream battered at the doors of his sanity.

He could hear their urgent whispers as clear as any spoken word. Calls for him to stay. Pleas, entreaties, threats. Somewhere, deep inside their dreams, these creatures knew he was amongst them and they were determined he should stay.

He knew his very presence was disturbing them and

he should leave before he compromised the safety of the group. Then, a huge bubble of pure blue light coalesced and rose like magma from the chamber. It towered oppressively over him, a distended orb of pure power.

Even though Violet couldn't see the reason for their sudden lack of progress, she halted behind D. He knew they couldn't move forwards. He also knew that their goal must be very close, judging by this show of strength. The unstable tower of light trembled unsteadily before abruptly lurching forwards and collapsing in a wave of brilliance that exploded in his face like a million flashbulbs. It surged over and through him, thundering into his chest, pummelling his heart and draining all his strength away as it eddied out behind him.

D held his silence, but staggered under the onslaught. A hound stirred fitfully at his feet and he froze. The spectral creature tucked its nose beneath a slender paw and fell quiet again. Surely it could smell him? Then D noticed something out of place, a small foot sticking out from under a flimsy shroud. The foot was illuminated by the blue light, but it did not emanate it.

D knelt and drew back the cloth. The boy was about three and he bore a superficial resemblance to the creature in the sack, but his Thomas the Tank Engine pyjamas proclaimed him as human. D grabbed the child and quickly stuck him with a prepared sedative. He didn't give so much as a whimper as the needle went in.

D waited for agonized minutes, in absolute stillness, shutting down his mind, trying not to think, feel, or be anything other than the words, *'Don't see me.'*

Nerves exquisitely stretched, he eventually judged it safe to pass the now deeply-sleeping boy to Violet. She strapped him into a harness close against her and slowly made her way back to Paddy. They nodded and swapped places. Paddy stepped into the crowded gallery, carrying the thing in the sack.

Shaking the fog from her mind, Violet redoubled her scanning up and down. They had rescued the hostage and she couldn't bear to blow it now. Hardly daring to breathe, she inched past Jockey, on guard in the main chamber and heart stopping moments later, she finally exited the barrow.

Prateeka folded open the lightweight stretcher and Violet laid the sleeping boy upon it. It wasn't safe to check him out here still so close to the barrow, so the women raced the stretcher back to the Land Rover.

Inside the gallery, Paddy noticed the gentle stirring. He had seen this before, there was something about D in particular that just seemed to rouse them. The entire barrow was becoming very unsettled, their gently increasing activity threatening to spill over into wakefulness and instant death for all of them.

Paddy motioned D to go. But D lingered, gesturing like a diver, pointing in complete silence, insistently showing Paddy exactly where the boy had been found and the specific orientation of how he had lain under the cover. Paddy acknowledged the mimed information and then gently pushed D away.

The moment D left, the assembly settled again into deeper sleep. To Paddy's relief, the effect was instant. Now at least he had a better chance of living to see another day. He swiftly cut the ties of the sack and poured the limp creature out depositing it directly onto the floor. He covered it with the shroud and straightened. Nearly there.

Paddy took another look around the sleeping figures. Just in case he saw - what was that?

The breath caught in Paddy's throat.

Sunlight from some tiny fissure in the earth had

seeped through. Such healthy, natural light in this dark place warmed his heart. It spoke of normal existence, of carefree days and nights without tormenting dreams.

Of all things, the finger of light had touched something quite familiar. It was glinting off a tiny golden bracelet. Even though he had bought it many years ago, he remembered it had a bluebird on it.

Soundlessly Paddy crept between the sleepers. Fixed on the tiny speck of light, he gently made his way into the farthest corner of the gallery. Tears blurred his sight, but he found his way, stepping across numerous bodies undetected, until at last, he stood and looked down.

With the fresh bloom of youth still upon her, Paddy's faery wife, Elin, lay sleeping upon a low couch of spring green silk. As beautiful as a sleeping princess trapped in a fairy tale, her arms were wrapped lovingly around their two children, Finola and Fiacre. The golden bluebird glinted from the bracelet on Finola's tiny wrist. Paddy knelt at Elin's feet whilst silent tears coursed down his face. Fiacre awoke and smiled at his father and all at once Paddy knew what he must do.

Outside the barrow, D restlessly checked his watch. Paddy was taking too long.

Jockey knew it too, he crept towards the gallery and peered in. Shocked, Jockey took in the scene. Paddy had taken off his goggles and sat with three of the creatures wrapt in their arms, bathed in utter delight, utterly bewitched and looking happier than Jockey had ever seen him. The fool had allowed himself to be trapped. He was lost and didn't even know it. Jockey shook his head, staunching the flow of angry words rising up from his heart into his mouth. Smiling serenely over the heads of the sleepers, Paddy looked straight at him and shook his head. At long last, he was at peace, he would not be coming back. Torn between fury and disbelief, Jockey could only watch helplessly as Paddy lay down to sleep.

Jockey staggered alone out of the barrow. D raised an eyebrow. Jockey shook his head. They left without a further word and made their way back to the Land Rover. The second they were out of the silent zone, Jockey spoke up.

'We have to go back! We can't let a man of his calibre go to waste like that, trapped by those things! When you think of what he's been through. To be caught like that? It's all wrong!'

D's reply was calm and measured. 'We are currently

engaged on another mission.'

'Then when it's over…' Jockey started and stopped himself. His anxiety was bringing him dangerously close to insubordination. He knew D would deal with it in his own way. He always did. He wanted to rescue Paddy, because he would never leave a mate behind, but he had to content himself with the thought that D would get Paddy back, even if he might send someone else to do it.

D remained tight lipped, he had no intention of rescuing Paddy. He had an insight into his troubled history and he fully understood the reason for this apparent defection. Loss had fuelled Paddy's self-destructive bravery and this had first brought him to D's attention. D had offered poor, lost Paddy some hope that his desire to find his missing family wasn't a crazy fantasy.

Letting him seek what he had lost had made him one of the best at his job - intuitive, thorough and very, very vigilant.

By the time D and Jockey returned to the Land Rover, Claire had slipped away to get some proper rest. Violet and Prateeka were shocked at the news of Paddy's capture, but they were determined to save any outpourings, until the current job was done.

The child was shivering. Torn from the mesmeric attentions of the creatures, he was in shock. They had all seen this before, it was almost as if some addictive drug had been withdrawn and he was going cold-turkey. Prateeka swathed him in warm blankets and kept talking gently to him.

'He's stronger than most, we got to him quickly.'

His case had come to light when his replacement changeling had been admitted to the children's hospital for his eye condition. Once there, the true nature of his 'ailments' had been uncovered. Between them, Violet, Jockey, Claire and a couple of Aranars, had scanned the likeliest locations and it had taken six similar, dangerous missions deep into the enemy territory of barrows and ancient earthworks before locating this one. Success had been hard won this time. Even before Paddy had been lost, one of the Aranars had succumbed to elf shot. His death had been publicly registered as the result of an undiagnosed, but long-standing heart condition. That he had died directly outside this barrow had been signpost enough that this was where D9 should be looking.

Distressingly, during one of the searches, a child had been found whose fairy counterpart had died in the human word. For her there could be no escape. Without a replacement to host the exchange, she was trapped forever in the wrong world and they'd had to leave her sleeping. These were the head-working missions Violet and Jockey hated the most.

The boy they'd just successfully rescued had only been missing for a scant few months and this would be an easy resolution, he'd slot right back into his real life and would soon forget the people under the hill.

After a brief spell 'in theatre,' the child would be returned to his hospital bed and his parents would find him looking a lot better and miraculously cured of a host of ailments and sudden behavioural issues and another victory would be notched up to the brilliant doctors at the famous children's hospital.

The brevity of this little boy's capture would hide the fact that he hadn't aged a single day in the months he'd been away.

Although D knew of one mother who had accepted a four year old back after her child had been missing for twelve years, such cases were rare. After a certain time had passed, even D had to admit it was impossible to fit the child back into its original family.

Bitterly opposed to this cross species trafficking, he had taken it upon himself to grow D9's links with the Aranars, and to return stolen children hopefully in such numbers that the metahominids would eventually abandon the practice altogether. He had seen so many unhappy ever afters and endured heartbreaking interviews with victims of charms and spells. He was coldly furious at the mindless, parasitic nature of these beings, the way they infiltrated and stole people's lives away.

One day there would be one last changeling and then there would be none. In the meantime, D was doing everything he could to bring that day closer.

The boy visibly coloured up.

'Heartbeat stabilised,' Prateeka probed the boy's ear, 'temperature dropping back to normal. He's good to go.'

D nodded. 'Report when you get back.'

Prateeka smiled and settled her charge for the journey back to the hospital. Violet slid behind the wheel and Jockey jumped in beside her.

Everyone was tired and uncommunicative. Acknowledging their leader, Jockey smiled his quick, tense smile and Violet gave a clenched fist gesture of defiance.

Mission completed, one man down.

D waved them off and then drove home slowly. It gave him little pleasure to know that the barrow would awaken later and be in uproar over their 'stolen treasure' and that the changeling would bear the brunt of its clan's resentment.

As the Saab covered the miles, his mind jumped from thought to thought and he considered how people never linked up the clues. Even bluff Jockey had voiced his doubts about how many people incarcerated in psychiatric half-way houses, living drug-induced half lives were not victims of psychosis, but enchantment. What a word! D's hands tightened on the wheel, with an uncharacteristic flash of hot anger. The amber petrol-pump and green, flashing arrow lit up on his dashboard and broke his thought pattern. He pulled into Frankwell services.

Whilst he filled the car, D was 'buzzed' by a little girl, sporting a pale lilac fairy dress and glittery-pink nylon fairy wings, darting and dancing about the forecourt. Her furious mother grabbed the child out of harms way and bundled her back into their car. D turned, hiding his grim expression, he couldn't bear to see fairy wings any more, even nylon ones.

'It's been declined, Sir,' the cashier handed D's credit card back to him. 'Got another one, or cash?'

D opened his wallet, he had some notes in there and for once it was enough. He handed them across.

'Want a receipt?'

'Please.'

'I'd get on to your bank if I was you, Sir.'

D nodded, but he knew it wasn't the bank that had pulled the plug. Somewhere in Whitehall, his funding plea had fallen upon deaf ears.

He'd never sought recognition for vital tasks well executed, but equally, he'd never looked to get kicked in the teeth either. What had been a challenging day suddenly turned a lot worse. At the stroke of an anonymous pen, his difficult, dangerous, but necessary job had become impossible.

Plunged into a mood of deep depression, D drove home.

15

PC Dylan Watkin wasn't faring much better. It had been weeks since the incident at Kew and the lead hadn't so much gone cold as completely frozen and then snapped off in the bitter chill.

The first month had been easy. Every dead end had only spurred him on. Back then, with his enthusiasm fully geared up he'd seen every block to his progress as just another sign that 'they' were responding to him, countering every move he made, closing down every line of investigation he opened and he was *thrilled* by it all. He'd pursued ghosts of clues with dedication and diligence, disciplining himself to thrive on the most meagre of results. But apart from briefly finding - and by a grandiose but stupidly short-sighted gesture - *losing* the girl who'd called herself Sarah Deakin, he'd had no results.

He'd gone back to Kew many times without finding any further leads. He'd chatted to the girl on the cosmetics counter in the department store, but she only remembered his stunt with the roses, not their recipient. He'd even trailed round every department she had dragged him through, ironically clocking up many more hours in those hellish halls than even she'd originally subjected him to, but all had proved spectacularly unrewarding.

Frustratingly for Watkin, the woman he believed wasn't really called 'Sarah Deakin' had been careful to pay cash for everything she'd bought that day.

Within just a few weeks, Watkin's strict regimen of long nights and early mornings, of spending every available moment he had dedicated to 'OpAl,' (Operation Alien), had eventually run out of steam. Now his fall from the wagon had become pretty total. The rot had set in when he started allowing himself the odd lie in before going to work and stopped re-reading his notes quite so thoroughly every night. He reasoned that he knew them off by heart anyway, the embarrassing fact that he had absolutely nothing new to add to them just made him squirm.

He'd been so close, but now that very proximity had become a bitter, twisted stick with which he beat himself. The odds of ever bumping into Sarah Deakin again by accident were as likely as him winning the lottery. Sure he could get lucky, but the chances were vanishingly small.

The entire incident and its aftermath had been absorbing and, before it had got painful, fun. Now it was over. Lack of evidence was simply that - lack of evidence. It was lacking because there was none to be had.

A conspiracy theory needs conspirators at the very least and they, whoever 'they' were, they had stopped rolling the ball back to him. It was as if they'd packed up their big secret circus and run away to mystify some other poor dupe.

Watkin remembered what had happened in great detail, but the sheer repetition of going over and over the happenings of that strange night, had dulled the bright immediacy of the events.

Although they'd had a huge impact upon him at the time, even as the 'spider bite' scar on his arm faded and his cut healed, without a regular top-up of fresh facts, that night had settled into the box in his memory marked 'weird' and more immediate, every-day events had taken his attention. As the host of mundane worries had overtaken him, he'd consigned his investigation to a mental back burner.

Watkin had initially kidded himself that all it needed was one, bright spark of renewed interest to set OpAl alight again, but the dead-end days had piled up and eventually the fire of interest had snuffed out.

'Excuse meh Offissah, but whort's *heypening* ohvah thah?'

The middle-aged woman wrinkled her nose in distaste. Every precise syllable oozed disgust at the presence of uniformed policemen in her expensive environs.

'There's been an incident, Madam.'

Watkin answered carefully. She was of the type that made him nervous, a typical, 'Hilda Headscarf.' Bitter experience had taught him that *Hildas* were prone to be more troublesome than the foulest mouthed slapper on the poorest estate.

'Thayt tells me nothing! I *deymahnd* to know whort's going orn! Are thah criminals in thah? Is my herme in any daynjah?'

The woman hovered on tiptoe, peering past him up the drive to the open door of the smart detached residence.

'It's police business, Madam. Your home is perfectly safe. The incident is being dealt with. That's all I can say…'

'Thayt is just *nort* good enough!'

She cut across him with a commanding tone

bordering on the Thatcheresque, 'You have done *nothing* to reassure meh. How do I know I'm safe, when you're concealing the faycts? Are thah *terrorists* in thah?'

All Watkin wanted to do was slope off for a cold lager. He had been standing outside the house for hours, mostly in bright sunlight, in full uniform, with his ridiculous Noddy helmet on. He'd have given anything to lean casually against the brick column of the gatepost and tell this grizzled harridan to mind her own business, but he quelled the wildly rebellious thought.

Apart from any official censure, he could imagine Mrs. Headscarf's vicious hand-bagging, accompanied by her shrill insistence that he should, '*Storp* slouching!'

He beckoned Hilda closer with a slight inclination of his head, as she bent in closer, he whispered confidentially, 'I'll tell you one thing though…'

'Whort' Her eyes narrowed. Hilda was intrigued, but unwilling to show it.

Watkin tapped the side of his nose conspiratorially. 'I bet this'll be on the news tonight and you'll *so* get papped on your doorstep.'

The woman's face wrinkled in puzzlement.

'You know,' Watkin explained helpfully, miming clicking a camera, 'The paparazzi? They'll want to know what you know. You can *truthfully* say you were the first on the scene, *but* you're not at liberty to mention anything.'

Mrs. Headscarf, who'd been leaning in, taking in every word, straightened. 'Well. I can quite see *thayt*. Of course one would be *heppy* to speak to an organisation like the BBC. *But nort to the tabloids!*'

Watkin weighed it up and then spoke slowly, to let the words sink in. 'Yeah, but think about it… they *pay more*.'

Hilda's were always all about the money. He watched her face light up, then withdrew the bait, 'Not that *you* need it, of course.' He watched her try to keep her face from falling, allowed a further beat and cast the prize back to her again, 'But any extra is always *handy*, isn't it?'

The woman gave him a sternly appraising look and turned on her heel, hurrying home to await the worlds' press. Hilda neutralised.

Watkin smiled, he was learning. His radio crackled into life. The team were coming out with the suspect. This was a delicate one. Some woman had lost it and tried to kill her kid. The child had survived and been taken to hospital.

A specialist team were inside with the mother and they had just ascertained that she was unfit to be questioned. She was going straight to hospital herself.

The psychiatrist came out of the house first. His feet scrunched self-importantly down the gravel drive as he barked into his mobile phone.

'Internet bride I guess... Eastern European, lots of cultural baggage. You know... superstitious hang-ups. Yes, Stranger in a Strange Land... Looks like... Husband? Nah, too busy to support her. Not like that. Pots of money. Refuses to accept the child is hers. Not insurmountable, but it'll take time.'

He slipped into his BMW. Still talking, he started the engine and eyed Watkin, daring the lower status male to challenge him and say something about him driving whilst on a mobile.

Why not, Sunshine?' Watkin thought cheerily and took out his notepad to take down the vehicles' registration number. At that moment something exceptionally strange happened.

Watkin had often found it easier to identify whatever actor was doing the voice-over on a TV advert when he wasn't watching the screen and now as he heard a familiar voice, a similar scenario began to unfold.

That voice had been burnt onto his memory.

It was a voice he'd been looking for.

Maybe that was why he hadn't found it, until now. Instead of looking, he was shocked to realise that, all along, he should have been *listening*. If he had been looking at the speaker, chances are he would have been distracted by the visual and would not have made the necessary connection.

He'd traced 'Sarah Deakin,' not from the fake ID she'd left, but from remembering what she looked like, after seeing her during brief bouts of consciousness in the back of the 4x4.

But he hadn't seen the man who'd operated on him and he'd passed out cold when they'd taken the alien artefact out of his shoulder.

Frozen, Watkin stared down at his notebook, listening to the man speaking quietly in a smoky Scottish accent.

'It'll live… just. But we can't hang about. Claire's already scoping out a likely hidey-hole for its counterpart.'

Watkin stopped breathing. It was one of the men from that night at Kew. The one 'Sarah' had called 'Jockey.'

Being careful not to show too much interest, Watkin cautiously looked up from his notebook. Jockey was still on his mobile and holding the door of a 4x4 open for the suspect. The accused mother exited the house, a spindly broken doll supported on the arm of a woman police officer. With ragged tufts of yellow hair, anguished red-rimmed eyes staring out from her chalky, grey face and clad in a simple white, linen shift, she already looked like the classic inmate of a Victorian lunatic asylum.

'Aye boss, I will.'

Jockey finished his call and quickly tapped another number into his mobile. This time he spoke so quietly, Watkin had to strain to catch -

'Gee Gee's on his way to Aintree.'

Watkin trembled as he copied Jockey's words down and the registration of the 4x4.

He didn't hold out much hope for the trace. No secret organisation would be so stupid as to drive around in fully traceable vehicles. It probably belonged to some innocuous transport pool.

With his heart in his mouth, Watkin ambled casually across to the vehicle. He nodded at the WPC. She was busy herding the suspect into the back, making sure the distraught woman didn't hit her head as she got in and so didn't bother to acknowledge him. Watkin covertly checked the interior.

His fingertips tingled with a surge of adrenaline as he recognised the cloth of the seats. *He'd been in this car!* Even though he suspected there were hundreds of identical 4x4's, how many of them were driven by a bloke with the exact kind of Scots accent as this driver? It shortened the odds, but that was just logic speaking.

Watkin knew, with the instinct that had made him want to be a copper, *knew* in his bones, that this was the right man in the right car. He couldn't help but stare at Jockey who was still on his mobile with his face turned three-quarters away.

'Aye,' Jockey finished. Without looking at Watkin, he swung into the vehicle and roared away.

It took every ounce of Watkin's resolve not to break away from his duty, bolt to the nearest car and follow them. He'd got the policewoman's number. He'd chat her up the moment he had the chance.

That evening, Watkin stirred his tea thoughtfully and reviewed his hand-written notes. His PC had abruptly started making a non-trivial sounding whine and fearful of losing all his files, he hadn't used it in days.

In the light of Watkin's recently assumed indifference, any surveillance upon him had been downgraded to an occasional snoop. It would be a while before D9 found it had lost its inbuilt spying capability upon him.

OpAl, fully revived in the light of the new information, was looking very interesting. He studied the words in his notebook:

'It'll live, just. But we can't hang about.'

It'll live? Why would they refer to the injured child as an 'it.' Was Jockey just using careless language, or was there more going on here?

Watkin tapped his teaspoon against the rim of his mug and pondered the title '*It.*' Not a word generally used for humans. The mother had battered the child after refusing to believe it was hers.

'Claire's already scoping out a likely hidey hole for its counterpart.' *Claire* - another name, could that be Sarah

Deakin's real name?

What was meant by its *counterpart?*

A wild thought struck him. *The mother knew the kid wasn't hers!* Were humans being replaced by aliens?

Was this a real life invasion of the body snatchers? Excited, he took a gulp of tea. Now he *knew* he was definitely onto something. Perhaps he could get in to see the mother and question her? He frowned, that would be risky. He still had his job to think about. In the current climate he couldn't risk losing it, not yet. One day when he had the whole story, he would happily turn in his Noddy hat and baton. In the meantime, maybe there was another line of enquiry? He studied the words, *'Gee gee's on his way to Aintree.'*

A gee-gee going to Aintree could simply refer to a horse in transit to the racecourse. But why? How would a racehorse connect to all this? If the horse/Grand National course connection was a red-herring, could Jockey possibly be referring to someone with the initials G.G?

Watkin had spent most of that remaining weekend putting in some solid police work, but not all of it was official. He'd made a discreet search and the vehicle was registered to a hire firm. It was on a long lease to a small company based in Brighton. After that, he followed a line of accommodation addresses and eventually ended up coming full-circle to the one in Brighton. He'd found nothing, but it thrilled him. Someone, somewhere, was determined not to be found. That alone made Watkin burn to find them.

He'd sought out the attending WPC, and had plied her with a great opening line, but all he got back was a stony stare. Unbeknown to him, she was on her bitter second divorce and deeply distrustful of any sweet talk. Watkin changed track and ventured his hope that the papers would be kind to the woman who'd gone beserk and hurt her kid.

Ohhh, coincidence! Hadn't *she* been there on that case? Didn't she support the poor lady into the car?

The effect of Watkins wisely chosen words was astonishing. The WPC opened up and told him every detail of her journey with Jockey to the unit. She seemed oddly touched by Watkin's interest, but all she could tell him was that Jockey had delivered the distraught mother into the care of the nursing staff, hung around for a bit and then left. He hadn't made, or taken, any calls during their time together.

She had then recounted details of the woman's

mental state and how she kept saying her beautiful baby had been stolen and the wicked fairies had left a twisted changeling in its place. She hadn't used the actual word *'changeling'* employing some sort of foreign equivalent instead, but the WPC had got the gist.

As she continued to expound upon how the woman had expressed profound and bitter feelings of abandonment, Dylan began to detect the needy desperation in the WPC's own reality.

Realising she had only revealed this much because she had labelled Watkin as being 'in touch with his feelings,' he spotted the trap and neatly side-stepped it.

He rubbed his hands together briskly and observed brightly, 'Still, even in that state, you could tell she was a right *looker* though! Eh?'

The portcullis behind the WPC's eyes crashed back down. Her withering sigh of disdain would have frozen a lesser man as, without a further word, she rose and stalked away from the canteen.

Now, just forty-eight hours after he had heard Jockey's voice for the second time, convinced he was about to break open a reality-shattering case of alien abduction,

Dylan Watkin stood nervously beneath the giant clock of Liverpool's Lime Street Station, at the start of his 'day off.'

Six very tenuous, but possible leads juggled restively in his head. Six addresses, all in and around Aintree. All garnered from local letting agencies who had recently rented out properties in the area. All extraordinarily long shots. Experience had taught him that people who wanted to stay hidden usually rented rather than bought. If the party of interest had simply taken up residence on a mate's floor, he was sunk.

Watkin hailed a cab.

'I want to go here first,' he showed the cabbie an address.

'No problem, mate.'

Watkin got in and the cab pulled out from the station. The cabbie continued, 'Then where to?'

As Watkin rattled off the various addresses, the cabbie began to laugh.

'Rent collector are yer? Nudge-nudge, wink-wink!'

Watkin was shocked, the cabbie was blatantly accusing him of being a drug dealer.

Affronted he blustered, 'No! I'm - '

'A Bizzy. Relax, me bro's one.'

The cabbie caught Watkin's puzzled frown in the rear view mirror and chuckled, 'Bizzy? Copper to you. Never heard that one?'

Chastened, Watkin shook his head, 'How did you know?'

The cabbie smirked, 'Yer not a dealer, too official. But yer lookin for someone. But what it's *not* is an internet romance gone wrong...'

'Why not?'

'There's no romance in your soul.'

'Really?' Watkin couldn't hide a faint note of disappointment.

The cabbie roared with laughter. 'Ay, I'm not saying yer a dud in that department, but ye've got the look of a man on a different kind of mission!'

'I might be a solicitor, legal-exec?'

'Nah… not slimy enough.'

Watkin smiled, the cabbie continued, 'So you'll be wanting a receipt for all this running round then?'

Watkin hesitated.

'Eh now! Yer going to have learn to be a bit quicker than that lad, if you want to nab some ne'er-do-well on the q. t.'

'It's a sensitive issue.' Watkin responded tartly.

The cabbie chewed on that one for a bit. 'And they've sent you here on yer own, with just a handful of addresses?'

'Looks that way.'

Over the course of the morning, Watkin visited all the recently let properties on his list, growing more forlorn with every closed-off lead. He wasn't at all sure what he was looking for, but his police training told him that each and every one of the people who'd helpfully been in and answered any of the various doors he'd knocked on, weren't conspirators of any kind. He hadn't missed anything, he'd just run into another dead-end.

'Back to Lime Street, please,' he smiled grimly at the

cabbie.

'Hang fire, Chief.' Before Watkin could react, the cabbie pulled over.

He punched a number into his mobile and waited for a reply.

'Don't give me none of yer DCI crap! Its yer brother! Didn't me number come up?'

The cabbie had upped his already considerable decibel level by some degrees and was now declaiming at full volume. In the confines of the cab, the man's sudden, powerful laugh made Watkin wince.

'Some detective you are! Got a fellow officer here. Man down. No, not literally, but he's in need of some assistance on the q. t.'

Winking in the mirror at Watkin, he turned the cab around and headed back into central Liverpool.

Over alfresco coffee and sandwiches, looking out across the Mersey to Birkenhead, the cabbie's brother, Alan, listened to Watkin's scant tale.

'All we know is that the person of interest was involved in a recent incident in Richmond,' Watkin ventured only the barest of information, 'and has recently settled in or around Aintree.'

'*Incident?*' Alan queried, his Liverpool accent a little lighter than his brother's.

Watkin nodded.

The DCI went on, 'Terrorism? If one of them bad boys has arrived on our patch, we want a heads-up. Give me something.'

Watkin shifted uneasily, he was already far deeper in than he wanted to be. If it came to out that he was working on a personal whim, he would be booted off the force without notice.

'All I can say is…' Watkin hesitated.

DCI Alan McArdle grew impatient. 'Look Detective, I'm having a bite of me dinner and we're just having this nice chat right? I'm not on the clock. This isn't official as far as I'm concerned.'

'Okay,' Watkin conceded, 'I can tell you that it's not terrorism. It's… something that compromises national security.'

'No name?'

'Just the initials G G.'

'And he's somewhere in Aintree?' McArdle exhaled noisily, 'Needles, haystacks, what else can I say? Give me yer contact deets and I'll ask round. Someone on street level may have clocked this scumbag.'

Watkin nodded.

'But I wouldn't hold out much hope,' McArdle added.

'Thanks for trying.' Watkin scribbled down his mobile phone number and handed it to McArdle. They shook hands.

The older man brushed the sandwich crumbs from his suit and as his brother had long gone, left Watkin waiting for another cab.

Although he believed the man he'd just spoken to was indeed a policeman, even before he had reached his office McArdle had checked out the man's given name and supposed detective status and found both to be false.

As he took the lift back up to his offices, McArdle was bemused. He couldn't begin to imagine what all this was about, but whoever he turned out to be, this young idiot wasn't secret service. No-one from M15 would ever be that sloppy. So however unbelievable, it was just *possible* that he was a lone operator, a young guy with a London accent, who looked, acted and smelt like police, but who was operating way beyond his regular patch.

So the question was this: why would some young bizzy go maverick and hang himself out on such a potentially dangerous limb? This young liar had been naïve and not a little stupid, but his investigation obviously meant enough for him to risk his entire career. Misguided though his actions undoubtedly were, it seemed clear to McArdle that he hadn't been a 'wrong 'un' *and* there was at least something commendable about the chutzpah of a young man who could look a senior officer straight in the eye and lie like that.

Even as he ordered his own investigation, McArdle inwardly smiled at the notion of finding a G G in Aintree.

What odds would the bookies give on that one?

16

The November of 1590 was proving to be even whiter than the last, and the Faerie Queene awoke to the soft light of a snowy morning. Her chamber was filled with the reflected brightness of pale winter sunshine and she stretched with the pure pleasure of living. How many mornings had she woken thus?

Once, when she had been so much younger, she had found herself a prisoner in the Tower and had not expected to leave it alive. Today she was, and had been for many years since, a queen. Elizabeth regarded her still fair complexion in the mirror and smiled. She had outlived many enemies, yet the years slid from her, the radiant heroine of Spenser's, 'The Faerie Queene.' To her utter delight, he had presented her with the first three books of what was to be his epic poem about her and England. Even though the distinction was unclear.

Elizabeth *was* England.

Today she would make a progress with great pomp to her fairytale palace at Richmond. On the way, the Royal barge would halt at Mortlake and she would pay a visit to her astrologer and confidante Dr. John Dee.

Some twenty years before, this same Dr. Dee had placed her at the head of a vast over arching concern that stretched trading links clear across the globe. He had coined the strange expression, 'The British Empire,' and it had caught her imagination and intrigued her, being at once so fantastically modern a concept, and yet with the quaint overtones of history, as if she were an Empress, akin to a modern Cleopatra.

The term she found so pleasing could only have come from the very man who encapsulated ancient and modern in one broad sweep of learning and achievement, and in whose company she was looking forward to being.

The Queen's gilded chamber filled with yet more light and laughter as drapes were drawn and her maidens danced in attendance. They bore with them her breakfast of sweet honeyed cakes and small beer. Elizabeth lay back upon her sumptuous brocade cushions and ate and drank whilst they carefully presented the jewels she had chosen the night before.

Musing as her ladies-in-waiting chattered and laid out her gowns for the day, she held a perfect droplet shaped pearl between her thumb and forefinger and gazed at the hints of pink and green in its softly glowing pearlescence. This beautiful jewel had once belonged to her mother, Queen Anne, and had featured in her most famous portrait. Although Elizabeth had long since outlived her murdered mother, she had been as scarred as much by Anne's reputation as a whore, as she had been by her father's horrific vengeance.

Her more shrewd observers understood that this could be why Elizabeth had so conspicuously celebrated her lifelong virginity *and* been so publicly reluctant to behead her enemies. Should she have ever compromised either value, her many vociferous supporters, coupled with her own natural discretion, had colluded to keep her reputation intact.

Self preservation had taught Elizabeth long ago to become a resourceful tactician in her own right. In this, she was served well by her favourite motto, '*See and say nothing.*' She stroked her mother's lovely pearl against her neck whilst her thoughts turned to darker things.

Despite the defeat of the armada two years before, England was still engaged in a whispering war with Spain. How much longer it could be contained was anyone's guess. The shaky peace between the nations was like a keg of gunpowder. Safe enough for a bird, a baby or a kitten to sleep in, until someone lit a spark. When they did, and surely one side would, it would be such a conflagration that would scorch the very gates of heaven.

It was late afternoon and already dark before her arrival at Mortlake. Elizabeth had been in conference for most of the day with Secretary Walsingham, her spymaster. He had imparted the deepest secrets that the various ambassadors at court erroneously considered to be 'safely concealed,' and now she was to see one of her most formidable cipher-breakers, John Dee. When engaged in such private work, this very public man hid his true identity beneath the secret name of '007.' The zeroes represented eyes and the encoded notes he passed to Elizabeth, his much loved monarch, often bore the inscription, 'For Your Eyes Only.'

Dr. John Dee waited as his monarch disembarked by torchlight. A handsome, scholarly man, Dee appeared the perfect magician with his flowing silver beard and his unfashionably long velvet robes. His interests included navigation, astronomy, astrology, and the sciences of alchemy and mathematics, as well as magick proper.

All Dee's academic and practical endeavours were focussed upon one ultimate goal, to understand the creatures that peopled the invisible world and underpinned reality itself. He had even developed a special language 'Enochian' with which to converse with the angels.

Dee's continuing studies of the forms he called 'pure verities' had confirmed the Elizabethan world view of the order of things - that the Universe was held in perpetual balance between good and evil and God sat at the apex of a vast hierarchy of angels and powers. Beneath it there existed a perfect, albeit dark, mirror image of negative entities with Satan at its nadir.

That these creatures existed purely to influence mankind for good or evil was not in question. The matter that was of current concern and not a little alarm to Dee, was the apparent growing imbalance. Of late, he had detected a significant rise in the evil deeds of the malevolent fairy people.

Queen Elizabeth accepted Dee's greeting gracefully and swept past his line of bowing servants, pausing to greet his latest protégé, a foundling boy whom Dee was instructing to become a mage like his master.

Finally turning back to take her host's proffered arm, Elizabeth allowed herself to be guided to Dee's restored library. This was the very same one from which many of the more valuable books had been stolen whilst he'd been away in Europe. With the Queen's valuable intervention, he had recovered at least some of the lost titles.

Elizabeth settled herself on a stately cushioned chair and waved away the fine wine and costly fruits candied with luxurious pure sugar.

Dee saw the last of the servants away himself and set his most trusted man, his protégé, to guard the door alongside four of the Queen's own men. He then set to personally tend the huge crackling fire that lay like a golden monster in its massive grate. Its low roar would serve to confound the keenest listening ear.

Dropping her habitually guarded demeanour, Elizabeth glanced about her with an enthusiasm that was childlike and unfettered. Haunted by death plots all her life, even during her childhood, there were pitifully few people in her life that she could genuinely relax with, but Dr. Dee was one of them.

As her most trusted advisor on astrological and scientific matters, she'd allowed him alone to select the most auspicious date for her coronation. Judging by the length and continuing success of her reign, he had chosen well.

With unfeigned delight, her eyes shone as she studied Dee's shelves. The excellent restoration of this fine library gladdened her heart. A keen scholar herself, she recognised many of the Greek and Latin titles, and even a few of the many hermetic and cabbalistic tomes as well.

With the fire stoked to Dee's satisfaction into a full voiced roaring, he drew up a small footstool and despite his advancing years, sat at the feet of his monarch. Dee, too, was of Welsh descent and she almost felt a sense of kindred with him.

He pulled a linen stopper from a cylinder of fine leather, tipped out the content and handed over his latest acquisition. Flattered by his complete trust, Elizabeth smoothed out the vellum scroll and arched an eyebrow, 'I have seen men beheaded for less.'

John nodded and pursed his lips like a naughty child being told off, but his eyes twinkled.

Elizabeth chuckled, 'Well, well. No further war with Spain then?'

'Unprecedented peace... amongst men.'

She caught the gentle emphasis in his word, *men*.

'And then?' Elizabeth studied the glyphs.

'Ma'am, your next war will not be with flesh and blood. Take heed, my Lady, and arm your archers and your swordsmen with silver. Let halberds be foiled in the substance. Then raise your Royal standard and have your armies march upon the secret lairs of the grey and green folk.'

'This is not the audience I expected to have with you, John,' Elizabeth's words were light enough but her smile was steely. 'The last speech we had concerned Prince Madog and my rights to the New World. What of those things?'

'Majesty, I laid my entreaties before you at that time. Now I suspect such unknown territories are far from your thoughts.'

Dee was right. The new world held little interest for Elizabeth. She laughed, her full throated merriment cutting the sudden tension between them, 'So you have discovered my disinterest in *unknown territories* Dr. Dee. Yet you would have me make a war upon *unknown entities*?'

She caught his pained expression and relented. He was often right. 'Very well John, you shall have what you wish. A war.'

'Majesty!' Dee's heart leapt, but she continued. 'However, it is to be a very subtle and discreet war. You have previously selected pilots and trained them in the arts of navigation?'

'Yes Majesty.'

'Then you shall recruit many agents to do your bidding. These said agents shall suffer to go into these diverse and secret lairs and deal with the denizens therein.'

'Majesty,' Dee faltered, 'That asks much of a mortal man.'

'But not *too much*, John.' She turned the full force of her personality upon him, 'Many men have died for England. For me. You do this very work, yourself, even now? Surely there must be yet more brave men?'

Humbled, Dee nodded. Elizabeth sighed, 'I understand you would wish for an army. But many men have many tongues and thus are secrets spilt. Be assured, I have nothing but contempt for that puffed-up papal prince sitting in Rome, but even he knows that only God or his priests can declare war on such supernatural evil. For the sake of my fathers' church in England and as its head, I cannot be seen to engage in matters of such dark metaphysic.... It would reflect badly upon my institutions.'

Her argument was persuasive. The fact that there would be no alternative offer was decisive.

She stared into the bright embers of the fire, her blue-grey eyes delving into the depths of the glowing caverns. 'You will create a brotherhood of invisibles, John. For this you shall have full access to whatever monies and other divers resources you require.'

Dee nodded, grateful for any help.

'However,' she raised a slender forefinger to emphasize her point, 'All of this is on the understanding that this new work must be kept up alongside your other duties of spy and mage.'

It would be a heavy additional burden, how heavy even the great Dr. John Dee could not yet calculate, but it was a work he was keen to do.

'You shall impart nothing of these doings to Walsingham, these matters lie solely between yourself and your Monarch. Secrecy is paramount.'

Dee remained silent as she continued, '*Video et Taceo*. 'I see and say nothing,' my own favourite motto shall be your watchword. My spymasters have kept me safe throughout my long reign, *every bit as much* as my many thousands of fighting men. Let your brotherhood of agents be as wise and resourceful as you are and I shall fear nothing.'

Thus was instigated the official government department known as 'Counter Metaphysics.' In the future it would become CM, then 900 after the Latin numerals CM represented. Over time even that would shrink to the more prosaic Department 9 or D9.

Later, as Dee stood by the landing stage, watching the lights of the Royal Barge retreat into the night, he shivered slightly, not from the cold, but from the direction Her Majesty's journey would take. She was *en-route* to her palace at Richmond and as far as Dee's studies had revealed, this was a favourite haunt of the very enemy they had just declared a secret war upon.

17

The day after Dylan Watkin had been chasing a G G in Aintree, less than a mile away Gnat Greville looked out of the huge greasy window at the grey skies of Liverpool.

When he grew up he'd have a son and they'd never flit about from place to place like this. They'd find somewhere nice by the sea and they'd live in the same house forever. Then his son could make good friends like Matt *and* be allowed to keep them. He wouldn't have to be the much picked on 'new kid' in every new school he ever went to. Unlike Dad, because they weren't forever on the move, they could even sign a contract thingy and have broadband and get even more friends on the internet.

Dad could carry on travelling as much as he wanted. After all, it was in his blood. Granny Di was a traveller. But all Gnat wanted to do was stay put somewhere and plant things. Things he'd be around to see grow and blossom. He'd make sure Dad knew where he was. Probably not Granny Di though. Dad didn't like her, but Dad could visit anytime.

Gnat turned away from the window and reviewed his mess of a room. Dad had just dumped all of Gnat's things in there and put his bed up. The rest was up to Gnat to sort out. The first thing he did was to look for a place to stash his secret stuff.

This was a bland modern flat in a dispiriting concrete block. There was no loose wainscoting, no wobbly floorboards, just smooth newly plastered walls and hard plastic laminate flooring.

Gnat scrambled under his bed, there was just about enough room, it would do for now. He dragged the Christmas tree box in after him.

His Dad always complained about it, but Gnat had argued that at least they could have the same tree every year. Even if it was almost always put up in a different place. Then he hauled in his old suitcase marked 'toys.' Most of the toys were long gone, sacrificed to make room for the artificial Christmas tree. The Christmas tree box only held a couple of sprigs, put there to disguise what the box actually contained – Gnat's precious fairy wing.

He couldn't resist popping open one end of the box and staring in, then he reached in and touched it. It was still there, stroking its fragile ribs he could tell it felt intact. It was safe. Gnat crept out from under his bed and stared in fascination at his fingers. He turned them in the light, examining the dull pink and green silky residue.

Like a word on the tip of his tongue, a memory tripped in Gnat's mind. That girl in his last school. What had they called her? He couldn't remember. He stared at the wing dust again. Why should this remind him of someone he'd barely noticed? Hang on… hadn't there been something in her hair? Maybe that was it. She must have worn a metallic pink and greeny ribbon thing in her hair, or something.

Gnat shrugged off the sudden disquiet and jumped up. He flung open his window and scrubbed the dust off his fingertips onto the harsh brickwork just under the exterior windowsill. Withdrawing his hand, he turned away, failing to notice the shadow flit behind him across the balcony.

'You done?' Dad came in, holding a glass of orange. Gnat's eyes gleamed. It had a slice of orange *and* ice cubes in it.

'Cheers Dad!' Gnat grabbed the drink and gulped. If Dad was doing his best to make things up to him, this was a good start. He'd made it with *real* orange juice mixed with lemonade and it tasted wonderful!

For his part, Gnat's father was less than impressed, 'Gnat, you've been in here hours and you've barely started sorting your stuff out!'

Keeping the glass to his mouth, Gnat pointed out the books tumbled out of a box onto the bookshelf and indicated the small rug he'd put down.

Another shadow crept past the window.

'If you don't get the bed cleared you'll have nowhere to - '

Unaware of his father's suddenly bloodless face, Gnat drained his glass and crunched on an ice cube, 'But Dad,' he began.

He didn't get the chance to finish. The door crashed in, Dad shouted in alarm, and suddenly there were dark bodies everywhere.

18

This bed was clear of stuff at least, but as Gnat got into it, he knew he wouldn't be able to sleep.

The people at the house had been very nice to him. Gnat hadn't been allowed back to get his stuff from the flat but they'd got a new toothbrush, a hairbrush and some new pyjamas ready for him.

No one would tell him exactly what had happened to Dad. The police had taken him and he was talking to them about Mum. Gnat had been brought here in a police car.

They'd driven through a tunnel under the River

Mersey, and now that impassable barrier of churning grey water flowed between them, cutting him off from wherever his Dad was.

Gnat lay in his snug pyjamas in a warm bed in a well ordered home, but his whole world was in disarray. He relentlessly turned things over in his mind. His Dad may well have had lied to him about the biggest thing ever. If Mum wasn't dead, she was missing.

A voice haunted him, someone, some woman had once said, *'She's not in heaven.'* Whoever had spoken these words seemed to know something. So if Mum wasn't in heaven, where was she?

Gnat pondered further, and slowly it dawned on him that his Dad might not have lied after all. Trying to recall the very few, painful and stilted conversations they'd ever had about Mum, Gnat could not recall Dad ever using the actual word 'dead.' Not ever. When it came to Mum, his father had always swerved away from that word. The few times he'd said much, Dad had employed evasive terms like 'left us,' or 'left the earth.'

At some point Gnat must have been told that something had been wrong with her, and because of it she had 'passed away.' Gnat had always taken this to mean that his mum had cancer and she had died. But now, looking back, he couldn't remember ever being told this in actual words.

Finally Gnat saw that this version he had grown up with and taken to heart must have largely been a construct of his own making. All he definitely knew for sure was that Mum wasn't around any more and she hadn't been since Gnat was a baby, but now that he thought about it, Gnat had absolutely no firm proof in words or otherwise of how these events had actually unfolded.

With the kind of precise reasoning most children have, but are never credited with, Gnat finally understood that Dad hadn't really told lies. He'd just avoided the truth.

Then a really bad thought came into his head. If Mum *was* dead, might Dad have had something to do with it? That must have been why the police wanted to talk to his Dad now, and that's why they had always kept moving. All this time, without Gnat even being aware of it, they had been on the run.

19

I attest that my name is John Meagher and this is my true account, the year is 1855and I am a man of sixty five summers, being from the parish of Edge Hill in the noble town of Liverpool.

Let it be noted that the happenstance I recount here concerns matters occurring some twenty years previous. Yet still is my memory accurate and my telling sincere.

I am giving this truthful and full account to Mr. Martineau who is writing down these histories. Having returned from the Peninsular Wars I came hither to my home town of Liverpool. Though but a boy, I had fought bravely alongside my comrades in the defeat of the monstrous tyrant Napoleon Bonaparte. But now, amongst many men, I did find myself turned out of the army being of no further use and was sorely aggrieved at being so dismissed and suddenly reduced to such a pitiful state of poverty.

So many of us returned at that one time from those foreign wars that we discovered ourselves to be a veritable flood of labour and no work, however humble, could be got.

The parishes of Liverpool were unwilling to support us and we were without aid or charity. Our children and wives went hungry and we were without hope.

Our prayers were answered by an extraordinary man of native nobility, wisdom and vision.

Not high born, Mr. Joseph Williamson had risen through society and had become a singularly rich man on account of his dealings in the tobacco business and he was kindly man who became popularly known as 'The Mole of Edge Hill.'

Mr. Williamson gave us much work to do and paid us well. It can be said with all verity that he returned pride and joy to our forlorn and saddened hearts. He set us upon a vast project, directing us to excavate great tunnels and caverns beneath the city of Liverpool.

Under his direction, we proudly created wonders including a subterranean banqueting hall and divers other chambers. During the navigation of one particular tunnel it is rumoured that Mr.Williamson stretched out his hand and shook the hand of Mr. George Stephenson who was building an underground railway in another tunnel at that time. Beneath many houses within certain streets of that city, we excavated cellars, then cellars beneath these cellars until some properties extended further into the earth than they did above it. Some houses had seven cellars stacked beneath them.

Mr. Williamson paid for all this work directly from his own pocket and we were glad of the labour. Many asked his motives, but he was known to be a very secretive man. It was said he was from a secret religious sect who laid great store in the belief that the end of the world was coming, and that the tunnels were to be a refuge against that dreadful time. Most held that he was an honourable man who wished to benefit the needy without the attendant curse of stifled self-respect.

I worked happily and without let or hindrance on these projects for a number of years until one drear day in September 1835 when I watched a number of my colleagues take fits and commence jigging as if possessed of the devil. What bewitching music they responded to I could not hear, myself having been rendered deaf some years previous during the said Peninsular Wars by my extreme proximity to repeated canon fire.

I noted five men dance into a tunnel we had previously dug, one which I refused to go down then and could not go down now. Their faces were greatly afeared yet still they tripped like marionettes as yet directed by invisible strings. The sight of their wretched expressions still fills my heart with great sadness and pity and although I was given to understand that many searches were made, not one man was found or did come to light ever again.

Being the sole witness and survivor, I spoke at length with Mr. Williamson who by this time was not a well man, and he revealed the true nature of his tunnels. He was of the opinion that the sudden growth of the city of Liverpool occasioned by the influx of so many of the starving Irish fleeing the first potato famine in that land, which was, at that time nearly a hundred years before, had effected an imbalance of a spiritual nature upon the environs and landscape of Liverpool town.

What he would have made of the most severe and yet more recent famine is only to be guessed at, but at that earlier time, poor Mr. Williamson held it to be true that many an immigrant Irishman had not only disturbed fantastical beings native to our own country, but had also brought leprechauns and fairies and all manner of unnatural creatures here to our land; literally borne upon their backs, with them.

After great consideration, and inasmuch as the citizens of the Americas have since laid by reserved encampments for their indigenous folk; in his earlier time, Mr. Williamson had sought to create a similar measure by way of these underground havens for his miraculous beings.

However, being a shrewd man he also had laid by a great stock of silver with which he believed he could quite subdue these apparitions should they resume their warlike habits. I took it from him that they were ungrateful creatures and not minded to be thankful for all his help, even though they took great advantage by it.

He spoke to me in all confidence saying that the liberal application of silver rendered them as drops of rain and although I did not take so much notice of his words at the time, it has always struck *me as strange that when he died in 1840, his death was from 'water on the lungs.'*

It made me wonder.

Back then though I knew for certain what I had seen, and bethought similar sights had rendered Mr. Williamson's demeanour somewhat deranged. I noted how his quirks and habits had become entitled by others as 'eccentric.'

Though I could not contemplate any solid truth coming from Mr. Williamson's quaint imaginings, neither could I reconcile my dark recollection of those five men dancing seemingly into hell.

With my nerves thus shattered, I was greatly afraid and shook at the memory of what I had seen; though I had witnessed far bloodier destructions wrought on the mortal flesh of men upon the battlefield. Accordingly I quit my work with Mr. Williamson and his tunnels and although it cost me dear, I could never go underground again, nor could I now. I am a very poor man and needy, but I could not do it, not even for a thousand guineas.

20

'They've pulled the plug?' Jockey was shocked. 'I knew it was coming, but it's still hard to credit. Don't they realise what we're doing?'

He met D's level wordless gaze and shook his head, 'No, of course not, no-one does. We're easy to overlook. Every last thing we do is invisible. Even the enemy's invisible.' Jockey sighed, 'all ye ever hear is "Cuts and more cuts" in the British Army. What's the thing those damned politicians are calling it?'

'Army 2020,' D murmured.

'Aye, that's the culprit. I thought we'd be safe in D9. What do they want us to do? Go to war with no weapons? All it'll take will be a crisis and then they'll wake up, you mark my words!'

They were sitting in one of their 'offices,' this one was a coffee shop in a plush hotel close to D's home. At the check-in desk, a weary looking man in his mid thirties shouldered a bulky blue bag and handed over his credit card to the desk clerk. Beside him a rather more animated, slightly older man conducted a row on his mobile phone. D's deceptively casual gaze dissected the size and shape of the blue porta-brace bag and their shabby expensive clothes. Cameraman and director/presenter, a two man team, probably documenting some hitherto unregarded slice of life as schedule-fodder for the late night viewers.

Scowling at the money men's lack of foresight, Jockey took a gulp of his coffee. A slender, sylphlike waitress cleared crockery from the next table. Jockey shot D a questioning glance.

'I checked her,' D said, 'She's clear. There's arboreal in her DNA, but way back. Somewhere, a meta got into the mix, like Aled.'

Aled and his partner Andrea ran a jewellery shop in Llangollen, North Wales. Apart from the fact that he could handle silver and anyone could see him in ordinary light, it was obvious to the trained eye that Aled came from an arboreal bloodline. Ironically, whatever his ancient forebears' fealties may have been, Aled had become the chief armourer to D9. It was he who tipped all the arrows, darts and crossbow bolts with silver, and he and Andrea were the only people Violet had ever trusted to silver Baby's blades.

Jockey's complaint sliced through D's reverie.

'We can't just let hundreds of years of tradition go to rack and ruin - not like this.'

D studied the other occupants of the lobby over the rim of his coffee mug, 'Regiments get disbanded, Jockey,' he said without emotion, 'they lose their history along with the regimental silver.'

'Aye, they do, but sometimes they get re-combined with other regiments and live on. They don't all go completely. We've got to fight those mealy-mouthed penny pinchers!'

'We will. *I* will continue fighting on two fronts, bureaucracy *and* metas, but anything big, like a reprise of the exercise at Kew will break us.'

'We're running low on everything!' Jockey grumbled.

As Quartermaster, he knew exactly what scant resources remained, 'If we're let off with light duties for a while,' he ventured, 'maybe, we'll last another month?'

D shrugged, 'In four hundred and twenty odd years of service, we've only ever faced a handful of what you might call major actions.'

Jockey slurped the foam from the bottom of his cappuccino, 'Aye. How likely is it they'll hit us whilst we're on the ropes?'

D thought it better not to share the unsettling news that had been coming in after the distribution of the new scopes. A host of traditional haunts and barrows had been revealed as being abandoned and yet not one sighting of where the displaced metas had relocated had been recorded.

On home ground they were bad enough, but if they were to start invading human territory... D pondered, remembering how he had been critical of Phil Dunford's likening of them to urban foxes. Now he reconsidered. Foxes had the habit of getting into henhouses and running amok with bloodlust, killing everything in sight, tearing the heads off the remaining chickens even when they had already killed far more than they could ever possibly eat. If humans were the chickens, then maybe it wasn't such a bad analogy after all?

Jockey caught D's sombre mood and fell quiet for a moment. He chewed his wooden stirrer thoughtfully and mumbled, 'Vi's running late.'

Violet hurried down to the platform and boarded the tube. She hated half-term. All immature human life was here, with every pupal stage represented. Babies bawled, bigger kids shrieked and moody teenagers deathstared at one another across the carriage.

She threw herself into a seat and caught her breath. With a rising whine, the train pulled away from the platform. Looking but not seeing through the window, she composed a mental 'to do' list. Baby needed a new coat. That meant a trip to Llangollen. Violet didn't ever send Baby anywhere, they always travelled together.

She considered for a moment. There was a big hill looming over the town that had intrigued her since her first visit. Strangely, even grazing sheep seemed to avoid Dinas Brân. She'd always wanted to investigate the place, and D9 would certainly get more value out of her trip if she took the opportunity to scope out 'Crow Castle' with D's latest toy.

Even as she planned all this, in her bag lay a small case. Inside rested what looked like vintage sunglasses. Except they weren't.

Opposite her a drunk lolled in his seat. His long ragged hair, gaunt face and bedraggled beard accentuated hollow eyes shaped by years of suffering. He was rake thin and shrouded in a greasy outsized raincoat. He looked like a dirty grey Jesus. Through thin blue lips he chanted softly. The carriage had thinned out and it had gone a little quieter and although Violet could clearly see his lips moving, she still couldn't make out his words.

The train juddered to a sudden stop. Then the lights flickered and went out. A teenager screamed and then giggled. All became deathly quiet. Finally Violet could hear the man was reciting a poem with a weird intonation.

'They *STOLE* little Bridget for *SEVEN YEARS LONG* . When she *came down again*, her friends were all *GONE*. They took her lightly *back* between the *dawn and morrow*. They thought that she was *fast ASLEEP*... *But* she was *DEAD* from *SORROW!*'

A light body flung itself down beside her.

Instinctively, Violet reached inside her coat, but a strong lithe arm stopped her.

'Up the *AIRY* mountain, *DOWN* the rushy glen, We *daren't* go a *HUNTING for FEAR of LITTLE MEN!'*

The arm withdrew, and there was silence. Violet recoiled but the man grabbed her again.

'They're here! There! And everywhere!' The drunk half-sang right into her face and the stench of his breath was sickening.

'They took me!' he hissed, 'and when I woke up *my kids were older than me!* They took me and they'll take YOU! Look!' He rapped on the window and howled like a demented banshee.

Violet flung off his arm and jumped up, just as the train lurched forwards. Unbalanced, she toppled towards him. Bracing herself she thrust out her hands, but all she fell upon was the hard velour seat.

The train stopped again and the lights stayed resolutely out. All around her in the almost total darkness, people were beginning to grumble and mutter, but she could no longer sense the presence of the drunken man.

He had gone.

His fetid smell and fervent chanting hung in the air like a memory, leaving just the unsettling echo of his scream in her ears.

Grappling with her rattled nerves, Violet sat down and folded her arms, hugging her worries away. Had that just really happened? No one else in the carriage had made any kind of move or even reacted to the guy. Was that because she'd imagined him, or was it just the accepted phlegmatism of most London tube travellers?

Had it been some kind of random PTSD episode? Violet's mind raced. She recalled how her oppo, Halliwell, had lost it at Kandahar. She'd never had post traumatic stress disorder, not that she was aware of, not even after they'd cut her foot off. That had been long after their encounter with the local version of chunkheads, and even that hadn't fazed her, but what if this was some kind of weirdly delayed reaction?

She deliberately calmed her breathing and forced her mind to stop focussing on worst case stuff. She'd seen more otherworldly weirdness than any old hippy caning it on acid ever would and she hadn't gone bonkers yet. As she steadied herself, she fiercely determined that she wasn't about to now. Regaining her calmer centre, Violet peered out of the window into the blackness beyond.

They had drawn up alongside an intriguing side tunnel. An unexplained shudder ran down her spine. There was movement out there. She scrabbled in her bag, all the time inwardly scolding herself that it was just a track crew, but still reaching for the case and its sunglasses.

Violet put them on and scanned the side spur. Nothing. She heaved a sigh of relief. She had behaved like a rookie and let some pathetic drink-crazed casualty get to her. Violet took the glasses off and relaxed. As she folded them, her fingers detected a small switch on the left arm. She hit it, flicked the glasses open and put them back on.

This time when she viewed the tunnel, she could clearly see the grey body of the drunk being borne away by multiple small figures. Everywhere she looked creatures clung to the walls of the tunnel or crawled around on the ceiling. Terrified but mesmerised, Violet watched. Held in a hypnotic fascination, she shuddered but couldn't look away. She found their insectlike movements physically sickening, like massed spiders crawling through her hair.

Every surface was shrouded with an infestation of creatures. In a perfect picture of hell, bodies skittered over one another, making inhuman movements in a slow inexorable surge of grey green like ragged moving moss. She could almost feel their chattering high voices vibrating through her body. Violet's hand shot to her mouth and she gasped. As one, the skittering bodies froze. All heads whipped up and swivelled her way. Rows of black, glittering eyes narrowed, targeting her.

Abruptly the lights flashed on and Violet found herself frozen, staring at her own reflection. The train squealed and shot forwards and a cheer broke out as palpable relief surged through all the passengers. All except Violet. Shaken, she put the glasses back into their case.

21

'Nothing you have said reassures me, Constable.'

Watkin shifted uneasily, he knew he'd probably hung himself already by saying far too much.

'I've reviewed your last appraisal, you weren't doing too badly. Pity.'

Watkin hung his head like a schoolboy accused of stealing sweets.

'Haven't we got enough to deal with on our home patch without *you* looking further afield?'

Watkin's heart contracted with a pang of fear. Had they found out about his Liverpool trip too?

'It's the police or the little green men, Watkin. Time to choose.'

In the great scheme of things, Watkin's error had been slight. He'd allowed himself to be drawn out on the subject of UFO's by the malign Sergeant Seward.

Within six weeks he'd been indelibly labelled with the tag of 'station weirdo' and subjected to all manner of jovial contempt. Then the petty schoolyard politics had solidified into something more serious, and now Watkin found himself under the attentive eyes of the station's most senior officer, Superintendant Alice Reidy.

Her hooded gaze displayed less compassion than the grand inquisitor as she fixed upon Watkin, waiting for his reply.

'My job comes before everything, Ma'am.'

'It has to, Constable.' The Superintendant nodded, dismissing him. Watkin turned smartly on his heel and marched out. As he reached the door, Reidy couldn't help herself, she called out with cold glee, 'May the force be with you, Watkin!'

Watkin pursed his lips into a thin smile. The term 'force' hadn't been used for years within the police, but still she'd dragged it out to make a lame smart Alec comment.

Is this what he had come to? The blighted years stretched out joylessly ahead, starring him as the butt of every tired old pun for the rest of his career.

He stood before his locker, changing his shirt, mentally going over the pros and cons of requesting a transfer. He could do with a change, nothing of great interest happened in Richmond, ever. An inner city beat would offer excitement and challenge and even the odd bout of fisticuffs. But if he went now, he'd look like he couldn't hack a bit of mild banter. The reason behind it would soon become clear and the taunting would follow him. It wasn't like he could call himself a keen ufologist any more, anyway.

He hadn't read a single article, much less a book on the subject since his failed trip to Aintree. His enthusiasm had died a death. Before long the bullying would too.

'Oi, Watkin! Phone home!'

The laughter rang down the corridor. Watkin didn't even turn to look.

22

'And they made no move to leave the tunnel?'

D's odd eyes looked questioningly into hers.

'No,' Violet shook her head and took a sip of the warming coffee. She cradled the mug between her hands, but couldn't shake off the chill that had seeped into her bones. 'They clocked me, but they didn't follow. It was like they were… waiting for something?'

By the time she had arrived at their rendezvous in the hotel's coffee shop, Jockey had gone and D had taken her news quietly.

'They've *never* got it together like this before, not ever. Someone must be organising them. Someone human?'

D shook his head, 'Half-human at best, they've only got contempt for full humans. They want everyone dead and the land back for themselves.'

D rubbed his aching neck thoughtfully, 'They've traditionally harried and upset mankind for millennia, but only in small, disorganised groups.'

'With respect, Sir,' Violet always prefaced any borderline insubordinate remarks with this opening, 'Excepting the disorganised bit, isn't that just how we're fighting back? In small groups?'

'It is,' D conceded, 'The SAS proved long ago it's the best way to tackle insurgents and for what we've been dealing with, it's been adequate.'

'Yeah, it *was*, but you should have *seen* them,' she heaved a hollow sigh, 'Sir, we need personnel… and a ruck of kit.'

'We don't need to engage them.' D was thoughtful. Violet shot him a questioning look.

'Not yet. You said they made absolutely no move to follow you, even after they spotted you?'

'I did - and no, they didn't.'

'So they could be using the quieter service tunnels as impromptu roosts?' D mused, 'urban barrows?'

Violet shifted uneasily, her foot tapped ceaselessly, leaking anxiety, 'It's a possibility, but I still got the feeling that they were waiting.'

'Perhaps.'

'So that's why we've got to hit them now.' She hit her balled fist into the palm of her hand, '*hard* - before they're ready!'

Her eager bright eyes were met by dark shades of resignation from D's. 'Violet, *we're* not ready and we're not likely to be anytime soon!'

His quiet words were like a slap across her face. Violet slumped back in her chair, 'I guess not,' she conceded quietly.

'So they work.' D lifted the glasses from their case and examined them carefully, turning them gently in his large hands.

'Yeah,' Violet murmured, 'they work.'

That night, D sat down to write the most forlornly urgent appeal to the highest authority for the restoration of his department. He didn't hold out much hope, but he had to make one last attempt.

23

And finally, one day in 1945 it had been the end of the end. V.J Day had come and long gone and although a mood of optimism had broken out in many quarters, it hadn't here at Chartwell.

Sitting behind his familiar old desk, the one he'd had brought back from Downing Street, Winston Churchill surrendered to a crushing sense of utter defeat.

Anti-climax. It felt like the aftermath of the world's biggest party, with a lot of clearing up left to do. The hangover was that the whole of Europe - and huge swathes of Asia - now clamoured for immediate attention.

Some clear up. Some party.

The mood Winston called 'Black Dog' had settled upon him. Black Dog brought with it a bleakness of spirit that leeched away all sense of satisfaction, achievement, or even redemption. His very recent election defeat had conspired to feed the beast and further rob Winston of any sense of victory.

All week, Clementine Churchill had insisted to her staff that every newspaper proclaiming the new Labour government should be kept well away from her husband's study. Inevitably her instructions had led to a surreptitious ban on *all* newsprint.

Winston snapped out of his bleak reverie and cast around for his missing papers. Of course she'd had them removed. Irritated, he reached for the house phone, but just then a familiar, gentle knock interrupted him.

'Clemmie, have you had *every* last one of my newspapers away?'

The tiny, birdlike Clementine smiled guiltily as she entered. Her elegantly upswept hair was succumbing to grey and her lovely face to lines, but all Churchill saw was his beautiful girl. Irritation gave way to sentimentality and unbearably moved by her tender concern, tears welled in Winston's eyes.

As the hem of her skirts brushed past it, the spectral Black Dog bared its teeth. It hated Clementine. She loved Winston with a fierceness and protectiveness that broached no opposition, and she was the only one with the power to occasionally banish it.

To Winston's vast amusement, Clemmie's fragile hands bore a tray carrying a china cup and saucer. Bearing it before her like an offering, she followed it into the room. The tea was doubtless long cold from the draughty Chartwell corridors, but rather more promisingly, a side plate bore not one but two of his favourite biscuits, shortbread. Clemmie playing house-maid? This would be good. What was she after?

'Winston, we have a visitor.'

'Your department I think, my dear.'

'He's come to see *you*, silly,' Clemmie laughed.

The studied lightness of her tone put Winston immediately on his guard. He'd habitually dealt with men far more treacherous than his sweet, well-meaning wife. Some of them had even been on the opposing side.

'Quack, is he?'

'No, Winston. It's Major Edward Maltby.'

'Oh that's alright then, not a quack, just a witchdoctor.'

'Winston, Maltby is a...'

Clemmie faltered as she caught Winston's impish eye. He wasn't cross at all, in fact he didn't suspect a thing. She relaxed.

'Get him in here then.'

Much relieved, Clemmie left the room. 'Oh, and Clemmie? Better leave the tea and biscuits.'

Clemmie's slender hands snaked back guiltily round the door. She dumped the wretched tray on a side table and unable to face him, fled before Winston could change his mind.

Winston got up from behind his desk and ignoring the cold tea, retrieved the biscuits. He sat down again heavily and a huge weight spread across his chest as the spectral hound pinned him to his chair with its massive body. It growled breathily and its words formed in his mind, it seemed to say, 'You do know you can't get rid of me, don't you?'

'It's the bargain I made, and I will keep to it.' Churchill replied evenly.

'Then send this man away.'

Winston caught the fleeting impression that the Black Dog understood Maltby and that it actually feared him. He shifted under the dog's weight, not from discomfort, but to mask any rising energy of hope.

A sharp knock on the door, and the spectral dog jumped down, crouching beneath Churchill's desk.

'Come in.'

The energetic Maltby practically bounded into the room. In spite of his bearing being that of a frenzied puppy, Edward Maltby was a preternaturally discreet man. No one better matched the job he did at the fledgling MI6, after all, no-one else had accrued so much experience working in Department 9.

As once-warring countries redefined their borders and loyalties, Europe was awash with spies. Churchill understood it was imperative that everything he had fought so hard to preserve in 'war, war' should not be lost, or even caught on the back foot, in the consequent, devious politics of, 'jaw, jaw.'

Still youthful for a man in his forties, Major Maltby was the centre of a huge network of information. He had earned his 'witchdoctor' reputation after recruiting psychics to persuade Hitler not to commit his full forces to The Battle of Britain. To Maltby's satisfaction, it had worked spectacularly well.

One of the most interesting sensitives, Cecil Williamson, was currently working with an American General called Eisenhower.

Winston admired the native cunning the army had failed to knock out of Maltby, and cherished the fact that the physically restless man standing before him defined the expression, that with some people at least, there could be far more to them than ever met the eye.

Winston shot him a quizzical look, 'Trouble?'

'Eastern Europe will always be difficult, Sir, but it's more of the ongoing domestic matter at the moment.'

The spectral hound growled from its hiding place. If the Major heard it, he registered nothing.

'Metaphysical business? D9 stuff?'

The Major nodded.

'*Metahominids* taking advantage of difficult times, are they?'

'The late harvest will not be a good one, Sir.' Maltby admitted, 'they continue to promote food shortages.'

'History has it, they milked cows through a sieve until the unfortunate beasts ran dry and their reputation for blighting crops is very much the stuff of legend.' Winston shook his head. 'I am no longer in Government, my influence is not what it was. But we will fight them… Wherever we find them, we will fight them.'

Maltby lingered.

'You have whatever support I can give. Do you need anything further Major… Money?'

'No, Sir… well yes, but that's been taken care of. I just wondered if *you* needed anything?'

'Indeed I do…' The dog growled, in anticipation of a fight, exactly as Churchill had hoped it would. He might be in its power, but he still enjoyed baiting it. Ignoring it, he rose and slowly crossed the room. 'You are probably aware that The Savoy Grill doesn't allow thirteen to dine? Not since the death of that Boer!'

'The Wool Joel incident Sir?'

'Indeed.'

Churchill unlocked a cabinet, and took out a splendidly sinuous figurine of an elegant, black cat.

'Is that…?'

'Kaspar, yes. The Grill needs him back, to sit with parties of thirteen and make them *fourteen.*'

Handing the heavy statuette to Maltby, Churchill returned to his chair, his spirits lightened by the thorough fright he'd given that blasted Black Dog.

'Silly damn prank by some RAF boys. I promised I'd help get him back. There's some liquid reward I understand. Best not to share that last piece of intelligence with Clemmie.'

'Sir…' Calmly surveying the huge, barely visible Black Dog, Maltby picked his words delicately, 'may I render any further assistance?'

Now the beast's hackles rose. Listening at the door, Clementine held her breath. The huge, echoing house fell silent, waiting for Churchill's pivotal reply. The pause was answer enough. As the spectral hound roused itself and put one huge paw on Winston's knee, claiming ownership, Maltby swallowed down despair.

Churchill finally spoke. 'Once such an agreement is made, it cannot be unmade.'

A host of objections rose in his throat and died, leaving Maltby bereft of any reply.

If Winston Churchill had willingly rendered himself hostage to the metahominids to keep them out of the war and save the world, then there was nothing further anyone could do.

'Sir.'

Maltby left and the house breathed again. Clementine wept silent, bitter tears and Churchill returned to his reverie.

England must be kept safe from the ancient enemies within. But now there was danger from outside interference too, from displaced metahominids. The Balkans, Eastern Europe, Ireland, all were in uproar. All were hotbeds of traditional superstitions warning about the malevolent 'little people,' 'fairies' or 'Grey Folk,' and each had very good reasons to fear their indigenous creatures.

Later, in a north London street, as Maltby approached the car, he could see the man from D9 was inside. He flashed a quick look in and as their eyes met Maltby gave the briefest shake of his head. The man's features set stern as he turned the ignition, and drove away.

They both knew if Churchill was determined to keep the Black Dog, it was just as well the election had been lost. At least the astral hound, a shape-shifting metahominid that presented itself as a *metacanine*, would no longer be so close to the heart of government.

24

Under the cover of darkness, Diamond expertly picked the door lock. She gently reached her hand through the tangled cat's cradle of blue and white tape and pushed against the wood. The patched up door opened with the slightest squeak. She froze and shot her companion an alarmed glance. He returned her look with a serene gaze.

Ignoring the tape's stern message *Police Line Do Not Cross*, Diamond pulled a few strands away, then bent under what remained and stepped through into the flat beyond. Clothes and books lay scattered across the floor.

There had been a struggle.

Her accomplice made his way directly to Gnat's room. Diamond scurried after him, then dodging ahead of him she flung the door open.

'Nathan!' the hoarsely whispered word faltered in her throat as it dawned upon her that the flat was empty. She looked about the room in wild panic. Following her companion's gaze, Diamond dived under the bed. She retrieved the Christmas tree box and ripped it open revealing the beautiful rainbow wing.

Gnat had never been without that wing before. He'd never let it out of his sight and it had been one of the things that had helped them to keep track of his whereabouts. Diamond's mind was in a whirl.

Typical! Now they really needed him, he had somehow become parted from it. Her foot brushed a discarded comic. As an afterthought she spoke in a loud whisper, 'He is alright, isn't he?'

Her silent companion looked down, gazing at the comic, studying the manga characters. Intrigued by their huge oval eyes and pointed faces, just like his own kind, he nodded absently.

'Good. I've got to find him and bring him home. It's my right. I'm family!'

25

The following is a verbatim extract from the autobiography of Reverend Dr. Edward Williams, co-editor of The Evangelical Magazine and one of the founders of The London Missionary Society:

1757: On a fine summer day, (about midsummer), between the hours of noon and one, my eldest sister and myself, our next door neighbour's children, Barbara and Anne Evans, both older than myself, were in a field called Cae Caled near their house, all innocently engaged at play by a hedge under a tree, and not far from a stile next to that house, when one of us observed on the middle of the field, a company of - what shall I call them? Beings, neither men, women nor children, dancing with great briskness.

They were in full view less than a hundred yards from us. Consisting of about seven or eight couples, we could not well reckon them, owing to the briskness of their motions and the consternation with which we were struck at a sight so unusual. They were all clothed in red, a dress not unlike military uniform, without hats but their heads tied with handkerchiefs of a reddish colour, sprigged or spotted with yellow all uniform in this as in habit, all tied behind with the corners hanging down their backs, and with white handkerchiefs in their hands held loose at the corners.

They appeared of a size somewhat less than our own, but more like dwarfs than children. On the first discovery, we began, with no small dread, to question one another as to what they could be as there were no soldiers in the country, nor was it the time for May dancers, and as they differed much from all human beings we had ever seen. Thus alarmed, we dropped our play, left our station and made for the stile. Still keeping our eyes upon them we observed one of their company starting from the rest and making towards us with a running pace. I being the youngest, was the last at the stile, and, though struck with inexpressible panic, saw the grim elf just at my heels, having a full and clear, though terrific, view of him, with his ancient, swarthy, and grim complexion. I screamed out exceedingly; my sister also and our companions set up a roar, and the former dragged me with violence over the stile on which, at the instant I was disengaged from it, this warlike

Liliputian leaned and stretched himself after me, but came not over.

With palpitating hearts and loud cries we ran towards the house, alarmed the family, and told them our trouble. The men instantly left their dinner, with whom still trembling we went to the place, and made the most solicitous and diligent enquiry in all the neighbourhood, both at that time and after, but never found the least vestige of any circumstance that could contribute to a solution of this remarkable phenomenon.

26

Gnat waited for the microwave to ping and fidgeted. He hated waiting. He'd never been any good at it. But there was a bigger waiting going on here.

A burdensome freight of unknown expectation bore down upon him, making him edgy and restless. Like a spring fret aching deep in his young, green bones, it urged him to run, to run as fast as he could, forever.

This waiting had been going on all his life. Every child growing up knows things change and bigger events will one day fill their lives but now, suddenly, in Gnat's case it seemed more urgent.

Somehow, something was building to a head. The old chronic ache he had almost become used to had grown and become even more acute of late. As if his present situation wasn't bad enough, like living under a perpetual black storm front, Gnat really couldn't shake his sense of foreboding that something truly awful was coming.

He looked around at the bright friendly kitchen. It was just another nice place where he didn't belong and he found its warmth and lively colours alienating rather than welcoming.

He stared at the daubed artwork of Mrs. Elderry's previous foster children. A pink fairy with blobby legs and a crimson grimace gash for a mouth shed its glitter on the countertop. He blinked back sudden tears and turned away. Living beneath the threatening darkness, Gnat realised somehow he had lost the knack of connecting with the brighter things any more. Memories of Matt and the raucous coach trip were in grey tatters, as if lived a lifetime ago and he couldn't imagine ever smiling, let alone laughing ever again. Nothing cheered him up. He was enduring a living death oppressed beyond bearing by the suspenseful sense of gathering gloom.

It had been three days and he'd seen nothing of his Dad. He hadn't been to school either.

Nothing was right.

Nothing had been right for ages.

His mind didn't seem to be working properly either. There were the sudden unexplained holes in his memory whenever he tried to recall Matt and his last school. As if that wasn't enough, his dreams had become increasingly troubled, but they'd been doing that for weeks before the police had come and taken Dad away.

Gnat drew swirls with his forefinger in the pile of shed glitter on the countertop. Half watching the mug of milk gently waltzing in a juddering circle inside the microwave, he tried to recall the last ordinary thing that had happened.

It had probably been the school trip to Warwick Castle and even that had faded blips of imperfect recollection. He'd somehow found himself in a strange room all alone, although he couldn't think why he'd gone off on his own like that.

There had been a wing just like his.

Gnat stared at the glitter on his fingertip, his heart ached for his wing almost as much as it ached for his Dad. For so long this hidden mystery had felt almost a part of him. Now it was gone, he felt bereft.

The ping of the microwave made him jump. He'd caught himself doing that a lot lately, being startled by the least little thing, like some stupid small kid being scared of the bogey man.

Gnat pulled his pyjama sleeve around his hand and carefully picked up the mug of milk. The handle always got too hot. He manoeuvred it onto the work top and stirred in a towering scoop of hot chocolate mix, carefully bursting each powdery bubble, then he added a bit more 'for luck,' mixing his drink with all the focussed intent of an old time alchemist.

The phone rang as Gnat was carrying his cup of hot chocolate upstairs to bed. He scooted into his room and crept behind his open door, carefully retrieving the stolen biscuits from his dressing gown pocket whilst they were still vaguely biscuit shaped.

He sat as quietly as he could and listened to Mrs. Elderry as she stood in the hall, just in case the call was about him or his Dad.

For the first couple of days it was almost always about him and Gnat had grown adept at eavesdropping. But despite his hovering within earshot of the telephone, there hadn't been anything about him or his Dad all day today, so Gnat was relaxed and only half listening at first.

Within the first few words, he had switched to fully alert mode.

'He's anxious. He wants to see his Dad....' Her tone rose, shocked, 'Why? That's ridiculous! This child has every right to see his father... You don't understand, he's got no-one else in the world.... *Grandmother?*

Gnat's heart sank, he'd never met Di and he didn't want to. Not after everything his Dad had said about her. Even though Dad had never spoken that much about her, he remembered it was all bad. Gnat frowned fiercely, he *wouldn't* go. They couldn't *make* him!

Downstairs, the call continued and Mrs. Elderry's voice became combative, 'No, he's never mentioned her, never.... Does he even *know* this woman? What if there's been some kind of family breakdown? ...'

His heart leapt, 'That's it!' he thought, 'you tell them! I don't want to go with her!'

However, judging by Mrs. Elderry's agitated finger tapping on the telephone table, her intervention seemed to be to having little success.

'I can't believe you're unsettling him again when he's barely had time... I'll bring him. But I can't say I approve of this boy being pushed from pillar to post, he's been through enough!'

Gnat sagged. Closing the door, he shuffled across the floor. Dragging himself into bed, he sat with his head beneath the duvet and chewed his biscuits thoughtfully. Every night he'd retrieve his mobile from one sock and its battery from the other. He didn't dare leave his phone on in case it went off and got confiscated. Plus he couldn't let it waste a drop of battery as he didn't have the charger with him. He reassembled it and checked for messages from Dad. There weren't any.

He really couldn't stop the tears coming this time. He'd never felt so alone in all his life. It had always been him and Dad against the world, as far back as he could remember. Why hadn't Dad tried to ring him? He thought hard trying to make sense of his father's apparent abandonment of him. He'd watched loads of DVD's round at Matt's house and although he couldn't remember any of the stories, Gnat knew that when people fell foul of the law they always got one phone call.

So why hadn't he called?

A consoling thought crossed a corner of his mind. Maybe it was because Dad had used his call to get some hot-shot lawyer on his side? That's what they always did in the movies. So maybe Dad had used up his telephone allowance that way, and that's why he hadn't called? Gnat marshalled his scattered ideas and thought it through carefully. In the movies, people sometimes got bail. Gnat pondered. As far as he could see bail worked just like a *'get out of jail free'* card. In lots of American films it seemed that they had to 'post' bail, so it made sense that 'bail' was just some kind of official card.

If Dad had got his postcard then he'd be here. If he hadn't been able to get one, then he would be in a police station somewhere in Liverpool. Gnat imagined a cartoon light bulb hovering above his head. Breakthrough! Now he knew exactly what he was going to do.

27

He'd been wrong. The bullying from his colleagues hadn't stopped, if anything it had got worse. Still Watkin held his tongue. His working days were miserable now, and Watkin found more and more that he lived for any precious time off. Then when it came, he wasted his time allowing himself to be drawn into computer games until even the most vicious of vicarious fights began to lose their appeal. He couldn't stop though. Even though he ended every night with his contact lenses seemingly lasered onto his retinas and his endless gaming becoming a chore, still he couldn't break the habit.

There was simply nothing else to do.

Without his ufology he had very little to fill his time. Chloe had been gone for nearly three months now, but

Watkin still didn't feel like trawling for the 'plenty more fish' that were allegedly out there.

At the end of another depressing shift of writing out reports and barely contributing to public order, he dragged his jacket onto his despondent shoulders and headed home for another pointless night of killing zombies and aliens. This was not what he had signed up for.

Apart from the usual rubbish, he had five emails from contacts waiting for him at home. Watkin slid behind his stark white desk in his stark white flat and began reading them. One was from Chloe, who plainly thought it time she forgave him for finding out what she had been getting up to with his now ex-best mate. Two were updates from the UFO group he no longer attended. One was from 'new best mate' Dave and a plaintive one was from his sister Katy asking him to make it up with her new husband Rhodri.

They hadn't *quite* come to blows at the wedding.

That one had been over Chloe too, Watkin mused. She was *chaude noir*, too hot to handle. Trouble followed her like a heat-seeking missile. He hovered the cursor over the 'delete' icon, thought better of it, and went on to read Dave's latest piece of news.

A couple of years younger than Watkin, Dave acted ten years older and presented himself, elbow patches and all, as an über-geek. Although he preferred his maths lite, his heroes were Einstein, Bohr and Feynman. He could quote Carl Sagan's 'Blue Dot' speech word for word and was hopelessly in awe of Professor Brian Cox. They'd met once at a science road-show and Dave had been thrilled to the very core when the Professor had smilingly singled him out to call him a 'nobber.'

Dave's email was full of his usual UFO ramblings. For as long as Watkin could remember, Dave had been trying to write a book on the history of alien abduction. His latest news was that he'd discovered a report concerning an incident in North Wales which dated back to 1757. He'd included a link to a site about the case.

With nothing better to do, Watkin idly clicked on the link. A page opened headlining the case as a probable failed attempt at alien abduction. Half interested, Watkin read on. The source appeared to be impeccable, a church minister who had been the central figure in the incident when he'd been just seven years old.

Watkin sat back and pondered. His police training cut in and he began to ask questions about the witness. How safe was his evidence? Within a few clicks, Watkin had accessed a biography of the man. His name was Reverend Doctor Edward Williams. The fact that he was a founder of The London Missionary Society suggested he had a well organised mind. The fact that he had published various religious writings could count against him as a potential crazy zealot.

Watkin accessed another biography and reassessed the subject of his investigation. Williams had been educated at a grammar school and had originally been interested in the law. This suggested a certain sobriety and precision of thinking. So why would this upstanding man, founder of an august body, a preacher and publisher put his hard-fought-for social standing on the line for a whimsical tale?

Williams had been writing his autobiography at a time when a lost reputation meant more than just a few harsh words in a newspaper. Williams had risked total financial ruin and real hardship. The fact that he had been prepared to wreck his presumably comfortable life over such an unusual story convinced Watkin that this witness was in earnest and his story was certainly worth more than just a cursory glance.

He clicked a few pages back to Dave's email:

So could you drive me up to Bodfari next time you've got a few days off then? I'll pay my whack of the gas. I need photographs of the field where it happened - Cae Caled - and I want to talk to the locals. It'll be great! Cheers! Dave.

Watkin grimaced, he just knew he'd pull off the road and cheerfully batter Dave to death somewhere within the first fifty miles. Not that he hated Dave, no one did. It was just that no one liked to be around him for very long.

The 'new best friend' tag was Watkin's attempt at irony. In reality, Dave's entry in his address book was *SDD* - code for '*Small Doses Dave.*'

He emailed a reply stating flatly that he had no leave due for a few months and he'd see about it then. This was a lie as he had to use up some paid holidays within the next two weeks. He mentally worked out when would be the best time to take it whilst re-opening his sister's email. She and Rhodri lived in a place called Corwen. Watkin checked an online map. If he drove up via Shrewsbury, he could drop in on them just off the A5.

On his way back from Bodfari.

28

Gnat swigged the last of his long cold chocolate. He'd lain in bed for at least three very long hours waiting for the house to grow silent. He didn't dare put the light on, so he felt for his clothes. He dressed silently, talking the pillowcase off one of his pillows to act as a swag bag and crept down into the immaculate kitchen.

He couldn't reach the top shelves for the bread without dragging a chair across the squeaky tiles, so he abandoned the idea of taking sandwiches with him. His eyes alighted on the instant noodles, but he grimaced when he realised that without benefit of a kettle full of boiling water, he'd have to eat them cold and hard. The fridge offered up a treasury of choice including golden scotch eggs. Gnat grabbed a couple and thrust them into his pillowcase. He broke a corner off a flat slab of cheddar and took a couple of bananas from the fruit bowl. He fancied some crisps, but he thought it wiser not to. In the quiet of the early hours, the noisy, crackly packaging would surely sound as loud as firecrackers?

He reviewed his loot, how long would that lot last? Until he got to Liverpool? Gnat grabbed a packet of digestives and added them to his hoard. He padded down the hallway in his socks and turned the handle on the front door. Nothing. Suddenly hot with rising panic, he tried again. It was locked in a way that he couldn't work out. Increasingly agitated, he pressed the button in on the handle and tried again.

This time it opened effortlessly. From the doorstep Mrs. Elderry's cat, Oscar, chirruped a greeting. He was waiting to be let in. Gnat shooed him away, but Oscar was persistent. Gnat frantically stuck his leg out to bar the cat from getting inside the house. If Oscar went upstairs and woke Mrs. Elderry, the game would be up. In silent terror, Gnat juggled with the cat, his shoes and the pillowcase. Softly closing the door behind him, he soundlessly shed the pillowcase and carefully placed his shoes on the step. He picked Oscar up, burying his face in his thick plush fur. Oscar purred and Gnat steadied himself. Lost and alone on a stranger's doorstep, it was all he could do to stop himself from crying all over again. He rubbed his face against Oscar's velvet cheek and sat down with him. He then pulled his shoes on whilst the cat rubbed around his legs.

'Bye, old mate, take care,' he whispered giving Oscar's ears a final friendly rub. Getting up, he shouldered his bag of stolen food and slipped out onto the quiet road.

29

In the early hours, D took the printout from the ATM and stared at it. How could he go to war with so little in his coffers? Apart from running his network, he had other pressing matters to attend to, simple things like getting more darts and bolts silvered by Aled and Andrea in Wales.

Then there was the upcoming visit to Japan regarding their new initiative, *Operation White Stone*. How could he continue to operate without any backing? On an impulse he calculated the time difference, figured it was a decent hour to contact someone in that part of the planet, and rang a number.

Richard answered in his customary breezy tone. He always spoke with a smile in his voice but he was particularly pleased to hear from D. Years ago, D had identified a metahominid clan who were using the beautiful river Cherwell as a refuge. Then he had detected a hot spot of activity just north of Oxford in the village of Shipton-on-Cherwell. He had cleared an old Manor house of a particularly vicious nest of chunkheads and iron-staked a stream of geopathic stress away from the property. That manor house had belonged to Richard who, at that time, had been all but flat broke.

Almost from that moment onwards, Richard had shaken off the bad luck that had dogged him and his business had begun building steadily and impressively. Whilst holding a clear picture of his own hard work and acumen, Richard still thanked D for the help he'd offered and the subsequent turnaround.

He listened carefully to D's request. Richard owned an airline, so getting his old friend to Japan was hardly a problem. The smile temporarily left his voice as he contemplated his metahominid enemies.

'Just get them D. Get them all wherever they pop up. They burnt my house down!'

30

Rhys Greville couldn't figure out how they'd found him. He was unaware that Watkin's heavy-handed interest had led the police straight to the latest of the many doors he'd been hiding behind for the last decade. He had assumed his mother Di's continual hounding had been to blame.

And *what* a chase he'd led his mother! Up and down the land since Gnat had been a baby. Dodging all the little calling card mementos she had so thoughtfully left for Gnat. Countering every attempt she had made to influence him and lure the boy away into her sick existence.

Di, he refused to think of her as *'Diamond,'* had always been there like a wicked fairy – oh, how she would have *loved* that title! Plain old Diane Timms transformed into a magical being. Di with her stupid airy fairy ideas and daft books on dragons and cutesy fantasy figures. He recalled the hangings, the dream catchers and the continual fug of incense and dope in her living wagon, and shuddered.

Rhys sighed. If his mother hadn't been so fixated upon paranormal mythology and the occult and left well alone, he would have had half a chance.

He would have married someone normal and never had to live like a fugitive. Now he was alone and unable to make contact with the one person who could help him out of this mess, D. The taped recording started again.

'Interview recommenced,' the detective checked his watch, 'at 10.30 hours, subject Mr. Rhys Greville. Officers attending, Detective Constable Jackson and myself, Detective Sergeant Dean. Duty solicitor Ms. Emily Turner is also present. Mr. Greville can you please explain the whereabouts of your wife?'

Rhys shook his head.

'For the record, Mr. Greville is shaking his head. When did you last see her?'

'Ten years ago.'

'Have you had any contact with her since then?'

Rhys hesitated, and then shook his head.

'You seem uncertain, Mr. Greville.'

'No, I haven't seen her or heard from her.'

'Mr. Greville, you have two sons, Nathan and what's this... Carden?'

'Cayden,' Rhys corrected.

'And Cayden is Nathan's twin?'

Rhys nodded.

'Mr. Greville, for the benefit of the tape recording, could you please vocalize your reply?'

'Er.. Yes... Cayden is Nathan's twin.'

'Yet when you were arrested, you only had Nathan with you. Where's his brother, Mr. Greville, where's Cayden?'

'With his mother.'

'And she is...?'

'Alive and well, as far as I know.'

The Detective opened a slender file and laid several pieces of A4 paper out on the desk.

'I am showing Mr. Greville his wife's bank and credit card statements.' He straightened up, 'Not much of a paper trail is it Mr. Greville? Not much to show for a life?'

Rhys shrugged. Then remembered he needed to speak. 'No,' he murmured.

'Your wife arrived in this country as a stateless refugee, married you, acquired a passport, national insurance number, credit cards and a bank account. Then, less than a year after she gave birth to your two sons, the paper trail stops dead. There are no further records of her. Her bank account lies dormant, the credit cards unused. She has apparently vanished off the face of the earth taking one of her sons with her.'

Rhys stared stonily at the Detective.

'She has disappeared Mr. Greville, with one of your boys. If I may say so, you don't seem that concerned.'

Ms. Turner, the young duty solicitor hired to speak on Rhys' behalf finally spoke.

'My client has clearly stated he has no reason to believe his absent wife and child have come to any harm and his demeanour is congruent with this.'

Tight lipped Rhys stared out of the small window, its thick frosted glass only hinted at the cold grey rain falling outside.   He knew Gnat must be kept safe, hidden away. If Di snatched Gnat it could mean the end of everything. Since his arrest, he had made several calls in an attempt to contact his handler, but all to no avail. When the police had applied to a court for further time to question him, Rhys had tried again, but he had met with no better luck.

The truth was that his case lay gathering dust, his handler victim to the swingeing cuts. There was no safe pair of hands to catch him any more and try as he might, there seemed to be no way of getting through to D, the one man who had shielded him and Gnat all these years.

D was the one person who knew every element of his history and who needed to know what was happening to him and Gnat right now.

31

Gnat eyed the ticket inspector nervously. The man was making his way down the carriage whilst Gnat hovered at the doors, willing the train to pull into the next station. He chewed the frayed cuff of his sweatshirt and wondered if he should bolt further up the train? No, that would be a dead giveaway. There were no toilets to hide in on this train, Gnat had already checked. He hung onto the steel pole and sucked at his cuff, it tasted of Mrs. Elderry's washing powder. From the corner of his eye he could see the ticket man was getting closer.

If they caught him, they'd call the police and he'd be shipped back to Mrs. Elderry, or worse, and then he'd never find his Dad. Gnat hovered at the door, fidgeting with anxiety.

He'd only managed to get this far by walking for what seemed like hours. The sun had eventually risen and by looking at the street signs, he'd discovered he was still in the same postcode area. Disgusted, he'd slumped on a shop's wide windowsill and tried to formulate a plan.

Walking was no good.

Overhead an early train clattered across a bridge. It mocked him, he had no money. Sighing, he had watched the commuters and shoppers queuing across the road at Bebington station and inspiration had struck.

He had darted across the road, running straight past the ticket office and hurtled up the steep slope to the platform, shouting, 'Mum, mum!' He had barrelled past a startled old man, but no one else had seemed to notice him at all. He'd coolly sat down next to a lady in a red coat, hoping people would think they were together and although his heart was pounding so loud he felt sure she'd notice and report him, no one came after him.

Now though, it felt as if his luck was running out. From the overhead speakers, a posh lady's voice announced that they were approaching Green Lane. Gnat chewed furiously, trying to stay as calm as his rapidly stretching nerves would allow. The ticket man strode towards him, Gnat dropped his head blushing bright pink.

'Er…eh, mate?' A tousle headed student tapped ineffectually at the ticket man's back. The ticket man jumped and turned.

'Er, sorry,' the student rambled, 'I know this is a bit random, but *where am I?*'

He ran a trembling hand through his trendily tousled guinea-pig-in-a-hurricane hair and blinked in bewilderment. The ticket man sternly appraised the spindle legged apparition standing before him.

'Green Lane!' he barked and turned to deal with Gnat.

'Yeah, but where's *that*?' the student persisted.

The train doors hissed open and Gnat hurled himself out and raced up the platform, waving at absolutely no-one and shouting, 'Mum, *mum!*' his voice cracked by a relieved giggle.

It didn't take him long to realise that this station was harder to slip through. Gnat turned back from the vigilant staff at the gates and returned to the platform to look for other ways out.

Escape presented itself in the shape of another train. Gnat jumped onboard and rode it until another ticket inspector got on. This time he got as far as a place called Moorfields. There was no way out of this station without a ticket, so he hung about the platform for a bit and considered his options. A man came and sat down next to him.

'So why aren't you in school?'

Before Gnat could answer, a burly bald man ran down the platform and started punching the first one. Gnat took to his heels and ran for his life. He vaulted the ticket barrier and raced out of the station onto a busy city street. He had no idea what had just happened or where he was going, but he continued running. He crossed a very wide street and ran alongside some dock buildings until the stitch in his side forced him to stop. Breathless, he sat on a big black metal bollard on the dockside and steadied himself.

He was hungry. He'd managed to conserve one of Mrs. Elderry's scotch eggs and had only eaten a few of the digestive biscuits, but he had a raging thirst and the biscuits only made him thirstier. He wished he had a nice cup of tea to dunk them in.

A police siren knocked all thoughts of thirst out of his mind. Gnat dipped his head, suddenly finding something in his pocket very interesting. He'd made very slow progress through the night and early morning. He'd only really got going the moment he'd got onto the train and that had been undercover of morning rush hour. Gnat guessed it must be some time after ten o'clock. The police were bound to be looking for him by now. He just hoped the ticket man on the first train hadn't got a good look at him. Gnat pulled out his battery-less phone and pretended to be texting someone. He deliberately dawdled, looking as un-purposeful and as less like a furtive runaway as he possibly could. The police car dashed past and Gnat turned and headed in the opposite direction.

After walking for a few minutes, Gnat spotted across the road one of the biggest police stations he had ever seen. He sagged. This was the bit he hadn't thought through. How could he go in there and ask for his Dad if the police were looking for *him?* Gnat stayed on the opposite side and scurried straight past, the road curved to the left and started to climb and he followed it. He needed to think. He needed to ask someone to help him.

Gnat eventually crossed the road, sank onto a low wall and tried to think who he could ask for help. He cursed himself for being so stupid, he should have asked Mrs. Elderry when he was at hers. She seemed nice. Then he thought about how she would have been forced to hand him over to his Granny Di and he shuddered. Maybe he hadn't made such a bad set of decisions after all?

A policeman was walking towards him slowly and deliberately. Gnat sat quite still and waited for the inevitable. The long crocodile of a school party ambled past, the kids all chatting brightly. Some had important looking clipboards for a project. All of them were without a care in the world, each and every one of them belonging to someone and to somewhere. They had stuff to do and things to see and Gnat wished with all his heart that he was one of them.

The policeman's hand descended on his shoulder and Gnat faced him, waiting for his fate to be pronounced.

'Now then, soft lad, don't get yerself left behind.'

Gnat stared open mouthed as the young constable indicated the retreating party of school kids. Dumbly Gnat nodded and scurried to join the tail end of the party.

A thought struck him, maybe the teacher might help him find his Dad? No, that was no good, he would end up having to tell the whole story, then they'd take him back, then he'd end up with Granny Di.

The party boarded a waiting bus, Gnat made to walk past but the teacher pushed him back and told him to wait in line. Gnat was alarmed. He considered making a run for it. He had no idea where this bus was going.

'Sir, when's dinner?' a girl asked.

'Soon. *Lunch* will be the very next item on our itinerary, Miss Palmer, in the cafeteria.'

Gnat's stomach growled, dinner, lunch, whatever, sounded good. Maybe he should tag along after all? When his turn came he scrambled aboard the bus and opted for one of the unpopular seats at the front. *No one* wanted to sit there on the school bus. No one would bother him. Gnat kept his head down and fiddled with the half empty pillowcase, twisting it so it suddenly acquired a narrow neck, trying to make it look like a homemade gym bag.

After a very short journey the bus drew into a large courtyard. The helpers ushered everyone straight into the odd looking vaulted building that appeared to be part huge curved brick tunnel and part greenhouse. There they joined another two school parties and Gnat was thankful for the welcome extra cover. Anyone who bothered to notice him now would simply assume he belonged to another party.

Gnat was constantly surprised at how people were really bad at noticing things, but right now he found he was very grateful for their slack vigilance. A missing boy would surely draw someone's attention, but an *additional* boy somehow didn't seem to be quite so noticeable.

Lunch was a free-for-all buffet in this sun flooded atrium. A welcome glass of orange squash allowed Gnat to slake his raging thirst. He ate discreetly, hovering at the edge of knots of excited children. No one asked him who he was, or where he had come from. The teachers hadn't done a head count yet and Gnat was feeling confident he could slip away into the exhibition and back out the way they'd come in.

It wasn't that easy.

He had to sit where he was whilst the food was cleared away around him and a pair of screens flickered announcing the start of the lecture on The Mole of Edge Hill. Gnat fidgeted, he was full now and no longer thirsty and he wanted to find his Dad, not listen to some stuff about the tunnels under Liverpool.

Gnat pursed his lips and waited. He'd think of something. But before he knew it, the tour had started and he was following the class along a broad walkway. It narrowed abruptly, descending into the tunnels.

Gnat wondered if he'd have a better chance slipping away from the party down there. He deliberately slowed his pace, discreetly opening the gap between himself and the tail end of the group.

'Stop that!' Gnat's hand shot to the back of his head. Someone had given a spiteful tug to the back of his hair. He peered around the dimly lit walkway. There was no one there. One of the helpers approached.

'Hurry up, you're going to get lost!' She muttered fiercely. Drawing her unbuttoned cardigan protectively around her body she eyed the tunnel suspiciously, 'Creepy. God know what's down here!'

She herded Gnat ahead of her.

'Ow!'

As he rubbed the back of his head and looked round, the woman nearly tripped over him. 'Stop messing about you little creep!' she hissed and pushed past him.

Gnat looked up. Uneven buttresses of sandstone loomed high above the enormous chamber. Something flitted high ahead. Gnat tried to follow the movement but it was just too quick. Whatever it was, it was bigger than a bat but sounded like a bug.

Gnat hung back, hoping the party would move further away so he could really listen. A shiny perch of rock drew his attention. It had been powdered silver pink as if someone had brushed it again and again with his secret wing. He wanted to touch it, to see if it really was the same fine dust he'd rubbed on his fingers, but it was the other side of the cavern opposite the walkway and there was no way of climbing across to it.

Ahead of him the noisy school parties turned a bend and their chatter was abruptly cut off. Gnat was alone in the Williamson tunnels.

He started walking back the way they'd come in. It wasn't far. A faint scattering of sandy particles made him look up. Gnat gasped. The whole roof of the cavern was alight with eyes. Hundreds and hundreds of them looked down upon him. A whispering grew like the first whisper of the wind through dry grasses at the onset of a storm. Words formed. As if on the edge of a dream, the more he chased them with concentrated attention, the further the ghostly words retreated.

Gnat hunkered down fascinated, to listen to the vast whispering chorus from the gallery above. They sang him the most perfect lullaby he had ever heard, words of such heart stopping sweetness his whole body was swept by a deep surge of emotion. After all his years of wandering, tired, heartsick, lost and alone, Gnat had finally come back to himself. There was no other place he could be. As they sang, Gnat slowly understood that the unfamiliar sense of growing contentment and ease was what other people called *'coming home.'*

They called down to him, creeping to collect him, urging him to join with them, to rest and rejoice in the beauty of pure being.

Gnat recalled a dream where he flew on rainbow wings high above the woodlands near his last real home. Echoes of recognition thrilled through his veins and warmed his aching heart. Their familiarity made sense of every strange path that had led him this far in his short life.

'Oi!' Gnat turned his tear stained face to the man, but he hadn't even been aware he had been crying.

'What are you doing? You hurt?'

The helper was from one of the school parties and he was concerned. 'Gotta go in the accident book if you've been hurt. There'll be forms to fill in and claims and stuff.'

Dumbly, Gnat got to his feet. The gently rounded man was short of stature and breath. Abruptly his feet began tapping. Gnat stood back and watched as the man pirouetted nattily, completely unable to control his own body. Only his face seemed to retain a degree of control.

As he danced, his round dark eyes bulged with the outraged expression of an angry pug dog.

'Stop!' the man shouted, then pleaded, 'No!'

He was dancing perilously close to the edge. With one leap he vaulted on top of the safety rail and tapped up and down it, a drop of sixty feet behind him. His face was terrified but he didn't seem to be able to stop. He was already leaning back at an extreme angle. He began to flail, then wildly windmilling his arms, he toppled backwards into the void.

There was an abrupt, terminal thud followed by a dreadful silence. Horrified Gnat fled. Clutching his pillowcase, he pelted along the walkway, his hammering footfall on the metal mesh masking the awful thud replaying on a loop in his mind's ear.

Gnat crashed through the doors back into the canteen. He careered between tables, knocking over chairs in his flight, barrelled out through the atrium doors and tore out of the courtyard onto Smithdown Lane.

The bright sunshine mocked him as Gnat pelted along the road, crying. Panic stricken, he ran straight into a pair of patrolling special constables.

32

The Right Honourable Nemone Althea Clarissa Featherstonehaugh-Lyle cut a curious sight as she strode purposefully across the neat turf of the parkland.

Habitually dressed down to minimise her class and age, she was tanned deep mahogany and wore a khaki vest and camouflage pants. With her woolly, grey ponytail escaping messily from under a Fidel Castro hat and looking more like a guerrilla than a theatre director, she carried a heavy stage weight in each gnarled, muscular hand.

The evening sky was a fathomless deep blue, still as a mill pond and the weather was set fair. On such an enchanted night, Charlecote Park in Warwickshire with its Shakespearian connections seemed the perfect setting for one of his plays.

Nemone was making her way towards a towering timber framed canvas. One of a pair, looming above the acting area, they stood just as they would have done on an indoors stage. She was regretting going with the idea of classic *indoor* staging outdoors. The huge canvas 'wings' were meant to disguise messy entrances and exits to and from the acting arena.

Now, rather too late, she realised it would have been better if she'd employed her original idea of woven rainbow balloon arches. It would certainly have been less dangerous.

Nemone had dismissed the balloon option, unable to live with the lost element of surprise as the actors entered. That she expected there to be an element of surprise for such a well known play was testament to her stubborn inability to be gainsaid.

Then horror of horrors! Two hours previously on this apparently calm afternoon, one of the huge canvas frames had somehow caught a sudden breeze and crashed down onto the head of the lead actress. Felicity was now in A&E being seen for a concussion.

Swearing gently in her cut glass accent, Nemone dumped the heavy stage weights so as to add ballast to the stage flat's base. She would have to get someone to tie the wretched thing off to that sturdy oak.

Straightening, she tugged at her waistband, hoisting up the seat of her combats, hiding her only slightly regretted slag-tag and turned to address her assembled crew.

'Okay, chaps and chapesses, as preev stated, we can't help what's happened. Flea would want the show to go on, so go on it *must!* How's it going, Willow?'

Willow suited her name. Felicity's understudy for Titania was whip thin, pale and drooping in both physical stance and mental disposition.

At mention of her name, Willow raised her huge suffering eyes and nodded in her irritating, simpering manner. A martyr to her various ailments, certain more robust members of the crew had started referring to her as 'Marge' or '*I can't believe she's not better.*'

Nemone resisted slapping Willow and barked, 'How are the fairies?'

Dorcas, the portly lighting lady had appointed herself the official child-wrangler.

'Tucking into pop and crisps!' She smiled toothily, 'Honestly, it's fine, they didn't see a thing.'

Nemone's tanned face darkened, 'They're eating? *Again?*

Offended, Dorcas retorted, 'They're kids!'

'Aren't they fat enough? Those guzzling little gluttons are supposed to be *fairies!* If any of them are sick on stage, I'm holding *you* responsible!'

With less than an hour to go before the audience were to assemble, Nemone's best laid plans were in chaos. She'd lost it, shouted at a few innocent, 'we're doing our best,' victims and a couple of slacking 'that's not in my job description,' culprits and somehow, like it had always done in countless, previous productions, the show had slowly garnered its own special energy and coalesced into the start of a coherent event.

By the time the last audience members had seated themselves on the grassy hill overlooking the stage area, Nemone was daring to hope she might be steering a directable machine again. The little band of fluting recorder players piped an enthusiastic medley of cod period tunes and the play began.

In the second act, Titania called her fairies to her. The little girls and boys dressed in diaphanous silks with sparkling net wings had caught the hearts of the audience.

It was at this moment four year-old Sophie chose to act up.

'What *is* she doing? That's *not* in the choreography!' Nemone hissed from behind the oak tree, 'Scene stealing little witch!'

Dressed in a lilac tutu with sugar pink wings, Sophie was executing a complicated little dance, twirling like a tiny fragile butterfly and pointing dainty, lilac satin toes at an enraptured crowd.

Nemone gestured fiercely at Titania. Unseeing, Willow looked straight through her, smiled wanly and turned to watch Sophie's solo dance.

After five minutes of very carefully executed, very delicate dancing, the little girl fluttered back to Willow's side. The audience erupted into rapturous applause and the scene continued.

Titania was in her bower gathering and then sending her fairies scrambling, to collect treats for her donkey-headed lover.

As she breathlessly ran from the stage, Nemone caught Sophie by one tiny arm, 'What was all that about?' she hissed.

Alarmed, Sophie stared back blankly, tears starting in her eyes.

'That was wonderful, Sophie!' Dorcas whispered softly as she gently took Sophie's other arm and shielded the little girl with her bulky body, 'the crowd *loved* it!'

Dorcas exhaled deeply and planted her feet square and bull-like and glared at Nemone, willing her to rise to the challenge. She was not by nature any kind of a confrontational character, but Dorcas simply could not allow any of her little chicks to suffer the full force of Nemone's severe directorial style. Her fingers tingled, itching to slap Nemone's face.

Nemone snorted and turned on her heel.

'Dorky,' Sophie tugged at Dorcas's hand, 'did you see us?'

'Ssh! The big boys and girls are acting now, we have to be quiet,' Dorcas replied, 'yes darling, it was a lovely performance.'

'Weren't the fairies *pretty*, Dorky? *They* taught me that dance!'

Dorcas hugged the little girl. It was so sweet that she thought her co-stars were real fairies.

Dougal the Scottie dog snuffled in his master's pocket for another biscuit. The damp grass had set off his rheumatism and his poor old hip ached. 'A Midsummer Night's Dream,' was just as incomprehensible to him as most human activities. Why they were all sitting here whilst there were ducks to chase was quite beyond him. Massed ranks of mallards had all hauled out of the nearby lake for the evening and were resting, heads beneath wings, a heavenly horde of possibilities, just sitting there for the taking.

Dougal heaved a sigh at the wicked waste of such an appealing opportunity. He laid his big head on his short paws and gazed soulfully at a human girl on the stage. She was surrounded by those nasty spiteful things that flicked his ears when he probed the long grass with his nose. Dougal watched the clear flickering flames dance around the girl and softly growled in the back of his throat.

'Shh! Dougal!' His master flicked his nose, Dougal covered it with a reproachful paw and sniffed. It worked! As if by magic, a crunchy biscuit was drawn from his master's pocket and Dougal happily seized his prize and settled down again.

In his restless fidgeting, Dougal had rucked up the picnic blanket so that one corner lay folded back, exposing the plastic waterproof lining. Just as he snuffled up the last vestiges of biscuit, something small and gritty pattered loudly on the hard plastic fabric next to him. Dougal jumped and nuzzled at what had fallen. It was a small piece of pointed flint. Puzzled he watched whilst his Master reached for his umbrella and put it up.

Finding his view of the stage all but obscured, a man behind them tutted loudly. Dougal snuggled, smug and dry, shielded from the sudden smattering of what sounded like hailstones. The same man's abrupt shout startled Dougal and through all his four feet, he felt the impact as the noisy human suddenly keeled over.

Blind to the sudden disturbance in the audience, Willow sat forlornly watching the dancing figures. She had lingered here for *so long...* She just wanted to go home. To be with her people away from this world with all its brightness, its sudden loud noises and shocks and all the multitude of modern things that tortured her nerves.

She knew she could never go back. Her human counterpart had died years ago, back in Willow's home barrow. Although she too was dying, it was taking longer and Willow was condemned to live here for however long it took, on what felt like the wrong side of the mirror.

Missing her cue, she lay down and surrendered to her misery. Nemone was aghast. What on earth was happening? Willow's actions were a mystery to her. One leading lady falling ill was bad enough, but the understudy collapsing too was an unmitigated disaster.

Nemone would have to go onstage and appeal to the audience to come back another night. Worry harried her from every quarter, there were no curtains to close, so they'd have to heave that stupid, flaky girl offstage in full view of everyone. Then there would be the refunds. Nemone's hand shot to her brow. Finally, she had to admit she was defeated.

Somewhere in the audience a woman screamed. A ripple of disturbed excitement seemed to be travelling wavelike through the crowd. Unbidden, Dorcas swung a powerful spotlight onto the spectators. Nemone glanced across to the seated watchers. People were jumping up as if stung and just as quickly collapsing. Others were scattering, abandoning the coats cushions and picnic rugs they had been sitting upon and fleeing the scene.

What was happening? It looked like they were being attacked by a swarm of insects.

'Come back,' Willow called to Sophie. The little girl giggled, shook off her new friend's hand and darted back. Her new fairy friend tried to grab at Sophie, but despite her apparent fragility Willow was just too quick as she pulled the little girl away.

As Willow lay back, propped up on the silken cushions and hangings of Titania's bower, Sophie thought she looked very ill indeed. Concerned, the child bent over her and stroked her lovely hair.

Their eyes met and Willow smiled. Years later Sophie would recall it was the saddest smile she had ever seen. Suddenly, Willow reached out and touched Sophie's little silver necklace, the one Santa had brought her. Then something very strange happened. Sophie saw, but her eyes could not make sense of it. Willow turned to water.

Then fell like rain.

Screaming, Sophie ran to Dorcas who swept her up and carried the hysterical little girl to the safety of the 'green room,' a tent. Dorcas settled her safely with Lal the stage hand and hurtled off to gather the rest of her brood. She gathered up seven of the eight children, but spotted Ben wandering off into the bushes.

'Ben!' Dorcas screamed, but little Ben didn't even look back. He moved trancelike but purposefully through the shrubbery heading deeper into a wooded area.

'Ben!' Dorcas shooed the other children into the safety of the tent and turned to pursue the small retreating figure.

Dorcas heaved her way through the undergrowth. Branches stung her face like whips and toothed cables of thick brambles tripped her and ripped across her shins, but she could see she was gaining on him and where he was heading. He was making his way to a huge oak tree with a gaping hole in its trunk that seemed to be luring him in, with its offer of a dark and secret hiding place. Despite her bulky body, Dorcas moved as fast as she could.

Gasping with the effort, she lumbered through the scrub and grabbed Ben mid-step, his foot hovering over the threshold of the tree.

Panting, she gripped his shoulder and spun the child around. Ben started in shock and terror. He burst into tears and Dorcas clutched him to her, ignoring the sudden sharp sting in her arm.

His brow was pale and he was sweating and shivering.

'How did I get here?' Ben asked in bewilderment. Dorcas shook her head and tried to reply, but she was extremely breathless and suddenly felt very unwell herself.

'I want to go home.' Ben said tearfully. All Dorcas could do was nod and squeeze his hand. Through sheer stubborn strength of will, somehow she got to her feet and staggered away from the oak, dragging the crying boy with her. She set her sights on a tree some fifteen yards away, concentrated and pushed herself hard, tottering towards it. Crashing against its damp trunk, she leaned her sweating face against the rough bark.

Ben stared up at her, his eyes filled with fear. Only six years old, he understood it was his turn to lead. Setting his face into his best Superhero look, the one with the grim chin, he announced bravely, 'Come on Dorky,' and led her to the next target.

They tacked through the wood, pinballing from tree to tree, using each one as a resting place before pushing off towards the next one. With each head-spinning step, Dorcas willed her failing heart to hold out until her charge was safe. She finally fell at the edge of the wood and Ben ran shrieking straight to the nearest grown up, a bewildered parking marshal.

The first car out was driven by Viv Fox. She had pre-empted the rush for exits, grabbing her children at the earliest signs of trouble. Out on the main road, she swung her car into a layby and ordered her kids to keep all the windows closed and sit tight. She'd already explained the event away to them as an unseasonal swarm of wasps and the casualties as victims of extreme reactions to stings.

She even introduced the term 'anaphylactic shock,' as that would be the likeliest cover-story to explain the night's casualties. An ambulance siren sounded nearby and various police vehicles were already driving along the lane to Charlecote.

Viv was one of D's watchers. More usually in charge of a humble iron post disguised to resemble an innocent mile marker, she regularly checked it was still doing its job.

A very junior member of D9, she had still received basic training. What had just happened was a definite anomaly. She rang in an urgent report to her line manager. Despite the fact that Viv was reporting on matters way above her rank and personal responsibility, he listened carefully. He then contacted his distant boss, a man he'd never met, but who went by the name of D.

33

As the first arrows were falling on Charlecote, D was still deep in conversation with his Japanese counterpart, Mr. Shiraishi. It had taken them a night of carefully chosen words and a bottle of sake before diplomacy had given way to open discussion. Now at 5.00 a.m. Shiraishi was finally speaking freely about his work.

Although the Japanese had always been careful where they built, employing Shinto priests to prepare the ground, sheer population pressure had demanded at least some structures should disturb hitherto unaffected metahominid homelands.

The recent collapse of a newly built block of flats had been attributed to an isolated but severe earth tremor and seismographs had certainly picked up a sudden churning of the earth directly beneath the building, but Shiraishi knew better.

He was spearheading a new initiative called *Operation White Stone*, wherein he and his department had been tasked to effect the complete eradication of all metahominids in Japan.

That metahominids had been known to cause sudden building collapse had been recognised ever since man had first tried to build tall structures. They had interfered in the early stages of construction of more than one medieval English cathedral and their acts had been encoded in British mythology when Merlin had been consulted to discover why a castle kept falling down.

Much of the devastation wrought upon Japanese structures was seismic, but a recognisable percentage wasn't. The latest Japanese counter weapon was now placed before D. It was a small cylinder, the size of a squat aerosol can. D eyed it with interest, but resisted the urge to pick it up and examine it.

Shiraishi clicked a button on a slender notebook and handed it over. D watched the screen flicker with the shaky images.

Some of the footage had been taken by a camera presumably mounted just above the cameraman's eye level.

The rest appeared to have come from another, unseen operative. The harvested images appeared to be from the twisted bowels of a wrecked building.

The cameras were meta sensitive, picking up fleeting figures of arboreals and greys as they darted through the tangled wires and broken blocks of concrete. Gaping voids in semi-destroyed masonry revealed them as they danced triumphantly between the jutting ribs of metal reinforcing rods.

Raising a cloud of dust as he went, an operative dressed in a full body suit of Kevlar carried a canister identical to the one Shiraishi had just revealed.

The man walked slowly, with great deliberation into the centre of a rubble clearing. D couldn't decide whether this slowness was through intense calmness or sheer terror, but he could hear the tiny impacts of flint against the armour. The man flinched when an arrowhead chipped his visor, but otherwise he appeared unmoved.

He armed the device by twisting the bottom section of the canister and then retreated back to where his colleague continued filming.

Very quietly, a gentle plume of grey rose volcano-like, filling the dusty air with fine, shifting veils of mist. The smoke continued to gently spark and crackle out, pluming upwards as the device vented the toxicant as if from a fumigation bomb. Light caught the dancing motes as the space gently filled with tiny particles of pure atomised silver. The effect was a slap in the face of reality.

Water exploded in small bursts everywhere.

Small plumes of spray fountained out from every nook and hidey hole as the deadly silver found its targets. Before long, the devastated cellar ran with streams of water. This was the very same, simple principle as D's spray, but on a far grander scale. How had they managed to suspend and propel particles as heavy as silver so far?

He turned a wondering face to his host.

Shiraishi shrugged proudly, 'Water, just like after our fire brigade have visited. Just what anyone would expect to see in the aftermath of such a disaster! But D, imagine it in one of your English barrows!'

D nodded sombrely, 'I can. And I can imagine the revenge. The metas would go on the rampage.' He stared at his odd eyed image in the now darkened screen. 'There will be a calling to account for this action of yours. Cold retribution. People will die.'

'But D, people have always died. Let these be the last deaths. Lose some to save many. The lost are just part of a bigger picture.'

'I can't make those sort of decisions.'

'Soon you will have to. These creatures want us all dead and the planet to themselves. They have only to push their Varroa programme further…' Shiraishi shrugged and fell silent.

D folded his arms and stared up at the impressively high ceiling. A decade or so after Myxomatosis had been introduced into the barrows, as if in answer, *Varroa Destructor* had first appeared on honey bees. Not properly identified until years later, the deadly parasitic mite had continued spreading through the bee colonies of the world.

Some years ago, at a covert meeting of representatives from the nine governments signatory to the secret *Reykjavik Accord*, Shiraishi had posited that the timing indicated that

Varroa was a counter weapon that had been deliberately deployed by the metahominids.

The creatures lived close to nature and, to a degree, appeared quite capable of manipulating other species to their own advantage. Many of the signatories listening that day considered Shiraishi's theory on Varroa to have some foundation.

Without any bees to pollinate them, crops would fail causing worldwide starvation. Then the vast edifice of human civilisation would be all but wiped from the face of the earth, in a little less than four years. Only the insects would remain.

Making up an astonishing twenty percent of the planet's biomass, following any catastrophe that might befall planet Earth, the last creatures standing, or crawling would be certain varieties of insect.

After the second world war, at Auschwitz where even the grass refused to grow, where no birds were seen to fly overhead for many years, only the cockroaches flourished.

Shiraishi had answered his critics, including D, agreeing it was a very high risk strategy for the metahominids.

Then he had pointed out that the metas were *just insectlike enough to probably survive.* They would be free to re-colonise a world cleansed of humankind.

'Varroa is not a programme,' D said quietly, 'Their petty factions and infighting leaves them with no clear leader or direction. They're simply not that organised.'

'They appear to be becoming so.'

D refused to countenance the idea. 'For now, we have a different approach in the UK. A balancing act.'

Shiraishi was already opening and inspecting a crate of canisters for D to take with him. 'You cannot appease these creatures. You must understand, D, before it is too late,' his voice was quiet, his manner that of a kindly teacher, not a dispenser of life and death, 'they must be destroyed.'

Then D's mobile rang. The unusual sound snapped the tension. Someone in the UK had some very urgent news.

Back in his apartment, D rubbed his aching neck and clicked on the enormous TV. He didn't watch much television, the flickering images affected his sensitive eyes and this screen was the dizzying size of something from a multiplex. However, he urgently needed confirmation.

The lingering chill left by Shiraishi's parting words had been bad enough, but the news he had received from England was worse. As his eyes settled and made sense of the giant images on the wall, he got a shock as cold as if someone had poured a bucket of ice water down his back.

Images from a muddy field somewhere in Warwickshire played behind the neatly sincere Japanese anchorwoman.

The wreckage of what must have promised to be a pleasant evening lay under the harsh glare of floodlights. Generators growled running the work lights and standing outside an area cordoned off with blue and white police tape, a terse young man spoke his piece to camera. The Japanese interpreter talked directly over him, forcing D to listen hard.

The camera threw up images of scattered coats, picnic rugs and lost shoes. People had scrambled, abandoning everything in an onslaught of... what was he saying? *Insects?* Then a shot of a line of ambulances. *Dead?* Did he say there were unknown numbers of dead people due to an *insect attack?*

D reached for the phone. He kept the conversation to the operative posing as his sister upbeat and his tone happy, despite the fact that her light hearted responses carried coded replies confirming his worst fears.

Information was coming in all the time from the site, none of it good. No, he reassured her, there was absolutely no reason to cut his visit short, he just missed home and he'd be back as soon as he could.

34

Within an hour, the four deaths at Charlecote had been widely reported clear across the globe in every kind of media. Measured analysis of 'what went wrong' and questions about it would no doubt be raised in Parliament within a few days, but for now the idly-interested amused their curiosity by watching blurry, pixelated phone clips on the net.

All of them showed the effects of the attack, people jumping up as if stung. Others just running away, brushing things from their clothes and hair.

Of the few shaken eyewitnesses already interviewed on camera, some had agreed that the cloud of stinging things had been vicious but must have been small. Some had stated that they did not see any insects, but others argued that they had plainly seen hornets, bees or wasps. One man blamed a plague of craneflies, he was *certain* he had seen large wings.

One thing seemed certain, more people had been injured by other people panicking and stampeding away from the site than had been hurt in the 'attack by a swarm of insects.'

Within forty minutes of the event first being reported, the internet buzzed with arguments raging amongst the conspiracy theorists.

More by luck than good management, the full heat of the debate centred on the exact species of insect that had attacked the crowd and D9 watchers were relieved to find

289

there was not even a whisper of suspicion that it might have been attributable to any other agency.

Anti-gm protesters blamed 'Frankenstein crops' for morphing benign bees into killers, whilst another faction blamed the apparent, abrupt onset of complete and absolute weediness in modern man. They cited the rise of deaths from anaphylactic shock due to peanuts or insect stings and threw in a host of random food intolerances that hadn't bothered previous less well-fed generations in the least. In a triumphal outburst of shattering condemnation, the Righteous Robust blamed the victims for their pathetic inability to last a single night out in the open air.

Through it all, nobody had a good word to say about wasps. By the second hour, a certain gallows humour had grown up around the event and someone started a site called *Putting the Sting into PoSting*' and invited the swapping of any previously filmed amateur footage of the frenzied movements of those made nervous by the appearance of a wasp. Limbs flailing, the victims would howl, flap their arms and jump about like demented Morris dancers.

With breathtaking speed, short films of the very best 'wasp dances,' attracted multiple hits on film sites and were being passed from phone to phone around the globe.

In D's absence, it wasn't as if what little was left of D9 had closed down, but the lack of his exacting presence and the inability to fund any emergency overtime combined to compromise one or two key areas.

The first was that many protection cases such as Rhys Greville's were catastrophically lacking in vitally important follow-up work, and the second was that the lockdown at Charlecote was neither as precise nor as completely checked as one personally supervised by D would have been.

The four victims and numerous witnesses were immediately subject to the full force of D9's dwindling resources. Even then it should have been enough, but somehow in the melee, a fifth victim lying some distance from the immediate centre of the incident had been overlooked and her body taken to a separate morgue.

35

'Wo-oh!' The boy on the bike was impressed, he hadn't expected this for just a regular drop. He stroked the tickets to his chest, and eyes shining, gave a heartfelt, 'Thanks mate!' and rode off.

D had got the earliest flight back, but it had still taken him a day to get home and containment of the Charlecote tragedy was no longer an issue. The story had already appeared in every newspaper and a public enquiry was to be opened. D wasn't unduly worried, it would be immediately adjourned for many months until all those present had been interviewed. There would be time for a carefully executed cover up.

D shelved the clutch of encoded notes he'd just been handed, made himself a strong pot of coffee and sat down to study the newspapers. The heavier titles carried interviews with naturalists. In one, a couple of amateur bee keepers in the locality of Charlecote had been questioned about swarming. The lighter publications concentrated on how a family entertainment had become a night of horror and featured interviews with witnesses and the victims' families.

D had already caught up with most of the stories on the net on his way home, but was relieved to see the man who had spotted all the 'cranefly' wings had not made any further comment.

Everything from killer bees to environmental poison to panic had been blamed for several incidents of fatal heart attacks all in the same place on the same evening. The gathering had not been large, and credibility simply would not stretch to comfortably encompass the premise that all these cases were purely co-incidental.

The conspiracy theorists continued to gnaw at the marrow of the story but so far no 'hard evidence' had emerged and D was relieved to see they were still just chewing on the wrong bones.

Purring loudly, Magnus jumped up onto the table and sat directly on the article D was reading. He considered batting the cat gently away, but gave in and stroked the plush black fur. Taking this precious moment for himself, he began to realise just how tired he was.

He had been battling on just too many fronts for too long with meagre resources and little hope of more to come. Abandoning the coffee as a bad idea and yawning hugely, he climbed the wide stair to his bedroom, it was only mid afternoon, but he was exhausted.

With every step, the recent events spun relentlessly around in his head. The attack at Charlecote and the massing in the underground didn't feel like the usual population pressure issues. D reluctantly recalled what Shiraishi had said. Maybe they had finally found some sort of organising principle, some sort of figurehead to rally behind. Whatever it turned out to be, D had neither the financial nor physical resources left to deal with it. Overwhelm enveloped him.

Still in his coat, he flung himself down onto his bed and surrendered to the reality wipe-out of sleep. At that exact moment, the phone that never rang, rang. D struggled up from the depths and flung an arm out to answer it.

The voice was severe and precise, the tones of an old Etonian. Cold as frozen acid, it excoriated him for being on a jolly in Japan when he should clearly have been at home in the UK preventing domestic mayhem. After the verbal drubbing, the man from the Home Office cordially invited him to visit their hallowed halls for a more formal carpeting. Replacing the receiver, D knew he wouldn't be able to sleep now.

D wrapped his coat around his large frame and sat on the edge of the bed. He didn't need this. Maybe he should let them get on with it without him? The thought was only fleeting. He had nowhere else to go and nothing else to do. He did this job because he was uniquely qualified to do it and he had accepting it knowing that, like the old spying cliché, this would be the one job he simply couldn't resign from.

Sighing, he clomped downstairs to decode the notes he'd been handed by the Street Biker Irregular.

One was from his airline-owning friend Richard, he had recognised the Charlecote incident as a metahominid attack. He was of the same mind as Shiraishi and considered dusting the barrows as the only option. To that end he had made a light aircraft armed with the appropriate equipment available. It was hangared, waiting, at Biggin Hill. All D had to do was collect it.

D pondered. It was still a sledgehammer to crack a nut. They hadn't quite come to that yet and he hoped they never would.

The second set of notes came from a vigilant operative. Posing as a junior reporter from the Leamington Spa Courier, he had interviewed the majority of the cast and crew from Nemone's production and had been alarmed to discover a metahominid had actually been within the cast.

The operative had made the discovery after taking especial interest in a small child who had talked about dancing with the fairies and how someone called Willow had turned to water. He had concluded that it was hard to believe that in such a large audience no one else had spotted this, but if they had done so, then they must have considered the vanishing of a slender woman lying down, half hidden by cushions and with Sophie blocking whatever was left to see, to be a very poor stage trick indeed. No one else had mentioned the incident and the young woman known as Willow remained untraceable. No one had, so far, reported her as missing. It appeared that everyone including the director, had assumed Willow was at home. The operative noted that this was unlikely to become an issue until the public enquiry. In the meantime, no one was at all concerned with the whereabouts of the depressingly tiresome girl. The operative concluded his report expressing horror at the apparently seamless integration of a metahominid into the cast.

D wasn't quite as surprised. Performing came naturally to them, fakery was their stock in trade. Many metahominids passed themselves off as human and they made excellent actors and sublime musicians.

He set the notes down. He'd decide what fate he'd invent for Willow's non-appearance before the public enquiry later.

The next set of notes from another operative made him sit up. Frowning he looked back through the reports. Then he went back through the list of names.

He had been sure there had been only four deaths, so who was this Dorcas woman? He had been confident that one of his tame Home Office pathologists had retrieved the four victims and prepared the reports. But here it was in black and white, Dorcas Beresford, a crew member had suffered a heart attack.

There had been *five* deaths that night, not four.

A further victim whose unaccounted-for body could well be carrying all kinds of definitive evidence. The full weight of his woes hit D and he momentarily slumped. How could this have happened? Rubbing his eyes, he pushed his chair back from the table. He had to trace that fifth body.

He opened his notebook and began searching for morgues within a twenty mile radius of Charlecote. He gathered a few numbers and wrote a hasty note. A whistle from the door summoned another BMXer.

'Got any more tickets?'

D nodded, reached behind the door and gave the boy an entry ticket.

'Wow!' The boy's eyes swept from the precious ticket to the note that urgently needed delivering, 'This for the white house?'

D shook his head, 'Blue door.'

'Cool,' the boy levelled his handlebars like gun sights and hurtled away.

Jockey would start a search within the hour.

D returned to his encoded messages, scanning for more anomalies. The remaining notes were simple updates on non critical issues. Violet had been keeping an eye on the underground gathering and whilst she found it all skin crawlingly creepy, she still could not detect any anti-human activity. D had been right, it seemed they were using empty tunnels as urban roosts.

He rubbed his eyes and stretched his aching neck. Maybe he could sleep after all? Hardly daring to hope, he turned to the final scrap of paper. A basic report from a hard-pressed operative. The cuts had meant that some of D's colleagues were now forced to survey larger areas than perhaps was safe. The operative hadn't had the resources to deal with sensitive matters he now reported.

The facts were stated simply.

Rhys Greville had been arrested for the murder of his wife and his son Nathan had run away from his foster home. Diamond was travelling north, presumably to collect the boy.

The cold shock of sudden fear chased through D's body making his spine tingle. If the other side found Gnat before he did, the boy would be lost forever. A simple human loss, but a huge metahominid gain. He might be exhausted, but this task could not be delegated, he had to get to Liverpool, get Rhys out of custody and find Gnat.

He looked out of the front door, a flurry of hopeful BMXers hung close by. Word had got round that D had free tickets for the exclusive ramp arena. Their wait was rewarded as D sent them scurrying in all directions to deliver his encoded orders to the few D9 cells left within the city.

36

It was already late, but Alice Irwin was in no hurry to get home. She had one last case to attend to, and had decided to work later than usual. Alice was of the opinion that the human heart was the cause of every misery. Hers had certainly caused her a lot of pain over the years. Mainly through its habit of fixating upon unsuitable men.

She and Charles had started the day with an explosive row and she had left him cradling a half-empty bottle of whiskey, crying on their sofa. Surely his liver couldn't take much more?

Like any good, but time-compromised pathologist, she started with the woman's heart. Cutting swiftly, she isolated it from its supports of veins and arteries, then lifted it carefully through the sawn-out cradle of ribs. She always weighed the heart before dissection. Alice gently placed it on the scales, and checked.

It seemed strangely light.

Intrigued, she began her dissection. Alice had commenced the post-mortem, reasonably confident it was another dreary MI. However, this was already proving to be a little more interesting, because as she cut through the tissue, she began to see the reason for the anomaly concerning the weight. Its owner, the subject, Miss Dorcas Beresford, 52, was displaying symptoms of the phenomena known as 'empty heart,' a sign of anaphylaxis.

Alice took bloods. The lab would test the samples for raised levels of tryptase. Intrigue over, she sighed, back to boring routine.

She idly scanned the body for signs of the sting, and spotted a curious entry wound, on the upper right arm. It was ringed with blue. Alice peered at the wound through a magnifying lens. It was an evil, little puncture mark, and Alice could see where the stinger had presumably gone right into the flesh. She wasn't an expert on insects, and couldn't say what had done it, but it was the probable culprit.

Then she stopped dead. How remiss. She wasn't thinking straight today, she had carelessly plopped the dissected heart back on the scales. Considering her own, bruised heart, she crossed the lab and carefully retrieved Dorcas's.

Something dropped with a faint, bloody splat back into the scales pan. Alice peered at it. What was that? Holding Dorcas's heart in one hand, she dabbed up the tiny object with a gloved forefinger and stared at the thing clinging to her fingertip. It looked like a pointed piece of dark glass, maybe flint. She needed a closer look.

Alice wiped the tiny object onto her note book and hurriedly replaced the heart back into the chest cavity. Then she took a pair of tweezers and picked up the object. She delicately rinsed Dorcas's blood away and then placed what was left onto a prepared slide. Magnified, it was a thing of evil beauty, looking for the world, like a finely knapped piece of flint. Alice interpreted the faint blue fire at its edge as a prismatic by-product of the magnification.

She stared, but didn't see. She was busy with her inner thoughts. Charles would have cracked open last nights' champagne by now. The bottle she'd been given as a 'thank you' for her exemplary work on the Draper case. She shouldn't have accepted it really, but she had not benefitted from the gift. It would all be gone by now.

Alice's vision returned from her troubled inner world to the outer one and she saw the stone again. Just another unnecessary complication, like Charles.

The subject could have unknowingly carried this tiny, flint splinter around with her for years. Alice was always digging old pieces of gravel out of even older men who'd been keen bikers in their youth. Literal hard evidence of hard falls. They wore their scars and tattoos on the outside, whilst under their skin they bore objects just like this one. Mementoes of long forgotten skids and crashes.

Alice had excised many similar, and bigger, pieces of stone and metal. Things that body tissue had grown around and hidden. She dropped the tiny fragment into a small, clear plastic canister and labelled it with the code for Dorcas's other samples. Alice didn't for a moment consider linking it to the stopping of the woman's heart. After all, she hadn't dissected it from inside there.

She recorded the object in her notes as, *'A stone chipping, probably historical, unlikely to have had any bearing on the cause of death.'*

Alice looked up as the door opened.

'You're working late. Those ready for downstairs?'

Her visitor inclined his head towards the samples for the lab.

'Yep, I'm all done here,' Alice handed her notes to the orderly. He was new and handsome, in a rough kind of a way. He smiled. Alice was startled. Not many people smiled in a morgue. He laid the folder of Alice's notes on top of the subject's legs, collected the few sample canisters, and lined them up on the trolley alongside the body.

'All accounted for?' he asked.

Alice liked this, he was good looking and competent. One to watch out for. She nodded. Jockey turned and began to wheel the body away.

'One moment!' she called after him. Jockey paused.

'What's your name?'

'John,' said Jockey over his shoulder, continuing to wheel Dorcas away. Alice could hear the smile in his voice. She smiled too as she carefully peeled off her gloves. She was still smiling in the changing room as she washed her hands and brushed out her hair.

She'd go to the pub on the way home. Simon would be there.

37

Normally, he would have handled this a lot better, but tonight Jockey had the shakes. He'd had a busy day and the siren-call of drink was luring him to scotch on the rocks. Still he resisted. One day at a time.

Never a great communicator, Jockey had willed himself to keep it light and businesslike. As he had walked into the room, his own dour mood was affecting him badly, making him expect a hard time. He was ready for some show of hysterics and been taken aback by the pervading air of calm.

Still his ragged nerves played with him and he'd had to force himself to bite down on his many questions. Wanting to know extra details would just plant the suggestion that there may have been something more to this death after all.

Against all his darkest expectations, the notes were anomaly-free and perfectly passable, and for once, Jockey was content to leave the victim's body at the morgue. He felt like he'd been granted some kind of free pass and was grateful for this welcome piece of simplicity in an otherwise tricky day of going solo up against the metas.

Jockey unsealed one single sample canister and replaced the flint arrowhead with a similar looking, innocent stone chip. That had been all he'd had to do this time. He rang in an all-clear to D's house. D didn't answer, so Jockey assumed he too must be out, working late. Jockey stripped off his coverall and left, grateful that his work was done.

The kid on the bike found Jockey just as he was about to enter his favourite late night café, The Blue Door.

'Hey Mate, you dropped this.' The boy held out a crumpled piece of paper. Heart sinking, Jockey took it and thanked the boy who sped off, leaving Jockey at the café door.

He ordered a strong mug of tea and sat down to open the scrawled note. Suddenly, he wasn't hungry any more. He took a gulp of the hot tea. D was off to Liverpool. Gnat Greville was missing and D was deeply concerned that his grandmother was after him, indeed might even have got him by now.

Jockey sighed, he knew Diamond was a crazy cow. She was a fully signed up member of the *'Strangers Are Only Friends You've Never Met'* brigade, and was the kind of person who'd happily release mink into the countryside. As long as the poor mink were free, she'd turn a blind eye to the slaughter they'd bring to the indigenous wildlife. She felt exactly the same way about metahominids.

All remaining operatives had been called to find her. Jockey stared at the encoded details, stopped and re-read the final line. He could barely believe what he was reading. The stupid woman was travelling in a *multi coloured campervan!* Jockey shook his head. How hard would that be to trace? From the nobbiest Special up, any fool, in or out of uniform, could find her in that vehicle. People would turn to gawp at something like that. She might have well have painted, 'LOOK AT ME!!!' all over it!

Heartened, Jockey pocketed the note and ordered an all day/all night, full English breakfast. The sausages here were just lovely, speckled with herbs and very tasty. Jockey grabbed a greasy newspaper from another table and sat down to read the football results. Not brilliant. He flicked back, through the rest of the paper.

A bright advertisement, taking up half a page,

caught his eye. A special train, running from Euston, had been laid on for enthusiasts of the VW. The city of Liverpool was hosting a rally of vintage hippy campervans, and a photograph showed hundreds and hundreds of multi-coloured vehicles, all lined up at a race course.

Jockey stared grimly at the relentlessly cheerful colours. The city would be awash with campervans, all looking like Diamonds.' Her van was now just a single, rainbow needle, in a multi-coloured haystack. Every plate would have to be checked.

His mind played the freakily realistic sound of the clink of ice in a glass and Jockey crunched down hard on his fried bread.

38

The train sped through the Staffordshire countryside, *en-route* from Euston. For the first part of the journey, Violet had nervously scanned every tunnel the train had swept through. All had been empty, leaving her to suspect that mainline tunnels were probably far too busy and noisy to double as metahominid roosts.

Eventually, as she travelled further away from London and from what she'd witnessed on the Underground, her uneasiness had slowly abated and she'd finally allowed herself to relax a little.

Violet stretched out comfortably. She would have to change to a smaller local train at Chester for Ruabon and then take a taxi to Llangollen, but for now, there was still plenty of time for her to enjoy the experience of travelling First Class. Sipping her latte, she smiled. She could get used to this. Despite the seriousness of her mission, the unfamiliar luxury had sent her giddy, even down to the way she had ordered her coffee James Bond stylie - two shots, whole four per cent milk, warm, not hot. She had no idea how D had wangled everything on expenses. Maybe he knew the guy who owned the train company? It wouldn't surprise her.

Idly skimming the pale foamy top with her spoon, she mused that if this was D's idea of cutbacks, she could probably live with them. Beside her, Baby slept in her own special, hidden compartment, tucked away under the false floor of a vintage vanity-case. Her silvered blades still appeared pristine and unblemished to the naked eye, but Violet knew her Baby's coat was riddled with microscopic holes and leaving Baby so shoddily clad for much longer was simply not an option.

Especially if there was a war coming.

She gazed out at the green tracery of hedgerows, speeding past in the late morning sunlight. The gathering sense of her shattered nerves calming was palpable. Inwardly she accepted she was only running away from the inevitable, but it was still good to be getting away from the brooding threat of the huge gathering of metas, sitting it out in the London Underground.

By synchronistic happenstance, that neither of them would ever be aware of, Violet's train crossed a bridge at the exact same moment Dylan Watkin was driving under it. A scant hour later, Violet changed trains at Chester. Juggling a bag, a suitcase and Baby's case, she settled herself on the local train for the penultimate leg of her journey. By the time she had reached Chirk, Dylan Watkin was pulling into a large car park in the middle of the tourist trap town of Llangollen.

He had made good time and this seemed a likely place to stop off for a trip to the lavatory and a top up of coffee. As the CD he'd played in his car had promised, it was indeed a bright, sunshiny day.

Following the signs to the river, he wandered down a darkly shaded, narrow lane, bordered by flower-laden stone walls and came out into full sunlight again, facing a large stone mill, now converted into a pub.

A couple of helmeted canoeists padded past in neoprene slippers. Making exaggerated steps, like cartoon cat thieves, they carried their lightweight craft on their shoulders. Watkin stood back to let them past and looked to his left. In a nearby courtyard, a couple of young backpackers were posing outside a caravan, gaudily painted to resemble a country cottage.

Watkin entered the cool interior of The Corn Mill, and ordered a pot of coffee. He took it out onto the decking and sat in the full sunshine, crunching an almond biscuit whilst watching the gleam and ripple of the River Dee rushing past.

Across the tumbling river, at the story-book station, one of the tiny trains on the heritage railway snorted like an impatient pony. Excited children lined up to take a trip on their blue faced hero, Thomas. Watkin grinned, this was beginning to feel like a real holiday. He closed his eyes and turned his face to the sun. The train hooted wistfully, and something buzzed past his nose. He opened his eyes to see a huge, blue dragonfly hovering above the table, as beautifully coloured as any kingfisher. Thrill and wonder hit his heart and brain simultaneously and he gasped like a delighted little kid. The dragonfly hovered for a second and then darted away, and he lost sight of it in a tangle of riverside willow. In the distance, a duck quacked ruefully, like a laughing automaton he'd once heard at a vintage fairground. He chuckled at the memory, making a long-overdue reconnection with happier times.

Feeling more positive than he had done in many months, Watkin drained the cafetiere into his cup and stretched idly. There was no rush, the sun was warm on his back and this was just the therapy he needed. He'd finish his coffee and wander up the street into town.

Watkin was staring at the workings of the mill machinery as Violet's taxi halted at the road works on the A5, a mile from the golf course. She was going to be later than she'd hoped, but she wasn't unduly worried. Andrea had closed their last call with her customary, 'We'll expect you when we see you.'

In Llangollen, Watkin took another narrow lane and emerged onto Castle Street. The looming hill of Castell Dinas Brân wasn't quite visible from where he stood, but he felt the pull of its presence. He'd spotted the castle ruins atop the fairytale hill on his way in on the A5. From across the valley, the breastlike swell of the steep, green hill had appeared, framed by an escarpment of layered rock that resembled a cutaway-diagram from a geology book.

Watkin couldn't believe he'd never come across such a beautiful landscape in Britain before. The valley and its romantic hills were the perfect backdrop to legends of swords and sorcery.

Turning away from the river and its pretty stone bridge, he made his way up the main street and through the town. He played tourist. Bimbling along, looking aimlessly in shop windows at nothing in particular, thoroughly enjoying the contented feeling of not really needing anything much.

Drawn inexorably, to the dizzying tarmac switchback of the Horseshoe Pass, a phalanx of Harleys drove down the street, their beefy exhausts popping flatulently. Watkin turned to watch the gleaming machines glide by and caught himself grinning like a little kid watching a big parade.

He'd been crazily, pointlessly motivated. Busy all his life, he'd bought into all the self-improvement books, got 'massive leverage,' on himself, always worked harder than his colleagues and striven to be better than he secretly judged himself to be - and where had it all got him?

Not very far. Now this was his time. A time to kick back and just 'be.' He crossed the street, for no particular reason, took a left at the traffic lights and ambled across the road.

Dylan Watkin wasn't a man who believed much in coincidence. He'd read about synchronicity and had gone so far as to keep a *'coincidence diary'* in his youth - at the bidding of one of his more esoterically-minded girlfriends, but Watkin had come to the gradual conclusion that coincidence was just a normal part of life. Only noticeable by comparison because it never happened on the stage, or the screen, or in books. Seemingly, in fiction, it was always considered 'the easy way out' and was creatively banned.

The same girlfriend had once told him, if something in his life happened that he wouldn't have believed had it occurred in a novel, then it must be 'metaphysics at play,' and he should sit up and take notice. He never had. But now abruptly, he did. He stared across the road, and chuckled in amused wonderment. He was a *Watkin* in search of the Reverend Dr. *Williams's* 'Beings at Bodfari' and the sign above the door read *Watkin and Williams!*

Surely a sign he was on the right track…?

Thoroughly pleased with the gentle way this lovely afternoon was panning out, Watkin folded his arms, and stepped back, allowing a deep shadow to cut the sunny glare and let him see the sign better. He hugged himself and rocked gleefully on his toes. Richmond, with all its frustrating, mind-bending troubles was suddenly a million miles away.

Then he saw her.

No. That would be too bizarre. It *couldn't* be her!

But it *looked* very like her.

Just across the street, right under the Watkin and Williams sign, the young woman who had called herself 'Sarah Deakin,' hurriedly jumped out of a taxi. The driver retrieved a small, wheeled suitcase from the boot. She juggled a small vanity-case to her other hand and took charge of the suitcase.

In the bright sunlight, Watkin was at least ninety-eight percent sure it was her. Keeping stock still, so as not to draw attention to himself, Watkin watched Violet shoulder her bag and extend the retractable handle on the suitcase. Whatever was in the vanity-case must have been important, because she held it clamped tightly beneath one arm. Watkin waited for her to pay the driver and start walking down a side street, before daring to cross the road and follow.

Heart pounding and mouth dry, all thoughts of Bodfari forgotten, Watkin trailed her as she took a left into a less touristy thoroughfare, Oak Street. Not once did she look back, but Watkin was on his toes, ready to dive into any one of the open shop doorways as he passed them. By now, she was almost back onto the main street through town. Maybe she was heading for the hotel on the river? Suddenly her head turned and Watkin dived into a florists shop.

The display of flowers effectively cut off all hopes of him spying on her through the window and so, after a couple of moments, Watkin was reluctantly forced to go back out onto the street. But by then, Sarah Deakin had disappeared.

Trailing a party of energetic hikers, Watkin headed for the main street. Ready to duck back behind a rack of newspapers, outside the corner shop, he scanned the street in both directions. She had vanished.

Watkin retraced his steps back into Oak Street, there was no sign… then, yes! There she was, inside *'The Oak Chest,'* a jewellery shop. Watkins eyes flicked left as he walked past. Now he was a hundred percent sure it was her. Sarah was talking to a blonde man, whilst an attractive, dark-haired girl tipped over the *'Open'* sign to *'Closed'* on the shop door. Watkin almost caught the girl's gaze, but averted his eyes to the pavement just in time. Then he caught the sound of someone rapping on the glass behind him and his heart almost stopped. Had they seen him after all?

'Sorry no, we've had to close for the day.'

Marching smartly away, Watkin just caught the fragment of conversation on the breeze. He didn't hear the girl's excuse to the frustrated, would-be customer. He raced round the block, and collected his car. Returning to Oak Street, he parked a few shops down from the jewellers, spread a road atlas across his knees and pretended to study it, all the time watching for Sarah to emerge.

Keeping his eyes firmly on the shop door, he called his sister. She didn't pick up and he was grateful to avoid any prolonged excuse-making. He left a brief message.

'Sorry, I can't make it tonight. There've been some developments on a really important case.'

He wasn't exactly lying.

39

No-one worked on D time, it seemed. It would be of no use whatsoever if he arrived anywhere in the very early hours. D was forced to wait before he could go after Gnat and Rhys and so chose to get some much-needed rest. Not that he slept, he just passed time, waiting for the world to catch up with him and emerge into useful wakefulness.

Finally, the sun had come up and he had been able to begin his journey northwards. He all but sleepwalked to the car, but by the time the old Saab poked its long nose out of the underground car park, D had regained some of his spark.

'The game's afoot, follow your spirit,' he murmured, as he threaded his way through a very early London morning.

After a long and pleasantly uneventful journey, an incoming text-alert sounded on his phone. The rare noise startled D. He had warned his colleagues never to use texts. He reluctantly pulled over. The information was stark.

Rhys Greville had been located, Gnat Greville had not, and Diamond had vanished.

Half an hour later, D hurled the coins into the basket and watched the barrier slowly rise. Driving through the Birkenhead tunnel, he found it hard to keep his speed down. He took the Albert Dock spur and arrived at the Police Headquarters on Wapping, the street opposite the dock. After a flurry of telephone calls, Rhys was no longer in custody. He sat in a side office, waiting for D and rose with a grateful smile as D entered the room.

D shook his proffered hand, 'I'm so relieved,' Rhys began, but D waved away his enthusiastic greeting with a heated, 'You should *never* have been put in this position! It's my fault.'

'D, you've consistently done your best for us.'

'Not this time.' A further incoming text-alert sounded on his phone. Warily he read the message.

GG SAFE. UPPER STANHOPE ST. NICK.

'Gnat's safe,' D stated simply. Rhys registered his relief with a huge sigh.

Still on his guard, D was anxious to get Gnat and

Rhys to a place of safety, only then could he rest. His aching neck reminded him he was still missing a nights' sleep. Under the dubious gaze of the desk sergeant, D signed off the paperwork and took Rhys away. Looking down morosely from his office window, a senior policeman eyed Rhys with the hard-done-to, rheumy eyed gaze of a bloodhound robbed of a juicy morsel. He watched them cross the concourse and stalked back to his desk muttering, 'Witness Protection, my backside!'

D and Rhys arrived at the police station in Upper Stanhope Street, within fifteen minutes. The Desk Sergeant was helpful and efficient. Nathan Greville had been held there briefly, having absconded from his foster home. The Sergeant was happy to confirm that Nathan was now in the safe custody of his paternal grandmother, Ms. Di Timms.

D took a deep breath and softly explained his fatal error to the Desk Sergeant. As the policeman grew more ashen, D used terms like *'unfit guardian,'* and, *'family feud,'* and threw in *'Place of Safety,'* and *'Witness Protection.'*

He didn't tell the man, that under his own mother's malign guidance, Rhys had unwittingly chosen a fairy as a mate and had fathered twins, Gnat and Cayden, by this fairy mother. How that same fairy wife had vanished, returning to her kin within a year of the babies' births. How she had taken Cayden with her into the barrows to be raised as a meta, whilst he had helped Rhys keep the other child Gnat, safely hidden all these years from her *and* the boys' misguided human grandmother. A foolish woman bent on reuniting Gnat with his brother, with his clan and ultimately, with the destiny D was trying to keep him from.

D asked what vehicle Diamond had left in. Eager to make up for his mistake, the sergeant was quick to find the relevant piece of film from the car park surveillance camera. In grainy black and white, it showed a sullen Gnat, being led by the hand to waiting campervan. Whilst the Officer concentrated on deciphering the number plate, D stared hard at the space beside Diamond. She was consistently moving so as to allow space for something, or someone, beside her.

Once the number had been deciphered and a trace set up, D played and rewound the same piece of tape, slowly building in his mind's eye a picture of Diamond's companion. Tall for a meta and powerfully built, D eventually recognised him as belonging to the same clan as Rhys's long-lost wife, Maeve.

The Sergeant confided to Rhys, that Di's vehicle

was high priority and could well be traced within the hour. D wasn't so sure. Rhys paced the floor, in a state of high anxiety. Eventually the call came. Diamond had been stopped at the exit from the Wallasey tunnel. Gnat had been taken to a police station in Birkenhead.

'Keep him there!' D stormed, and turned to see Rhys hugging the visibly moved Desk Sergeant.

D grabbed the moment and used the Sergeant's telephone to ring a Llangollen telephone number.

Aled answered, 'Vi's here,' he confirmed and handed the phone over to her, 'Wait until I get there tomorrow morning,' D ordered.

'Problems?' Violet queried cautiously.

D simply countered with, 'Can you hand me back to Aled?' The moment he heard Aled's, 'Hello,' D continued. 'We've got something of a problem job on at the moment. How's my credit looking?'

'Not good!' Aled laughed, 'But I'll help all I can.'

'See you tomorrow.'

With a huge sense of relief, D took Rhys to collect his own car and they drove in convoy to Birkenhead. D had already activated a dormant Safe-House in Chester for now, but he knew he'd need something more permanent within the week. Gnat had to have a proper place of safety where he could grow up - safely unhindered by his unhinged grandmother and her misguided plans for metahominid integration.

D had watched over this little family for some time and seen how the metas had kept close surveillance on Gnat as he had grown. He obviously meant a lot to them and that alone was the best reason for D9's interest.

Lack of funding meant D would probably have to pay for their next place out of his own pocket, but if it thwarted any meta schemes, he knew it had to be a good investment.

Although he'd know Rhys for years and they had met on many occasions, D had always been careful to avoid meeting Gnat, face to face. He didn't want to become an object of curiosity to Gnat. He shook hands with Rhys outside the police station and wished him well.

Inside the police station, Gnat sat eating a great slab of chocolate cake. He licked the cool, chocolate buttercream from his fingers, before biting off more of the darkly-moist sponge. It was heavily laden with chocolate sprinkles and by now Gnat was sporting his own quota of decorative chocolate sprinkles and smudges too.

There were formalities before he could be reunited with his father. Gnat had been settled in an interview room, as there wasn't anywhere else safe to put him. Paperwork completed, the father stood for a moment, watching his son on the monitor, tears of relief streaming down his face. The attendant policewoman had enough sense to leave him be.

Tucking into his cake, and so obviously enjoying himself, Gnat was a picture of normality, an ordinary kid caught up in an extraordinary situation. Rhys had always kept Gnat's genetics quiet, the boy had never seen a non-D9 doctor. To his great relief, the one time he'd seen the school nurse after a fall, nothing came of it. He gazed at his son, innocently absorbed in eating a cake, his skinny legs swinging contentedly.

What should Rhys tell him? It would have to be everything, or nothing. What if it wrecked Gnat's peace of mind? What if he chose to go off with his mother's kin? Rhys knew he would never see him again.

Rhys had lived years skulking in the shadows, hiding, running, telling half truths. He didn't want this for Gnat. Not yet. Time would come when he'd have to tell him, but not now. Not today. There would be time. There would always be time.

Rhys signalled he was ready. As he entered the room, Gnat cast aside the remains of his cake and flew into his fathers arms. They hugged fiercely and both cried.

They clung to one another for long moments, Gnat finding it impossible to speak. Eventually Rhys found the words, 'I'll never leave you. I promise, I won't let them split us up again.'

When they were finally able to unclasp and leave the room, a pretty young WPC thrust a note into Rhys's hand. 'It's from your friend,' she whispered, 'there's been a change of plan.'

D had waited an anxious twenty minutes for a beaming Rhys to come out, with a very happy-looking Gnat, before starting the engine and following them onto the M53. Keeping a discreet distance, he relaxed when they peeled off the motorway and swept down the sliproad.

Within a very few miles of leaving the Wirral, exhaustion swept over him like a grey, blanketing wave, and D considered stopping. Yet Llangollen was less than half an hour away so he pressed on, reaching the comfortable out-of-town hotel by mid-afternoon.

A cooling shower and a comfortable bed were all he could fix upon right now. Drawing the curtains against the strong light, he lay down to sleep.

Everything else would have to wait.

40

It had been at least two hours before Violet had left the jewellery shop. Watkin noticed that she no longer had the vanity-case with her. From the way she'd clasped it so fiercely, Watkin surmised that some kind of important delivery had been made.

She'd gone to a parallel street and entered a pub called 'The Wynnstay Arms,' re-emerging less than half an hour later, changed and without her suitcase. So now Watkin knew where she was staying.

Having thoroughly learnt his lesson from the last time he'd attempted to tail her, Watkin kept a long way back as she crossed the bridge and headed out of the main body of the town.

Without D to give the alarm, Violet was unaware of her discreet shadow. She was looking for trouble of a different kind.

Climbing the steep road up to the local school, Violet kept her eyes open for the sign for the public footpath that led across the fields and up to Castell Dinas Brân. She found it easily and began the laborious climb up the steep field that skirted the school buildings. She carried a small day-pack on her back, containing her carbon fibre prosthetic 'fighting foot.' Without Baby, she couldn't afford to stir up anything vaguely confrontational, but she carried the spare foot because it made climbing easier, plus a silver spray *'just in case.'*

Clear of the buildings and with no one about, Violet sat on the short rabbit-cropped turf and took a drink from a small bottle of water. Buzzards yelped overhead in the cloudless blue as she unlaced her walking boot and swapped her plain foot for the stark, black fighting spur.

Loitering back down by the school buildings, Watkin was so far away he couldn't see what she was doing. He didn't see her take out the 'vintage sunglasses' and hang them on a string about her neck. But when she stood again and continued the ascent up the smooth, green slope, he could immediately see she was moving a lot more easily.

Eschewing the zig zagging path, Violet took the direct, if far steeper, route to the summit. Within just a few feet of the well worn track, she spotted a few of the metas favourite plants, *fey herbs*, artfully arranged so as not to suggest deliberate cultivation, and suddenly she couldn't help feeling edgy again. Alone and unarmed, she was deep within enemy territory without the reassuring weight of Baby hanging from her belt.

After a nervous ascent into the unknown, Violet finally reached the summit. Standing by a grey, ruined wall punctured with strange, craggy arches, she stood in the sparkling sunshine, feeling very dark and sombre indeed. From the *accidental* arrangement of mounds, the gallitraps, the traces of wing-dust left upon their favourite perches, to the strange quality of stillness in the air, it appeared her hunch had been spot on, there was evidence aplenty of a thriving meta-population in residence here. Despite the warm weather and the likelihood that the metas would be sleeping soundly beneath the hill, Violet suddenly felt very cold and unsettled. This was their place, not hers. Unwilling to linger on hostile ground, she began her descent immediately.

There were few places to hide on the towering conical hill and looking up, Watkin was alarmed to see Violet start back down. He took to his heels and tore a few yards along the weaving path, then vaulted the low handrail, and raced into the shadowy dark-side of the hill, putting as much of its bulk as he could between them.

By the time he was forced to stop and catch his breath, Violet was completely lost to his view. It hadn't been his best move. Realisation dawned and he cursed his foolishness, he had given himself the distinct disadvantage of being unable to see her exact whereabouts and she could happen upon him at any moment. Skulking in the shadows, Watkin chided himself, he was getting dangerously close to blowing the whole enterprise again. If he was to keep hidden, yet remain able to observe, then the only way was up. If he could race up the unseen side, to the very top of the hill, it would give him back the advantage again - he would be able to keep an eye upon Violet in relative safety.

He'd always been fit, easily outclassing all the other police recruits on his intake, especially on the gut-busting shuttle-runs, but even for Watkin, running the best part of two-thirds of the way up to Castell Dinas Brân presented a serious challenge.

Fully fired with the enthusiasm of finally getting somewhere with this enigmatic puzzle, Watkin took a huge gulp of air and sprang up the steep slope. Narrowly missing ankle-breaking rabbit burrows, pushing his lithe frame as far and as fast as he could, fighting gravity with every step, he hurtled upwards. Muscles screaming, lungs bursting, he ran like a man possessed. At the back of his mind, he knew he'd regret it in the morning, when his legs would complain after suffering this workout from hell, but for now, if he could just find out what was going on, it would be worth every drop of pain.

He was close to the top, but his lungs were nearing collapse. Panting heavily, Watkin was forced to move more slowly.

What was up here? What had she been doing? What was in the small case she'd handed to the jeweller?

As he staggered the last few feet, he wondered if he was about to be confronted by a shiny silver UFO. He couldn't help comparing the steep, punishing hill to the Devil's Tower in *Close Encounters of The Third Kind*. A green rise promised the end of the torture, but it was a false promise as another ridge rose above it, then a third. His breath was coming in short, ragged bursts now.

At the very edge of his frayed stamina, the ground finally stopped rising beneath his feet. Sweating, Watkin stumbled through the ruins. He sagged against a rugged, grey wall and rubbed a forearm across his gleaming face. Senses taut, he glanced about him. His keen anticipation was met with…. nothing.

There was nothing here but jumbled walls and rock. Too breathless to laugh, he gasped. Another wild goose chase!

That little minx!

Watkin flung himself down on the short turf and gazed down to see how far away Violet had got. She was moving steadily down the slope. She didn't even have the grace to look back. Watkin shook his head. She didn't have to look - somehow she *knew* he was there. Watkin lay back and gazed up into the blue depths soaring above him. He couldn't imagine how he'd given himself away this time. He'd kept hidden and been very careful to tail her at an enormous distance. Not once had her head turned in his direction, but somehow he'd blown it.

He rolled over onto his stomach and looked again at her retreating figure, grudgingly admiring whatever brilliantly-honed training had alerted her to his presence.

He'd get his breath back and start down again in a moment. Lying on the lumpy grass, his head propped on his arm, Watkin watched Violet move across the gentle green landscape. He'd catch her up. After all there was no need to worry about her seeing him now. Yeah, maybe they'd even have a nice chat? Yeah, like *that* was likely...

Watkin sighed, closed his eyes and lay back in the glorious sunshine.

Disappointed after all that wasted effort, he felt depressed and empty again. An insect buzzed close by and then a curious thing happened. Music began.

Beautiful music. Haunting and teasing him, it seemed to be playing both inside, and outside, his head. Wow, this was amazing! Watkin's foot began to tap to the driving addiction of the rhythm.

Violet eventually slowed down and stopped in the sunlight on the lower slopes of the hill. Just like leaving London, the moment she'd moved away from the malign summit, she had instantly begun to feel a lot better. It was as if they had known she was there. Just like when D had been in the barrow, unsettling the denizens with his presence.

Although the effect of her physical presence, up on Castell Dinas Brân, had been considerably lighter than that of D's in the barrow, it was as if some essence of D9 still hung about her. The enemy had caught it on the air and it had awoken them.

Violet opened the water bottle again and took a leisurely drink.

High above her on the hilltop, the already exhausted Watkin was fighting for control of his body. It leapt and spun and jigged *so* fast, and would *not* stop. It did things he swore he could not do, bending and flexing, leaping and landing, with a grace he knew he would never naturally possess. All around him, the maniacal music grew and grew, to an accompaniment of light, tinkling laughter. Whispers were softly dropped into his ears. He could eat, he could drink, he could rest here, he could stay here and take his ease. Instinctively, Watkin knew he must resist the voices and the music. To give in would be to die, but still he could neither catch his breath, nor stop his body's mad, capering, jerking dance. His heart was hurting and he felt he would faint on his feet, and yet he understood his senseless body would just keep jigging, whilst his heavy, unconscious head, would loll and threaten to break his neck. He gathered what little breath he had and wailed brokenly in a shudderingly, forlorn whooping cry.

'What the..?' Violet glanced up. Scrambling to her feet, she shielded her eyes against the bright glare and stared up at the summit. Against the sky she could see the silhouette of a man dancing like a demented dervish. She raised her scope sunglasses and saw immediately that the hapless figure was ringed about by jubilant metas.

Without hesitation, Violet started back the way she had come. She snapped her head up to take quick glimpses of her target, but mainly kept her eyes down. She would be of no use to him if she tripped and fell on the uneven terrain.

Violet had only ever seen film of this typical metahominid Death Dance, but she understood that what would have started as being something more akin to mere dancing, had already entered the second stage of the enchantment. Any hitherto graceful movement had now descended into fit-like jerking, suggesting this victim was, literally, on his last legs. The third stage was death, or capture.

Violet made a split-second assessment. It was going to take her around fifteen lung-bursting minutes to clamber up to him. Time that would be hellish for the both of them.

Watkin's nose was bleeding. He'd smashed his face a few times with his own madly flailing arms and every part of him hurt. He tried everything to stop. He tensed his body, but the charm just worked against his every effort, grinding his cramping muscles agonisingly against themselves into unwilling action. If he relaxed, his suddenly heavy limbs just moved faster and his arms became wild weapons to beat himself with. He could control his face and his mind, but that was it.

He closed his eyes and opened them to find he had jigged very close to the edge of the steep hillside. Someone... was that someone? Abruptly his body spun and took him away from the edge again. He'd only caught the faintest glimpse, but hope flowered in Watkin's heart, that someone was coming. He didn't know if it was Sarah or some other walker, but maybe another person could drag him out of this endless exertion and rescue him from himself.

His back ached, his teeth hurt from grinding them, he'd bitten his tongue, his legs were on fire and his arms felt like all the sinews in them had been stretched beyond recovery. He wanted to fall to the floor, but all he had to do now was to hang on.

Trying not to think about her own wracked body, Violet hauled herself up the slope, occasionally skidding on her false foot, but never losing ground. Her head felt like it would explode with the blood bursting pressure, but she forced herself up the shortest possible route she could find.

Pushing the sunglasses back onto the bridge of her sweating nose, she pulled herself up onto the summit plateau, and ducked behind a low stone wall. Hands shaking with adrenalin, she plucked the silver spray from her bag, silently gathered herself and on the inner count of three, deftly vaulted from her crouched position clear across the wall. She landed directly behind Watkin, in amongst the metas.

Casting her silver-spray in a wide arc, the chunkheads, arboreals and greys caught in its fallout appeared and instantly melted as rain. Crouching low, she circled the jerking victim and directed the vicious droplets towards the enemy.

Before his rapidly settling eyes, Watkin saw evil insectlike faces appear then melt away as clouds of rain. Grey faces with slanted alien eyes, old wizened faces, beautiful faces, bodies with and without wings, all of them bursting into tiny showers of water before the fierce blast of

Violet's spray.

Released from the enchantment, Watkin found he could no longer stand and sank heavily to the floor. Whilst his body was utterly exhausted, his mind was not. He stared in alert interest, as numerous bizarre forms appeared clearly in the face of the strange, grey spray Violet was directing at them. Each of them struck angry, warlike poses before feebly dissolving into mist. Unseen by Watkin, a single archer on a high wall drew his bow and sighted on Violet. She caught the movement and directed what little was left of the spray upwards. Watkin saw the archer materialise and fall. His spent arrow missed its mark and skittered across the back of his hand, the lifeless flint leaving a harmless blue trail on his skin. Watkin stared at it. He still bore the same blue on his shoulder.

At Kew, he had been aware of the clear flame beings, but he hadn't got close enough to see exactly what had been going on. Now he finally understood that this is what that strange party of people had been doing there.

Violet shook the canister. Its precious payload was running out. Without looking at Watkin, she screamed, 'Got any silver? Ring, chain, belt buckle, *anything? Hit them with it!*'

Violet pulled a slender silver chain from her neck

and swung it into empty air. Metas materialised and died. Watkin polished his silver signet-ring against his chest and painfully jumped to his feet. Not really knowing what he was doing, he punched hesitantly into clear air...

... and made contact. As the arboreal materialised, its shocked face gaping, Watkin jumped back disgusted.

Initially yielding, and then offering some strange resistance, it had felt like he'd just punched a jellyfish. He struck out again and again, fighting back to back with Violet. Battling against an unseen enemy, he fought on, waiting for the sharp sting of an arrow. None came, but before long, his blind flailing seemed to be having a lot less success. Either the aliens were evading them, or they were winning the fight.

Behind him, he could sense Violet's movements becoming less frenetic. Eventually she stopped swinging the chain and appeared to be scanning the scene through her weird thick sunglasses. Violet pocketed her necklace, and took a deep breath. 'Time to go,' she half whispered.

Turning to face Watkin for the first time, Violet gaped in shock. She slowly lowered her glasses, shaking her head in wonderment.

'*Suckerfish!*' she gasped in a whisper.

'What?' Watkin began, but she furiously motioned him to be silent, then took him firmly by the arm and dragged him back down the hillside. Without stopping, Violet hauled him down the long, green slope, through the fields, down past the school building, over the hump-backed canal-bridge and back towards the river.

Feeling close to mental and physical collapse, Watkin staggered alongside Violet back into town. Outside a coffee shop, her furious pace slowed and a gasping, wordless Watkin finally took the opportunity to motion her to stop with an outstretched hand.

He was fit, but she was steamingly angry, both at her unwanted shadow *and* at her own lack of vigilance. All that extra adrenalin firing through her body had made her all but superhuman. Even half-carrying Watkin, she had flown back down the hillside in double-quick time. Watkin threw himself down into one of the metal chairs on the pavement, slumped back, then fidgeted and retrieved a sweat-soaked tenner from his pocket. He dumped it on the table. His defiant gesture a small challenge, a gentle reassertion of his will. 'Mine's a latte,' he said quietly, but firmly.

'So's mine,' she answered coldly and swept up the

note. Violet went inside to order, leaving Watkin wondering uncomfortably if there was a back door to the coffee shop and that was the last he'd ever see of her, or his tenner.

She was back out in under a minute, even before he had time to gather his wildly scattered thoughts. He rubbed his eyes. 'What just happened?'

Violet reached into her bag and brought out a tissue, she leaned across the table to wipe Watkin's bloody nose. Instinctively, he swatted her hand away. She glared at him, Watkin was eyeing the tissue warily.

'It's not chloroform!' she snorted, shoving the tissue back across the table, 'Your face is a mess.'

Humbled, Watkin wiped his bloodied nose. Dark speckles of dried blood flaked off his skin. His nose clicked now, it hadn't done before, but he didn't think he'd broken it. He shivered and the shiver turned to a shudder, as his mind replayed the Death Dance. Violet dug in her day pack again and pulled out her other boot, and foot.

She turned her chair away and bent to take off her fighting spur. Watkin watched the muscles flexing in her slender back as she pulled her walking boot on. He sighed, and patiently repeated his question in an urgent half whisper.

'What - just - happened?'

Violet straightened and turned her chair back. She looked at him for a second and then cleared her throat. She seemed to be making up her mind.

'Are those things aliens?' he prompted.

'Far from it,' she began quietly, 'they're *natives.*'

Watkin nodded slowly, 'And you're not called Sarah?'

Violet shook her head. 'No, I'm...' Then her training cut in and she finished curtly, '...not Sarah.'

'And you're not going to tell me anything? Just leave me hanging?'

'Something like that. It's like this, Dylan...'

He flinched at her casual use of his name.

'....We're not 'Men In Black' and we don't have any magic biros to make you instantly forget all this.'

We? Who are 'we,' then? A specific organisation?'

A girl in black brought their lattes and the moment was lost. Watkin glumly sipped.

'Did they ever do that to you? Control you like that?'

Violet shook her head.

Watkin continued quietly, 'I haven't been a copper for long - but of course you know all about me.'

Irritated, Violet folded her arms.

'I've been caught up in a couple of fist-fights, a riot and been threatened a fair few times. Sometimes by my own side, sometimes by the villains, but through fire or fight, or riot, or whatever, I have never, *ever* felt such raw, helpless terror as I did on that hill less than half an hour ago.'

Violet drained her latte glass.

'So you're just going to leave me, without any explanation?'

Tears of frustration welled in Watkin's eyes.

'I don't see what else I can do.'

'*Please!*' Watkin's voice cracked as he pleaded, 'just tell me what those things are up there.'

Violet shook her head, 'I'm bound by the Official Secrets Act.'

Watkin leaned across the table, 'So am I.'

He took a deep breath and continued, 'You hear about people finding God. "The Damascene experience." I just found something quite the opposite. Something very bad. Things that I never knew existed…'

He shuddered in the warm sunshine, '….Got into my head. And now I don't know if I'll ever be able to sleep peacefully again.'

Humbled, Violet lingered.

'And you know what they looked like? *Fairies!*' Watkin laughed hollowly and slumped on the table. Violet reached out to touch his arm, thought better of it and withdrew her hand.

Watkin looked up, his face a mask of misery.

'*Please,* don't follow me again. Don't pursue this,' she urged. 'No one will believe you. People will laugh at you. You'll lose your career *and* your family. I've seen it happen. Please don't be stupid.'

Around them, the busy town bustled as people went about their business, scurrying, shopping or chatting in the late afternoon sunshine. Watkin looked up. From where they were sitting, he could no longer see the dark bulk of Castell Dinas Brân looming impassively above them, but he felt its presence.

He began slowly, 'Then I had better go back up there and confront those things.'

Violet rolled her eyes, 'You think?'

'At least I'd find out something.'

'Like a really agonising way to die?' Violet responded coolly, 'Go for it, then. Knock yourself out, be my guest. Maybe then you'll die happy!'

'Solve one of your problems, wouldn't it?' he responded, suddenly quiet and dangerous. Violet narrowed her eyes questioningly, Watkin continued, 'Your bosses aren't going to like it that I found you so easily.'

Stung, Violet rose to go. 'Forget all this. Forget that!' she pointed in the direction of the hill, 'but most of all,' she said pointing at herself, *'forget me!'*

Watkin sat for a long while after she had left, eventually rising with a groan as his over-exerted muscles leaked pain throughout his body. He felt like he'd taken the beating of a lifetime. All he wanted was a really hot bath, and then bed.

A skein of men, all about his age, wandered past his table, heading for one of the many the pubs in town. On an impulse, Watkin staggered to his feet and followed them.

Long after sunset, several hours and many drinks later, Dylan Watkin staggered back up the dark street. He hadn't booked into any of the B and B's, and no-one would have him now, he was so drunk and dishevelled. It was looking like he'd have to sleep the night in his car. He didn't care, it didn't bother him in the least.

Shrugging exaggeratedly, he tried not to think about the hulking hill somewhere behind him, an eerie black berg floating in a darkly, starless sky.

A high-pitched squeal rattled his ragged nerves. A gaggle of shrieking mini-skirted girls were tottering down the street towards him. All in their best plumage, they clasped bright bottles of luridly coloured alcohol. One broke away from the clutch and approached him.

He eyed her warily, but she abruptly flung slender arms around his neck.

'Hey, you're nice! Wanna dance? Yeah? We're all going to the dance! C'mon, come with us!' In a flash, they were encircling him, ensnaring him with their sinuous arms and floaty boas. Swamped by what seemed like a sudden mass of bodies, engulfed by the din of their squeals of glee and jangling bracelets, overwhelmed by their cheap perfume and clinging arms, Watkin lost it.

Afterwards, he found it difficult to recall, but he had panicked when he'd suddenly seen one of them had pink, sparkly wings and he had bodily hurled her away from him, and had started striking out at the skinny forms.

The girls screamed and one fell heavily onto the pavement. Watkin tripped over her and staggered backwards, lurching against a shop window. Another girl leapt on his back, pulling his hair, screeching at him for punching her mate. Then all hell let loose. Watkin, still with the girl on his back, spun around, swinging her, howling, until she flew backwards into the road.

Stumbling, Watkin lost his balance and crashed through the shop window. An alarm wailed like a furious banshee and instantly he was surrounded by a host of fairies. Unnaturally huge, slanted eyes stared down at him impassively. In utter terror, Watkin began screaming at the top of his lungs. Howling like a man possessed, he instinctively struck out in all directions, tearing down dreamcatchers, hurling fairy statuettes and fantasy figurines out into the street.

The girls fled crying and in a haze of blue light, the police arrived to find Watkin's bloodied and inert form. At the height of his demented fury, he had smashed his head against a low shelf and now lay passed-out, in the wrecked remains of the window display in a New Age emporium.

41

On London Underground maps, the Bakerloo line shows up as brown. A sombre hue for an undertaking that had seen such a colourful inception.

Originally entitled *'The Baker Street and Waterloo Railway,'* it had been financed by an eminent entrepreneur called Whitaker Wright. A man who had grown rich from mining silver Whitaker Wright committed suicide in 1904, when his past had finally caught up with him. As a consequence, work stopped on *The Baker Street and Waterloo Railway* for many months. Only one curious detail of his involvement remained.

Unlike any other underground railway, the line that became known as *'Bakerloo,'* adhered to Wright's insistence, that the polarity of the conductor rails should be reversed and although this strange rule was never fully explained, it remained strictly adhered to for many years after his death.

Every night, at a certain hour, the power is cut to the rails on the London Underground. In the stillness, the silence is broken only by the occasional water-drip. Floating ghostlike through the darkness, small teams of people walk the tracks, checking, clearing rubbish and ensuring all is safe for the millions of passengers the Underground carries every day.

Jockey introduced himself. Smiles were exchanged and hands shaken, but the tight knit group were suspicious of their new member. Although he wore a high-viz jacket and carried a bin-bag and broom just like they did, they knew exactly what he was.

A boss sent to spy on them.

An air of resentful efficiency pervaded the group, as they all went the unwilling extra mile to show this snooper their mettle. Meanwhile, all of this was lost on Jockey, who'd only come to check out the metahominids roost. Falling back, he checked his map against the location Violet had given to D. He quickly scoped out the area. It didn't take him long to find what he was looking for.

Just a quick glance, as he skirted the opening of the side-tunnel, was enough. The sight of the massed bodies peeled back the lid on Jockey's anger. His desire to annihilate every last one of the creatures rose like a dark acid at the back of his throat. He bitterly resented having to wait, but he could not go against D's orders this time. Swallowing down the impulse to act without back-up, Jockey hurried to catch up with the rest of the night cleaning team. They were all busy, head torches down, cleaning fluff and litter from in-between the rails. Jockey's thoughts ran to another type of cleansing.

The numbers of metas down there in the side tunnel already looked to be approaching what had been estimated as the total population figure for the whole country. Assuming it was possible, spraying every last one of them with silver would immediately create an awful lot of water.

An instant, tidal torrent would be sent crashing through the tunnels. Jockey approached the team leader and asked the question that was, if not at the very top of his list, somewhere in the top ten.

'What would happen if there was a flood down here?'

A couple of heads popped up, someone laughed.

Another voice asked, 'Is he for real?'

The team leader didn't like the disruption Jockey's presence had caused, but he answered him carefully, 'We have dedicated pumps running in relays on the system here, coping with ground water. We don't anticipate them breaking down any time soon. But you can be assured that, whatever limited flooding might, or might not occur, it is completely under control.' His reply sounded like something akin to an official press release.

'But what if there was a flash flood?' Jockey persisted.

'Is that likely to happen?' A nervous young voice asked. From somewhere in the darkness, a cheery voice piped up in perfect imitation of the team leader, 'If it does, you can be assured we might, or might not be swept away, but we'll certainly all drown!'

This was met by a chorus of laughter. Even Jockey managed to raise a rueful smile.

42

In the darkness, over the noise of the engine, Rhys reached out and squeezed Gnat's hand. He could have wept when Gnat squeezed back. They lay together on the lumpy mattress, both pretending to be out cold, whilst Rhys was busily working on an urgent escape plan.

The note had re-directed them to an alternative Chester 'safe house' - a note that hadn't been from D. Uncharacteristically relaxed, believing himself safe after all their recent ordeals, Rhys had unthinkingly followed the instructions left for him there and had travelled to an address in Whitchurch. That was where Diamond had been waiting for them.

'You awake, Gnat?' Diamond called out.

Rhys could feel Gnat freeze like a terrified mouse. Then he heard his mother say, 'get him here!' A weight landed on the bunk and Gnat was gone, dragged into the cab by an unseen force.

Rhys lay still. He might be able to work on the cable ties binding his wrists now he was alone in the back of the campervan.

In the front, Gnat rubbed his eyes and tried to figure out where he was. He could still taste the vile chemical in his mouth, the one Diamond had knocked him out with. Sounds were phasing in and out, his head was heavy and his unfocussed brain felt as if it had turned to grey wool. It was like that time he'd drunk a load of his Dad's beer when he'd been four.

He pulled his head back and tried to focus with one eye shut, like he'd done that other time when he'd come home from the dentist, still woozy.

His bound hands were suddenly free. He stared at the ragged slices of cable-tie as they fell away to the floor. Someone must have cut through them.

'You see it's like this, Gnat. People zig and they zag.' Diamond hauled at the knobbly steering wheel, guiding the campervan onto the motorway. The quiet, blonde man shot her a questioning glance, Diamond winked, 'Less likely to be stopped.' The man sat back impassively and Diamond continued her lecture to Gnat.

'Now your Dad's a zag, and I'm a zig. You're a zig too. You see, my Dad was a zag, horrible bloke, full of rules and regulations, and timetables and that. His zagging decided me to be a lot less bossy and more come-day, go-day with *my* kid. I let your Dad be as free as the wind, as free as I'd always wanted to be. But no!'

She sighed dramatically, '*that* didn't suit him. He wanted *structure* and *rules* and *boundaries*. Turned into a right zag he has. And because he imposed all that on you, it's only natural you want to be a zig just like me and get away from every last bit of it!'

With his mind beginning to clear, Gnat bit back his reply. He didn't want to be a zig at all. If anything, he wanted *more* rules if that meant he could feel safer.

With more rules, there'd be fewer oddballs like Diamond, free-floating about to collide with and ruin normal peoples' lives.

She hadn't introduced the tall blonde man, but Gnat understood instinctively that he was a fixture. There was something weird about him. Sometimes he pulled faces at Diamond, but she made a great play at never noticing. Sometimes she'd seem to address the space just by him, her eyes a few degrees off, like a blind person.

He'd caught the man staring at him and returned his gaze. The man had smiled and nodded, as if just by looking at him, Gnat had done something he should be proud of.

'*Rhys!*' Diamond almost spat out her only son's name. 'I'd planned so much for him, married him into Royalty. We'd have been sorted for life, if he hadn't been such an ungrateful fool!'

Royalty? Gnat was confused, Dad had married Royalty? Diamond chuckled mirthlessly and asked, 'What's your Dad told you about your Mum?'

Suddenly aware of the man's keen eyes upon him, Gnat did his best to gather his thoughts and pick his words carefully, 'A little,' he mumbled, adding quickly, 'But not that much.' That final comment was at least truthful.

'And what did he say about Cayden?'

'Cayden?'

'Your twin brother?'

In the back of the campervan, Rhys could only think his vehement reply. If he didn't get free soon, his mother would ruin his son's life forever.

Now thoroughly awake, Gnat was shocked to the

core. Cayden! He didn't even know he *had* a twin brother! He fiddled with the zip on his jacket, 'Mm, not much.'

He shifted in his seat, doing his very best to keep his tone neutral and disinterested. Diamond was not impressed by Gnat's ignorance.

'You don't know a blind thing do you? He's told you nothing!'

Gnat studied his shoes.

'Righto, let's get this over with now then, shall we?' Diamond's tone was brisk and dangerous, 'Here's the skinny… I introduced them at a festival years ago, when they were kids. They grew up and one day they 'accidentally' found each other again…'

In the back, Rhys had stopped struggling and was listening intently.

'…With a little help from me. Your Dad married your Mum, not knowing she was a real Faery Princess. Can't think why, but she loved him and vowed to stay with him. And she *tried*, she really did! But then you two boys came along and the pull of her old home was very strong, so she went back to live with her people! Got that?'

Gnat nodded dumbly, this was nuts. Dad had once said that too much skunk had clearly flaked Diamond's brain. It seemed his words were shaping up to be correct. There probably was no twin, and Mum had been dead all along, without there being anything sinister about it. Why else would the police have let his Dad go? Judging by how nice they'd been to him, they must have realised his Dad was not a *'bad man.'*

When the police caught up with them, this time, it would be Diamond who'd have to answer for her actions. Then she'd be put away forever.

As the miles drifted by, still she rattled on. 'Have you heard about King Arthur?' Gnat nodded, wondering where on earth all of this was leading to. Diamond was behaving as if kidnapping him and his Dad was the most natural thing in the whole world.

Diamond continued, 'In the old days, in his time, great store was laid by Royal bloodlines. A King could never guarantee his wife was faithful, *that's* what all that Guinevere and Lancelot argy-bargy was about!'

Cackling, Diamond elbowed Gnat in the ribs, 'So that's why the *son* of the King's *sister* was *always* next in line. Not his *son*, because he could never guarantee the kid was

356

his. His *nephew* inherited, because his sister was deffo of the Royal line, get it?'

'Like Fata Morgana and Mordred?' Gnat ventured, doing his very best to sound enthused and fully engaged, attempting to keep the mad, old bird calm and stay on her least-worst side.

'Ish… remember, King Arthur was his dad *and* uncle. Seriously creeps me out, all that Arthurian… Lost my thread, where was I? Oh yeah, anyway, the title is *Sisterson*, it goes back a very long way. You, Nathan, and your twin Cayden, are Sistersons.'

'You mean we're *important?*'

Diamond threw her head back and cackled, 'I should coco! Your Mum is the only sister to a dying King. By faery tradition, she can't inherit the kingdom, *but you can!*'

By now, Rhys was bruised and bloody and close to admitting defeat with the cable ties. He felt about for a loose spring inside the mattress, a nail sticking out of the plywood cladding, *anything*. There was nothing and he couldn't even get to his keys.

In the front, Gnat had been listening intently.

'Okay so I'm heir to a kingdom! Coo-ool!' He said brightly. At last, Gnat fully understand why his Dad had always said his grandmother wasn't anyone he wanted anything to do with.

The line from a song Dad used to play whilst he did the washing up, came into Gnat's head, '*Shine on you crazy Diamond...*'

'Listen, Gnat, this is *serious*!' Diamond hunched over the wheel and stared intently at the road ahead, 'Two boys of the Royal bloodline. One raised human, one raised faery: *between them, making one whole human, and one whole faery*. Each with a foot in both worlds, and insights beyond both peoples! Gnat, you and Cayden can heal the rift, and unite the races!'

Gnat caught the mocking grimace on her companion's face. He obviously thought she was barking too. Undeterred, Diamond forged ahead with her pre-planned speech.

'Gnat, I have watched over you for so many years now. Ever since you were a tiny baby, I made sure there were reminders of your heritage. It was me who made sure you had a photo of your Mum.'

Gnat's heart gave a lurch and his hand instinctively went up to his chest where the photograph lay. Diamond had had a hand in getting it to him and somehow, now, it was tainted. She missed his pained expression and continued. 'There's something else too. It's in the back.'

Gnat turned and looked over the back of his seat into the crazy jumble of clothes on the floor of the campervan. On top of it all, sat the old Christmas tree box.

'I rescued it from that last flat of your Dad's.'

Before they could stop him, Gnat had scrambled over the back of the seat and grabbed it. He desperately regretted that he had no knife to palm to his Dad's inert form, so, appearing to steady himself, Gnat just touched his Dad's arm reassuringly as he passed.

Gnat made a great show of being fixated solely upon the box. Torn by the sudden pang of having betrayed his Dad by not destroying it, he still couldn't deny he was thrilled to see it. He unlaced the cardboard end and checked his precious wing was intact. It was.

He reached eagerly inside the box and touched it.

'I made them leave it for you. Like a calling card.'

Struck by a sudden thought, he hesitated and slowly withdrew his hand. His reflex of joy had abruptly winked-out and was gone. His wing wasn't his any more. It was Diamond's. Maybe that was why Dad hadn't wanted it in the house? Gnat stared at the mesmerising powder on his fingers. It was changed, tainted somehow by its provenance. It was a zig, when all he wanted was to be zag.

He filled the awkward silence with a question, 'Is it hers? My Mum's I mean?'

Diamond roared with laughter, 'No prizes for guessing which lad's been brought up human! *Is it hers?* Goodness me no, it's been ripped off the back of … oh I dunno… some other fairy I expect.'

Enamoured of all insects, the notion of ripping the wings off *anything* made Gnat shudder. He considered the cool brutality of Diamond's statement and fell quiet.

As he stood up, he dislodged a tray from the small countertop. The tray tipped, hung for an instant, then fell shattering upon the only exposed piece of floor in the whole vehicle. It had been an old tray, made of butterfly wings pressed behind a sheet of glass. The glass broke, with a delicate tinkling sound, into long, linear shards. Gnat immediately bent to pick up the pieces.

'Gnat, leave it! You'll cut yourself!' Diamond shrieked, seeming genuinely concerned.

'Already have,' Gnat examined his glistening thumb. Diamond shrieked again. 'It's okay,' Gnat sucked at his thumb, 'It's not coming out blue though!'

Relieved, Diamond chortled. Gnat slowly rose, with his thumb still in his mouth. Leaning against the bunk to get up, he slipped a jagged piece of glass under the bedclothes, as close to his Dad's hands as he dared.

Gnat slowly returned to his seat and slid down beside his demented Grandmother and her companion. Diamond took a hand from the wheel to ruffle his hair. 'Should be blue! Faery Royalty, you are!'

Gnat let the words wash over him, wondering if his Dad was out cold.

On the bunk, Rhys was painstakingly insinuating his bound hands, towards whatever Gnat had just planted by him. Keenly aware that this might be their last chance, he was desperately anxious to take this precious opportunity slowly and not blow it.

'That's why you see things other people can't.'

Gnat was exhausted, but Diamond persisted with her mad-talk. The blonde man smiled and nodded, Gnat stared at the floor.

Maybe it was the proximity of the strange man, but a sudden rush of memories bubbled up, as if from some long, lost wellspring, hidden deep within Gnat's mind. It was as if he'd been happily splashing in the shallows one moment and then suddenly strayed far from the sunlit surf, out over some vast, dark continental shelf the next. As the depths had opened up to engulf him, the land of everyday normality had plummeted away. Suddenly he remembered everything. From the dream of flying, to Neave and her Mum and the near-miss, when they'd tried to lure him into the hill. The hill!

Suddenly, Diamond didn't seem so deluded and crazy after all. Gnat felt sick with fear. Sick at the memory of that green hill and the two beings who had so clearly tried to lure him inside it.

He especially remembered his feelings of terror and regret and of missing his Dad.

A sudden pang of fear shot through him. What if they were taking him somewhere like that? *Fairies* though? No! It couldn't be!

Then he clearly remembered the label on the wing at Warwick Castle:

Fairy wing. Found Flintshire 1724

The young woman curator had thought it had been a fake, but he had known better. Now Gnat bitterly wished it had been a fake.

Biting his lip, he ventured a question, 'Granny Diamond, where are we going?' He asked it with as much lightness and innocence as he could muster. So far he'd been quiet and compliant. This was not the time to kick up.

'I'm taking you to claim your kingdom, Nathan. About time too.'

Gnat sat back, imagining a life trapped under a green hill and shuddered. He caught the man's gaze again, and shifted uncomfortably in his seat. Maybe the stranger could read his thoughts?

'You cold?'

Gnat thought it better to nod, and Diamond turned the heater up. The cab instantly filled with the smell of hot oil. Maybe Diamond's van would break down? Gnat could only hope. Then again, maybe he could push things along?

Get her to speed up? Then again, if they didn't break down, they'd only get to where they were going that much faster. Gnat slumped, thinking hard.

What did his Dad say about cars? He remembered one old heap of a thing his Dad had owned a couple of years ago. Dad's running joke was that he called it, 'Flattery,' - because it didn't get him anywhere. Poor old Flattery had hated stopping and starting. Gnat gazed ahead as the weak headlights delicately probed the uninterrupted grey lanes of the motorway. Diamond was unlikely to be doing a lot of stopping and starting. Irritated at his powerlessness, Gnat fidgeted.

'What's up with you?' Diamond demanded.

Inspiration hit. 'I need to pee!' Gnat said urgently.

'Oh Nathan, it's fifteen miles to the next services!'

Diamond leaned forwards as she depressed the accelerator. As the old van picked up her skirts and scurried faster, the hot oil smell grew. Satisfied, Gnat wrinkled his nose, and fidgeted convincingly, like a boy desperate to go.

43

'Your shirt's ruined, Dyl! You'll have to have one of Rhodri's!'

Watkin groaned, his eyes refused to open. He rolled over and gave a loud 'Owww!' as every muscle fibre complained. He ached like a penitent couch-potato who'd recklessly shown off at the gym.

'It's all your own fault! I've got no sympathy!' Katy grumbled, bustling around downstairs, her voice still loud through the guest bedroom door. Watkin shifted his body again and waves of dull, aching pain held his lower back in an inescapable bear hug. The events of yesterday began to clear in his mind. Whilst his brain was still processing the visuals, his body remembered every sinew-stretching, muscle-milking moment of the climb, the near-fatal encounter with those *things,* the flight back down and... oh yes. Oh no! ... The aftermath.

'Breakfast in ten, Dyl!' His sister shouted up the

tiny stairs. She was getting a Welsh accent. Katy loved her brother, but this wasn't the first time he'd shown he couldn't handle his drink. The previous time had been at the wedding, when Dylan had brought that awful Chloe creature with him. This time, it had been left to her and Rhodri to pick up the pieces.

They had collected her contrite and teary brother from the police station at Wrexham. Rhodri had been brilliant, but then again, he was a solicitor. He'd lain great stress on an incident from some months back, that had seen Watkin hospitalised for three days. It was obviously still affecting him.

He had cited Watkin's previously unblemished police record and with only a little collusion from a senior officer, who happened to be one of Rhodri's golfing buddies, they'd been allowed to bring Dylan back to their cottage in Corwen. Not that he was out of the woods. Watkin had committed several public order offences, criminal assault *and* criminal damage. Whilst Rhodri was certainly silver-tongued, as good as he was, Watkin had been made to fully understand that even *he* couldn't make all this go away.

During the nightmare drive back from Wrexham to

Corwen, in between gaps in Katy's excoriating tongue lashing, Rhodri had managed to convey the seriousness of Watkin's position. His brother-in-law had been reasonably certain he could keep Watkin out of prison….

But…There would be a sizeable fine, reparation for damages, a suspended sentence… he went on. For Watkin, the worst was unspoken, but he could imagine it. Rhodri's fat, serene face forever floating over him, grinning like a Cheshire cat, exuding all the sneering superiority of his fake benevolence, forever reminding Watkin just how deeply indebted he was.

Nodding penitently, whilst Rhodri listed off all the favours he was doing him, Watkin had never so wanted to kill someone in all his life.

Assuming he didn't - and so wouldn't be facing a murder charge - then the worst case scenario was that he'd lose his job. Best case scenario was that he'd be suspended on full pay - and then he'd lose his job.

Watkin grimaced at Rhodri's shirt. Apart from being a couple of sizes too big, it was white, with sprigs of small, periwinkle flowers and looked like busy wallpaper. Still, he raised his leaden arms and somehow got into it.

He was shocked at how many bruises were coming out on his body, but considering he'd fallen into a shop full of spiky dragon and witch ornaments, *after* crashing through a plate-glass window, he was preternaturally fortunate not to have cut himself more, or worse.

Watkin had once attended an incident where a young idiot had, brick in hand, punched a hole through a large shop window. His scheme had worked, but as he was reaching through the hole to grab a games console, the entire remaining top section of glass had dropped like a guillotine and sliced the youth's arm clean off. He'd been found, ashen faced, still standing but rapidly bleeding to death, staring at his own arm on display behind the fallen glass. Watkin shuddered at the recollection and continued dressing as quickly as his own damaged body would allow.

He ate his breakfast in silence. Katy couldn't find the words to give vent to the full extent of her anger and frustration with Dylan.

In the past, she had begun all her improving talks with, 'What would Mum have said?' As if their own, dead mother was somehow looking down and habitually judging and condemning him for never being quite as good as his sweet little sister.

Now he'd come here, got bladdered, and thrown everything away.

Katy bit her lip. If she hadn't emailed him, he could have been a complete idiot somewhere else and she wouldn't have had to even see, or begin to deal with, the total mess he was making of his life.

For his part, Watkin was sincerely grateful for the silence. It gave him time to work out what he was going to do next. 'I thought I'd go and get my car back.'

Katy almost spat out her tea, 'You're going back to Llan? Are you *mad*? Those girls will have brothers and they'll *kill* you if they see you!'

'I've got to get my car,' Dylan persisted, 'must've got a ticket by now.'

'Well I'm not taking you!' Katy snorted, 'there's a bus in eight minutes,' she pointed a warning finger at him, '*don't* go near any pubs!'

'I wasn't going to!' Watkin snapped.

Grabbing a piece of toast and sliding his arms through his battered, leather jacket as painlessly as he could, he added, 'I need to go and see a jewellers.'

'You need to go and see a head doctor!' Katy sniped back, but the cottage door slammed behind him, and he was gone.

44

D hadn't moved since collapsing into his bed. Now, he rose quickly with complete, instant wakefulness and stretched the stiffness from his shoulders.

He was desperate for a swim. The coursing waters of the restless Dee had beckoned as he had driven the short distance out of Llangollen, but D couldn't risk wild swimming. He had a knack of attracting all manner of aquids. A walk in the woods was bad enough, but a swim in a lake or river would expose him to nixs and fossegrims, merrows and dryads - the aquatic branch of the metahominids.

After a light breakfast, he finally opened the letter he had carried with him for the last three days. It gave a date, a time, and the Whitehall Office he was expected to attend. His face betrayed no reaction to the contents.

He made a quick call and arranged to meet Violet in the coffee-shop by the bridge. The fine weather persuaded him to leave his car at the hotel and walk into town.

The summer had progressed past its peak, but the sunshine still struck warm upon his back as his long, loping gait carried him into town. A country bus passed close by the narrow pavement, momentarily enshrouding him in a hot breath of dust and diesel fug.

D only got a split second glimpse of the passengers. It was enough. Watkin was onboard.

D called Violet. 'That wretched cat? The one you hadn't fed?'

Violet's silence condemned her.

'…Appears to have followed you. All the way here.'

'Erm…Yeah.'

D could imagine Violet fidgeting with the phone, leaking guilt.

'It's a bit…tenacious… I guess.' She ventured.

'You *knew?*'

'Yeah,' Violet felt physically sick. She had wanted

371

to dissuade Watkin herself in her own way. She feared D would make sure Dylan Watkin was permanently discouraged from any further interest in D9.

Whatever it took.

D's tone was curt, 'The coffee-shop's not an option now. See you at Aled and Andrea's.'

45

'Steel true and blade straight!' Aled smiled as he handed Baby back to Violet. She took her precious knife, admiring the gleaming cruelty of her finely honed lines and smiled ruefully.

Aled cocked his head and regarded her solemnly.

'Trouble?

Violet sighed softly as she stowed Baby snug inside the vanity-case. 'You have no idea.'

The door shrieked in protest as someone wrenched it open violently.

Watkin stormed in, '*That!*'

He pointed threateningly at Aled, 'You see, *that* is what messes with my head!'

'What the hell..?' Andrea jumped from behind the counter and stood between the intruder and Aled. In a flash Baby was unsheathed and Violet stood behind Watkin, her blade at his throat.

'I told you to get lost!'

Even with the cold steel pricking his neck, Watkin's eyes never left Aled. Andrea raised her dark eyes to his, 'He thinks you're a meta.'

Aled nodded. Picking up a nugget of solid silver he walked around the counter. Rolling the silver between his lithe fingers, he waved it under Watkin's nose.

'Having a bad fairy day are we?' he asked lightly.

Watkin would have sagged, if it weren't for the proximity of Violet's blade. 'What are we going to do with you?' she sighed.

Watkin would have answered, but moving his jaw was not the safest option.

'There's a man coming here,' she continued, 'and if he finds you, you'll wish you were still on top of that hill.'

To Watkin's unutterable relief, she took the blade away, turned her back on him and packed Baby away in her case. 'Get lost, Dylan. No one wants you here!'

There was very little emotion in her voice, it was light and level, but Watkin sensed the faintest echo of regret.

'I'm going to lose my job over this,' he began.

Andrea folded her arms and pursed her lips. She was a sucker for a sob-story, and she already felt desperately sorry for the confused figure before her.

'Tough. Goodbye, Mr. Watkin.' Violet held the door open and he trailed miserably out into the road. He hesitated for a moment, his face taut with strained resentment, then he turned and walked straight into a tall, ungainly man. As they collided, the man had to grab Watkin's shoulder to steady himself and keep upright.

'Ill met, Mr. Watkin,' the man said in a familiar voice.

'You were there… at Kew!' Watkin gasped. D smiled and Watkin was taken aback at the genuine warmth.

'I was indeed. Your point being?'

It suddenly struck Watkin that the man's studied pleasantness might not be that sincere after all. Now that he had been acknowledged, he wondered if he wasn't in a far more dangerous position than he had been when they were telling him to go away.

'Shall we?'

D held the door open. Spellbound, Watkin nodded and walked back into the shop.

'I thought I'd told you... oh!'

With her back turned to the door, Violet had only caught Watkin's reflection in the display cabinet. Turning, she was shocked to see D was with him.

'Sir, I found him... on the hill...he was beguiled.' Violet faltered under D's critical gaze.

'Clearly.'

Violet squirmed. D's single word answer and his steady scrutiny were worse than any interrogation. Watkin drew his breath to interrupt. Without even looking at him, D silenced him with a single, raised finger. Violet studied the floor.

'Poor fieldcraft.' Her heart sank at D's simple summation.

Mystified, Watkin watched the tense scene, then sudden realisation dawned and he protested Violet's innocence, 'I didn't follow her! … Well I did….. but just up the hill! I didn't follow her *from London!*'

D finally turned to face Watkin, his cool smile seeking to strip away Watkins lies and excuses.

'*Excellent* fieldcraft!' D pronounced, his sudden smile sliding into hawk-like fascination. Watkin felt like his bones were being picked clean by this big, weird-looking man's shrewd gaze. He fell silent. There was no way his keen observer was going to believe he was there by coincidence. Maybe that wasn't such a bad thing after all?

Then a strange thing happened. Watkin's mouth opened and words came out, but Watkin wasn't at all sure he was making them.

'Look, okay, I'm tenacious. But surely I could be a real asset? I'd work day and night for you! And I wouldn't be doing it for the money!'

This, at least, raised a smile from Violet. There was no money.

Lives change on the flip of a coin or the turn of a wheel. Time makes indelible the small acts that contrive to lead on to glory or despair. This was the moment when Watkin's heart gave an enormous lurch. Suddenly he realised that this was what he really wanted. This was what he had been born for. All his curiosity, his conviction that something more than ever met the eye was going on behind the façade of day-to-day reality, each and every path he had thus far travelled, they had all led to this point.

Whatever these people were involved in, more than anything he desperately wanted to be a *part of it*. He knew he had to plead his case and give the speech of his life.

Maybe he wanted it too much.

At the one moment he needed inspiration the most, the muse left him, all his fine words dried up and he might as well have had mud in his mouth. His next utterance was a complete disaster. 'I'm very discreet!'

The silence that followed these words was condemnation enough. Aled cleared his throat, Andrea bit her lip. Only Violet stood stock still. Eventually D spoke.

'Falling through shop windows?' his tone was a study in pleasantry, 'hitting young women?'

Watkin cringed, blushing schoolboy scarlet, but D's softly spoken and merciless summation continued, 'initiating your own cack-handed investigation, thereby compromising the secrecy of a protected witnesses' home and endangering the lives of those within?'

Now the blood drained from Watkin's face and suddenly, he felt sick.

'None of your endeavours appear to be sterling recommendations… Or evidence of your possession of any useful abilities.'

D turned to Violet, 'Make sure our Mr. Watkin gets home safely.'

He pointedly waited for them to leave, before opening his negotiations with Aled.

Summarily dismissed, a mortified Violet ushered Watkin out of The Oak Chest before her. The test that lay ahead - and it was test set for her by D, she was certain of that - was to sit with Watkin, in his car, for the several hours it would take them to get to London and not let a single thing slip.

From her name onwards, Watkin must not learn anything. She was confident she could turn any topic back onto Watkin and let him spend most of the time speaking about himself, but she knew she couldn't relax.

That was a pity. Dylan Watkin was growing on her.

What?!

Violet strangled the shockingly flirtatious thought at birth with a tourniquet of inwardly directed scorn.

'Am I for real? *Suckerfish?* A jobless, flying-saucer-fixated ex-copper? Oh *c'mon, Violet!*'

46

Despite all his very best efforts, with no sign of the funding they still so desperately needed, D9 was all but dead in the water. The metahominids were massing in the London Underground and Jockey was wanting alcohol.

He resisted as he had done these past twenty years, but still the pull was strong. Drink had always brought him trouble. It made him feel invincible, and perform wildly reckless acts to prove it. It had made him champion at *tomb-stoning*. On his cold home surf, the young Jockey had been adept at hurling himself from huge rocks, into a wild, wild sea.

It had damn near killed him too, when the undertow had rolled him around mercilessly, sucking the strength from his body and crushing the air from his lungs.

She had come to him, then. A vision of extraordinary beauty, with a song of such wistful ululation that hearkened back, to ancient times, of loss and sadness. She had taught that same song to a blind Irishman called O'Carolan and he, in turn, had taught it to Vivaldi. A song that now encircled Jockey's doomed heart.

As his lifeless body slowly tumbled down into an underworld of grey-black rock, and green-red weed, she had caught him. Stepping delicately from a forest of kelp, she had held her lips to his. Jockey's eyes had opened and stared into those of his saviour and they had momentarily hung together, wrapt in the green depths, held in a shard of emerald sunlight. Even as she had guided him up, up the dizzying heights, up into the sunlight and long before he rose, gasping, through the surface and collapsed back into her slender arms, he knew he had irrevocably fallen.

The simple act of near drowning, of finding, falling for, and ultimately losing the love of his life, had brought him such a complete sense of abandonment, that Jockey had long believed he would have been better off drowning on that fateful day.

When, after all his wild, drunken stories of silkies and mermaids had worn thin and even his mates had decided he was a bit 'touched,' Jockey's anger had taken a different direction. He no longer risked his own neck. He vented his woes on other people instead.

Back, when he had still been in his teens, but was already feeling bereft and that the best part of his life was irrevocably lost and behind him, his favourite form of self-expression had become the cold execution of spectacular acts of mindless violence.

Magistrates had necessarily given way to judges, and even his fellow inmates in a series of young-offender institutes had admitted Jockey had a real talent for hurting people.

After a lot of counselling, Jockey had almost believed the drink and lack of oxygen had played tricks with his mind, and he had imagined his various encounters in the deeps. Almost. But although Jockey was stubborn, he wasn't stupid, and he knew what he knew, and he'd seen what he'd seen. He refused to lie down and be brainwashed into thinking that this life-shattering event was an empty illusion, he just learnt to be more discreet about it.

The army had taken his raw, unformed talent and shaped it into a thing of efficiency and precision. D had finally saved him from a lifetime of wondering if his sanity was indeed compromised, and for that he would always be grateful. However, even though he had found people who believed his version of events, events that had spun his world so disastrously off-course, it hadn't made him any happier.

An encounter with a nereid, a nixe, a mermaid, or a melusine, whatever she had been, had warped his day-to-day existence into something far different from that of his fisherman father and his brothers, and it had blighted his life forever.

If anything, fully trained and armed, the present day Jockey was an even more dangerous man. Just now he was in a dangerous mood.

He perused the enhanced picture. It clearly showed Gnat, pale-faced and unhappy, sitting next to his grandmother, Diamond. The date, time and location of the roadside camera that had captured the image, ran along the bottom of the picture.

It had been taken within the last half-hour.

D had set Jockey to keep as close an eye on Diamond as he could given her nomadic lifestyle, and over the past few years, they had kept track of all her wanderings. After the latest incident, once Gnat was back safely with his father, the immediate threat had appeared neutralized, so Jockey had relaxed and lost contact with her. Now he was kicking himself for his lack of vigilance. He had known she was tenacious, but two abductions within the space of a few hours was rather more than he had expected, even of her.

The moment he had received the latest picture, Jockey had attempted to alert D. All he got in reply to his calls was *'this mobile is switched off.'* Its signal had been swallowed by Welsh geography.

Unable to talk directly with him until D got on the move again, Jockey left a terse message about a *'gee-gee in trouble,'* on Aled and Andrea's answering service and considered his options.

The police cameras had tracked Diamond to a rural area south of Oxford. He could simply have had her rearrested and Gnat reclaimed by the boys in blue, but that hardly satisfied his ever-present ache for retribution.

Suddenly grateful for the Welsh landscape that created network blind-spots, he found himself grimly gleeful at the prospect of operating solo again. Jockey revelled in operating off-grid. It was what he did best. His next vital act would be ridding the earth of that persistent crazy old cow Diamond.

She'd always be a threat. Enough was enough, time for one mad old bint to leave the planet. Jockey punched *Wantage,'* into his sat-nav and joined the slow, Friday night exodus from the heart of London. This was going to be one easy clean-up job.

47

Aled ignored the blinking light on the phone, he was too busy to deal with customers just at the moment.

He motioned D to stay seated in the back of the shop and began loading the boxes of silvered ammunition into the Saab.

Still not entirely having made up his lost nights' sleep, D was worn out. He'd managed to negotiate a great deal with Aled, swapping valuable books from his personal collection for these latest armaments. He knew the number of boxes fell far short of the optimum needed to deploy against that number of metahominids - probably by an order of around twenty times.

Head bent, Andrea was kneeling on the floor, going through a box of scrap, salvaging anything that held even the least silver content, bits that could be chopped into lethal fragments and scattered.

Ever alert to the subtle changes in D's demeanour, she was thoroughly alarmed. She had never seen him so resigned to defeat before. He looked like a beaten man, even before the first shot of battle had been fired.

She looked up, and eyed him steadily, inviting a response to her unspoken question. D rubbed his eyes, and slowly turned his head, making the vertebrae in his aching neck crackle.

Eventually he spoke, 'I have no idea why they are suddenly gathering like this now. Nothing I know about them is answer enough on its own.'

Cradling her tea, Andrea ventured suggestions, without prying. 'Maybe it's more than one thing, what if all the bits of the puzzle all contribute in different ways? Then again, could something be happening that's being deliberately hidden from you?'

'Sabotage?' D's eyes narrowed. *'Cui bono?'*

'Eh?'

'Who benefits?'

'I couldn't even begin to hazard a guess about their politics. I have no idea who's who, or even whether they have politics or factions anyway.'

D said, 'I wasn't talking about metahominids.'

Andrea stared, her eyes wide with sudden fear. 'You mean they've turned one of us...' she hesitated, unwilling to form the words, '... into a *traitor?'*

'It wouldn't be the first time in D9's history.'

Andrea sat back on her heels in shock.

Aled breezed in, 'All sorted! There's a lot of weight over that back axle, take your time getting home.'

The bubble of quiet reflection burst, D nodded, finished his tea and rose to go. At the door of 'The Oak Chest,' he solemnly shook hands with Aled and briefly hugged Andrea.

As the shop door closed behind D, all were left wondering if they would ever meet again.

48

It took Watkin a whole seven minutes to stop being flattered by Violet's keen attention and realise she was manipulating the conversation.

When the penny finally dropped he was disappointed for the both of them. Her for doing it, and himself for taking so long to see what she was up to.

'Well, well! What shall we talk about now?' he asked brightly.

'You?' Violet ventured.

'Again? Ah yes, silly me!' Watkin's hands gripped the wheel a little more tightly. 'You'd have thought my immediate problem was my impending lack of employment, wouldn't you?'

Violet shrugged non-committaly, folded her arms and feigned serenity.

'Thank you for your keen lack of interest, Ms. Notdeakin.'

This was his new name for her. Violet refused to rise to the bait and correct him, but it was still irritating. D had *known* Watkin would be like this, she thought bitterly. She could either take her medicine and put up with Watkin's relentless digging, or duck out, and face D's wrath.

Neither option enthralled her.

'However,' he continued, 'My immediate concern is discovering what has actually happened to me. Twice, now, I have been exposed to events that have led me question my own sanity.'

Getting no further information from Violet was not going to stop Watkin marshalling his scattered thoughts. Maybe, if he could step on enough nerves, she might react and give herself away?

Very unlikely. He reconsidered - worth a try, though.

'So, we've got a covert operation at Kew. A group

of shady people, working under the cover story of the accidental excavation of a wartime bomb. This group of shady people, lets call them .. ooh, I don't know… something like Unidentified Fighting Operatives? Yes! Let's call them UFO, shall we?'

Violet registered nothing.

'Anyway, there were four of them. Your boss. Nice bloke, bet you're glad he's sent you to keep an eye on me, eh?'

Violet stared at her own, bored reflection in the wing mirror.

'Then there was Jockey.'

Violet stiffened imperceptibly, unaware it was she who had let slip Jockey's name during the operation.

Watkin continued, 'He's the ex-army bloke. Very capable. Then there was the posh bloke with the fiddle, and then there was you, Notdeakin. You with that beautiful Gerber knife. Boy, did I get a good look at that baby today. Lovely piece of kit, quietly flash if you know what I mean. Beloved of the SAS. Vintage 1970's, might even have been your Dad's. Your pride and joy, I expect?'

Violet sat as motionless as she could, he was right on every count. If he'd managed to keep his job, Watkin would have made a formidable detective.

As his latest verbal dig hadn't worked, Watkin went for broke.

'And what were you doing there? Not picnicking in the rain, Notdeakin, no. You were all busily destroying other life forms weren't you? In a ruck with all those 'beings,' weren't you? So this is the thing, isn't it? The core of everything. Those things. For now, let's call them *'fairies,'* shall we?'

Violet brushed a stray hair behind her ear. This was the tell Watkin had been waiting for, he was getting somewhere.

'So these fairies can infest places. Some places it's cool and you leave them be. Other places are *inappropriate?* Would that be the right word to use, Notdeakin?'

Violet stared steadily at her own reflection in the wing mirror.

'These fairies have been around since at least 1757. The Reverend Doctor Edward Williams wrote about them in his memoirs. He came across a group of things like garden gnomes, dancing about a field not far from where I did my own little dance, Notdeakin. *Hey!* You know what?'

This last exclamation was made at such volume, Violet turned, shocked, to face him. 'I never thanked you for saving me! Oh, Notdeakin! How remiss of me! Thank you, thank you!'

Before she could stop him, Watkin grabbed her hand and kissed it. She indignantly snatched it back and raised it to thump him.

'Baby, you could always slit my throat!'

Violet burst out laughing. She laughed long and loud, and although puzzled, Watkin relaxed and smiled broadly, enjoying the full-throated charm of her genuine, bubbling glee.

'Oh, Suckerfish!' she wiped her eyes, 'you'll never know...'

'Nice to know you're not always so steely, Notdeakin.'

He kept smiling, but started wondering which part of, *'Baby you could always slit my throat,'* was the relevant bit.

She'd already held a knife at his throat. A thought

struck him. Could it be she had actually named her knife Baby? Just like when the Viking heroes named their swords? It made some sort of weird sense - a play on words. When his sister had been little, she had been fed baby-food out of a jar. He could just about remember that the label had borne the name 'Gerber.'

Violet gathered herself, alarmed that this man was getting to her. She considered dumping him at the next services and hitching back to London. She had failed the test. Watkin continued with his relentless summation.

'So these fairies that need to be cleared out of certain places have, like us, strengths and weaknesses. There are a lot of them, they move like lightning. They are all but invisible. They abduct people. They can infest places - including the human brain and turn your own body against you. They have surprisingly sophisticated weaponry, like arrowheads that work like heat-seeking missiles. They only have one weakness, silver. That's like radioactivity is to us, except it kills them quicker.'

He paused momentarily. 'When we were fighting them together, back-to-back, remember?'

Violet said nothing.

'I was seeing, but I wasn't *believing*. Afterwards… After I'd made a prat of myself, that is, I had a good think and lots of stuff came back, but it wasn't the way they trapped me in my own body that left the biggest impression. No. It was the way they died. *That* made the biggest impact on me. You know what it reminded me of?'

This time, he didn't even wait for her non-answer.

'It reminded me of some film I'd seen as a kid. Old footage of Hiroshima and Nagasaki. It showed shadows on the pavement. Just shadows, but those shadows were the imprints of real people. They'd all been vaporized on the spot. Real, living bodies reduced to just a stain on a pavement. Do you think they knew anything about it, Notdeakin? Was it fast, a flash and all over? Or did they feel what was happening?

'The faces on those fairies Notdeakin, *they* were suffering. For the split second I could fully see them, I could tell they were in torment, feeling every last atom of their bodies turning to water. Is it water, Notdeakin?'

Before she could begin to answer, he ploughed on, 'They might be nasty, evil people-stealers, Notdeakin, but isn't all this unbelievably harsh? Why aren't we investigating these beings, Notdeakin? Working with them? We could share technologies, Notdeakin. And you're not telling me, that if more people knew about this, there wouldn't be a 'Save the Fairies,' lobby within seconds of the news breaking? Anyway, how do you know I won't do a Nick Pope on all this and tell the world, the minute I'm home?'

Again he barely stopped to draw breath. 'I've got nothing to lose, remember. My job is gone. I'm already a laughing-stock. Somewhere, someone on the internet is going to believe me. Even though I'm an ex-copper, *I'm still a credible witness!*'

His eyes pricking with defiant tears, Watkin finally ran out of steam.

Violet had been through every emotion, from anger to pity, and still she did not know how to deal with this broken man. The signs were all there and none of them were good. He'd already shown an aptitude for drowning his sorrows in drink.

In all likelihood he would go down the same route as Jockey but, without D9 to save him, Watkin would become just another casualty of the ongoing war.

'It's all over the internet already, Suckerfish,' she said quietly, 'If it's not all about celebrities, the vast majority of people just aren't interested.   Add your stuff to it, say what you want. It won't make any difference.'

They spent the rest of the journey in silence.

49

'I'm not going without Dad!' Gnat wailed.

They stood in the deserted car park.   Face off. Gnat stared at Diamond and her companion.   Something buzzed in Gnat's ears.   No, not his ears.   He suddenly realised the insect-like skittering was happening *inside* his skull and chest, and he shuddered.

Diamond's companion was staring at him levelly, mouthing an incantation.   It didn't seem to be working. Gnat stood his ground.

The twilight, serene and blue, was overtaking what had been a glorious late summer sunset. The huge, red orb of the sun had slipped gently into its nightly cradle beneath the planet and the warmed earth exhaled rich, mossy breath into the cooling air.   The chalk chippings they stood upon glowed ghostly white in the fading blue of evening-tide.

'Don't you want to see your Mum?' Diamond whined.

'I do. And so does Dad!' Gnat replied stubbornly.

Diamond's companion turned to her, apparently negotiating, and Gnat held his breath.

He'd done his level best to delay whatever Diamond had in store for them, but closely guarded by the companion every second he was away from the campervan, Gnat had been unable to escape. He'd been unwilling to leave his Dad anyway.

After his third attempt at a prolonged toilet break, Diamond had finally snapped and lost her temper. Except Diamond's idea of snapping was more of a slow bend. She had subjected Gnat to a stultifying, boring speech of right-on-ness and self justification.

She had gone on and on about his opportunity and privilege, his heritage and his debt of honour to his peoples'. One side had been continually under attack of late, and he and his brother could sort everything out. Her whining tones grated on his nerves and depressed him beyond words. He would sooner have been shouted at, or even slapped about a bit. At least it would have been done and over with far more quickly.

His Dad had been totally quiet through every stop. In the rare glances he had shot in his Dad's direction, Gnat hadn't detected the faintest movement. Now Gnat was seriously worried about him.

'Okay!' Diamond's smile was honeyed with fake sincerity, 'I think it would be great if your Dad came too. Reunite the whole family that would!'

Gnat studied the chalky ground, anxious to appear that it was no big deal and he wasn't tense beyond belief waiting to see if his Dad was okay.

Diamond's companion slid the side door open and waited. Nothing happened.

Wide eyed, Gnat peered through the gathering darkness at his father's inert form. Only then did he become aware of the shapes that were approaching and encircling them. The low chatter of their insectlike voices and the delicate click of their wings was like a living river of sound as they slowly surged up the steep sides of the Iron Age hill fort.

Gnat could see a huge assembly gathered, waiting.

'*Rhys!*' Diamond shrieked, 'Stop playing silly beggars, and get here!'

Still nothing.

'Go in there and untie him.' Diamond moaned at her companion.

From the dark interior, something exploded into movement. Rhys shot from inside the campervan like a dark comet, grasped Gnat's hand and turned to run.

The creatures were on him in an instant.

Rhys found himself suddenly encased in air as heavy as treacle. Mystified, he turned to Gnat, but even the act of turning his head was a profound act of strength against some unseen, nightmarish resistance. Every limb weighted down by an invisible freight of metahominids, he sank to the floor and they held him there, face down.

'Let him go!' Gnat yelled. They looked to Diamond's companion, who nodded, and suddenly Rhys found he could get up.

He grabbed Gnat's hand, 'What's happening?'

'Dad, we're surrounded. By hundreds of them.'

Diamond cackled, 'You can only see 'em when they *choose* to show themselves. They ain't gonna do that for the likes of *him!*'

'Then they can do it for me!' Gnat demanded.

Before she could answer, he turned to address the assembly. 'You know me! I am your heir! A Prince of the Royal Bloodline. Show yourselves!' Gnat commanded regally, 'reveal yourselves to my father!'

Like lights suddenly blinking on, figures began to appear across the broad swathe of landscape. Above them the ancient, cut-chalk figure of the Uffington White Horse, its sweeping white outline glowing against the darkening landscape, began to disappear, obliterated by a sudden mass of condensing bodies.

Rhys clutched his son's hand and slowly turned to look at the multitude. A vast crowd of glittering beings stretched like an uneven sea, right down the valley and over the surreal, inverted basin shape of Dragon Hill.

The creatures exuded a soft, transparent light, so that even in semi-darkness, Rhys could clearly see individuals. As a human, Rhys was an object of distain. As Gnat's father, he was a focus of curiosity. Rhys stared and tens of thousands of eyes stared back. Diamond's companion motioned them to move and started up the hill. Hand in hand, Gnat and Rhys followed.

'Can't you just tell them to let us go?' Rhys said.

'Careful!' Gnat whispered urgently, 'I think they can read our thoughts!' Rhys glanced nervously around, Gnat continued quietly, 'I can ask them to let *you* go.'

'Not you, though?'

'No, I don't think so. They want me for something.'

Rhys gripped Gnat's hand fiercely and hissed vehemently, 'Then they'll just have to get used to the idea that you're not going anywhere without me! Yeah, I hope you all heard that!'

Within twenty minutes, they had gained the top of the hill and far below them, the flattened landscape stretched out like a great, dark map of fields and small settlements, half-hidden in the shifting grey mists. In the far distance, friendly lights of farmhouses twinkled, speaking of warmth and normality, of families settling down for the night, of fathers reading their children fairy stories. Rhys's breath caught in his throat. If only they knew what was going on up here.

He was ushered, with Gnat, to stand on the eye of the Horse. They stood, waiting, and Rhys could not help but let his mind wander. This was not the first time he had been here. He had visited Uffington when Diamond had taken him to a festival, The Big Green Gathering, one year. She had insisted they come up here. He'd watched a woman walking with a young black cat on a lead, and he'd stroked it.

Diamond had been talking to a girl. The girl hadn't seemed quite right somehow. She didn't like the cat, and wouldn't come near until the woman had led it away, down the hill. That had been the first time he had met Maeve. The words of an old poem came to him:

They took her lightly back, between the dawn and morrow...

A hush fell upon the chattering creatures and Rhys became aware of them parting like a slow wave. Someone was coming. Diamond rubbed her hands together with glee. For the first time, Rhys noticed his mother had swapped all her silver rings for gold ones.

Surrounded by an honour-guard of grey-clad archers, the approaching party made its way solemnly up the hill. Rhys craned his neck to see what was happening, but Gnat wasn't interested, he hung sullenly close by his father's protective side.

The greys glided to a halt and stood aside.

Then he saw her. His long-lost wife and, although he hated himself for being so weak, the breath caught again in Rhys' throat. Maeve approached in a haze of diaphanous, azure silks and scintillating leaf-green jewels. She solemnly regarded Gnat.

Gnat stared back in wonder. The mother he had so fervently wanted to find out about was... what was she? Gnat tried hard to fathom his own thoughts. Even more beautiful than her picture, she carried the preternatural youth of the faery folk.

She was, if anything, far better than the photograph of her in a plain blue dress. But there was a cold emptiness in that perfection. A missing dimension that he could not identify, but the lack of it went so deep it touched Gnat to the core. She smiled, but her timeless face was without anything as human as true emotion. Its empty coldness chilled him and he gave a little shiver.

He could see how shallow people would be taken

in by faery glamour, the photograph in his breast pocket suddenly felt clammy and unwanted against his skin. He looked at her again, the one being he had burnt to see and know, but her icy smile held no motherliness and little humanity and it made him feel ashamed that his father had been so easily fooled. From behind her, another form stepped forwards and Gnat found himself face to face with a boy so like him he gasped.

Beneath them, the very earth seemed to wake and tremble, as yet more battalions of his clansmen left their barrows and lined up to greet the half-bred boys who would be their twin kings.

Cayden wasn't quite identical. He was almost an inch taller than Gnat, paler and if anything, a little skinnier, but it would still have been hard to tell them apart. His twin approached Gnat who instinctively drew back. Then Cayden did a curious thing - he sniffed at Gnat's hair. Gnat froze and looked fearfully at his Dad, but he was staring at Maeve with a mixture of fascination and hatred.

Whilst the boys stared at one another, Diamond's companion rallied the watchers with a great whooping cry. From across the hillside they answered in a huge multi-tongued agreement. Something was being settled.

The creatures were restive, brandishing bows and other weapons and Gnat could plainly see they were preparing for war. He looked again at Cayden, who was surveying the massed ranks of warriors. Gnat stared at him and Cayden turned and spoke to him for the first time. He didn't move his lips, but the words formed clearly, not inside Gnat's head, just a foot or so away, like real speech.

'Now they have brought us together, the truth is, there's no stopping this. We are mere figureheads, not really needed. The gathering has gained its own momentum now. Vengeance will be meted out.'

Cayden's accent was strange and clipped.

'Then they can let us go?' Gnat asked.

Cayden shook his head, 'Where to? It's so easy when you are raised human, but where would I go?'

'Don't you want to stay with your -' Gnat caught himself, ' - *our* Mum?'

Cayden looked at her, she was watching Diamond's companion give his rallying speech to the assembly, uplifting their hearts, gearing their minds for the conflict to come. Cayden turned away from his mother, his huge eyes dark with troubled thoughts.

'Nathan, I have always wanted to be you.'

Fear gripped Gnat's heart. If Cayden was to be swapped for him, would anyone notice? He looked up at his Dad, but he was fixated upon Maeve. Surely his Dad would notice the difference?

Still staring at his wife, as if in answer, Rhys gave Gnat's hand a small squeeze. It was enough to encourage Gnat to venture to his twin, 'Come with us. We're going to get away.'

'From all this?' Cayden's whispering voice was all but lost in the sudden clamour of a huge cheer. The crowds were hanging onto every word the companion was uttering. Gnat slowly turned and looked around the vast assembly, Cayden was right, there would be no chance of escape.

'Who is that?' Gnat asked, nodding towards Diamond's strange, speechmaking companion.

'Thyllym. Our cousin. The dying King's son.'

'Doesn't he hate us for stealing his crown?'

'It was never his, for we are the Sistersons,' Cayden's voice took a deeper tone, 'but he doesn't like us.'

'We're like the Princes in the Tower.'

Gnat shuddered.

'What?'

'The nephews of Richard III? Oh, it's a made up story… from human… our history.' Gnat shrugged lamely, embarrassed he'd used the word 'human,' to his more alien-looking brother.

Thyllym vented a long ululating cry and clear across the valley a hundred thousand voices answered him. Turning, he approached Gnat and Cayden and bowed low, his eyes anything but obsequious.

Maeve slipped her arm though Rhys's. The shock of the contact sent his heart tumbling and fluttering, like a trapped bird behind the cage of his ribs. It was all he could do not to faint.

In that instant, he was parted from Gnat.

Gnat found himself thrust, with Cayden, into the only bit of clear ground. The grey guard formed around them and before he could turn back to see his Dad, they were on the move again, back down the slope.

At the bottom of the hill, the old campervan stood, looking faintly ridiculous, in the car park, an incongruous backdrop to the multitude of extraordinary beings that steadily moved past its gaudily painted flowers, butterflies, and toadstools.

Gnat managed to glimpse his father's pale face. His mother was clinging to him, saying things Gnat could not hear and, to his horror, he could see his Dad was openly weeping as he walked.

Diamond reached her campervan. It seemed this was going to be the parting of the ways. As she pulled open the door, it gave a harsh metallic squeal. Then Gnat was aware of a flurry of movement. There was a sudden explosion of water where his Mum had been, his Dad ran two steps and fell screaming, then with screeching tyres, a car hurtled out of the darkness and slammed into the campervan. In an instant, the air was full of arrows that skittered off the car like hail.

Gnat threw himself upon his father's fallen body. 'Dad!' he wailed. Hands dragged him back, but Gnat clung to his father. Cayden slipped away and was bodily pulled into the car by the driver. The car was being rocked as they attacked it.

Inside Jockey shouted at Cayden, 'Hang on Gnat!'

Terrified, Cayden pawed at the windows with his pale fingers, like an anxious dog. He didn't have a clue how car doors worked. He banged on the glass and screamed across all frequencies. The noise made Jockey feel physically sick.

'What the hell have they done to you?' he asked, hanging on to the steering wheel of the wildly bucking car. Surely it would be tipped right over soon? He had kept the engine running, but couldn't push through the mass of bodies. Without his goggles the eeriness of an invisible attack was terrifying enough, with them, he would have seen just how far he'd underestimated what he'd be up against, when he'd foolishly decided to fly solo. He'd brought some silver spray, but he didn't dare open a window to deploy it.

Long, spindly fingers were beginning to exploit every loose part of the vehicle. He'd lost both wing mirrors and a number plate. Now they were working on the lights.

Gnat crouched over his Dad. He had to get him to the car, but it was too far… then maybe he could get him to the campervan? His Dad was heavy. Gnat pulled at one arm, but it was no use. Then Diamond was there.

'We've got to get him into the van!' Gnat screamed

over the clamour. Stricken, Diamond nodded and helped Gnat carry Rhys the few steps to the van. From inside his car, Jockey spotted them.

'What the…?' He shot a furious glance at Cayden, 'So ye're a scumbag changeling?' He sprayed the silver at Cayden, who screamed again. But he didn't die. He didn't fall screaming into a sudden rush of liquid. Red blisters rising on his skin, he stared back at Jockey with a look of utter hurt and shocked bewilderment.

'Okay,' Jockey said shocked, 'so ye're not a changeling. Which one is Gnat?' Cayden pointed at the boy labouring to drag Rhys inside the van. Jockey hit the horn, and the car fell back heavily, rocking on its springs. The relief lasted a split-second, as instantly, they were upon it again. He quickly dragged a pair of goggles from the glove box and put them on. Now he could finally see what he was up against. Mouthing curses, he took a canister from out of a small case, armed it and simultaneously dropped the window as he hit the horn again. He hurled the canister out of the window and hit the 'close,' button.

The window rose agonisingly slowly, as a fusillade of arrows hit the glass. Four came into the car. One hit him on his gloved hand and Jockey felt it pierce his skin.

He whipped off his glove and before it got a chance to burrow any deeper, clamped his teeth around the affected area of skin. He could feel the arrow head moving, nosing and probing for a way out, like a mouse held in cupped hands.

Jockey pinpointed the exact spot it had entered, and trapped it with his teeth. There was nothing else for it. Jockey bit harder until his teeth came into contact with the hard piece of flint. Squeezing his eyes hard shut, he bit through his own flesh and spat out blood, tissue, and the vicious arrowhead. Then he quickly pulled his glove back on, to stem the rush of blood.

Outside the car, the canister had created a small clearing, but Jockey had wasted precious time dealing with his injury. He could see Gnat and Diamond tending Rhys in the back of the van. Assuming his own car wasn't rolled, he had to get Gnat to safety. He armed another canister, then another. He hadn't a clue what he was going to do next.

'My mother is dead. My father killed her. He is hurt. He is dying.' The boy in the back spoke in a strange clipped voice. 'They will take my brother. Let me go from this place.'

'You can't go out there, they'll shoot you.'

'They'll shoot *you*, not me.' Cayden insisted quietly.

Jockey thought for a second. He had absolutely no escape plan. Against his better judgement, he touched a button and with a low click the doors unlocked. The boy sat waiting until Jockey realised he had to show Cayden how to open the door. Twisting in his seat he pulled on the lever. The door opened and Cayden slipped out into the clearing.

Breathlessly, Jockey watched as the beings quietly fell back, their full attention upon the boy. He approached a tall arboreal who appeared to be some kind of leader. They both approached Gnat and some kind of discussion appeared to be going on.

Gnat tearfully agreed something, then nodded and called Diamond over. She listened, nodded and then crossed back to her van. Slowly she dragged Rhys from her campervan and hauled him to Jockey's car. As he was in no hurry to get out and help her, Diamond motioned Jockey to lower the window. He shook his head.

'Do this and you live,' she shouted through the glass.

Reluctantly, Jockey lowered the window.

'If you take him you can go,' she indicated Rhys, 'free passage out of here for both of you.'

'My Dad needs to go to hospital!' Gnat wailed in the distance.

Jockey fixed his eyes on Diamond and quietly clicked open his door. He cautiously circled the car and lifted Rhys's lifeless body into the back. Almost without daring to breathe, he made his way back to the driver's seat and got back in.

'Now go and don't look back,' Diamond cautioned fiercely, 'you've done real harm here tonight. I only want peace!'

It took every ounce of Jockey's self composure not to punch the old hag in the face, let rip with the remaining canisters and drag Gnat back into the car. But he knew when he was beaten. Outnumbered, he would only succeed in getting himself killed, then Rhys would be left to die an agonising death and without a witness, Gnat would be lost forever.

Jockey was keenly aware that he was more than fortunate in not being killed anyway. His throbbing hand was a reminder if he needed one. Now time was running out. He had to help Rhys.

Swearing softly, he pulled out of the car park and drove like a demon away from the White Horse at Uffington. Maybe he could save Rhys. For now, at least, he knew he couldn't save Gnat.

50

It has often been said that the trick to busking is finding the one, right song that can be played repeatedly, without giving torture to either the player or the listeners. For Yelena and Maria it was a deceptively tricky little tune by JS Bach, from his Partita number three.

Yelena lifted her violin, Maria, from her case and rescued the shoulder rest from under her elegant neck. As Yelena rosined and tightened her bow, she looked out across the platform and made the last fine adjustments.

The trick to busking on the London Underground is to find a place where music can be heard above the rumbling of the trains, yet is close enough to waylay the scurrying commuters without being helplessly swept away by the tidal crowd. Yelena had been displaced from her more regular, favourite spot and Baker Street was unknown territory to her. She wasn't at all sure what her reception would be like, either from the station staff or the commuters, but she had her hard-won licence to fend off the former, plus all the usual student debts as motivation for contending with the latter. She knew she was good and that talent-spotters had been known to haunt the tube. Until she was discovered, at least busking was helping Yelena keep her head above water.

Unaware there were no official busking spots at Baker Street, she had chosen it simply because it was such a large station. She made her way down to the lower concourse, but it didn't look promising. A young man was crouched over a semi-acoustic guitar. He would have drowned out all her best efforts. She didn't see that he was packing his guitar away, having been told to go by station officials. A simple matter of mistiming saw her take a second escalator down into the depths of Baker Street, to platform eight, the old Bakerloo line. This was the line that had seen the demise of its creator, the silver millionaire Whitaker Wright: enemy of many, including his Surrey neighbour Sir Arthur Conan Doyle.

Not knowing the layout of the station, Yelena was disheartened to see that there wasn't that much space at the foot of the escalators. Sighing, she decided to go, but then she stopped herself. She had bills to pay.

Her mother's stubborn resolve had seen her through far worse situations in Srebrenica than that of a little musical opposition and a compromised busking pitch. Chiding herself, Yelena chose a spot on the narrow reservation, between platforms seven and eight.

Finally, she set her bow against Maria's strings. The opening notes of the Gavotte en Rondeau lifted into the air, perfectly balanced, crisp and sweet. Like fine wine for the ears. The light and lilting music danced far from its creator. Threading its way gently through the tunnels, it penetrated deep into the dark recesses. It tiptoed *en pointe* between sleeping figures, roosting batlike, deep within the earth. Delicate, pointed ears flicked, limbs bestirred and slowly the sleepers began to gently awaken.

En-route to a recording session with the rest of the orchestra, September was in danger of running late. Vasily was probably the most critical conductor September had ever worked under, and the thought of not being on time and having him throwing one of his quiet, but deeply

415

sarcastic, fits made September nervous. He scurried across Marylebone Road, past the Rath-bony statue of Sherlock Holmes and entered the assault course that was Baker Street Underground station.

His violin would be waiting for him at the studios, so September was unencumbered for once. He ran across the smooth wide floors, past the shops, between the pillars, through the gate, hopped past more patient travellers on the first escalator, skirted the lower concourse, swept down the second escalator and emerged breathless onto the Bakerloo platform.

Even in his hurry, his trained ear caught the notes of the Gavotte en Rondeau and he immediately appreciated that the young girl playing it was giving a faultless performance. Spirits lifted, he caught his breath and smiling, dropped a handful of change into her open violin case then, without a second to spare, he hopped lightly onto the waiting train.

Before he sat down, September dug into a deep pocket of his oversized raincoat and brought out a small, cylindrical parcel that had been waiting for him for days in his pigeonhole at work. Sitting, he turned it over in his slender fingers before ripping it open. It was from D and it contained a natty pair of retro-looking sunglasses.

He'd wanted a scope like Jockey's, but had to admit drilling holes in a Stradivarius to mount the thing was probably not a good idea, so he'd had to content himself with these as an alternative. Pale ivory butter frames with large dark lenses, they looked like they'd been designed for the baddie with the cod Germanic accent in an old black and white movie. Around him, people started murmuring. September surfaced from his reverie and glanced up. What was going on?

The train stood waiting, its doors still open, long after it should have moved off. The notes of Yelena's violin floated along the platform, she had elegantly negotiated the polyphonic sections and was on the home stretch. September glanced down at his watch and tutted.

He became aware of a skittering noise on the train roof. He looked out of the window. There was no dark side here, just a brightly lit curved, tiled wall. The train fitted its single track snugly. He stood and peered out of the open door, into the gloom of the tunnel ahead. A strange, smoke-like dust hung in the air and there was some kind of indistinct movement going on in the midst of it. Instinctively, September put the glasses on and peered out.

Recoiling in horror, he scrambled back screaming, 'Stop! Stop!'

At that moment the doors hissed closed. The girl with the violin was proving irresistible to the metas. She was drawing them inexorably from some huge, central roost. Thousands of them.

The train lurched forwards.

Yelena looked up from her playing and spotted the crazy man on the train. The same one who had cast a shower of coins at her. He'd seemed nice and smiley then. Now he looked demented, he was screaming, the long palms of his hands hammering against the glass door.

'Nutty nutter!' she mused aloud. Still, she was grateful for his money. Turning her back to the platform, Yelena kept playing.

51

Jockey hammered on the door frantically. He'd tried to ring ahead, but had been met by squealing, crackling static. Every number he'd tried had failed. At last, the metas were on the march, and he'd been unable to contact D to warn him.

Jockey waited in agonised silence, straining his ears to detect the faintest sounds of movement inside the house. He winced as a salvo of hailstones scattered against the brass plaque that announced this to be the dwelling and business place of James Jarvis MRCVS.

A cold sting struck Jockey's neck. He shuddered, but for once it was nothing more than hail Just as he became aware of the scuffling of slippered feet, the glossy, black door opened and Jim stood there. Pushing back his incongruously youthful fringe of blonde hair away from his bronzed, weather-beaten face, he filled the doorway, his tall form towering above Jockey.

'I tried to ring…' Jockey began, but Jim was already out of the house and striding towards the car.

'Still alive?' Jim barked in his best Sandhurst manner. Jockey managed to stammer a 'Yes.' He respected Jim Jarvis, but even though he must now be in his late sixties, there was something about the man that always reduced Jockey to a blithering raw recruit.

'How many hits? When? Where on him, *or her*?'

'One, I think. About forty minutes ago. His back.' Jockey had to resist adding a smart salute accompanied, by a foot stamp and a clipped, 'Sah!'

As Jim hauled him out of the car, Rhys gave a low moan. He had a high fever and his lips were beginning to show blue. Big Jim Jarvis hefted Rhys into his arms and carried him like a small child back into his house. Jockey jogged after them.

Deep inside the warren of Jim's veterinary practice rooms, Jim kicked open a door and laid Rhys down on one of the larger examination tables.

Jockey helped Jim turn him over.

'Not elfshot. Poisoned blade. Nasty.'

'Will he make it?'

Jim shrugged unwilling to say. Jockey watched. as Jim injected Rhys with adrenaline and flushed out the neat puncture mark on Rhys's lower back with a weak silver solution.

Allegra, Jim's perfect army wife, elegant in cropped pyjamas and silk dressing gown, floated in with a tray of coffee. Through their forty-three years together she had seen a lot, and handled everything with a unique grace.

'Oh dear!' She exclaimed at Rhys's damaged back, completely unfazed.

'Jockey! Darling, so lovely to see you! Would you care for a sandwich?'

He hesitated, he was ravenous as he hadn't eaten all day, but somehow the idea of sandwiches in the midst of all this trouble was faintly ridiculous.

'Now, don't be polite,' Allegra chided gently, 'there's some absolutely gorgeous Wiltshire ham and a wonderful mustard, and some chutney from the Farmers Market! Now *don't* let me down!'

Jockey nodded gratefully.

'Might as well make myself useful and have some excitement, eh?' Allegra grinned conspiratorially, 'wretched telly's been off all night!'

Jockey's blood ran cold. As Allegra headed off to the kitchen, humming an approximation of a Gary Barlow tune, Jockey turned to Jim, 'What if they're jamming everything? TV, mobiles, everything?'

Jim cocked his head to one side, considering. He was deftly sewing up the wound in Rhys's flesh, 'They're not capable of anything like that. Metas simply don't have that kind of kit.'

'But what if it wasn't down to any kind of a device?'

'Meaning?'

'They're on the move Jim. A multitude of them. What if the sheer weight of their numbers was enough to create some kind of an energy field?'

Jim deliberated for a moment before admitting, 'I see what you mean. Single ones drive EMF meters bonkers. Enough of them might be able to broadcast some kind of an effect. But the scale would be extraordinary, the numbers would have to be biblical!'

'A crowd so big even Cecil B DeMille would baulk at it?' Jockey sighed nodding, 'Aye. We've just been tangled up in one like that.'

Jim set up an old army camp bed and gently lifted Rhys onto it. Perfectly choreographed, Allegra came in with a quilt and Jockey's sandwiches. She thrust the plate at Jockey before turning and tenderly spreading the warm quilt over Rhys. 'Poor darling, who is he?'

'Rhys Greville,' Jockey said. Allegra nodded, none the wiser. Jockey took a huge bite of his sandwich and chewed for a moment before adding, 'His son's half meta.'

'What! This man is in collusion with the enemy?' Allegra was aghast. 'Far from it. He's as much a victim as…' Jockey faltered and finished quickly, 'any of us.'

He turned back to his sandwich and continued eating, stuffing down the sudden, stark emotions that threatened to bubble up and engulf him. Allegra touched Jockey's arm, a sorrowful look on her face. She was well acquainted with Jockey's troubled past.

'Poor man,' she was looking down at Rhys, but she squeezed Jockey's arm.

Satisfied Rhys was as comfortable as he could make him, Jim turned to Jockey and demanded, 'Where's D?'

'Let him eat for pity's sake, James!' Allegra insisted.

Jockey swallowed hard and gave a thumbs up, 'It's okay, Allegra. D was in Wales, last time I heard. Getting supplies from Aled and Andrea.'

Jim nodded, Jockey went on, 'as Quartermaster it should have been my job, but we've had a run on ammo of late, and we're so short of cash he had to plead for time to pay, and he wanted to ask them personally. He should be on his way home by now.'

'And the metas? Where do you think they were headed?'

'Couldn't say, I just got the hell out of there.'

Jim fixed him with his fiercely intelligent gaze, 'Best guess?'

Jockey shrugged. 'The obvious place would be London. "Seat of power"… and all that.'

'So we are potentially looking at a huge coming-together of the cultures? D's missing and you've got limited arms?'

Jockey nodded and Allegra slipped out of the room.

'Their mood is warlike?'

'Yeah, you could say that. Just a tad. They've been properly stirred up.'

Jim sat in his captain's chair and carefully deliberated before delivering his verdict, 'Then we haven't got a snowball's chance in hell.'

He looked down at his pyjamas, 'Better change.'

He rose quickly and left the room, standing aside as Allegra shuffled back in with an enormous holdall and a picnic hamper.

'There's leek and potato soup in one flask, and coffee in the other. I've packed cheese scones, a couple of pork pies and more sandwiches. There's some lovely cold lamb if you're sick of ham, Jockey, and half of Mabel's very best Dundee cake.'

She countered Jockey's amazed look with, 'An army marches on its stomach!' She dumped the holdall in front of him, with a clangorous crash.

'Is that the family silver?' Jockey joked.

'Well, you're got to have something to fight those dratted pests with haven't you?' Allegra stated flatly. That floored Jockey. He just stood staring at the bulging holdall.

'This was Mother's,' Allegra pulled out an elegant gallery tray, 'I don't know what you'd do with it? Swat them I suppose?'

Allegra hopped about, wafting the tray around in an alarmingly aggressive manner, just as Jim reappeared, dressed in his country vet uniform of tweed jacket and corduroy trousers. Jockey had half-expected to see James Jarvis in full battle fatigues.

'Whoa there, Boadicea!'

Allegra gave a mock pout, winked wickedly at Jockey and dropped the tray back in the bag, whilst Jim gathered phials of silver solution and cast them in on top of the assorted silverware in the holdall.

'Come on man, stop staring and stir your stumps! Allegra, there's no need to be covert, if our guest takes a turn for the worst, you'll just have to call an ambulance. All secrecy will be shot after tonight anyway.'

He grabbed his wife and hugged her fiercely. Jockey looked away.

'Goodbye, my darling,' Jim said, breaking their embrace, 'I'll see you in the morning.'

Jockey smiled, waved Allegra a shy goodbye, picked up the hamper and shouldered the bulky bag of silverware.

She crossed the room and gave Jockey a warm hug. 'Look after him, silly old fool that he is,' she whispered.

Allegra stood, waving them goodbye on the

doorstep, stoic in her acceptance that she was unlikely to ever see her husband alive again.

52

When Gnat had been little, he'd been really, *really* ill. So ill, his Dad had taken him to see a doctor and that was something Dad never did. Except this had been a special doctor, a lady called Prateeka.

Now, carried along in the misery of the moment, Gnat felt that ill again. Like a fever, words kept coming into his mind, buzzing and humming and *bothering* him. He shivered and sweated and threw off the blankets. Diamond's old van stank of oil now and he felt sick. Gnat turned to the cold, metal wall and closed his eyes, waiting for his mind to clear, but it didn't. The buzzing and humming of half-heard words just kept scurrying through his mind like a pack of rats, nibbling at the edges of his sanity. There would be no rest, no break.

There was no fever to break. It just felt like one.

Gnat opened his eyes and leaned across to pull aside

427

the mildewed curtain. He stared out at the convoy. All around Diamond's van, the people from the hill were riding cars, coaches and lorries. Some flew above the horde, and others dropped down and jumped from vehicle to vehicle. They crawled and swarmed like an army of terrible insects, but the drivers didn't even seem to notice, they drove straight on, without the slightest tremor, when a fairy landed or lifted. The unwanted passengers were invisible.

Gnat looked up. Like a low bank of storm cloud, the sky was dark with a black gleaming rainbow of metas. When the sun struck their wings, they gleamed and shot dark auras, like black bismuth crystals. When he looked up, they always looked down at him, mesmerising Gnat with their dark fairy glamour.

Somewhere out there amongst them was Cayden. His twin had learnt the art of moving with mecurial speed like them. Gnat had not and was stuck with Diamond's stuffy van for now. Compared to his brother, he felt inadequate, useless. Gnat sighed and suddenly understood what the *spring frets*, the pure desire for movement that he'd suffered all his short life, were all about. His body had been urging him to jump and run and spin around in ways that he hadn't been aware that he actually could.

Gnat let the curtain drop and lay back. He didn't understand what was happening to him, but he knew that simply by meeting these people, he had changed. Thoughts of his Dad rose but he squashed them down. He would not think about him, or normal stuff. It was as if they held his mind, as well as his body, captive, and he knew that regret and longing only made the whispering humming far, far worse.

It didn't even matter that today was his twelfth birthday. Nothing mattered any more. They were on the move, an invisible force streaming down the motorway. The air was thick with them, their energy making every car radio crackle ominously. Satnavs lost their voices and mobiles failed as the army rode and flew towards the capital, gathering fresh followers from every open piece of countryside as they passed.

Like an approaching electrical storm, the combined static from the friction of their wings made hair stand on end and raised goose-pimples on human flesh. Car-bound dogs whined and fretted, eyeing the skies nervously, sensitive people felt waves of nausea but didn't know why, and those with faint traces of arboreal in their bloodlines felt strangely restless and discomforted.

On a converging northern road, even as he crossed the border from Wales back into England, D could feel the stirring. A sudden sense of oppression that was so strong, it had almost knocked the breath from his body and had left him gasping.

The old Saab carried every piece of silver Aled and Andrea had been able to spare. D knew with absolute certainty that this was a rising beyond anything D9 had so far encountered and whatever they had to throw at the enemy, it would not be enough. He felt sick. Nervous, stress-induced blisters were rising on his skin and he clung onto the steering wheel in a state of extreme agitation.

All the signs had been there, the extra sightings, the incident at Kew and the gathering in the tunnels. Gnat's coming-of-age in metahominid terms would also be a factor, but not enough to explain what had stirred them up in the first place. Whatever the reason might be for the onslaught, it didn't really matter now. D had failed. His troops were scattered and unarmed, just when they were most needed.

'See that?' Red faced with outrage, Brendan flicked a thumb at the fuel gauge, 'you *never* get what they reckon. Officially, this thing does forty-eight to the gallon. *Officially,* my elbow!'

Bredan snorted. Maz unfolded her arms, and stared out of the window, whilst she picked tiny wads of soggy crisp from her fillings. Twenty minutes into their trip and he was already off on one. Another three hours of Brendan's affronted, petrol-themed lament lay ahead, just waiting to be topped off by the inevitable, cataclysmic putting-up-the-tent row. An invisible payload of metahominids jumped from the side of a large truck onto Brendan's roof-rack, joining those already there and settled themselves comfortably amongst the soft lumps of the badly-packed tent.

'Look at it!' Brendan howled as the needle on the petrol gauge dipped even further, 'and we're not even going up a hill! The *money* this is costing.... I'm telling you, this old heap has *got* to go!'

Maz folded her arms and glowered, she knew which old heap she'd like to dump at the scrap yard. She glared at Brendan's outraged, scarlet profile. If they were married, she'd divorce him.

By complete contrast, Anil and Parveeta were driving along in a bubble of pure happiness, blissfully singing one of the old songs. Their youngest, Javed had passed the last of his exams and they were finally beginning to feel free again. Far from suffering the bittersweet sadness of becoming 'empty nesters,' they sang their hearts out like a pair of dippy teenagers.

Anil had always seen to it that their vehicle was 'ethnically neutral.' Despising the nodding deities, bells and other paraphernalia his father's car had accumulated, he had always stubbornly resisted hanging similar charms and good luck tokens in their car, but Parveeta had insisted on one tiny token.

Thanks to her, a tiny solid silver figurine of the affable and magnanimous Ganesh stood proudly on the nose of the car, right on top of the Mercedes badge.

As they sang, as usual Anil was getting the words completely wrong, mostly on purpose, just to hear her squeal and laugh at him.

'No, that's not right!' She began, but a sudden impact cut off her words. Parveeta's laughing eyes gaped wide with sudden fear and she screamed and hid her face. Something splatted across the windscreen, spraying liquid. Anil swerved and overcompensated, threatening to clip the car in the next lane. Somehow he managed to avoid a collision, only for the car to be impacted by another thud, and another splash of water. What the hell? He flicked on the windscreen wipers.

'Parveeta!' he screamed, 'can you believe it! Some damn idiot is throwing water balloons at us!' He darted a glance at her, 'Help me!' He pleaded, 'uncover your eyes, try to see who is doing this!'

As another juddering impact rocked their car, Parveeta reluctantly opened her eyes, dreading what she would see.

'I thought we hit someone!' she wailed, 'I thought there would be blood all over the glass!' Anil stared at the wipers, gathering and ejecting nothing but pure, clear water from the windscreen. Two more bucketfuls hit them head on. There were no bridges on this stretch of the motorway, they were not being water-bombed from above.

'It must be coming from the car in front, Anil!' Parveeta shouted, shifting in her seat, trying to see above and beyond the now regular inundations of liquid.

What *was* that? Parveeta leaned forwards in her seat, and squinted into the deluge. There it was again! She was sure there had been something in that last explosion of water. Something like a skinny arm, flung up from down by the radiator grille.

433

Dolls?

Was someone playing an elaborate trick upon them?

She tugged at her sari, arranging it defensively like a monk's cowl around her head. This was not good. Someone had singled them out for a silly trick. Now the school ground taunts of years ago came back to her, harsh words of hatred, used against a small, defenceless child.

Tears welled in her eyes, 'Stop Anil, pull over. Let them go!'

The agony in her voice snapped Anil out of his chase response. All thoughts of confrontation and retribution snapped and shattered with one look at his wife's agonised face. Humbled, he slowed and steered onto the hard shoulder. Coasting to a gentle halt, he took her hand and gently kissed it. He kept his tears at bay by staring straight ahead, as did Parveeta. The car was still rolling slowly and they clearly saw the shocked arboreal materialise as Ganesh's deadly silver sliced through the strange creature's body.

Bewildered, they leaned forwards as one and peered through the steam rising from the radiator grille. Dripping, the car came to a gentle halt. Anil made to get out, but

Parveeta's restraining hand on his sleeve delayed him until she had unbuckled her own seat belt. They were a team, they would exit the car and face this thing, together.

A moment later, the couple stood on the hard shoulder, buffeted by the slipstream of the passing traffic, with Parveeta's pink sari billowing in the torrent of dusty air. Before them Anil's gleaming Merc still dripped water, but there was something sticking out of the front of it.

Anil knelt and stared at the thing. The air vents on the front had harvested a bizarre souvenir from this very strange encounter. Dwarfing the accumulated bug splatter on the number plate, an enormous insect wing stuck out brokenly below the three cornered star badge, its curious beauty challenged Anil's belief in what he was seeing.

It looked like they'd hammered into the biggest dragonfly ever. Anil stretched out his hand to pull at the wing, but Parveeta gave a little cry of alarm and dashed his hand away. She took a few steps across the hard shoulder, towards the wooded embankment and pulled a whip-like branch from the dusty hedge. She solemnly handed it to Anil, who poked it at the wing, dislodging it from the vents.

Muttering her deepest thanks to Ganesh for protecting them from this unnatural entity, Parveeta herded her bewildered husband back into the car.

Then she did what she always did in a crisis, she fed them. With great solemnity, Parveeta broke out the food she had brought, and they ate in silence. After half an hour, Anil hazarded a slow creep along the hard shoulder. There were no more impacts, there was no more water. Barely fifteen minutes later, he joined the slip road and with a growing sense of relief, left the motorway and the unseen river of metahominids pouring into London.

53

The sickening dizziness rising within him reminded Gnat of how he'd felt one time when he'd wandered onto a cliff top path. The crashing waves far beneath him had exerted a fierce magnetic pull, irresistibly inviting him to gently step off the solid, rocky path. It took all his resistance to fight it, he knew he would tumble head over heels through the empty air for a few seconds of free flight, before being dashed to his death on the rocks below, but the siren call of the high place and deep water was so strong it almost made him jump. Standing safely on the path, he felt anything but safe. He could already sense the roaring wind rushing past his ears and it had taken all his concentration for him to keep his feet rooted firmly upon the solid earth.

Now Gnat wondered, if he *had* stepped off that narrow rocky ledge, would he have been able to fly?

Wordlessly, he crept from the bed in the back of the van and clambered over the seat into the front. Diamond nodded but said nothing.

He looked up again at the dark hordes as they raced across the skies and the same fatal magnetism seemed to be pulling at him. Only this time it drew him *upwards*, not down. They were compelling him to swoop up, to fulfil his destiny, to merge with the hive. Resist as he might, Gnat could feel their intrusive thoughts harrying him like a pack of hyenas. Bit by bit, they carried off great, invisible chunks of him, robbing him of his free will and stripping away vast swathes of memory. Everything that made him human was being destroyed as they absorbed him into themselves and slowly, Gnat the amateur bug-hunter, began to understand what it must be like to be an ant or a bee.

It was the ultimate sensation of safety in numbers. Without any sense of personal identity, need or peril, he felt himself begin to enlarge and dissipate. Boundlessly reaching from organism to organism, his body felt like it stretched for miles. His eyes could see further and his ears hear more clearly than they had ever done before. He reached far ahead of his own small, limited form trapped in the metal box on wheels and saw what those high up in the storm-front of the swarm were seeing. Fields and towns swept past beneath him, cattle looked up, people did not.

Then he diminished down again and with eyes grown black with sudden seeing, Gnat stared across the cab at Crazy Diamond.

Beneath contempt, she had reduced a full force of nature, a free and proud life-form, to a whimsical notion of sugary-sweet little helpers of mankind. Gnat's kin had as little need for her contact and approval as any wild creature would.

Feeling his gaze upon her, Diamond turned her eyes from the road and looked at Gnat. She screamed and the van swerved violently. In that split-second, she had seen her grandson was no longer human. Howling, she wrestled with the wheel as Gnat's black eyes narrowed in an insincere smile. With an insectlike skitter, he flung his bony body out of the open passenger window and crawled spiderlike up onto the roof of the campervan.

Diamond regained control of her vehicle and she peered cautiously upwards. Gnat's skinny legs dangled down from the roof, his heels pressed hard against the windscreen.

Diane Timms had courted occult phenomena all her life. She had prided herself on her abilities to sense auras and see angels and fairies. When she'd first had her son, Rhys, she'd told anyone who'd listen how he was an *'Indigo Child,'* born for greatness. She continued telling this story even after he had run away from his destiny - and her - to take up a variety of ever-changing, dead-end jobs. Now, as she saw the reality of her meddling wish for a fairy-child within the family, she felt unaccountably afraid. There had been something so inhuman in Gnat's huge eyes and his movements had been so batlike and creepy, it made her shudder. Gnat had changed forever and Diamond could not quell her sudden sense of growing dread.

Unable to stop or go back, compelled to drive on, she clung to the wheel. Rocking gently and weeping openly, she murmured the Tibetan mantra of compassion, *'Om mane padme hum.'* If she were to die this day, at least her eternal spirit would be prepared for its next incarnation.

Up on the roof of the old campervan, Gnat settled

himself amongst the metas. Grinning, they accepted him as a welcome, if exotic guest. Gnat looked at those huddling around him. He now found he could easily distinguish between the clans and tribes of each of the main species.

The more accepting, younger ones had gravitated towards the campervan that bore a future, if half-blood, king. Now they were thrilled he had come out to join them.

Gnat threw his head back and laughed with glee at the rush of the wind. The sense of anticipation was palpable. Old scores with the enemy were about to be settled, and just now it didn't really matter that the enemy were as much his kin as the ones that surrounded him.

He watched in fascination as they hopped lightly from vehicle to vehicle. A large supermarket lorry drifted up alongside and Gnat waved cheekily at the driver. The man stared back in abject horror.

It hadn't occurred to Gnat that what he was doing simply wasn't normal. He felt safe in amongst the mass of bodies, all travelling like so many extra passengers on the roof of a train in India. All any other driver saw was a lone boy, riding on the roof of a crazy old campervan as it careered at breakneck speed down the motorway, but the majority of them were far too busy grimly wrestling for control of their own suddenly, wildly misbehaving vehicles, to have time to worry about anyone else.

The lorry driver attempted to radio what he'd seen to the police, but his call failed. Annoyed, he cautiously pulled ahead of Diamond's van. When the inevitable happened and that crazy kid fell off, he really didn't want to be the first one to run him over.

As he drew level, the driver couldn't help but gaze across again. The boy's balance was breathtaking. There couldn't be much to hang onto, yet the kid was perfectly poised, with all the strength and bearing of an athlete…. Unless there was a hidden rig…? Suddenly, the lorry driver began to feel very sheepish. It must be a stunt. There was plenty of room for a hidden camera, if not an entire team of cameramen, in the back of that campervan.

He pulled in behind the van again, faintly disgusted at his own gullibility. Oh no…. they'd even got him to try and call the police! Pulling a rueful face, he shook his head, and turned his attention to the old dear in the nice, new but tiny, red car who obviously didn't know how to drive it. She was all over the place. If she carried on like that, he felt sure she was going to hit someone. He sighed, hoping it wouldn't be him.

As Gnat regarded a fellow passenger, a light-green skinned child, a name sprang to his mind 'Neave.' Once again, he remembered the walk towards the looming green hillside, only this time it wasn't so scary. Now he felt like he'd missed a real chance, an opportunity to go home. He could have met his mother sooner and spent some precious time with her.

Gnat grew sombre. Although he couldn't mourn someone he'd never known, he regretted all the lost opportunities for contact.

Personal peril, or individuality, was no longer an issue, but he began to feel a grievous sense of wrong. Vengeful anger thrilled through his veins and he understood harm had been done to them all, and it must stop. Goaded beyond bearing, his kin were swarming to confront their implacable enemy. Somehow, he knew that even now, water-beings were gathering around the shores, preparing to swim upstream to the great barrow of the humans on the southern river.

With a shock, Gnat realised they comprehended humankind as a single entity like themselves, many individuals driven by a single purpose. The head of this great dragon-kin lay on the great southern river and they were now engaged in full battle-quest to confront and kill the beast. If they attacked the great barrow of man, it would kill all of him.

Another signpost for London hurtled past.

That their concept of humanity should be so alien jolted Gnat, it blocked his further absorption into them. Disengaging a little, his mind snapped back and recovered some of its lost wholeness. Only now, considering himself an individual felt as strangely otherworldly and unfamiliar as being in the hive-mind had. He glanced down at his own skinny hands.

Colours shone back up at him. Not the glorious, pearlescent rainbow blush of metahominid flesh, but primitive comic-book colours where traces of a semi washed-off superheroes transfer still clung to the back of his left hand. A simple reminder of another world, but it brought him back to himself. If those surrounding him felt any change, they didn't register anything. Gnat somehow comprehended that they had already accepted that part of him would always be human.

He caught the level gaze of a boy with blue veined skin, who nodded at him, whilst pulling a grey hood over his white blonde hair. Gnat saw he carried a fine, white wood bow, and a quiver of slender, reed-like arrows. The boy beckoned and Gnat scooted across the roof to him. The boy handed an arrow across. Gnat took it and turned it over in his fingers. It was pale, slim and pliant, but apart from a gentle taper, it appeared to have no barb. Gnat tapped his forefinger on the tip where the arrowhead should have been and frowned, this thing would barely punch its way through a wet paper bag.

The youngster caught Gnat's questioning look and grinned. Opening a green silk pouch on the side of his belt, he invited Gnat to look in. Gnat peered down and hastily recoiled in disgust. Maggots! Or were they?

Gnat ventured a second, slower look. The green pouch was full of grey squirming things, restlessly churning around as if trying to escape. Puzzled, Gnat made to dip his hand in, but the boy hurriedly dashed it away. Pulling on a thick buckskin glove, he reached in, and plucked out one of the grey, squirming things.

Gnat could not believe his eyes. It was rock, but it moved like a living creature. Instinctively he understood this was the alchemy of the thickset mineral workers. The things he had seen in picture books labeled *'gnomes.'* He marvelled at their ingenuity and felt something akin to pride.

A body leapt and landed lithely onto the lorry behind them, making a space and almost immediately, another light body landed beside him to fill it. It was Cayden. He turned anxious eyes to Gnat.

'What will happen to our father?' he asked, then before waiting for an answer, he added, 'when you go back home, will you take me?'

Home.

The word stung into Gnat like a hot blade. He hadn't thought about his father in the longest time. Suddenly, he lurched forwards. He felt sick, and Cayden had to grab him to stop him falling from the roof. The black had disappeared in a flash from Gnat's eyes and he suddenly felt very vulnerable and afraid as the road rushed past beneath them.

Cayden deftly dragged Gnat's limp body towards the passenger door and bundled him back into the van through the open window. Gnat curled up on the long bench-like passenger seat and howled. He had no idea what had happened, or what was happening. All he wanted was to be with his Dad. Cayden clambered in through the window too. His burning questions unanswered, he slumped miserably beside his twin.

54

Just ahead of the procession, D sped towards the capital. His old car carried both a CD and a cassette player, and D eased the buzzing, sickening head noises that had been steadily growing all day by playing old tapes of gentle, melancholic music. In mournfully melodic tones, Richard Thompson sang *'The Ghost of You Walks.'* It helped a little, but D's skin itched and he longed to plunge into some calm, deep pool and escape the inevitable confrontation that could not be avoided. Or won.

Dog tired, D stretched his aching neck, and considered. Gnat's presence alone could not explain this event. The boy was no metahominid messiah. In all the long centuries, his case was not unique. There had been other half-breed boys, even twins. They may have been a fleeting point of focus, but there had been no such massed rallyings behind them. Something else was drawing the creatures out of the countryside and into the capital.

Someone must be guiding and enabling them.

Someone with far darker motives than Gnat's deluded grandmother.

Drawing upon his extraordinary memory, D meticulously analysed every recent conversation with every member of his team, plus those with any Aranars, Shiraishi, indeed, anyone who was aware of D9 and could compromise them. Sucking the meat from the bones of every exchanged word, he sought to find anomalies, clues that might reveal who was secretly working behind the scenes and helping the enemy.

All logic broke down in the face of one simple fact, no human would ever benefit from a metahominid rising.

The only person who appeared to believe that the races could ever live in harmony was crazy Diamond. D was right in his conviction that no-one in D9, or its affiliated services, could possibly harbour the same beliefs.

The thudding of the rumble strip thundered into his ears, making him respond by snapping his head painfully up into a more alert pose. This was no good. If he continued, he'd fall asleep at the wheel. He'd only just passed the sign for the services and was thankful it would only be a matter of crossing the lanes and coasting up the sliproad before he could grab a few welcome moments rest.

A coffee and the briefest break were all he could allow himself. Already feeling a surge of relief, D pulled into a parking space. An abrupt wave of dizzying nausea gripped him and the chattering in his ears grew even louder.

He took a step out of the car and stared across at the motorway in cold disbelief. A convoy of metas were screaming down the southbound carriageway. Free-flying, or attached to vehicles bucking wildly, chattering, shrieking - every one of them was fired up for war in their mad, careering flight. D ducked back inside the car and bent his head like a child hiding. Fingers of their consciousness stroked playfully across his mind. Outriders of their physical presence, these terrifying thought-projections had been sent to seek out whatever they might find.

They mustn't find him.

Pulling on the lever by his seat, D clicked the boot open. The silver had warmed in its boxes on its long journey and now it breathed out miniscule particles into the air. The tendrils of metahominid intention snapped back and were gone. Fleeing the deadly poison, the Thought Scouts retreated back to their senders.

D sagged against the steering wheel, watching an ugly rash of worry rise and bubble up on the soft flesh of the back of his hand.

He couldn't rest and now he would have to find another way home.

55

Elsewhere on the same motorway, Violet's fury with Watkin and their situation had hardened into a solid lump of calcified resentment. Now, to top it all off, her mobile had packed up.

She stared out of the car window. An Asian couple stood on the hard shoulder with a steaming Merc. They flew by so fast, Violet failed to see the man was tentatively using a stick to dislodge a fairy wing that was sticking out of its radiator vents.

'This wind's stronger than I thought.'

Watkin corrected for the slight buffeting. Violet pursed her lips. She'd been trapped in this car with Watkin for over three hours and right now, even the most inconsequential statement from him grated on her nerves. She leaned forwards and flipped on the radio, only to be met by nothing more than crackling static. Frowning, she pressed the tuning button, but the numbers raced up and down the wavelengths without settling on a single clear broadcast.

'Bust?' Watkin ventured.

Violet sighed and sat back, leaving the radio scanning empty air. Watkin leaned across her and fumbled in the glove box. Violet shrank back into her seat, determined to avoid any contact with this irritating buffoon. He dragged out a battered, early-model satnav, cocooned in a tangle of wire, and handed it to her.

She patiently untangled the cable and plugged the device into the lighter socket.

'Where to?'

'It speaks!' Watkin was triumphant.

Violet scowled and fiddled with the satnav. That was broken too. She unplugged it and crossly shoved the thing back into the glove box.

'Can't be bust as well!' Watkin wailed, correcting for another abrupt bout of buffeting. Violet watched him manhandling the steering wheel and checked out of the side window. In the passing hedgerows, the trees weren't even stirring. Biting her lip, she ardently cursed her short-sighted stupidity.

In her all-consuming anger with Watkin, she'd forgotten her craft. She'd ignored anomalies, signs and warnings. Her mobile, the car radio and satnav were all unresponsive and the car was being swept all over the road, without any obvious reason whatsoever. She had always prided herself on her finely attuned cognition of the unusual, knowing anomalies could well be the sentinels of metaphysical activity, but all day she'd let every clue sweep past her, like so much roadside scenery.

As Violet reached into her bag, the radio suddenly crackled into life. The whispering static rose to a whine, then it abruptly spat out several disjointed words at them

Early ...ports...bake...underground... teh...wrist...in sid...

Violet gave a choked gasp, Watkin shot a glance at her. She was wearing weird-looking sunglasses, and staring straight at the road ahead, but her expression was completely unreadable.

He turned his eyes back to the motorway, just as the tiny silver car in front swerved and clipped a lorry in the slow lane.

The car bucked wildly, pinballing from the truck into the rear flank of a sleek people carrier. The larger vehicle slammed into the Armco and slewed sideways into their lane. Just ahead of them, it hit the lorry and began to spin. Watkin checked his mirrors and hit the accelerator, heading directly for the point of impact. In the fraction of a spilt second it took them to get there, the other vehicles had bounced apart, creating a small window of space through which he accelerated.

'Nice,' Violet observed tersely.

Watkin checked the rear view mirror, another lorry was launching, seemingly in slow motion, over the now burning carcass of the people carrier.

Mesmerised, Watkin stared at the unfolding horror behind them murmuring, 'I learnt it off a racing driver.'

'What are you doing?' Violet yelled.

He had instinctively slowed down.

'Keep going! As fast as you can!'

Watkin uttered a mild, 'We can't just leave…' faltered, then obediently threaded his way, speeding between cars that nervously twitched and wavered across lanes, as drivers rubbernecked, or fought the seemingly crazy currents of the wild wind. Behind them, a sickening pall of black smoke was rapidly gaining bulk, swelling, and rising above the motorway. This was nuts. His whole life was nuts.

'Where to, Notdeakin?' His voice was weary, resigned to the crazy unreality he was being swept up in.

'The name's *Violet*,' Violet stated flatly, 'And we're going to an address in central London, Dylan.'

'We won't get near,' Watkin insisted, 'If I heard right, there's been a terrorist incident on Baker Street tube.' He couldn't help but add, 'Violet.'

She took off the weird glasses and folded them up, 'I don't believe it was a terrorist incident.'

Thoughts of that life-changing night in Kew flooded Watkin's mind, he imagined an underground platform swarming with the strange, clear flame-beings. Could she possibly think there a full scale encounter enfolding even now, on the London Underground? Watkin

453

pushed the accelerator harder, coaxing the screaming engine with renewed vigour. He was dying to find out.

Violet's thoughts raced ahead. They needed weapons. She couldn't get hold of D, but if the emergency directive, *Black Dog* was in operation, he would be waiting at his place. She would have to take Watkin. Trained or not, D9 were going to need as many extra bodies as they could get. Fighting back-to-back with her, he'd done okay on top of Castell Dinas Brân. After this, all secrecy would be blown anyway.

D could shout at her all he liked, some things were more important than a job.

56

In the green room, Vasily flung his jacket into the chair. He didn't do rage, but right now he was pretty close to it. His second violin hadn't just not shown up for a recording session they had spent weeks working towards. That would have been bad enough. But no, this paragon of unreliability, this *disgusting* man had had the unutterable gall to show, collect his violin, *and then leave!*

Vasily reached for the phone. It wasn't working. Taking a deep, frustrated gulp of air, he calmly flung it against the wall where it shattered and lay in blameless pieces on the tasteful carpet. He would have September strung up for this, preferably by his own strings.

The only piece of luck September had received so far that day was that Pauline, D's occasional cat-sitter had been in at D's. She confirmed that no one had called. Without D's presence, he surmised the Black Dog directive was not in operation. Still, he asked Pauline if she could hang about in case Jockey or Violet showed up.

Pauline was happy to help. She was watching a very nice Charleston style vase on eBay and she was content to settle in for the day and follow it there. She carried D's cat, Magnus, through to the comfortable study.

September had been texting and calling the team from his mobile for the last hour without success. He tried everyone again on D's landline, but could not reach D, Jockey, Violet or even the two other small cells he had worked with recently. Everything was jammed. Pauline popped her head around the kitchen door just as September replaced the phone in its cradle.

'Internet's down, too,' she said, trying to keep the fear from her voice. Their eyes met, they were both thinking the same thing, *where's D?* Neither of them said it.

'Will you be needing this?' She hefted a large box at September. He looked at it, and nodded solemnly.

'Armour?'

September shook his head, 'I've got my cloak.'

Taking the infra-sound generator from her arms, he shouldered his violin case, and quickly left.

57

Although D now found himself in London, he was stranded in a sea of paralysed vehicles, frustratingly close to his target. The traffic lights were down at the junction up ahead and obstinate drivers, unwilling to be sensible and give way, were paying the penalty by slowly going into meltdown.

D sat, tasting the diesel hanging in the thick dusty air and watched a man thumping a recalcitrant ATM machine across the street. He shook his head. Everything was breaking down. Caught by another wave of sickness, D gripped the wheel. Time was running out. Even without knowing they could get to him, they had got to him. Burrowing despair seeped into his soul. He had to hang on, to get the pitifully small hoard of silvered weapons back to his house.

If the team had followed the established emergency directive, Black Dog, they would all be converging there. That's even if they knew there was an emergency. D looked out at the unfolding chaos surrounding him. How could they *not* know?

A rap on the window made him look up. One of the Street Biker Irregulars grinned down at him.

'Mad or wot?' the boy indicated the traffic, 'whoa! You look proper rough! Bin on the lash?'

D nodded weakly, but as two more bikers skidded to a halt by his door, hope rose in his heart.

58

Jim and Jockey arrived at D's some ten minutes after September had left, they had just managed to slip into the neighbourhood on the cusp of the meltdown. Behind them, the traffic was building as London began to choke.

Pauline lined up Jockey's Kevlar armour on the kitchen table and busied herself looking for another carbon cloak for Jim, there was no way he was going to shoehorn his tall form into Jockey's spare armour.

Jim was helping Jockey into the jacket as D's key sounded in the front door. They looked up expectantly.

Young voices filled the hall and Jim steeped smartly into the pantry, dragging Jockey in after him. Pauline wandered out into the hallway, closing the kitchen door firmly behind her.

Three teenage boys were carrying boxes into the house. Leaving the gridlock in their wake, they had carried all the boxes *and* D, on the backs of their bikes. Racing through open parks, over footbridges and across pavements, gathering other Irregulars as they went, they had made quick work of the otherwise impassable distance.

D followed the youngsters up the steps and into his house, with the last load. As he stepped through the door, Pauline noticed with alarm how worn and gaunt he suddenly looked. His broad shoulders drooped, and his flesh was mottled with what she recognised as stress urticaria. She understood that D had given everything to fight those dreadful creatures, but now the worry of it was killing him.

He smiled gravely at her, and turned to address his saviours. 'Above and beyond the call of duty troops!' He pronounced proudly.

'But still no lager!' one of them complained.

'No. Just boring old season tickets to Bordenbyke Ramps Hangars, but if you'd rather have lager…'

'NO!' they shouted in unison, D smiled wanly at their eager faces.

Then the encoded knock sounded. D motioned the nearest boy to open the door. 'Nice timing, Mill,' the boy observed.

'Ginger Milly,' the only girl Irregular, stood on the top step, unsmiling and slightly out of breath. She had ridden like the wind to deliver a message from an important associate of D's, called Greg.

D gave her a quizzical look as he opened the note. Never a joker, she was still unusually sombre, even for Milly. D read, *'HG Wells. NOW!'* He surveyed the assembled Irregulars and murmured, 'There's just one more thing...'

After getting the Street Biker Irregulars assurances that they would weave their way speedily through the traffic without delay - *and* their solemn promises not to put themselves at any risk, D sent two of the Irregulars to deliver a small parcel apiece to the Station Supervisors at Regent Street and Marylebone stations. Then he showed the remaining Irregulars how to arm Shiraishi's 'fumigation' canisters and then gave details where they were to deploy them.

They were all to ride to Baker Street station and enter past the Sherlock Holmes statue on Marylebone Road. Greg, or one of his associates, would let them through the ticket gates and take them to the escalator down to the lower concourse. They were to follow the curving corridor and approach the second lot of escalators. There would be two sets of escalators, the one directly ahead of them accessed platforms nine and ten. The one a little way off to the right was flanked by huge, studded doors painted vibrant vermillion red and it led to platforms seven and eight. This was the important target, this escalator led down to the Bakerloo line.

They were to arm the devices and gently roll them down both sets of escalators. On no account were they to follow the canisters down onto platforms seven, eight, nine or ten. He made them repeat back his instructions, stressing that they must not go down to the deep level track.

'And what exactly will these do?' one boy asked.

'Turn on the sprinklers.'

'Cooool!' they chorused. Giggling, they stuffed a canister apiece into their hoodie pockets. D rocked! The Bakerloo Line was about to get the drenching of its life!

As Milly and the boys pedalled furiously away, Jockey emerged from the kitchen. D nodded wearily at the nine boxes. Scant munitions for what they were about to face. Jockey stood aside and Jim followed him out. D grasped his old friend's outstretched hand and shook it.

'Jim, this is the worst yet, I don't expect you to...'

Jim's blunt, 'Wouldn't miss it for the world,' cut across D's words and D fell silent, acknowledging his gratitude with a nod.

Jockey indicated the holdall full of silver.

'This'll stop a few of 'em in their nasty wee tracks,' he murmured grimly.

D assessed his troops. Both of them. An urgent rap sounded on the door.

'Mistah D?'

A small voice came through the letterbox. D motioned the others back into the kitchen. 'Mistah D? You dere?' The tiny, querulous voice sounded again, 'I din't get no tickitt...'

D opened the door, and looked down at Beeny, the very smallest Street Biker.

'Why aren't you in school?' D asked.

'Scloolded,' Beeny shrugged.

'Excluded? Again?'

Beeny picked at a scab on his knuckle, 'Yeah, bin fightin'.'

With Beeny, size was no indicator of fierceness. Despite his lack of stature, he was always the first in any scrap. D nodded, took a notepad from the hall table, and wrote a few scant words on a square of paper.

'Take this to Mr. Monksworth,' he instructed. 'Stay with him and help him if he needs it.'

Beeny nodded, 'No pranks like wiv the others? No water bombs?'

'No.'

'But I still get me tickitt, right?'

'Beeny do this, and you can have a ticket *and* a new bike.'

'Yeah, right, believe that when I see it. Just get me a tickitt, eh?' Beeny murmured, taking the note and frowning deeply, 'S'only a drop. What yer wanna go round promisin' bikes for? That could get me hopes up that could. That's cruel to a little kid, that is…' still grumbling, Beeny rode away.

As D closed the door, Pauline thrust a mug of hot tea into his hand. He gulped gratefully.

'September called.' Pauline ventured, 'I gave him an

ISG.'

'And he went off on his own?' D sighed, exasperated, 'he didn't wait?'

Pauline shook her head, 'There was no stopping him. He was really spooked.'

D's heart sank. September would be attempting to lure them back into the tunnels away from the station. Even if he managed it, it would leave September exquisitely vulnerable to attack himself. Lured by his music, the metas would follow him, but there was absolutely no guarantee they would remain passive.

After what he had seen happen during the disastrous Operation Gawain, in the Clocaenog Forest, even the impulsive Jockey appreciated September's foolhardiness.

'An' after he's led them like the Pied Piper of Hamelin, what will he do then?' Jockey snorted. 'They're gonna snap out of it – an' they'll be *murderous* when they do!'

A scatter of hail dashed against the windows. Only it wasn't hail. Jim strode into the hall, 'We're under attack!'

'Here?' Pauline shrieked. 'How did they find the house?'

At that moment there was a fierce hammering on the back door. Pauline checked the hidden spy hole. It was Violet, she was carrying a large holdall and she had someone with her. Pauline motioned D to look, but he just swept the door open.

Violet hurled herself into the room. Charging after her, Watkin skidded on the kitchen tiles, tripped over Violet's bag and fell sprawling at D's feet.

'Ill met *again*, Mr. Watkin,' D murmured, giving Violet a level stare. That look said everything. It condemned her for Watkin's presence… yet grudgingly accepted they were going to need him.

As another volley of elf-shot hit his windows, D looked up adding, 'Violet, you appear to have led Mr. Watkin's fan club directly to my home.'

Violet straightened, crossly brushing down her clothes and checking for signs of elf shot. 'With respect Sir, what with the gridlock, we've had to run for the last half an hour. They were already pouring into your street as we got here. *That's* why we ran around to the back door.'

Watkin got to his feet with a fiercely cheery, 'Hey! No! Really! I'm fine, please don't fuss!'

Jockey's loud tut was lost under a further onslaught of metahominid arrowheads clattering against the glass.

Wide eyed, Pauline shrank back. 'Will the windows stand up to that for much longer?'

D casually finished his tea, 'Should do. They're bullet-proof.'

Magnus was sitting by the cat-flap and growling at whatever lurked just outside in the back garden. Violet took one look, dragged a gauntlet out of her holdall and pulled it on.

'Don't let him out!' Pauline wailed, and hurried to pick him up, but Violet shot past her. Flinging herself to the floor, she simultaneously grabbed Magnus, whilst pushing open the cat-flap with Baby in her gloved hand. She made a few stabbing, slicing motions and was rewarded by a spray of water drenching her wrist. She handed the snarling cat lightly up to Pauline, whilst she firmly locked the plastic door on the cat flap.

'Looks like we're trapped...'   Violet surprised herself at how calmly she had said it.

59

In his younger days, Mr. Monksworth had taken charge of the Queen's flight of racing pigeons. Nowadays he was semi-retired, but he still kept one of the best pigeon lofts in the country.

Beeny rode straight through the allotments, raising clouds of complaint from the gardeners as he tore along the narrow pathways. He liked Mr. Monksworth, ever since the first time the old sod had chucked a chocolate bar at him. It had bounced off the back of Beeny's head and knocked him off his bike and they had been firm friends ever since.

Beeny found him snoozing in his shed. He carefully reached up to the narrow shelf and took down one of the brown paper bags Mr. Monksworth kept for putting over the huge pompom blooms of his prize chrysanthemums.

The old man was sound asleep in his deckchair and Beeny had only put two breaths into the bag when Mr. Monksworth spoke, 'You wouldn't be thinking of popping that, and giving a poor old man a heart attack would you, young Beeny?'

Beeny giggled, and thrust D's note at the old man. Mr. Monksworth lowered his reading glasses from his forehead and read:

Big Bird 2D>HG Wells.

He took a deep breath and rubbed his hands together, cracking his knuckles. 'Help me out of this, Beeny.' He held out a gnarled arm and Beeny hauled him out of his deck chair. 'We've got to send some of these here birds back to their proper homes.'

He crossed the small shed in a single stride and opened a drawer in what may once have been an elegant dressing table, but was now reduced to storing bird food, seed catalogues, labels and string. Mr. Monksworth took out a series of little silver cylinders.

London might have suddenly found itself lamentably cut off from all modern forms of communication, but D's distrust of them now enabled D9 to continue communicating off-grid with the rest of its operatives.

Mr. Monksworth checked the cylinders. They were

all pre-loaded with scraps of paper. He opened them, one by one and carefully wrote '*BBD>Wells*,' before rolling up each fragile paper and replacing it. Beeny watched, fascinated.

Mr. Monksworth showed Beeny how to attach the message cylinders to the birds' leg rings and together they flung the dozen pigeons, two at a time, into the lowering skies.

A dazzling shaft of sunlight pierced under the gathering stormclouds and Beeny shaded his eyes to watch the birds circle, pale grey and white scraps racing against the slate grey cloud. They swept around the allotments in another couple of circuits, circling, gathering magnetic information, like so many satnavs acquiring satellites.

Then they were off. A handful flew north, others scattered to all points of the compass.

Beeny sighed, 'How do they know where to go?'

'How do *you* know how to get home?'

'Dunno. Just do.'

'There you go then.'

Beeny hovered about expectantly in the hope of

469

chocolate, but Mr. Monksworth just shuffled back to his deck chair.

Beeny wandered outside and rescued his toppled bike. He lifted it, vented a huge, theatrical sigh and turned to go. As he did so the window in Mr. Monksworth's shed opened, and a huge bar of milk chocolate sailed out, clipping Beeny neatly on the ear. The boy fumbled and caught it before it hit the ground.

'Result!'

Beeny punched the air and flew homewards.

60

As with all previous Station Supervisors, history had demanded Greg Mallon should be in close touch with D9 and D, and he had received the same basic training as all the other watchers.

There had been nothing much to report in living memory, and Greg had assumed his guardianship of Baker Street Station would pass, as it had done for so many of his predecessors, without incident.

He had never expected to be the one. The one to send the note.

Events on the Bakerloo line had started with an accumulation of dust. It had happened before. It looked alarmingly like smoke, but always simply dispersed. A few announcements generally had to be made to allay any passengers' fears, and usually that was that.

This morning, the smoke had refused to disperse. Greg had trained the one CCTV camera with the meta-sensitive lens onto the platform and just before it malfunctioned, he had got the shock of his life.

A few bewildered and bloodied passengers had managed to make their way up to the lower concourse but they were already dying. The camera had already picked out bodies on the platform and more were lying on the escalators. He had all escalators shut down. They would recover the bodies later, if it could be done without risking the living.

Radios down, he'd gathered staff by word of mouth and instructed that they were to get everyone out that they could, and secure the metal gates so nobody else could get into the station. In the meantime, *under no circumstances* were they to let any fresh passengers down onto platforms seven or eight - *or go down there themselves*.

He'd split the available personnel into small patrols and directed them to sweep all the other areas and shuffle all the remaining stragglers out of the station. They were then to meet at the designated spot up the road near Madame Tussaud's.

He had been unable to ask the NOC incident desk to stop all trains coming into the station, but with no comms or electricity, the trains would have stopped by now anyway. He checked his watch. The emergency batteries would continue to light the station for another couple of hours. After that, they would become as black as the grave.

He reiterated, *no-one* was to venture down onto Bakerloo. They were under attack.

Greg carefully avoided the word 'terrorist,' but soon the whispers transmuted it into just that: a gas attack, a dirty bomb, who knew? It was bad and there were bodies down there, and more and more people trying to get into the station by the moment.

All of them would have to be herded slowly and

safely, back out onto the streets that were jamming with more and more cars as the traffic controls all broke down. Panic had to be avoided for those still in the station, or there would be a bloody stampede.

Whilst his staff patiently followed the emergency directive and worked to clear the station, Greg personally swung-to the enormous red doors at the top of the Bakerloo escalators. Like huge castle gates, they were made from the thickest wood and heavily studded. He took a deep breath as the two huge doors met with a dull and final thud. It made him feel a little safer just knowing they were closed.

Unaware of their previous sterling work in a similar situation, Greg thanked whatever ancient foresight had led to them being left *in situ*, when so much of Baker Street Station had been modernised.

He had already done his best, but with all comms down, Greg was working blind. A wary Station assistant entered his cramped office, just off the Metropolitan ticket hall.

'Them kids are back. Shall I let them through?'

Greg nodded, 'Bring them here.'

The boys, and Ginger Milly, all shuffled shamefaced

into Greg's office.

'We wuz only gonna set off the sprinklers!' Milly wailed.

'Hand 'em over!' Greg barked sternly.

Reluctantly, the Biker Street Irregulars handed over their precious canisters, already imagining the disappointment on D's face.

There would be no more tickets now.

'And how do these work, exactly?' Greg demanded.

One of the boys showed him, miming twisting the base. Greg nodded, and broke into a grin, 'That D!'

Shocked, the Irregulars stared at him.

'You knew he wuz gonna prank yer?' One of them asked.

'Yeah, he's a mate. Bit of a trickster. Set you up didn't he?'

They all nodded glumly.

'Well then,' Greg conceded, 'You tried, you got busted, not your fault. It's nothing to look so fed-up about

– I'll sort it with him, he'll be here in a bit. Get home now, we've got other stuff going on, as if you hadn't noticed!'

Chastened, the four youngsters pushed their way through the bewildered crowds and trailed glumly out through the station.

Back in his office, Greg lined up the four glistening canisters. He would have to leave the doors to Bakerloo shut. He'd roll two of these down the open escalator to platforms nine and ten. He'd cover platforms eight and seven via a way that would be far more effective. A way that would have been unreachable to the Street Biker Irregulars.

Crumpling his lightweight high-viz jacket into a ball, he stuffed it into his pocket and pulled an anonymous sweater over his uniform shirt. Oh his way out of his office, he grabbed a screwdriver from a shelf where banks of sullenly dead radios were charging pointlessly. Greg made his way anonymously through the milling crowds, careful to avoid any colleagues, lest they detain him with time-consuming questions.

He quickly found his goal, a door in the mid-circulating area. Donning his high-viz jacket to look 'official' again, Greg took a deep breath and unlocked it. Before him, a narrow shaft dropped out of sight.

Nervelessly, he turned around to face the doorway - and stepped backwards onto the metal ladder. As he climbed down into the gloom, his flesh was chilled yet he was acutely aware of the tickling fingers of sweat creeping down his back.

He only breathed again when he touched down into a long corridor. Not that he felt any safer in this place. He'd always considered the dimly lit corridor was a conduit for the *'heebie-jeebies.'* It had always carried its own distinct atmosphere and every time he had been down here, he'd had the definite sensation of being watched. Maybe he had been?

Greg slammed the lid shut on that thought. Engulfed in the clammy cold, with deep pools of shadow conspiring to unnerve him, he stood directly above the old Bakerloo line at a spot where the old, disused lift shafts were now serving as ventilation towers.

As he unscrewed a louvred wall panel, his hands shook very slightly. Try as he might, he couldn't dispel the fear that there was something here, just waiting to leap out at him. Prising back one corner of the panelling, he judged it to be just enough. He primed a canister and dropped it clattering down the deep shaft. He waited to hear it working, discharging its contents before quickly following it with a second one. Even as he screwed back the panel, Greg very nearly convinced himself that he could hear water running down there.

Twenty minutes later, he gratefully ascended the ladder, feeling he was scooting back up to something a few degrees more normal - yet still way off the chart. Pulling off the high-viz, so as to be not readily identifiable as an official person again, he hoped he could speed through the rest of his task and get back to his office without further incident.

Greg pushed his way through the door - and was shocked at the number of people still inside the station. He set off back towards platforms nine and ten and a fairly new, and very junior, colleague barred his way. She didn't recognise Greg as her boss.

Pulling up his sweater, Greg revealed his uniform shirt and ID badge and was speedily allowed through the temporary barriers, to the stopped escalators of platforms nine and ten.

He sent the last two canisters clattering and ringing down the shining steel steps, before hurrying back to his office to await D.

61

If there was something more important than his job, it would seem D had found it.

Somewhere in Whitehall, the Gatekeeper looked down at his watch again. D was way beyond late for his scheduled telling-off.

This would not do.

The Home Secretary had waited politely for a few moments and then she had left. For D to have furnished no explanation whatsoever for his absence was appalling. Only severe illness, or death, could be accepted as an excuse now. Along with the queries regarding the serious gaps in his Quartermaster's housekeeping, whereby it appeared a quantity of silver had apparently vanished. By not turning up, D had effectively rendered himself unemployable.

The Gatekeeper looked up as a great cast of hail battered against the large windows. He moved the anachronistic modern blind aside from the ancient stone mullion, and peered up into a late summer blue sky.

Another scatter of hail fell like rice at a wedding. But from where? There wasn't a cloud to be seen. His eyes narrowed, was this someone's idea of a practical joke?

A junior approached, 'Sir! There's an incident unfolding on the tube.'

Arms folded, the Gatekeeper turned away from the window, his raised eyebrows inviting the young agent to continue.

'Reports are patchy… er.. *all* communications are patchy, probably from the fallout. Early indications are that we've been hit by a dirty bomb.'

The Gatekeeper's mind conjured terrifying images as it reeled back over the years. He had been on the Japanese underground, on the very same platform where eleven people had died in a sarin gas attack. That had been bad enough. But a *dirty bomb?*

Apart from rocking back a millimetre on his heels, the Gatekeeper gave no indication of shock, or outrage.

'Suspects? Casualties?'

'Still working on it, Sir.'

'Operation Greengage?'

'In effect, Sir. The media have been temporarily DA-noticed. Frendlies have been contacted and they will be advising their own foreign nationals.'

'And all the *Less-Than-Friendlies?*'

'All non-friendly countries with a significant presence here have been misdirected, as far as is possible for now, Sir. However, we expect them to catch up sometime in the next hour. In the meantime, whatever the nature of the contact, it appears to have been tactile, but we aren't one hundred-percent sure what is going on. We have people on the ground, but they are failing to report back to us.'

In this, the last remaining office in the capital with a limited degree of remaining internet connectivity, a flashing screen drew The Gatekeeper's eye. Pixelated footage from Baker Street, taken on a mobile phone, had just hit YouTube. Figures appeared to be lying, scattered on wet tiles. Victims of the unknown 'tactile contact,' they didn't look real. Then again, the blurred image was so degraded, it was hard to make out whether these were scenes from a terrorist attack, or some esoteric art installation in a vast gallery. Other clips began buffering.

The Gatekeeper tensed imperceptibly. Gagging the media, for the sake of national security, counted for nothing when nearly every pocket or handbag contained a mobile phone. In the years since he had begun his ascent to his present, lofty position, he had seen how the populace had become a nation of newsgatherers, all well-versed in filming and uploading. Even The Gatekeeper had to accept the fact that somewhere on the net, better images would be getting ready to play to the world.

Then the screen went blank.

The Gatekeeper wondered if D could possibly be caught up in all of this. As far as excuses for not showing up went, it could be a reasonably satisfactory one.

62

Watkin couldn't help but flinch with every fresh scatter of arrowheads on the window. The man they called D seemed completely relaxed. He checked his watch, he seemed to be waiting for something.

'Okay,' D took mental stock, 'Everyone into the strong room! Grab whatever's in there and bring it all back in here!'

Ten minutes later, alongside the original hoard of the nine new boxes of ammo, Jockey's armour and Jim's cloak, there now lay on the large refectory table D and Jockey's crossbows, a quantity of arrows, darts and bolts, some phials of Jim's silver solution, a dozen hand held silver spray aerosol canisters and a further nine silver fumigation bombs. Jim's beautiful Hoyt bow, bristling with scopes and projecting balancing-arms, lay in stark contrast to an old battered composite bow and Allegra's silverware. Lined up alongside all of this, were a couple of infra-sound generators, together with Jockey's spare set of armour and the holdall containing the rest of Violet's armour.

Violet offered the composite bow to Watkin. D stayed her hand, asking, 'Have you ever fired a bow?'

Watkin reluctantly shook his head. D nodded to Violet, and she replaced the bow back on the table. Watkin would be of limited use to them if he shot himself in the foot with one of his own arrows.

'Going up against the multitude, armed with little more than a couple of tea trays are we? That's nice.' Jockey observed lightly.

Watkin made to take off his silver ring and chain, but Violet stopped him with a grim smile.

'Finish suiting up,' D ordered, 'and help him,' D indicated Watkin, 'into that,' he pointed at Jockey's spare suit. Jockey scowled.

D continued, 'You wanted to work with us, Mr. Watkin?'

Watkin nodded eagerly. D regarded Watkin's shining face and hesitated. A fresh flurry of arrowfall urged him to make his decision quickly.

'Now's your chance! Stick close to Jockey and obey his orders!'

D's fierce gaze stemmed any complaint from Jockey. He turned back to Watkin and continued, 'You are about to get a crash course in metahominid clearance. There will be no time for questions, just do what Jockey tells you and you'll have a better chance of surviving. If you lose your head, go solo and get into trouble, then you will stay solo. Any extra body has to render help, not become a liability.'

Still grinning, Watkin nodded and D reached out and shook him firmly by the hand. Watkin's enthusiasm was smashed by Jockey's casual, 'Aye, I hear tell he's only good for hitting girls!'

Watkin glared at Jockey.

'Children!' D chided, and left the room.

Watkin started pulling the Kevlar armour on. Jockey curtly showed him what went where and more or less left him to it.

Violet hurriedly strapped herself into her own suit. Tutting, she checked Watkin's straps, making small adjustments and hefting the back and breastplates, until she was sure they were properly fitted. Watkin found the Kevlar armour was light but still uncomfortable. Tailored to Jockey's body shape, it ill-suited his leaner, taller form.

Within moments D reappeared, similarly clad in protective Kevlar. His face looked a little better and water was dripping from his hair, a quick sluice down in the shower had calmed his raging skin condition.

'Feeling fit? We need this lot on the top floor!'

He nodded at the accumulated armaments on the

table. Even above the scattered, rice-hail sound of the arrowheads against the windows, D's sensitive ears had picked up the distant echo he had been waiting for.

At least one of the pigeons had got through to operatives outside what had transpired to be a localised communication blackout-zone. Phone calls had been made and help was coming.

Even as Jim, Violet, Jockey and Watkin grabbed boxes and started up the long staircase, a clattering whine approached, seemingly from all directions, getting louder until it resolved into a single point of noise directly overhead. Bouncing off other houses in the street, it sounded weird and otherworldly, phasing and echoing until it resolved itself into the regular chop chopping of a helicopter's rotor blades.

One of Mr. Monksworths's pigeons had summoned the Aranars and they had brought along this bigger bird.

D checked again, he was sure he'd had at least one more precious box of silver fumigation bombs, but no, he must have been mistaken. Not one for mistakes, this unexplained discrepancy bothered him, but there would be no time to resolve the matter now.

With elfshot pinging off his visor and armour, Jockey climbed out of the skylight, onto the roof. He had gaffer-taped a canister to a length of rope. Now he twisted the canister to set it going and then let out the rope, so it dangled off the edge of the roof by the eaves. Taking just a few steps, Jockey was able to drag the hissing canister, around the entire perimeter of the roof.

He laughed and shouted, 'If ye've come for me, ye'll be regretting it now!' Then he liberally doused the metahominid attackers below, on all sides, with a fatal dusting of silver. Within moments the volleys of elf-shot ceased. Even if he had time to do so, Jockey didn't need to look over the edge to know D's gardens were now running with water. He whistled down to the others and they quickly emerged onto the roof and began carrying their arms onto the expertly hovered aircraft.

Downstairs, D checked the table had been completely emptied of useful kit and turned to address Pauline.

'The little one, Beeny?' Pauline nodded, 'I believe I owe him a bike. There's money in the usual place to take care of it. Look after Magnus!'

Before she could answer, he spun on his heel and

loped up the stairs after his team.

D was not expecting to return.

63

High above London, Gnat looked down. He had no idea how he'd got there. The last thing he remembered was being sick in Diamond's van.

Now he was flying with the swarm, held by an invisible force high above the jammed streets of the paralysed city. But far from feeling the wonderful ease of self-propelled movement, the magical joy of his flying dream, he was as powerless as if he had been strapped into the world's biggest rollercoaster. Only this was far more terrifying.

With a sickening swoop, the flock of fairies dived and dragged him down with them, down past the tall buildings, down past windows where shocked office workers looked out at a small boy, apparently falling through the air, plummeting down to the street far below. Gnat flinched and looked away as the pavement rushed up to meet him, but the flock deftly jinked and flew on. The road now rose like a wall to Gnat's left. Swerving through a cracked, narrow opening, the multicoloured squadrons swept down even further, swooping and flowing like a living river through an old shaft, cascading down through an eerie abandoned station, making the peeling posters flutter in the wake of their flight, scattering, re-forming and sweeping through tunnels, deep into the living guts of the city.

Silver-blue rails swept beneath him in the half-light of the tube tunnels. An abandoned train lay silent and strangely mute, shocked people staggered along the tracks.

They came to another tube train that had halted just outside a station, and Gnat saw its roof was bristling with crawling figures. It was being rocked on its wheels by a furious horde of thickset, chunkheaded gnomes. Inside, the trapped commuters were screaming in shock and terror. With a shrieking howl of rending metal, the engine toppled over, crashing onto its side, twisting and dragging its carriages with it. One of them tore apart, spilling people onto the rails.

The sight was lost as the swarm was brought to an abrupt halt in alarm and confusion. A spent canister lay on the dripping wet platform. Here and there humans lay sprawled in the puddles, dead or dying from elf shot. With a barely-heard clatter, a second gas canister rolled onto the platform and began scattering its lethal discharge.

Those that could avoid the deadly poison scattered like cockroaches. To his horror, the supporting beings around him vanished into sudden explosions of water and Gnat's guts lurched as he dropped the full height of the tunnel, towards the rails. A skinny, preternaturally strong hand shot out and grabbed him, dragging him onto the platform. It was Cayden. He'd been hit by the fallout from one of Greg's silver bombs and was covered in livid, red weals. Both boys stood, crying and shaking. Similar weals were coming out all over Gnat now. Diamond stood wracked, wringing her hands.

She had arrived in Baker Street station by more conventional means, hoping to see a final ultimatum delivered by the Fair Folk to this historically important site, and witness the birth of an orderly truce between the races.

'I didn't think it'd be like this!' she wailed. She grabbed Gnat and Cayden and hugged them fiercely, whispering into their hair, 'Oh my boys, it shouldn't have been like this! They've *killed* people!'

64

Watkin, Violet, Jim and Jockey had grabbed places in the back of the ambulance helicopter with Aranars Scott and Ruby, and D had taken a seat in the cockpit.

Jockey spent the brief flight checking his scopes, whilst Jim sat impassively, looking commandingly patrician in his cloak like a classical statue.

Violet took it upon herself to instruct their newest recruit on meta strengths and weaknesses, and what weapons he was likely to encounter.

'So, that thing you dug out of me, really was just an arrowhead?'

Violet shrugged, 'Not *just*.' *Never* underestimate these things…' Unclipping her protective collar, she drew out what looked like a pendant on a fine, silver cord.

Watkin's hand instinctively stroked his shoulder as he stared at the miniature piece of finely-knapped flint.

'It looks Neolithic.'

'It's a bit more sophisticated than that. Think of them as *seek and destroy* missiles. All it has to do is hit a target, anywhere on the body, and this thing will work its way towards the victim's heart.'

'I was lucky.'

'Very.'

'Let's hope I didn't use it all up that night, then.'

Their eyes met.

'Luck doesn't work like that, Suckerfish,' Violet murmured.

Sam, the blonde, ruddy faced Aranar, who looked more like a young farmer than a rescue-helicopter pilot, briefed D of events outside London.

Elsewhere in the country - beyond what was already being referred to as *'the blind cordon'* - where communications were still able to run unfettered, rumours of a dirty bomb were escalating.

The communications blackout that hovered over central London, condemning it to a black hole of non-being, had been ascribed to various causes. These included government intervention, microwave emissions and radiation from the bomb blast, and even just simple multiple grid failures. Newspapers and TV stations had decamped, as far as they could, to the provinces, and were operating out of regional offices. *'Worst case scenario,'* fever was running high and it was being posited that central London had been destroyed in a cataclysm far worse than the destruction wrought by the Luftwaffe in the Second World War.

The army and emergency services knew better, having quickly found the edges of the communication hole. But once inside the capital, the army and police were working blind.

Co-ordinating personnel was proving impossible for the various officers in command. Even emergency meetings could not be synchronised. Directives not contemplated since WWII came unexpectedly into service. The army had built temporary barricades across roads and imposed restriction orders on all movement into the affected areas. None of this made much impact upon D. Even so, he was the nearest he could be to relieved when Sam told him that there had not been any simultaneous attacks on other towns and cities.

London was the sole focus.

Overwhelmed as they were, there was, as yet, only one area of conflict to deal with.

Then Sam told him that shoals of aquids had been detected swimming up the Thames. Now, D was sure, this was nothing to do with Gnat. Something else must have been added to the equation, to embolden the metas, and bring them to the brink.

'Can't say we were happy to hear it's Wells,' Sam's words cut through D's thoughts.

Wells was the code for Baker Street Underground. H.G. Wells had once lived above the station in the block of apartments there. Any reference to Sherlock Holmes had been avoided as being far too obvious. The oldest station on the London tube, Baker Street was the hub of five converging lines and carried ten platforms on various levels.

D had little more than a handful of people to wage a war in one of the most complex stations on the London underground.

In the back, Jim echoed his thoughts. 'Chins up, chaps! We can do this! Those Spartans were seriously over-staffed anyway!'

There was no way to discreetly land a helicopter in a London street, let alone one where confused and hysterical people were milling between gridlocked vehicles.

Sam had been unable to call ahead for the road to be cleared. Even if his communications had worked, all police radios were down.

D surveyed the chaotic scene below and groaned inwardly, he still felt sick and dizzy, and abseiling had to be his least favourite method of travel, even on a good day.

Sam hovered his craft just over the raised bus-lane on Marylebone Road, directly outside the station. He had to land them the correct side of the steep wall, or they'd have to waste precious moments jogging all the way around it. It couldn't be climbed with all their kit. Jockey caught Watkin's anxious look and grinned.

Simultaneously exiting the helicopter, camo-clad Scott toppled with Ruby. They swooped down on their lines, alighting gracefully as mystified commuters and tourists stood back, an apparent army presence bringing a sense of relief and calming them a little.

Violet and Jim went next to clear a space for the bags and boxes to be lowered. A harassed-looking constable joined them to help keep the crowd back. He was inordinately grateful for something constructive to do.

'Am I glad to see you!' he shouted over the ferocious engine clatter, 'Is is a dirty bomb? Are we getting fried standing here?'

Violet was unimpressed that he hadn't even asked who they were. For all he knew, he could be helping a bunch of terrorists. He took her noncommittal expression as both a reassurance and a professional cold-shoulder, a discreet warning about the need for secrecy. 'I get it, *mum's the word!*'

He reminded her of Watkin at Kew. After today the city would be full of Watkin wannabees. All hanging onto D9's coat tails.

Jockey stood at the door, thankful for the pilot's skill. With his navigation systems unresponsive, Sam was flying blind. He would have to find somewhere to land whatever happened, however long this took, without critical instruments, night flying was not going to be an option.

D reluctantly followed the penultimate box out of the helicopter and landed unsteadily, twisting his shoulder. He barely noticed. He was thinking.

Although they might be behaving somewhat differently than of old, he firmly believed his enemy remained a creature of habit and there were strong metahominid links with the oldest underground workings. Even before he met up with Greg, he knew where the enemy would be gathering.

Seventy feet beneath where they now stood, D9 had fought metahominids over a century ago, on what was now the deepest level of Baker Street station.

Above them loomed the substantial stone walls of Chiltern Court, home to H.G. Wells, friend of D9. Together with Conan Doyle, Herbert Wells had become an implacable enemy to Bakerloo's creator, Whitaker Wright.

D decided to follow his instincts and focus his scant resources on the south-bound platform of the Bakerloo line. He told himself that even if he'd had an army, he would have still done the same.

A boy pushing a bike was firmly held back by Ruby, whilst D unclipped himself from his line. D then nodded for the boy to be allowed through. He looked genuinely scared, but even so, D expected a crumpled note to be thrust into his hand, not what came next.

As D shouldered his crossbow bags, the boy blurted tearfully, 'Beeny's down there!'

D put his bags back down. The helicopter was still hovering noisily and Jockey was busy lowering kit, so D dragged the boy away to shelter in the sound lee of the Sherlock Holmes statue. Even so, it was still difficult to hear anything over the chopping and whine of the rotors, so D had to lean in close to catch the rest.

'When Beeny'd done his errand, he came here to see us. He wanted to do some mischief, wiv the water bombs. We were coming out and I told him you said not to go down there, but he wouldn't listen. Mr. D, *we didn't do the water bombs!*'

D's heart missed a beat.

The boy continued, 'The Boss-man in the office took 'em off us.'

'Which man?' D's tone was urgent, intense.

'The same one Milly brought the note from.'

That, at least was better news. Greg would have deployed them. D relaxed a little, 'So Beeny went into the station?'

'Not just into the station, he went down to platform eight.'

D exhaled patiently.

The boy continued. 'I heard him!   Hollering and screaming!'

'And that was because you went down there after him too?'

The boy hung his head and wiped his running nose with the back of his hand, smearing glistening snot absently against his trouser leg.

'Couldn't leave him,' he mumbled.   'Not wiv all them dead people! I could hear him, but his voice sounded ever so far away an' I couldn't find him!' The boy stared up into D's mismatched eyes. 'There's *things* down there, Mr. D! Scary things! Crawlin' round and hurtin' people, like summat out of a horror film!'

D nodded. The boy was slight and elfin faced, the genetic result of some long-forgotten crossing of the bloodlines. He had been able to perceive the enemy.

Loyal, and with natural meta sight, in an alternative world where D9 wasn't about to be destroyed, this boy would have had a fine future with the department. D looked down at the forlorn figure.

'We'll do our best to get him back.'

Downcast the boy nodded, then looked up with tearful eyes, 'Mr. D? Is this a war? Like against zombies or summat?'

'No,' D managed to raise a weary smile, 'Now get home as quickly as you can, I'll find Beeny.'

He had no guarantee that he could do this, or that this was not a war.

As the subdued boy wheeled his bike away, Jockey lowered the final ammo box and dropped lightly beside it. He was closely followed by Watkin, who just about managed to keep his feet upon landing. He danced on the end of his line for a moment, then gained his balance and unclipped himself. Jockey gave him a stern look. With a deafening, full-bellied roar, the helicopter powered up and flew off to land at nearby Regent's Park.

Jockey arranged his bow comfortably across his back and started divvying up their ammunition. Jim, Violet, Ruby, Scott, D and Watkin all had to carry an ammo box each. When D reached to pick up a second one, Jockey's hand stayed his action.

Jockey always kept the lions share for himself. D9's Quartermaster had served previously with a regiment that had chosen men, partly on their ability to carry a lot of heavy kit quickly over long distances. In past operations, Jockey had been D9's pack animal, this time would be no different.

Paying no attention to the mix of puzzled, unaffected, horrified or deeply shocked passengers filtering out of the station onto the street, D was let through the metal gates. It was done on a nod from one of Greg's colleagues, who had been set to watch for what a stressed Greg had described as, *'Serious wallahs led by an odd looking geezer.'*

They made a strange sight, hurrying past the shops, the Aranars in camouflage and D9 in black. Inside the station on street level, all was relatively normal, people were aggrieved at the apparent breakdown of the system and delays, but all were leaving slowly and no-one was injured.

A knot of angry passengers were still gathered around several Station Assistants. These junior members of staff had been tasked to direct people away from the station. One or two more belligerent and foolhardy members of the public simply pushed past them. Short of physically restraining them, there wasn't much the Station Assistants could do. One young woman Station Assistant caught sight of D's party and gave a relieved yelp. She raced towards them.

'Over here!' she cried, gesturing for them to follow her. She led them towards the Hammersmith and Circle line, past a queue of arguing passengers, to the office where the Station Supervisor, Greg Mallon, was waiting. Greg nodded his thanks to his junior and looked at D's companions wondering where the rest of them were.

After the Station Assistant left, he confirmed in rapid sentences D's theory that platform eight was the centre of activity. Then he told them what he'd done so far, that the massive doors were firmly shut, and that before the cameras had gone down he'd seen multiple bodies on platform eight. He did his best to describe what he'd seen on the meta-sensitive camera too. His stroked his glistening forehead and shook his head.

'I know you've always said to be ready, but I have no idea what's going on. We have emergency procedures, but we're blind, we can't co-ordinate. We've got no comms, no back-up, nothing. We've lost people *and* trains. It's like a black hole down there. D...'

He looked earnestly into D's strange eyes.

' …Bakerloo just vanished off the map.'

65

Service Control had gone spookily quiet, but Gayle kept telling herself that the radio would be okay any moment.

Then the signals went.

Feeling sick with apprehension, she slowed. She wanted to keep her train moving as she was operating in an area well known for large gaps in the power rails. If she got stuck down here, it could be over an hour before they towed her out again, but she applied the brakes and reluctantly brought her train to a complete stop.

In the utter blackness, she waited for the radio to splutter into life and offer much needed instructions. Gayle sighed softly. This one event would cause multiple delays and backups, throwing everything out of synch.

Not knowing the whole system was down, she

pictured the Controller telling trains to hold in platforms, if they were already on their way down, or diverting them if they were not.

Gayle forced herself to stop imagining the worst, she would have to be very unlucky to be completely *'off juice,'* the train would be fine. She patted the panel in front of her. Then again, staring into the darkness, there wasn't a single light. She ran through her checks again.

She couldn't even radio the passengers to reassure them. She would have to bite the bullet, and walk through a train full of irate people to the back cab, and see if the radio worked in there.

By the time she'd answered all their questions and fielded a fair few insults, the problem may well have resolved itself. Still, she resignedly shouldered her work-bag and rose out of her seat.

Something skittered across the roof of her cab. She grimaced at the thought of a rat dropping from the roof of the tunnel. Then there was another light thud, then another and a third. It was raining rats. A shudder of disgust ran through her.

Then a man came running, pale faced and sweating,

out of the darkness, staggering along the tracks. For a split second his maddened eyes met hers. He vanished below her line of sight, only to begin hammering on her locked door and rattling the handle.

The tube train driver had never had a *'one under,'* a body beneath her wheels before, and she didn't want one now. Even so, Gayle shrank back, unwilling to let him in. If this psychotic-looking guy was cunning enough not to get run over, or electrocuted, whatever his problem was - drugs or general craziness - she couldn't fix it.

As she cursed the useless radio, the man started making weird scratching sounds, rasping his nails against the skin of the train, like he was being dragged away by some inexorable tide. Then the noise stopped. Was he gone? Something smacked into the windscreen, and Gayle recoiled.

Straightening, she realised there was nothing there. Then multiple *things* started hitting the windows. *Invisible things.* Gail held her hands over her ears, and turned away from the window.

As a woman driver, she'd endured a fair few practical jokes from the lads, but this was no joke. Her mind raced. There were many strange stories about the Underground. Things seen. Things that weren't there.

In late night canteen sessions, drivers would spook one another with tales of ghostly encounters in dark tunnels. Gayle told herself she'd just had to wait, soon it would all be over, and then she'd have a tale to tell.

The impacts sounded again on the roof. This time they didn't stop. Hit after hit after hit echoed through the cabin roof as multiple things landed above her head.

As if in the grip of a giant hand, her cab suddenly began rocking from side to side. Tons upon tons of steel groaned and shrieked with the violent movement, and Gail howled in fear as the wild ride grew more extreme, and the arc of the swing grew longer. She could hear the muffled wails and screams of her passengers trapped in the carriages behind her. Struggling to recover her balance, she was hurled from door to door as the cab swung back and forth, like a small boat, cresting giant waves. If this was an earthquake, the bucking ground was moving with a bizarrely regular pulse. With each sway, the train poised for a split-second on the brink, struggling to right itself, before crashing back down onto its ruined wheels.

Gayle grabbed tight hold of the back of the driver's seat and clung on as the inevitable happened, and the whole cab toppled onto it side, dragging its carriages over with it.

Huddled against the wall of the tunnel, September raised his head as he heard the crash. From inside the folds of his cloak, Yelena looked up at him. This crazy man had not been crazy after all. He had come back for her. He had saved her from... what?

She had seen people dying on the station, seemingly beset by strange, clear flame spirits and she had seen how this man had controlled them with his playing. Oh, and *such* playing! She had joined forces with him, and together they had fought the ghosts with their music. Beating them back with Vaughan Williams, fighting for a little time and respite from the terrible onslaught of squirming missiles, giving people the chance to get off the platform and flee.

Then the black box thing had run out of power, and it had all gone wrong. The murderous spirits had surged back and overwhelmed everything again. She had grabbed him, and together they had run here.

Run and hide, that was the thing to do. That was what her mother had done in Bosnia. She had told Yelena how she had run and hidden and, unlike others, had lived to tell the tale.

Now they huddled, staying quiet, hidden within his magical cloak, whilst the angry spirits vented their wrath upon others. Her violin, Maria, and his beautiful Stradivarius lay nearby, but neither of them dared venture a hand outside the protective cloth to retrieve them.

They were waiting for the man he called D, a man who would save them. She deftly wrapped the folds to protect September's head, and they curled up together to wait. Whether for death, or rescue, Yelena could not say.

66

The escalators were stalled and the lower concourse at Baker Street had been all but cleared. A young man in a smart suit lay slumped beneath a garish theatre poster. Watkin stared at the fallen figure. Beneath the dead flesh, the man's forehead squirmed where burrowing elf-shot crawled, their inward progress checked only by the bone of his skull.

Violet dragged Watkin away, and D's raised hand quelled the rising exclamation of shock Watkin was about to vent. Unmoved, Scott and Ruby stepped over him, then stopped and stripped off their outer camouflage gear.

Beneath, they were wearing the same type of black armour as the rest of D9. D gathered them all in the centre of the concourse, and began his briefing.

'We have to concentrate on Bakerloo. In theory that's just platforms eight southbound, and nine northbound, but in reality we may have to deal with platforms seven through to ten. They run east-west on the lowest level. Seven and ten lie to the north of eight and nine.'

D continued, 'They will be concentrated on the southbound line, between here and Regent's Park.'

Violet wanted to ask how he could be so sure, but she obediently remained silent. If he was wrong… but even her thoughts faltered, she was unable to accept the magnitude of the task before them.

'There's fourteen and a half miles of the Bakerloo line in total…' Watkin murmured. Jockey frowned fiercely. Watkin's train-spotter's knowledge wasn't helping morale. D drew out a small notebook, and began drawing a map.

'Shortly, we will walk down the escalator ahead. This leads down to platform ten, northbound. We'll use Jim's family silver to establish a cordon across the foot of the escalators once we're down, that will keep them from migrating up into the rest of the station.'

Puzzled Watkin interrupted. 'What's to stop these creatures turning tail and travelling away up the tracks? Once they get onto the Jubilee line, there's that whole abandoned bit between Charing Cross and Green Park, and that's *before* they get onto the rest of the system...'

D quietened Jockey's tut with a look and explained patiently. 'Earlier tonight, I despatched two parcels. If our friends at Marylebone and Regent's Park have been able to do their job, at least two trains will have travelled down the line with canisters attached, laying down a fine spray of silver in the tunnels.'

Watkin opened his mouth to interject, but D continued, 'I understand the trains are compromised and we have no idea how far any of them were able to travel before the system broke down, but at the very least the enemy using the Bakerloo line are trapped somewhere within the space of these three stations. They cannot pass beyond.'

Violet nodded. She was glad of the containment, but not reassured. Now she would be facing a multitude of metahominids in a relatively confined space.

D continued his briefing. 'At the foot of the escalator, there will be a passageway marked *"No Entry,"* immediately to our left. Ahead, there are two passageways, one either side of a wall, both leading to platform ten. We'll lay lines of silverware across these points too.'

He indicated the mouths to the passageways.

'To our right is a short passageway. There is a passage off it on the left, here,' he indicated with the point of his pencil, 'that leads to platform nine. Lay silver there, but keep on straight ahead. There will be a single flight of stairs down to platform eight. *This* will be the hotspot!'

They all stared down at the place D had encircled.

'Platform eight has a pronounced curve, you can't see one end from the other, so groups will be unable to keep visual contact.'

Violet frowned, a difficult job was not getting any easier. Jockey shifted, eager for the off. Working solo suited him.

D then gave each of them a detailed map he had prepared of platform eight. Watkin swallowed hard, quelling his sense of rising panic. He was hopeless with maps at the best of times, that's why he had to study them so hard -

purely to get them memorised. Now there would be no time to slowly fix the features in his minds' eye - and this map, with its multiple exits, stairs going off in all directions, and its own set of escalators, was pretty much incomprehensible to him.

'If they haven't already spilled out onto it, we have to cover the exits to platform seven. We have to contain and destroy. Not let them get the chance to get away and spread out through the system.'

They all fell silent.

Privately, Jim thought the venture was about as realistic as trapping air in a sieve, but he gave a thumbs up.

Jockey gave an authentically cheery, 'Chunky dory!' and ripped open the ammo boxes.

Whilst Jockey, D, Jim and the Aranars filled quivers, pockets and bags with arrows, darts and bolts, Violet explained the infra-sound to Watkin.

'Think of it as a stun-gun. Multi-directional, it incapacitates them, but only briefly. It won't give you time to get away if they're right on top of you, and it takes time to regenerate the charge for the next blast, so use it wisely. You arm it here.'

Her gloved finger pointed to a toggle-type switch, folded back on itself into the body of the box. 'You pull it out, flick it down and the light above turns green when it's ready to go, then you hit this button, right?'

Watkin nodded. Violet added, 'It's useful, but limited. It takes a lot of juice and runs down fast, so only deploy when Jockey orders it, like this,' she showed him the three finger signal, adding, *'Don't* waste your charge!'

Jockey had been occupied, taping canisters to arrows. He handed one apiece to Ruby and Scott, one to Jim, and kept a couple back for himself. Both Jockey and Jim were armed with slender Hoyt bows. D carried his pistol crossbow and a larger, traditional crossbow slung across his back. Scott and Ruby both carried crossbows and reassuringly fat bandoliers of multiple silver sprays.

'Scopes and goggles on,' D ordered.

He hunkered down by a pillar and motioned Jockey to hand over the infra-sound generators, one to Watkin, and the other to Violet.

'After we leave this level, we operate in silence, Mr. Watkin.'

They moved off as one, pausing at the top of the

512

only way down left open after the closing of the great red doors. All seven of them stared down, into the face of hell. This was the only opening to the lower level - the escalators to platforms nine and ten.

The sound of sobbing floated up to them.

Jockey leaned forwards and peered down the steep incline. Someone was clambering up, making a lot of noise. D nodded to Scott, who lightly sprang away down the steps.

He reappeared moments later, with a very nervous station assistant. The man was white-faced and jabbering incomprehensibly about 'ghosts on the line.'

'You can go now. Thank you for staying at your post,' D said calmly.

The man stared at the black clad team. As amazed as he might have been to see them, they were stunned he had evaded a full-on meta attack unscathed. His astonished eyes took in their arcane weapons and, weird black clothes and unable to cope any further, he yelped *'Ghostbusters!'* and fled down the corridor. Watkin grinned, but D turned away from the retreating figure.

'We're looking for the heaviest concentration. I don't have to tell you there aren't many of us. So the drill is this: on every platform except eight, clean out if you have to. If not, don't waste a canister, just lay down the barrier of silverware. When we get onto platform eight, I want Jim, Scott and Violet to the left, Watkin, Ruby and Jockey to the right. Remember, you will be unable to keep within visual distance. Don't let them draw you away. Arm the ISG's. Deploy both at once halfway down the escalator.'

Then D stood and formally shook hands with each member of his team. When he came to Watkin, he handed him a small bronze cylinder.

Watkin took out the pair of meta-sensitive goggles, and stared at them.

Jockey pointed out the button on the arm and growled, 'Time to meet our little green men.' Before they moved off, Watkin voiced the ultimate, final questions.

'Why here? Why now?'

'The '*now*,' I am not sure of, Mr. Watkin. 'The '*here*' is a matter of history. We are dealing with creatures of habit, and they have simply gravitated to a previous point of major conflict.'

'They've been here before?'

D nodded, 'When the line was being built.'

Anxious to be off, Jockey cleared his throat pointedly. Watkin took the hint and despite many more questions, fell silent.

Jockey and Scott were the first down. Their grim task was to move any obstructing bodies out of the way.

Violet was next down the escalator, closely followed by Watkin. Her finger hovered over the switch on the side of her ISG. She turned wordlessly to indicate hers was powering up. Fumbling with his thick gloves, Watkin felt a flush of hot sweat as he struggled with the recessed switch. Finally he managed it, and within a few steps more, the light showed green. Violet nodded and they hit the deploy buttons together.

A wave of sound swept before them, echoing through the eerie corridors and passageways. Nothing moved.

Jim was the last off the escalator and he grabbed some pieces of flatware from his holdall and helped Ruby lay them across the foot of the stairs and the adjacent corridor. Ahead of them loomed the twin, tunnel-like walkways to platform ten.

Silver sprays at the ready, Jockey and Scott took one walkway apiece at a sprint. They hurtled along the parallel passageways and simultaneously burst out onto the platform, within a few feet of one another, but nothing lay waiting for them. Platform ten was desolate and empty.

Silently, more silver was laid across the open passageways and, one by one, D's team steeled themselves to turn towards the narrow tunnel to platform eight.

Something small and fierce shot from the tunnel and flung itself at D.

Baby flashed, and somehow, Violet managed not to kill Beeny who clung sobbing to D. As D patted Beeny's skinny back, great sobs erupted from his tiny frame. He was a tough little kid but there were limits, and he had seen more than enough this day. After motioning the others to stay, D carried Beeny back up the escalator. Halfway up, he stopped and put the boy down, but Beeny wouldn't let go. D gently unpeeled Beeny's arms from his neck, and held the boy in front of him, speaking gently in a half-whisper.

'Beeny, I can't spare anyone to take you back upstairs, but if you go now, you'll be safe, understand?'

Beeny's face crumpled, but he nodded through his

hiccupping sobs. 'Don't go down there, Mistah D! It ain't safe!' he wailed.

'We've got a job to do. Beeny, we're sorting this out.'

Beeny shook his head, and sobbed afresh, '*Please* don't go!'

'Listen, I've got a job for you, Beeny.'

The boy sniffed. Head down, he nodded, awaiting his instructions.

'Go home.'

'That's it?' Beeny was dubious.

'Tomorrow, a lady called Pauline will send for you. She's got something for you, but you have to be at home to get it, got that?'

'An' you'll be okay?'

D nodded. Beeny leaned in for another hug, thought better of it, and patted D manfully on the shoulder. Then he gathered his ragged nerves, and bolted back up the escalator. Bemused, D watched him go. His smile faded as he concentrated again on his task.

Rejoining his team, D motioned Violet and Watkin to hit the infrasound again. They waited in tense silence as the machines powered up, then the moment the sound wave was released, D shot through the tunnel and down the short flight of steps to platform eight. They all followed.

His machine had done its job of freezing everything in its path, but Watkin was still not prepared for the sight that met him. These were like the figures he had briefly seen coalescing before his silver chain, on top of Castell Dinas Brân, but here there were *thousands* of them - and they didn't vanish in a split second either.

The glasses gave him time to gawp at the heaving sea of sickly grey-green bodies shuddering under the onslaught of the infrasound.

The usually pale, tiled walls of platform eight were dark now. The tunnel bristled with strange bodies that covered every inch of the curved walls and roof, the numbers making a mockery of the fragile black boxes and few simple bows and arrows. It seemed as if D9 had brought some sorry sticks with which it hoped to beat down a multitude.

Watkin faltered, transfixed by the sheer, bitter malice glinting from their eyes, all seemingly directed straight at him. He would have lingered, but Jockey dragged him away to the right, to their position. Ruby raced past them both and stood poised, some twenty yards down the platform.

The instant Violet hit the foot of the steps, she veered left, taking Jim and Scott with her.

D stood full square to the enemy, facing them down. They knew him, and he knew above all that they wanted him dead. Pulling a respirator over his freshly mottled, ravaged skin, he gave the first signal by throwing a canister directly onto the line in front of him. The sudden, massive deluge was signal enough. Jockey fired two canister-laden arrows as far down the line as he could, then Jim and Scott sent the others in the opposite direction.

As each canister brought instant death to hundreds, up and down the track, a multi-tongued howl erupted through the cavernous tunnel. It careened through Watkin's skull, and pounded at his heart.

A trickle of dust sprinkled down from the roof. Watkin looked up. Directly above him, legions of creeping things crouched, frozen by the infrasound, but as yet out of reach of the canisters. They hung there in attitudes of pure hatred, daggers and bows drawn, ready to drop and kill. He grabbed Ruby's arm. She turned and pointed at the sound generator. In his terror, he had missed Jockey's signal.

Under Jockey's silent glare, with shaking fingers, Watkin hunkered down and set off the ISG. Firing randomly into the massed figures, Jockey was disgusted, this was no place for a rookie, and now the ISG's were out of synch. They couldn't afford another mistake like that one.

Jockey accepted they were all dead anyway, but he wanted to take out as many of the enemy as he could, before they got him. Ruby stood beside him, matching shot for shot, until water streamed and cascaded down the walls. Jockey approved. She was worth more than a thousand Watkins in this kind of a scrap.

Yet as many as they hit, ten more filled the space. Jockey couldn't figure it out, they were all still paralysed by the infrasound, he could tell that much at least - otherwise they would be on the attack. So where were the replacement metas coming from? Defying physics, somehow they folded out from nothing, blossoming out into the spaces left by their liquefied kin.

It was like trying to cut the head off the hydra.

67

Greg stared down at the small figure.

'Mistah D tol' me ter go home,' Beeny grumbled, 'snot fair. 'Ee needs help. It's ded scary down dere.'

Mystified Greg asked, 'What were you doing down there anyway?'

Beeny frowned furiously, 'I yonly wanted ter do sum water bombs like de ovvars.'

A thought took form at the back of Greg's mind. 'It would really help Mr. D, if you could deliver a shed load of notes asking for a bit of back-up.'

'Where to?'

'The usual places,' Greg improvised, bluffing crazily.

He had no idea of the extent of D's drop box system.

'Ain't got no pencil.'

Greg handed Beeny a pen.

'Or paper.'

Greg patiently handed over a notebook.

Satisfied, Beeny finally left.

Greg was careful to make sure Beeny actually exited the station, then made his way through the maze of levels, and unlocked a plain and unregarded door marked *'Private.'* It took him to one of the many linking tunnels the majority of underground passengers were unaware of. This one led directly to the closed and deserted Lost Property Office.

The main one for the city, it held vast shelves of unlikely items the British public had mislaid on the transport system.

Taking a little used and curiously wrought key, Greg opened the oldest of the three enormous safes. Ignoring the gold and jewelled items, he concentrated on grabbing anything that looked like it might be made of silver. There were a lot of small silver items, but a couple of large plates and an ornate tea pot and spirit burner really caught his eye.

He grabbed a tartan shopping trolley from a nearby shelf, and tipped them in.

The second safe offered just a little more, and Greg stared down disheartened at the tiny haul. He opened the third safe with a resigned air, but was delighted to find a quantity of silver chains and wristwatches. Greg knew his actions would play havoc with 'Sherlock,' the lost property office's computerised log, but he told himself 'needs must,' and in the midst of an apparent war, it seemed Sherlock was the least of his problems. He would have left an IOU, but Beeny had his writing materials, so he relocked the safes, and dragged the half-full trolley back down the passageway to the hushed station.

He knew Baker Street like the back of his hand. He had recently prepared a detailed map of it for colleagues new to the place, and it was a matter of moments before he stood again outside the door on the lower concourse.

He really didn't want to have to do this.

Steeling himself, Greg hung the trolley over his shoulder and started down the ladder for the second time that night. This time he carefully placed his feet as quietly as he could, stopping at every echo.

Nerves stretched, he inched his way down into the darker corridor, step by painful step. It took so long that he was shocked when his probing foot hit the floor. His sweat-slicked fingers slipped from the metal handrail and he dropped the shopping trolley, falling awkwardly against the corridor wall. The precious silver scattered, and Greg lay absolutely still. Not breathing. Waiting.

Seconds ticked into minutes, but no attack came.

Slowly, painfully he moved to get up. He had wrenched his arm badly, but was barely aware of the injury as he gathered together his sundered hoard.

Willing himself to ignore the squirming knot of fear that scurried in the back of his brain, Greg stuffed the oddments of silver back into the shopping trolley and carefully trundled it up the dimly lit passageway.

A sudden pang shot through him. The batteries for the emergency lighting would soon be reaching the end of their lives. Their failure would plunge the lower levels into the darkest blackness imaginable, and he would be lost down here, right in the middle of it. The thought added an impetus to his actions.

He had to move more quickly - and that would

mean more noise. He made a split second decision, if he was going to be attacked, it would have happened by now. Head lowered, Greg charged down the corridor dragging the wildly skipping and shimmying trolley in his wake.

Within a couple of moments, he stood panting, poised at the correct vented panel. Without bothering to unscrew the cover, he began stuffing the smaller items through the metal louvres. He discarded the tea pot, but the silver plates went through, as did parts of the burner and some of the jewellery. He moved on to another panel, and then a third, feeding each one with a deadly cargo of silver. Then he jogged some distance, and began the procedure again, targeting ventilation shafts much further down the line. Insurance in case the trains carrying the canisters hadn't made it.

It was just as well he did. They hadn't.

Far below, silver dropped, like liquid death, through the open ventilator shafts catching huge numbers of the creatures beneath unaware. The scattered pieces rained down onto the track. Lying like a baited trap, the silver spread its deadly breath through parts of the tunnels out of range for D and his team.

Massed metas began to liquefy.

With the final piece despatched, Greg abandoned the trolley and hurtled back up the corridor. His aching shoulder became a real burden as he hauled himself, grunting, back up the ladder, slowly gaining every inch with pain and sweat-wringing effort.

His eyes were just level with the door when something touched his foot. Greg screamed and kicked out. The unseen thing hung on and scuttled up his body. He screamed again and wriggled to dislodge it, but the rat ran right over his head and jumped onto the step.

Flinging open the door to the mid level, Greg watched it scurry away, a dark speck against the pale tiled floors, the sole survivor of presumably many more of its clan. Catching his breath, Greg sagged with relief. He had seen a lot of rats over the years on the Underground, but he'd never expected to be so grateful for such an encounter.

68

At the other end of the platform from Jockey, Jim was getting into his stride. With six arrows airborne at any one time, he was reliving his glory days as an Olympic marksman. Scott was thoroughly impressed. If they made it out of here, he would be sure to ask Jim for a masterclass.

Violet was busy, sliding up and down the water-slicked platform, slicing and hacking her way through anything within reach.

To Jockey's horror, something was moving from where it had no place to be. Indistinct, the dark mass was approaching from the far end of the platform. It emerged from a small area behind a grey gate marked with high voltage signs and warnings, and it was coming down the platform towards them. Something black had escaped the effects of the infra-sound. Jockey levelled his bow, and took aim.

Whatever it was, it didn't show up on his scopes. He stared again. It looked like absurdly comical - like a weird pantomime horse.

A pantomime horse carrying two violins.

He held his fire as September lifted his cloak, revealing Yelena and their two instruments. They ran past Jockey and the pair of them stood facing the rails. Bravely they smiled through their tears at one another, and began to play for their lives. Jockey shook his head in disbelief, and took aim into the heart of the massed metas again.

A shock of cold water hit Watkin like a freezing blow. It ran down inside his armour. He looked up. Ruby was using one of her silver sprays to clear the area directly above them. When he realised what was running down his back, Watkin shuddered. He felt sick and heartily wished that they had trusted him with a weapon of his own.

As if in answer, D's crossbow pistol skidded across the platform. He had discarded it in favour of his larger crossbow.

Watkin scrambled towards it, but his gratitude was short-lived. As he picked it up, he saw it only had one single bolt remaining on the four-bolt revolve. He would have to make that one really count.

Violet heard the sweet, faint notes rising from the violins above the continual explosions of water, and smiled. She could rest the ISG for wider stretches between blasts now. It offered the scrap of hope that the machines would keep going just a little longer.

Jim reached down into his quiver and faltered, all his arrows were spent. Shaking his head, he started hurling his tiny phials of silver solution like grenades, smashing them against the opposite wall of the tunnel.

The solution ran down the tiles, washing the metas before it, but in their wake, just a little away from the deadly streams, more of their evil kin seemed to blossom out of nothing. They weren't so much killing metahominids as making space for their kin to stretch into.

D's canister was disgorging its contents onto the tracks, effectively slicing the multitude into two groups and separating them with an impenetrable barrier of silver dust.

He jumped down onto the rails, and positioned two further canisters to widen the cleared area. Pinned down between the infra-sound and the music, those few metas that could still move a little, swung round to face him and hiss. D's task was overwhelming enough, but now all the dust was setting off his old allergy, and he coughed into the respirator. It was taking a lot of his energy to stand up, let alone fight. He reached into his ammo bag. The canister he had been relying upon was empty, either faulty, or someone had already discharged it.

To his right, Jim had jumped down onto the track between the frozen metas, and recovered a few precious spent arrows. Now he was expertly firing into the mass of figures, each arrow describing a shallow arc that skimmed close to the tunnel walls, slicing through multiple bodies and making every shot count for many.

After another blast of the ISG, Violet continued scything Baby's deadly blades through as many metas as she could reach. Her armour dripped with their residue, and the wet platform was getting treacherously slippery.

Reaching up to swing at a dangling meta, she skidded and fell heavily, bending her spur backwards beneath her. If it had been a real ankle she would have broken it. As she struggled to regain her footing, her spur's pent energy kicked out, flicking the heavy ISG away. Like a brick skidding on an icy pond, the sound generator skittered across the wet platform and slid towards the edge.

In one fluid movement, rugby player Scott cast his bow and quiver aside and hurled his body in its way. Balanced precariously, he wavered, teetering on the very brink. Just as a single, very determined, spindly arm fought the paralysis, and reached out to stab him. Somehow he defied gravity, and rolled back onto the platform towards Violet.

His arms wrapped protectively round the ISG, and his face wreathed in a triumphant grin, Scott relinquished the machine to Violet, and fell back. A poisoned blade sticking from the left sole of his non-regulation boots. He didn't even know they'd got him.

Violet lunged to grab him, but Scott toppled over the edge of the platform and was lost from sight. Aghast, Violet armed the generator and fired it.

Out of synch with Watkin's, her machine wasn't having the same effect, she could see immediately the spread had lessened, and the multitude of creatures as yet unharmed were still capable of movement.

Then they were gone. Just like at Kew. She knew what was coming next. So did Jockey and Ruby, they hunkered down, waiting for the onslaught of elf-shot. September stopped playing, beckoned Yelena, and she darted beneath the folds of his cloak. Watkin resisted Ruby's pull on his arm and wheeled around, looking for D.

Spotting him, he gasped. D was right out in the open, in the middle of the tracks. Watkin stared for a split second at D struggling to stand. Something was wrong, he was moving oddly. Maybe he'd been hit.

A rumbling noise approached down the tracks, making the tunnel walls shudder. Watkin thought a train might be coming, but the pummelling noise and the shaking was horrendous. With a crash, enormous torrents of water rushed from each end of the tunnel, to meet in a mighty clashing wave. Jockey grabbed Ruby, and hurled her towards the foot of the nearest steps. Then he turned back to look for Scott, but it was too late, he had already been swept away. Yelena dragged September after her, and Jim and Violet charged from the other direction. Scattering, they all raced back up the various stairs and passageways that led in different directions.

Watkin raced past the spot where Yelena had first taken out her violin, and charged up the escalator. The bodies here had not been moved. Watkin panicked. He was lost. This was a different escalator to the one he had come down, but in his mad flight he could see only one thing. The vision of D being overwhelmed by tons of water.

Watkin climbed past the bodies, to the top of the escalator, only to find his way was barred by a pair of enormous red doors. Uncomfortable in his armour, he tried to un-strap it, and failed. Almost wishing they had already shot him, he slumped miserably on the top step to await his fate.

Remembering his Death Dance on top of Dinas

Brân, he looked down at the small crossbow. He held it in an outstretched arm, judging the angles. Yes, it would just about work. If it came to it, he would take off his helmet and use it on himself.

The remaining half of the team regrouped on the lower concourse. No one mentioned D, Scott, Jockey and Watkin were missing. Ruby was shocked to find she was the only surviving member of her group.

'What have we got left?' Jim assessed their remaining supplies.

Violet flashed Baby. She had abandoned the useless ISG, but had grabbed Scott's dropped bow and quiver. She regretted she hadn't had the time to retrieve him and his bandolier of silver sprays. She presumed Watkin's ISG had been lost along with Watkin. Jim still had his bow, but no arrows and he gratefully accepted some of Scott's from Violet. September and Yelena had saved both their violins, but September had tripped over his bow and snapped it, on the way up the steps.

'You two can stand down,' Jim said bluffly, 'Your actions have been exemplary, but we can ask no more of you. Please, get home safely.'

There was no time for a formal goodbye, so September gave a gentle wave, and they took their leave. Jim turned back to face the remaining operatives, 'That inundation could well have taken care of the entire Bakerloo line,' he stated flatly.

'Are they all dead?' Violet asked.

'Most, perhaps not all.' Jim answered mechanically, 'Unless of course any of them were aquids, but that's not likely. They don't tend to travel with the land-based metas...' He trailed off, and bit his lip, thinking of poor, lost Jockey.

Violet shared his misery. After her dad, D had been her hero, and now they were both gone. 'If we don't know why they came here, we've solved nothing. We can't say they won't come back and try again now the silver's been washed away.'

'These things are sensitive to silver in parts per billion.' Ruby murmured, 'No Vi, that water may have taken D and the others, but it's done us a big favour.'

Violet shifted, uncomfortable at Ruby's choice of words.

'She's quite right. By spreading the silver further,

534

it's more than halved our work.' Jim observed, 'Right, we've still got a job to do. We have instructions to follow.'

He avoided saying that they had been D's instructions. He wandered over to the escalator and looked down. The water that had been lapping the bottom step had already ebbed away. Turning back, he addressed them briskly, 'In the unlikely event anything's now turned up on platforms nine and ten, I'd be inordinately grateful if you, Ruby and Violet, could help me see to it.'

He nervelessly set off, back down the steps, with the women following.

69

What *was* that? It was like a dull boom that Gnat felt rather than heard. Sometimes when the school bus had idled, the low engine notes had made him feel sick.

Jamming his fingers in his ears had done no good, as the low thrum somehow just bypassed his ears, and resonated through his chest, and all around his skull, making his cheekbones ache. On more than one occasion, he had been tempted to beg the driver to rev-up, just to stop the nauseating agony.

This was worse. The booming sound swept across him again. He shrank back with Diamond and Cayden, and shut his eyes.

He had felt the swarm stop dead. For a moment, he had got some respite from their vicious outpouring of anger. Then the moment grew into minutes, their voices thinned out, and now only the occasional lost cries buzzed through his brain.

Thyllym found them huddled at the bottom of some steps. They were just across the way, on platform seven, and within earshot of the events unfolding on platform eight.

When the black clad people had first come, Diamond and the boys had hidden, unsure of who to trust. None of them had shown up on the meta-sensitive scopes, because they were all sufficiently human.

Diamond looked up, 'It's you,' she said brokenly. All the intense interest had gone from her. His fairy glamour shattered by the cold reality of the dead bodies she had seen lying, just a few feet away, on the other platform.

One moment the boys were in Diamond's arms, then they were gone, the ghosts of their body warmth, leaking away from hers into the chill, damp air. Diamond crouched on the platform and howled, her cry lost in a sudden, thundering crash. Then the water had come and she had bolted up the steps. It had subsided again in moments, and she had tentatively made her way back down. She didn't know where else to go. If she stayed here, maybe he would come for her again?

She sat shivering in the damp air, lit by the frail and fading lights, listening to the dripping sounds. The sound of approaching feet froze the breath in her throat. She looked up and smiled in recognition.

'Thank God you're here! Now things will get sorted out!

He didn't say a word, just circled her and looked down with his cold, fish eyes. Diamond became aware that a second man had emerged from the shadows and was lurking some feet away, down the platform.

'They've taken the boys! Help me find them.'

He remained silent, he seemed to be weighing something up, she grew exasperated with him.

'You always knew where Gnat was!' She wailed.

The last time he'd seen Gnat was at Uffington. Jockey's mind flew back to the time he'd rung from Richmond, to tell her Gnat was going to Aintree. This time he didn't have a clue where Gnat was. He shook his head.

Diamond was taken aback by his coldness, and a sudden fear overtook her, 'We're in this together right? We both want peace?'

Jockey regarded her with open hostility. This stupid, troublesome hag couldn't have been more wrong. He wanted war. Nothing but war. He walked away, leaving her sobbing.

Then he turned, and levelled his bow at her.

Diamond gasped, finally understanding she had been betrayed. Just as much as Gnat, and all of D9 had been. She drew breath to speak, but didn't. Jockey's arrow slammed into her, stopping her words, and bursting her heart. Diamond flew backwards and slumped against the steps.

Initially drawn by the voices, Watkin had crept down the escalator, now he shrank back into the shadows.

A clatter resounded through the empty tunnels. Activity was starting up again on platform eight. Jockey quelled his sudden start and fixed the entrance through to the blackness of platform eight with a glassy stare. He removed a small hipflask from his quiver, took a hearty swig, and approached the entrance.

Just as Watkin was deciding whether to circumvent the blocked escalator, and take the stairs back up to wherever they led, Jockey passed so close to his hiding place in the shadows, that he could smell the drink on Jockey's breath.

Watkin let him pass and sidestepped back onto platform seven. He stopped in his tracks and stared for a moment at Diamond's forlorn shape, a broken doll in ragged ruffles. Watkin sighed and turned away. He hadn't a clue who this woman was, or what was going on. Or even why Jockey had murdered a civilian in cold blood. Reality was on its head, and he'd fallen rather further down the rabbit hole than he'd first suspected. He changed his mind about going up the steps and followed Jockey.

70

If a member of his species had a single mind, Thyllym had something approaching one. Everything was going to plan.

He had known the hated one, D, would bring his forces to the scene of the last great battle. In fact he had counted upon it.

It had been Thyllym's tactic to draw out their battalions and waste their foot soldiers and weaponry in a confined space, a space that had never been the goal anyway. If he'd had a word for it, Thyllym would have called his lost brethren *'cannon fodder,'* sacrificed for the greater good of the whole.

Despite the telltale signs of silver exposure on his flesh, he flew strongly and soundlessly along the narrow

Jubilee line. He carried Gnat under his arm through the dark underground tunnels, whilst Cayden flew at his other side. He had anticipated a greater resistance than the few humans they had come up against. If D had committed his full forces, then Thyllym knew he had already defeated his hated enemy. If D was hiding the greater part of his army in the barrow by the river, then Thyllym was prepared for that too. Either way he had won.

In a moment of exhausted abstraction, Gnat glanced across at Cayden and his uncle, and saw that, as they flew, their fingertips touched. Just like in Peter Pan. He wondered if the human in Cayden needed that extra help. Then he wondered again if he could fly too. He tried to twist out of Thyllym's grasp, but his uncle misread the action, and simply clasped Gnat tighter.

They swept past broken-down surveillance cameras and out into the daylight.

Gnat blinked, shocked it was still light. The great river Thames glinted beneath them in the late afternoon sunlight. Below them the massive clock tower pointed up, seemingly straight at them. The Houses of Parliament glowed warm, honeyed gold in the beguiling light and the river waters roiled and frothed with activity. Then the whispering in his head started up again and Gnat knew they must be getting close to the hive once more.

71

Roger ran thoughtful fingers through the shaggy grey microphone cover and went through his lines. They'd had a hellish time getting here, and now he was in danger of missing his deadline. He sprinted through his opening.

'The minister who has spent so long avoiding blah, blah, no-one from the treasury available, blah, blah.'

Straightening up, he cleared his throat, and began his piece to camera.

'The Minister who...'

'Mic in shot!' The cameraman cut across Roger's opening words.

'Haven't got six foot long arms!' Roger grumbled, attempting to hold the microphone a little lower. He raised his eyebrows questioningly, the cameraman nodded, and he began again.

'The Minister who has spent so... What do you think you're playing at?'

The cameraman had swerved off Roger, and was focussing on something to his left, and behind him. Roger turned to look.

Normally sedate ministers were galloping across Abingdon Green. Ties flying, jackets flapping, they looked like they were racing one another in some kind of bizarre comedy sketch. Roger giggled. It was the Ministry for Silly Gallops. As they got closer, his grin faded, now he could see all of their faces were stretched taut with genuine effort. Whatever might have passed for a grin, was the gurn of genuine pain from unfamiliar exertion, or from an imminent heart attack.

Roger reverted to his brief glory days in Srebrenica, hunkered down, and began commentating off-script on the event unfolding around him.

'Truly extraordinary scenes of confusion on

543

Parliament Green as Ministers fall prey to some sort of bizarre attack, or even mass hysteria.' He turned way from the camera to look at various individuals running maniacally, and flailing their arms.

'I can see seven people on the ground, but there is absolutely no sign whatsoever of what might be causing this outbreak. It looks like a vicious insect attack, and it could be a re-run of the recent incident in Warwickshire. But I can't see any.... Wait!' Roger slapped the side of his neck, like a clichéd, mosquito-plagued, ex-pat in some ex-colonial hot-spot. 'I've just been stung... Now that's incredibly painful...Gosh that's reall.... I can tell you it's some sort of burrowing. .. This is Ow! David! Help me can you?'

Roger turned his back and the cameraman focussed on the moving lump in Roger's neck.

'Don't just film it man! *Do* something!'

72

Revealed in the scything light of Jockey's head torch, platform eight had been swept clear of just about everything. Even some of its tiles lay scattered on the tracks. A movement drew his eye, and Jockey leapt from the platform, and hurried across to the thing that lay on the rails, gasping like a stranded fish.

D was bleeding from multiple, shallow wounds, but he was still alive.

Jockey made a great show of carefully removing the single remaining earpiece and the broken respirator strap from around D's neck. He stared at them, chewing his lip, biting down hard on his thoughts.

He had never felt so betrayed.

Finally, after checking D's shattered goggles were, as he expected, nothing but clear glass, he spoke.

'You?'

He found it hard to form the next words.

'A *meta?*'

Wearily D nodded.

Jockey sat back on his heels as the bitter taste of bile rose in his throat. He stared coldly at D.

Suddenly everything made sense.

D's appearance was odd. How odd Jockey had never really noticed until now. He shook his head, remembering D's clumsiness out of water and his grace in it. Then there was his aversion to silver, as evidenced by the open wounds all over him. But it was only an aversion, by rights he should have been dead. If D could build up a resistance to the stuff, what was to prevent the others doing the same? Humankind would be powerless.

Another thought struck Jockey, 'But I can *see* you!'

D nodded, and slowly sat up, 'Years of practice.'

Jockey's eyes narrowed, 'How many?'

'In human years?'

Suddenly feeling very small, Jockey flinched. D might just as well have said, '*In dog years?*' D flexed his large hands, Jockey kicked himself for never noticing the emphasised webbing of his fingers before.

'I knew the original John Dee.'

This meant nothing to Jockey.

'He was a code-breaker, and spy.'

D continued, 'For Queen Elizabeth the First.'

One being had blighted his whole life. Now her kinsman lay before him. Jockey spat out the litany of his most hated words, 'So what kind of *aquid* are you? A *merman?* A *merrow?* A *fossegrim?*'

'More to the point, what are you, Jockey? *A traitor?*'

Jockey jumped up, snarling, 'Not to my *own* kind, not like you!'

Taking a few steps back, he raised his bow.

D lifted his arms, and let them flop back on his lap in an open gesture of helplessness. Then he smiled his broken, lopsided smile, 'Why Jockey? Just, at least, tell me that.'

'*You* want answers?' Jockey chuckled humourlessly, keeping his bow aimed at D.

'All I ever wanted to know was *why*. Why have we got no resources? Why are we always reduced to playing Cinderella? Why do we have to creep round, begging kit?'

Jockey shook his head slowly, still keeping his aim. 'No,' he continued, 'there are no answers, at least none that make much sense to me.'

Jockey laughed hollowly, the grim noise surreal and

chilling as it echoed through the dripping tunnels.

'You know what? I *loved* operating solo. Casually tossing canisters into barrows, forcing them out into the open, driving them to this, stirring them up to a confrontation. No more hole-and-corner stuff! Just uncomplicated, open warfare! Now the public and the money men will *have* to sit up and take notice! Now they'll fall over themselves to give us money! And we can wipe out every last ...'

'Did I hear right? Because D9's strapped for cash, you thought you'd bring on a war? That's one *hell* of a tantrum, Jockey!'

Watkin's clipped tones betrayed his nerves. He snapped on his helmet-mounted head-torch and levelled it at Jockey.

'Lower your bow!' Watkin barked the order, but he couldn't quite match Jim's best Sandhurst manner.

Jockey weighed up his chances, Watkin might not have fired a crossbow before, but he was aiming at his bare head and at this range he was unlikely to miss.

Defeated, the Quartermaster's shoulders fell as he cast his bow onto the tracks. In the millisecond Watkin relaxed his aim, Jockey spun and pelted away into the darkness of the tunnel opening.

Unsure of what to do next, Watkin jumped down off the platform and wandered towards D, who sat shivering, his ungainly body in shock from the silver poisoning. Watkin looked away, staring out into the blackness of the tracks where Jockey had vanished.

'The best laid plans of mice and men..' he faltered, D, the creature wracked in agony before him, was neither a mouse nor a man.

'Mr. Watkin, I need a shower.'

D held out his arm, and Watkin helped him up.

Something small and metallic, clattered towards them. It skittered and bounced, striking harsh music from the rails.

Watkin's torch located it, and revealed it to be round and shiny, as innocent looking as a Christmas tree bauble.

Panicked, Watkin hauled D onto the platform, but they didn't make it as far as the steps, before an explosion rocked the tunnel.

With an enormous crash, a great crown of stone, earth, wood and metal erupted on the track, and tiles and damp masonry began falling from the roof. Watkin and D were bodily hurled, with the flying debris, into the void between the platforms and trapped by an avalanche of rubble.

D9's fleeing Quartermaster had succeeded where earlier would-be bombers had not. He had spent some of D9's budget on a quantity of that most efficient and waterproof of explosives, semtex, and now he was bringing Baker Street down on top of all of them.

73

Jim grabbed the girls before the first blast had finished echoing round the cavernous tunnels.

'Out! Now!' He barked, and they had scampered up both sets of escalators, and into the wide spaces of the eerily empty station.

As they approached the one man left waiting for them, Greg looked around for D. Jim shook his head.

Taken aback, the Station Supervisor made to say something, when a further explosion rocked through the lower levels. They felt it up here on street level, and Greg's face twisted in anguish as the guts of his station were ripped apart.

'Time to go,' he conceded quietly.

Like the captain on a sinking ship, he only relinquished his post after sending his staff out of the building before him. Jim, Violet and Ruby helped him check a few empty offices, and then they walked with him, past the deserted concession stalls.

The last they saw of him, as they hurried away, was Greg busily directing staff to move everyone away from the station gates.

They made their way across the still-jammed streets, to nearby Regents Park, and were relieved to find Sam waiting for them. His face fell when he saw how few of them returned, but as he inwardly admitted, he hadn't been expecting *anyone* to return.

As the sole survivor of D9, Violet now outranked Jim and the Aranars present. She quickly appraised their situation. A proportion of the huge numbers of metas in the tunnels may have survived and even escaped. If they had, the little of what was left of D9 needed to know where they were now, and what they were up to.

At best, all it could be was an obs mission. It wasn't just that they were without weapons - having seen what they were up against, they now knew they needed greater quantities of armaments than they had personnel to handle them, Violet shared her thoughts with Sam. He flew through his pre-flight checks in double-quick time, and fired up the engines.

Having donned their meta-sensitive goggles and visors, whilst Sam meticulously quartered the streets of the city, Violet and her team peered down at the streets below, looking for any signs of metaphysical activity.

74

Deep below the streets, D and Watkin sat out their remaining time in the hushed rubble. D was fading fast, his system succumbing to the poisonous silver seeping into his exposed flesh. The air was still full of it, burning his lungs, as he breathed.

Just behind him, Watkin lay where the blast had hurled him, half buried beneath a tumble of brick and timber. Crumbled mortar and earth mixed to make a cold slurry that seeped into gaps in his ill-fitting armour. Only his head and one hand were free. His ribs would have been crushed but for his back and breast plates, but he couldn't feel his other hand, or his feet.

Something very odd was going on with his right ankle, by turns it was on fire and then icy cold. When he tried to move it, spasms of agony shot through him. A gentle warmth spread across his shoulder, and comforted him, until he realised the warmth was coming from his own, leaking blood.

Above them, the escalator towered, still carrying its frozen burden of felled bodies. Beyond that, the stout red doors stood locked and impassive. Even if they could somehow make it up the escalator, these enormous doors effectively barricaded them from any further progress.

In the frozen heart of the captive city, with all communications down, they understood that timely rescue was unlikely. In the ordinary world, order would be eventually restored, and the army would come and find what was left of them. However, this was not the ordinary world.

The Battle of Bakerloo had been lost, the war still raged and, for all they knew, metahominids were creating chaos, even now, in the streets above them. So they talked, passing the precious time between life and death.

Watkin had told D how Jockey had killed Diamond and they had pieced together how he must have been her informant, always keeping her aware of Gnat's location.

D cursed himself for being so blind. He had recruited Jockey on exactly the same basis as he had done Paddy. Yet their life changing encounters with the other side had had profoundly different effects on the two men. What had made Paddy an excellent operative had been the driving force behind Jockey's lingering anger and lust for vengeance. It had made him commit desperate acts.

Watkin had spoken of his regrets. He'd been living a life of compromise, never really doing what he wanted. He told D about Chloe, his life as a policeman, how his encounter on a Welsh hillside had left him jobless, and slowly, but inevitably, their talk had turned back to D.

D told him of many old friends. How he had not been able to keep the metahominids from meddling in World War I, and how this had driven him to double his efforts when conflict erupted again.

He had worked with Churchill to draw up the treaty and keep the metas from complicating an already difficult Second World War - and he told Watkin the price Churchill had paid with his attendant 'black dog.' A creature put there to ensure he adhered faithfully to his side of the bargain and kept harm away from the barrows.

Alongside Conan Doyle and Herbert Wells, D had fought Whitaker Wright, the creator of the Bakerloo line, ironically the very place that now would become his own tomb. Together with Jim Barrie, he had attempted to warn Sherlock's creator of his blind addiction to metahominid glamour.

It was D who had persuaded Dr. John Dee to meet with Queen Elizabeth and set up D9. He had been Dee's 'trusted man.'

Watkin had assumed D meant the present Queen, and Dr. Dee to be a contemporary, but then D had finally admitted how old he was.

Shocked, Watkin stared through his fringe, thick with dust, at the being lying in front of him, as D continued.

'Dr. John Dee was the first human to fully understand what I was.'

'And what's that?' Watkin asked in an awed whisper. 'Jockey said some names. What are you really?'

'A *changeling!*' D spat the word.

Fascinated, Watkin forgot his pain, and quelled his laboured breathing. D continued, 'Dr. Dee saved me when my human hosts finally realised beating me wouldn't *'make me right.'* When they understood I was the unwanted cuckoo in their nest, they threw me out onto the murderous streets of Tudor London. Dee took me in. I helped him set up the proto-D9.'

'You turned against your...' Watkin searched for the word, 'People?'

'They didn't want me.'

'Neither did your human family.'

'No, they didn't, but Dee shielded me from all harm.' D closed his eyes, and lay quietly for a while.

'And in all these long years, you never thought of going back to be with your kin?'

D's thoughts returned to a place he had long wanted to forget, a cursed place, a beautiful glass domed place, a secret room beneath a lake. He smiled bitterly, 'I wanted to at one time, but…' he trailed off.

'But?'

'I couldn't. The human child I had replaced died in infancy *on the other side*. I can never go back.'

Watkin felt the full force of D's loneliness wash over him. The desolation at the core of this stranded creature's life left him without any words of consolation. He stretched out his free hand and grasped D's trailing one.

It felt cold and inhuman.

Nevertheless Watkin clasped it as tight as he could, with what little energy he had left. For once, D didn't pull back from human contact.

'It's been good to have known you,' he said.

Watkin was shocked at the unfamiliar warmth tinged with hopelessness behind D's words.

'It's not over, yet.' Watkin's attempt to muster brightness failed.

'I think you'll find it is, Mr. Watkin. I've waited a long time for this.'

D closed his eyes.

Watkin mentally cast about him. This wasn't the death he wanted, lucked-out in a tumble of blackened rubble.

If D was spent, he wasn't.

He had years in him yet. He'd go out in a triumphal flurry of white, off-piste on a black run. His DBS would describe a graceful arc over a mountainous ravine. His body would be wracked with age, but his face wreathed in smiles as his degenerate corpse was recovered from a legendary cat-house…

Anything, *anything* but the icy realization that they weren't going to make it that was seeping coldly into his soul. Try as he might to resist it, the whispering blackness finally overtook him, and closing his eyes, Watkin finally succumbed.

75

Jockey hauled himself up onto the platform at Regent's Park and took another drink. Distance, darkness, the curve of the tunnel, all had conspired to prevent him from being able to see the fruits of his labour, but he could imagine it.

The chrysanthemum bloom of fire, the blast wave, the shocked look on that inhuman thing's ugly face as it, and Watkin, were blasted into infinity.

It pleased him that he had got rid of the irritating rookie, Watkin. Two birds with one stone, he mused, raising his hip flask in a mock toast.

'Departed fiends,' he growled and started off up the platform.

The army unit found him just inside the entrance. He might have been shot as a terrorist, but for the fact that an old buddy from way back recognised Jockey.

'I heard the bombs go off down the line, and I stayed put.'

'What's this in aid of?'

The senior officer tapped Jockey's Kevlar breastplate.

'Need to know!' Jockey stroked the side of his nose dramatically, his eyes bright with drink. 'One word goes non-stop to fairyland!' he sniggered. 'Don't you know there's a war on? No one does... *yet!'*

The officer stared. The man before him was dressed like bomb-disposal, yet his hands shook. He turned with a questioning look to Jockey's ex-colleague.

'He's basically a good lad, Sir. Old school. Few problems.'

They escorted him up the steps to a waiting army vehicle. As Jockey climbed into the back of the truck, a soldier on a motorbike came breathless with the latest news.

In lieu of dependable radios, the army had adopted a mechanised variant of D's street bikers. A state of emergency had been declared, and London had been split into a series of small, administrative sectors. Each one had a central command post set up in whatever hall, church, office or even shop was deemed most suitable. These command posts were linked by motorcycle messengers and, slowly, order was being restored.

Throughout the paralysed city, people were being ordered off the streets and told to stay indoors, the jammed traffic was being untangled, and the panic was subsiding.

Very slowly, over the course of the afternoon, something like a picture was emerging.

Across London, hospitals had taken in only a slightly higher number of casualties than usual, mainly walking-wounded from minor traffic accidents, and the odd panic-induced heart-attack, plus a cluster of anaphylaxis cases centred on Marylebone and Westminster.

Without internal, or external, communications, London was held in stasis. Billions had been wiped off the economy and whatever the nature of this strange attack, it had proved effective, but bewilderingly inexplicable.

One small explosion, and a flood, had swept through a tiny portion of the underground rail network, but even now, army seniors were arguing that it could have been a chemical explosion on a freight train that had toppled a couple of passenger trains, and not, as initially thought, the work of terrorists.

If this was so, the communications blackout could be a natural phenomenon too. Extreme sunspot activity, solar flares, seismic activity with something emanating from the core of the planet. Maybe the poles were reversing?

These men were not scientists. They couldn't explain why any such activity should solely focus upon the capital, but in their area of expertise, that of mechanised warfare, they fully understood that no enemy had the capability to cause such widespread and lasting disruption *without obvious means.*

So what else could it be?

Little green men?

When the next piece of news came in, they began to wonder. Parliament had become the focal point of a bizarre phenomenon. It seemed a multitude of children had scaled the walls, and had gathered, like so many Midwich cuckoos, on every window ledge and crowded the extensive roofscapes. Beneath them, the Thames was boiling and churning, swept and moulded into fantastical shapes by some unseen force.

In the back of the vehicle, the nearest he could be to sober right now, Jockey listened intently to the latest incoming news.

The officer shook his head. The report outlined happenings that were beyond anything he'd ever dealt with in his professional life. 'Where's Professor Quatermass when you need him?'

'Sir?' The junior had never heard of a 'Professor Quatermass.'

'Have all districts been appraised?'

The runner nodded.

'And the orders are?'

'To stay put, and continue keeping order here. After all, they're only a bunch of kids, Sir.'

'Indeed.'

Unchallenged, Jockey slipped from the back of the truck.

76

They had picked up a lot of metahominid activity around the Thames barrier. Sam's nav systems finally came back online a little way north of Woolwich. Without navigation, he'd been flying by visual reference to the landscape below, crisscrossing the river, following it east.

The radio spluttered into life a few seconds later. Sam marveled, the communications black hole was enormous. Within moments they were being buzzed by a pair of Eurofighter Typhoon jet fighters and ordered to divert west and land at RAF Northolt.

Immediately upon landing, their helicopter was surrounded by armed personnel. Sam's door was flung open, and he was ordered out of the cockpit at gunpoint, as was Violet. Jim and Ruby exited the back with their arms raised, and lay face down on the tarmac as ordered.

All five of them calmly complied, and remained still as they were searched. Although it pained Violet to have Baby taken from her, it was preferable to a bullet in the back of the head. Then they were ordered to stand and led to a small, flat-roofed office in the middle of a cluster of buildings.

The Station Commander stared in fascination at Ruby and Sam. *Aranars.* He'd heard rumours. Stranger yet was the reference number the young black woman had given him. Classified above his clearance as a Group Captain, he had not been able to confirm it immediately. It had taken an encoded message to a senior Whitehall figure, holidaying in France, to establish Violet and her team were some obscure sub-branch of MI5.

As he handed Baby back to her, the Station Commander all but apologised to Violet.

'Utter mess. With you chaps, by necessity, the left hand doesn't know what the right hand's doing at the best of times, but in the present situation it's impossible.'

Violet nodded, 'Understood,' and sheathed Baby, reassured by her weight and unyielding form, pressing against her back.

A young officer brought in a tray of tea and sandwiches, and Violet was struck by the absurd normality of this small gesture of hospitality. Nevertheless, everyone grabbed the chance of a quick break, whilst the RAF, rather sportingly Sam thought, checked out his craft and refuelled her.

Jim was beginning to feel his age, and the emotional shock of losing his lifelong friend D. They had met when Jim had been a boy, still missing a father lost in the war, and D had become a great and lasting influence. Now it almost felt as if he had lost his father all over again. Ruby and Sam had eaten in exhausted silence, whilst Violet requested a map of London.

The Thames was proving to be the next hotspot. They would resume their search for meta activity from the east and begin at that traditional centre of activity, Mortlake near Kew. After the briefest respite, it was just a matter of a few handshakes and they were on the move again.

Violet and her team followed a briskly polite Flight Lieutenant down the corridor, past a huge notice-board featuring a large-scale aviation map of half of Britain. Another board was fluttering with 'Notams.' These *'notices to airmen,'* carried the updates for the day. Violet saw immediately that London and its environs were no-go. Two words drew her attention. 'Purple route.'

A clearly defined corridor leading to Balmoral was to be avoided by all other aircraft.

The Queen was on the move.

77

For the second time that day, Greg found himself briefing an elite force. They were already armed with maps of his station, but he was the only person topside who knew that platform eight had borne the brunt of the action.

Wordlessly they donned chemical protection gear, and made their way down to the big red doors. After testing for toxins, they began work on it.

It took them a little less than ten minutes to open it. There were bodies on the escalator and at the foot of it, a shallow rubble field. Two further bodies lay trapped in it.

Watkin raised his dusty head and one hand, and the team got to work freeing the rest of him. He had an obviously broken ankle, and couldn't help giving a wail of pain as they lifted him clear. His armour had taken a beating. Dagger-like shards of sleeper, tile and brick had hammered on his back plates, and a piece of wood had deflected and punctured his neck.

Though relatively shallow, this shrapnel wound was of more immediate cause for concern. It had driven some dirt deep into the muscle, and the area was red and angry from the onset of infection.

Prateeka assessed D.

He was trapped, but not crushed, and apart from the near-fatal silver poisoning, had only superficial cuts and bruises. Watkin's armoured body had effectively shielded him from the brunt of the blast.

She had brought enough saline to float a battle-ship, and she began dousing D's exposed skin with the solution.

The effects were dramatic. Within moments of his skin shrugging off silver particles, he began to heal with breathtaking speed. She'd witnessed similar with her other meta-blood patient, Gnat.

Whilst the Aranars carried Watkin away, again she watched the miracle unfold, as colour and vitality returned to D's body. She was only one of a handful of other living people to know of D's provenance, and understood his self-healing was the first attribute any life-form needed, if it were to last for centuries.

Within moments, he was unbuckling his armour. He stood, and taking another bottle of solution, carefully rinsed any part of his head, or hands, where he still felt the prickle of silver.

The red welts lessened, but just as there had been in his car when he had carried the silver from Llangollen, there were still sufficient particles in the air to prevent his skin from recovering completely.

Whilst he finished washing the poison residue away, Prateeka explained the regular army were on their way. Everyone was co-ordinating outside the capital, and working semi-blind within.

The Aranars had responded to a message from an Irregular. D raised his head, puzzled. He'd ordered all the Street Bikers home. Some little kid had disobeyed, and hung around the station.

Beeny!

D shook his head, exasperated. When it came to tenacity, that boy could give Watkin a run for his money. Beeny had been worried about D and had posted notes at all the usual places.

The Aranars had responded to:

cOm qwik mista Dee at Bayca StayShun weerd fings hapPn. TrUBLE!

Other notes had flown back and forth too.

What civilians had taken to be the slight forms of children, a Watcher had identified as metas. Long before the creatures had made themselves visible so that the army, amongst others, had become aware of them, this same Watcher had reported the new concentration of them around the houses of Parliament.

Whilst D peeled off the last of his armour, and brushed down his damp, crumpled clothes, he considered this latest piece of intelligence. If the metas had come to parlay for the terms of surrender of the land, they had come too soon. It was time to take up Richard's most recent offer of help. He thanked Prateeka and asked her to keep an eye on Watkin.

'You need to rest.'

'No time.'

She pulled his face close to hers, and stared hard, checking his eyes. They still showed some residual greyness, from argyria poisoning.

'Tip your head back,' she ordered and squeezed a few drops of saline from a pipette into D's eyes.

'Ow.'

'Big baby!' She smiled fondly.

'Better?' D blinked and Prateeka shook her head.

'You'll never be an oil painting, Sir, but yes, amazingly enough, better.'

He stretched his knotted neck, 'Gotta go.'

'Far?'

D pursed his lips. Prateeka knew better than to ask questions like that.

'Just thinking,' she continued, 'Would you find these helpful?'

She dangled a couple of keys, one red, one black. They hung off a key fob marked *Ducati*. D's beautiful, ugly face broke into a huge grin.

'Yes, I would, thanks.'

'Up top, by Sherlock's statue. You can't miss her. She's the bright yellow beauty. Play nice, not a scratch now, I'm warning you!'

Prateeka was left with her forefinger raised in warning. D had already gone.

78

Thyllym stalked the places that had been called, 'The Corridors of Power.' Places that were now anything but. Behind him, Gnat and Cayden trotted to keep up. Before him, a junior minister pranced and whirled like a court jester, his face a contorted mask of misery. Unwillingly showing them the way to the twin houses of government, he was unable to resist and regain control of his own body.

At Thyllym's bidding, every minister, secretary, clerk and mandarin scuttled out of his, or her, office or hiding place, and took their irresistible position in the growing procession to the Commons.

Like an army of court jesters, Thyllym's helpless puppets capered and jigged into the Commons chamber, advancing awkwardly between the long leather benches, filling the spaces with grotesque, staccato movement.

The great closed doors between the two houses flew open. The crash reverberated around the halls, jerking lords and ministers alike from sleep. Furious and unwilling, Lords Spiritual and Temporal, members of what the House of Commons traditionally referred to as 'that other place,' were half danced, half dragged into the House of Commons as if by some strange compulsion. They gathered and huddled in the space between the green Commons benches, filling the gap between the opposing sides, one that by ancient expedient had been ordered to be *'two sword lengths apart.'*

Thyllym raised his head, and began speaking in a

strange, skitterish tongue, full of clicks and insectlike humming. Some members of the house found they could hear clear words forming in their minds. Many could not, and for them, Thyllym now turned to Gnat.

Cayden was already translating into his head, so Gnat simply said what he heard.

That one from such an alien culture could begin to frame abstract human concepts, and create a coherent argument, showed how deeply Thyllym had studied his enemy.

'The old treaties have been ripped up, alongside the new. You have proven you cannot be trusted. My armies wait, poised to destroy you. This place shall be cleared of your infestation. Your Queen has abandoned your barrow, and left you to all to die!'

Gnat thought this was crazy. Even *he* knew the Queen had no real power. Thyllym plainly had no idea how the government worked.

It was lucky the Queen wasn't here. If she had been, Gnat knew she would be powerless to resist handing everything over to Thyllym. Then he realized, the people who ruled the country *were* all here, and *they* were powerless to resist too.

By a supreme act of will, a lady peer managed to finally speak. Although her tone was strained, and strangled, her words were clear.

'What do you want?' She asked.

Cayden translated.

Thyllym turned, and stared at the woman, consumed with hatred.

'Our land back!' Gnat said for him.

Even if they could have done so, the peers were too shocked to make an attempt at any answer.

Above him, Gnat could feel the intent of the hive mind, oppressive and listening, waiting for the call to swoop down and destroy, to strike the killing blow at the very moment of surrender.

'You have broken treaties that have been held since Domesday! We have allowed you to claim ownership of *two thirds* of this island on the *sole condition* that you were to guard the ancient places!'

Thyllym circled, lithe and dangerous, moving on his

toes like a dancer, poised and ready to strike like a rattlesnake, all the time his low voice carried his words and Gnat blindly interpreted them.

'Our races have intermarried. Your lineages carry our bloodlines! Your kin is our kin. Yet you have attacked us. You have sought our destruction, and now we seek yours!'

Thyllym examined the minds of those present, seeking out the most powerful in all the land. One by one, members of the inner cabinet, heads of certain departments, and a few with less clearly-defined roles, stepped forwards, propelled by an imperious compulsion. Thyllym scented the air like a bloodhound, his preternatural senses homing in on the faintest elements of the earth they habitually walked upon, elements buried deep within the cells of their skin and hair. He traced each one of them back to their provenance, their estates and their land.

It was easy for him. He was a creature who understood that the earth owned these people, every bit as much as they thought they owned it.

Two men were dismissed, modern politicians, not landowners. They danced back to their colleagues, and once relinquished, fell in a daze onto the Commons floor.

No-one in the hushed gathering could move a finger to help. Two more sauntered up to take their places and the bizarre investigation began again. After an hour of tense examination, one by one, Thyllym gathered those who owned the most.

The House of Lords had not been as full as it might have been. Today was not the State Opening of Parliament, but there had still been a greater number present than could be expected on an ordinary day.

Beautiful music began. So beguiling, even Gnat's foot began to tap. Cayden reached forward, and grabbed his arm, shaking his head, and frowning. Gnat found that he could resist the sound, only if he concentrated. If his mind wandered, his feet started tapping and his fingers began drumming again.

He watched in amazement. As the eerie sounds played through the Commons chamber, be-suited, respectable looking men began moving their bodies in startling ways. He began to laugh as they pirouetted madly, then he caught the shocked expression on one small man's face and he turned away suddenly feeling sick, assailed by an abrupt recollection of the loud thud made by the hapless tour guide in the Williamson Tunnels.

As Thyllym turned on his heel and strode away, Cayden grabbed Gnat's arm, and propelled him along in their uncle's wake. They followed Thyllym out through the double doors, and down a long corridor with the procession of jigging peers following behind, like so many children lured out of Hamelin.

They passed silently. Along corridors and up staircases, and past a line of etchings hung at shoulder height, scenes from, '*Iolanthe*,' but the irony was lost on Gnat. Some of the Peers were crying silently, Gnat felt very sorry for one young man who appeared far too young to be there. He looked terrified.

Only recently elevated to the Peerage, this had been only his second visit to the House of Lords. Now compelled by a strangely irresistible, otherworldly command, he capered along behind the tall creature and his child attendants.

Percival had heard through family legends, long told, how his kinsmen and women had conspired with the exquisite, secret dwellers on their land. Together they had worked to keep certain acreages all but invisible.

The beings had beguiled those government assessors who had come and sought to pry, confusing and compelling them to leave well alone. Metahominids had effectively hidden many family estates from the eyes of whosoever was perceived to be the enemy at the time.

From pre-Saxon, to Norman, then those of the acquisitive King Henry VIII - and later on the tax collectors, and more recently, even present-day government departments.

Despite its creation over seventy years previously and all the sophisticated, modern surveying equipment the twenty first century has to offer, meta collusion had meant huge swathes of Britain continue to remain unrecorded and invisible to the Land Registry. That this extraordinary fact, that half of Britain's landscape remains unregistered, should be 'overlooked,' had been an integral part of the deal.

Now, this agreement had seemingly gone sour, although the mystified Lords couldn't begin to guess why. Hopping and skipping wearily along, all of Thyllym's unwilling puppets had time to think.

Some danced, recalling family legends or more recent encounters. Others became suddenly acutely aware of the faery jewels, relics of long forgotten dowries, held in safety deposit boxes. One man had even proudly placed on display a fading green flag at home in his baronial castle.

This fragile, mossy piece of silk was a *fairy flag* - to be used in time of crisis, a legacy of the mingling of his family with the metas.

As hard and fast as they all thought, none of them could see how the treaties had been broken.

Guided by the faintest drafts, Thyllym scented his way through the labyrinthine structure to the upper levels. Making steady, if unwilling, progress, the spellbound members of the peerage climbed through yet another heavily carved door, and up along another, narrower passageway.

By now, most of the party were panting heavily. Looking back along the line of mainly elderly bodies, Gnat felt sure one or two of them couldn't go on for any longer. Even in the dim light of the passageway, he could see their lips had turned blue.

Just when the prancing steps grew more stumbling, and the ragged breathing seemed to be reaching a dangerous crescendo, Thyllym threw open another door, and stepped out onto a broad flat roof space. Gnat and Cayden followed obediently, and the train of bewildered men and women peers tumbled out of the narrow doorway behind them. All fell, gasping, to their knees. Unable to stand, they knelt, heads bowed, taking great gulps of the fresh air.

Wherever Thyllym moved, like iron filings drawn to a magnet, they scrambled upon their knees to keep up.

They were right on top of the Houses of Parliament. Gnat shielded his eyes against the suddenly bright sunlight, and took in the view of a strangely silent London. The great rotating eye had stopped moving, and abandoned cars and buses choked Westminster Bridge.

Slowly he became aware that they were not alone. A low hissing began, as the metahominids crept from their rooftop perches, and began advancing upon the humans.

Head down, Sir Henry was aware of their approach. It was a noise he had listened to many times before, dating far back into his personal history. As a toddler, he had heard his first fairy procession, passing close by the house, whilst lying in his cot in his nursery. His very young eyes had grown huge as he had stared with wonder at the fairy-tale shadows cast around the walls of his room. Nurse had been drunk as usual. When he had been old enough to understand, someone had told him that she had lost a child of her own long ago, and she had never recovered.

As he had grown older, Henry had begun to suspect the creators of the shadows had been the culprits, who had taken her child. These beings had haunted him all his life, he thought bitterly, and now they intended to kill him. The forced dance had not taken much out of him. Although overweight, and the wrong side of fifty, his ruddy complexion was that of a man used to long walks in the countryside. What had just happened was as nothing compared to the torture of the cross-country running demanded of him by his old school.

Clearing his throat, Henry tried his voice. 'Look here!' he began, still unable to raise his head, but pleasantly surprised at the sound of his own steady voice.

'I cannot speak for anyone else here today, but I know this. I have not broken any pact, or treaty, with you, or anyone. As far as I know, your kin have been left completely in peace, as agreed.'

Gnat nervously translated the words, unable to look Thyllym in the eye. He could feel the icy energy of anger rising within his uncle.

Henry continued, 'Destroying us will achieve nothing. Our heirs will inherit, and nothing will change. If you believe ownership of the land will be surrendered to you, then quite simply you are mistaken!'

White faced, Cayden spoke Thyllym's reply.

'We do not expect a swift conclusion to this conflict. Victory will be slow, but it will come. I can wait. You no longer have that option. For now the forfeiture of your lives will impress upon your offspring the need to keep us safe. With your fates as an example, they will *not* neglect their duties, as you all have done!'

Henry was dragged to his feet by an overwhelming compulsion, and the dance started again. Slowly, his prancing feet closed the long distance of lead roof lying between him and his destruction.

79

Jockey had scampered swiftly through the streets, avoiding patrols by ducking into doorways or dropping behind abandoned vehicles. He was sweating in his lightweight armour, but he didn't dare take it off. The metas were close. He could sense the humming energy in his bones. Like the build-up before an electrical storm, the air was growing thick with their presence.

He covered the scant few miles quickly, in an easy,

rhythmic jog they used to call, '*yomping*,' back when he was a kid. Within half an hour, he was skirting the squat outline of The Jewel Tower. Jockey stopped to catch his breath, and looked across at the Houses of Parliament. Activity drew his eye. The roof was bristling with metas.

One single canister nestled against his chest. Had they searched him when they'd stopped him, the army would have found it, together with a tiny detonator and a blob of semtex the size of a blackbird's egg.

There were no cordons here yet, and Abingdon Green lay silent with just a few suited bodies scattered upon the sunlit grass. Like a bizarre tableau of strangely posed tailor-shop dummies, they lay with their ties fluttering in the light breeze.

Jockey stared down, the blank face looking up at him was familiar. Then he remembered where he'd seen this man so many times before - fronting news reports on television.

'And it's goodnight from him!' Jockey quipped lightly, draining the remainder of his hip flask. He looked down at it, glinting seductively in his trembling hands.

Unnecessary weight.

He cast it away into the grass, then thought better of it and retrieved it. Just the smell of it was comforting.

Pugin's gothic embellishments offered a wealth of handholds as Jockey began his climb up the side of the building. The combined effects of weather and pollution had done their worst, and not all of the rocky extrusions could be relied on to hold his weight. As he jammed his fingers behind an ornate trefoil, it crumbled into sand.

The shattered fragments showered down onto the green, and he slipped and hung for a second, before locating a firmer hold.

Despite the setbacks caused by the uneven quality of the stone, Jockey climbed efficiently, exactly as he had been trained to do, keeping three points of contact at all times, whilst groping for the next place for hand or foot.

Completely absorbed, some of his anger left him as he focussed solely upon this single task. The initial hard climb was growing increasingly easier as the higher adornments sprouted further elaborate patterns, and allowed him an even greater choice of anchor points. Ducking into the dark space offered by a tall window, he assessed his progress. He couldn't see the metas from here, but that meant nothing. Even now they might have him targeted him with bows drawn ready, or even be creeping down, like so many spiders, to ambush him. He didn't want to climb up straight into an attack, but he didn't have much choice. He was about to set off again when the distant drone of a helicopter temporarily distracted him.

The skies above London had been as silent and deserted as the streets, and this had been the first air-traffic he'd heard all day.

80

Violet confirmed, 'I see them.'

'God God!' Jim exclaimed. 'They've got hostages!'

'What now, boss?' Sam asked Violet. He was circling the helicopter around the Houses of Parliament, careful to keep out of range of the deadly elf-shot. Sweeping out over the river, they could all see the unearthly water sculptures thrown up by the shoaling aquids. Jim was thankful for his failing hearing, and the clatter of the rotor blades, as he knew how compelling the siren song of the aquids could be.

'What have we got left?' Violet asked.

'A few hand-held silver sprays.' Ruby answered.

'They won't do much from this height.'

'Downdraft might help,' Sam ventured.

'Yeah, but only if we hover right on top of their heads.' Violet sighed looking back at their target. 'We've got to get onto that roof.'

'Two suicide missions in one day? You're spoiling us!' Jim said wryly.

' "This must be a Thursday," ' Ruby quoted with a grim smile, ' "I never could get the hang of Thursdays." '

Looking down, they could see a knot of miserable-looking people, half-heartedly jigging in procession along the roof top. They looked like a line of drunken sailors walking the plank.

As they watched, a man in a dark suit danced to the very brink, balanced there for a moment, and then toppled over the edge. His body cartwheeled through the air, impacting heavily onto the terrace overlooking the river. The paving cracked and deformed beneath him, and he lay breathing his last in a shallow depression that slowly filled with his blood.

Everyone onboard the helicopter held their breath, as the next body flew further out, into the river.

'What the…? Look! There's a man, climbing up! He's just about made it to the top. Hang on! It can't be?' Adjusting his goggles, Jim peered hard.

'Well, well, well, if it isn't our Jockey!' He finally announced, 'The devil really does look after his own!'

'Get ready, everyone,' Violet ordered, 'If Jockey can distract them, we may get a chance of not being killed the instant we set foot on that roof.'

As if he knew, Jockey chose that moment to create an explosion on the far side of the roof. It sent masonry and metas scattering, and created a fair sized empty space for Violet and her team to drop into.

Sam took the helicopter down very low, and they all hopped lightly from the craft. Sam rose again, and the three of them stood back-to-back, getting their bearings. Violet couldn't help but think of how she had stood like this on top of Dinas Brân with poor, lost Watkin. Blinking back tears, she unsheathed Baby and raced to help Jockey.

D9's Quartermaster had rushed into the thick of the metas, and was furiously gesturing Sam to follow in his craft. The reason soon became clear. He had managed to preserve one precious canister. Arming it, he waited for the first faint wisps of silver to appear and then continued to hang onto it until the plume was strong and established. Judging the moment right, he cast it into the thickest part of the meta crowd, and watched as Sam's swirling rotor blades broadcast the silver particles even further.

Within moments the roof was awash. Shallow eddies ebbed around the bewildered humans who had been released from their enchantment. Now they found themselves shivering, soaking wet, and completely unable to remember how they had come to be up here. Those nearest to the doorway down fled back through it, leaving the others to their fate.

On the dripping roof, the canister slowly ejected its final, deadly breath, and lay spent and inert.

Within a heartbeat, airborne metas surged down with a vengeance. Screaming multi-frequency battle cries, they thumped down hard onto the roof, and drew their poisoned weapons on the humans.

With neither music, nor infra-sound, to freeze the

metas, Violet was quickly becoming overrun. Dodging Baby's blades, her attackers sought to trip her. Their grasping, spindly fingers grabbed at her armour, and tried to prise off the plates.

She turned, and whirled on the spot, stabbing blindly at the heavy chunkhead who had leapt onto her shoulders and was attempting to drag off her helmet.

Jockey was fighting alongside her, armed with a small knife, plunging it arm deep, into the wavering wall of semi-opaque beings. Jim stood to the right, deploying the last few silver sprays, at very close quarters.

Ruby had retrieved a silver pocket watch that had been dropped on the roof and was swinging it hard into the metas that pressed in on every side. Undeterred, still they came. The last remnants of D9 were battling, half-blind, in a murderous hail of elf-shot. The few hostages left up on the roof were riddled with elf-shot, and dead, or dying.

Jockey had been trying to tell Violet something the moment he had spotted her. Something about D and the metahominids, but she couldn't quite catch it.

Above them, Thyllym directed the archers to the human male. Even from here, he could smell the barrows upon him.

Another pair of eyes had singled Jockey out for special attention. A denizen of the place called, '*Wayland's Smithy.*' Eirian had passed this very man on the way home, one spring day. He had been walking away from her barrow. When she had returned home, she had found it dripping with poisonous silver. If the metas had the word for it, they would have called Jockey a war-criminal.

Eirian sent out urgent thought whispers, announcing to the assembly that this human had even more of their blood upon him than any of the others here.

A dark cloud of innumerable metas formed mesmerising shapes over the rooftops as it gathered and reformed, like a flock of starlings. Then they dropped with deadly intent, falling silently upon him, as if falling from the sky to roost.

All Violet was aware of was that one moment Jockey was there, and then he was gone. She watched helplessly as he was taken, kicking and screaming, up into the fatal heart of the dark cloud.

They took him far out over the river, where the water formed arms that reached up to receive him. For agonising seconds, he was held swearing above the dizzying drop, then they let go.

Jockey dropped like a dark comet, and smashed into the turbulent surface of the green Thames. The water was full of movement, and instantly lithe bodies surrounded him. As he fought for the surface, they playfully tugged at his feet, dragging him deeper into the depths. He shook them off, and resolutely kept his head, struggling to dump his armour. Then the clutching arms grew helpful. Someone unclipped his helmet, and it floated free. His back and breastplates came off next, and he found he could move. Somewhere far beneath, a restful lullaby was being sung in a beautiful voice.

Then she was there, and all the years, all the hurt and rage, tumbled from him, sinking gracefully like calm benthos, to settle on the river bed.

Softly, reproachfully, she sang to him.

'I'm sorry.' Jockey mumbled in a dream, 'Forgive me…' and all the while, the precious air streamed from his nose and mouth.

This time she made no move to save him.

Then the next one came.

She was identical.

As was the next.

And the next. Until he was surrounded by them.

The nymph sisters were so alike, as to make it impossible for him to know which one had been his. If any of them.

Having found her, Jockey had lost her again.

One last scream of despair, and frustration, and Jockey was done.

His lungs filled with the alien element of water, and after the initial panic subsided, his body remembered it had come from amniotic fluid, and lived on for a few moments more. The last thing Jockey saw was the calm regard of their beautiful eyes as they watched him die.

At the first fireball, Thyllym had grabbed Gnat and Cayden, and risen up above the humans' flying device. Seething, he watched the massacre unfold beneath him. Even so, the roof had not been big enough to accommodate even half of them, and long lines of his kinfolk still hung in the air. Those beneath were just a fraction of their number.

He had to marshal them again, but they were wild

with glee at the death of the human, and even Thyllym was finding it hard to make his thoughts heard. He would summon the hordes from above the river, and direct them to snatch the remaining humans from the roof, and drop them from the heights onto land, or water. It didn't matter. They would all die.

Whilst the hive mind was focussed on celebrating the conflict, Gnat suddenly found he had been abruptly detached from its influence. Held fast under one long and powerful arm, he studied his uncle at close quarters, and shuddered. He wanted no part of this.

He wanted to be a boy again. A boy with a Dad, and a normal life. Even a life constantly on the move was better than this. Hanging high in the air above the Houses of Parliament, tucked beneath a supernatural being's arm, for some absurd reason he found himself wondering what Matt was doing.

Something swooped down from above and approached him. He recognised her at once. It was Neave.

Smiling, she took his hand, inviting him to pull away from the safety of his uncle's side, but as if in answer Thyllym's grasp tightened. Gnat turned to Neave, and shook his head. They were hundreds of feet above the river.

She smiled, sadly unwilling to leave, until Thyllym's stern frown ordered her away, but not before she vouchsafed Gnat a dazzling smile.

It brought to his mind a fragment of what Diamond had told him, about his Dad meeting his Mum. *'I introduced them at festival years ago, when they were kids. They grew up and one day they, 'accidentally,' found each other again...'*

Then, without a doubt, he knew they had already mapped out his life for him. Like some historical Prince, they had chosen his future bride already.

She would be Neave.

He stared down at the helicopter beneath him, twitching and sliding about on the currents. Sam's compensatory manoeuvres slowed into a gentle ballet, and the noisy blades grew silent and graceful, as Gnat studied their beautifully balanced lines. The black and white painted strips on the rotors created whorls of colour, and he stared down, drawn to them, as they beckoned him, as potently as any spell. The spinning rotors offered peace and an ending. They would cut him into so many pieces, even Thyllym would be unable to save him.

81

Prateeka's motorbike scythed through the eerily deserted streets, scattering an extraordinary number of rats that had ventured out into the unnaturally human-free city.

As D headed south-east, he crossed beneath the restive Thames, through the echoing Blackwall Tunnel, all the time mentally keeping his head down, watching his thoughts, doing whatever he could to avoid attracting the hive-mind.

He covered the twenty-odd miles in a little under eighteen minutes. The moment he passed the sentinel Spitfire and Hurricane at Biggin Hill, D started looking for his target.

'Lynmouth,' was tucked away in hangar ten. D drove around until he spotted a large white X painted on a brick wall. He coasted the bike to a halt and moved quickly and quietly towards the hangar.

Hunched over his phone, playing a game, a youngster in red overalls was sitting outside the huge double-doors on a blow-up chair.

He leapt up when he spotted D.

'Mr. D?'

D wheeled, greatly surprised he was expected. He nodded cautiously.

'Very pleased to meet you, Sir!'

The youth pumped D's hand enthusiastically, 'I'm Tim!'

The man checked out. He had the weird eyes Richard had told him about. Tim abruptly dropped the handshake and scampered to push open the huge hangar doors. They slid gracefully apart, to reveal a very shiny, very small aeroplane.

'She's not quick, but she's steady. I've kept her in tip top!'

D nodded appreciatively at the gleaming, bright red-and-white aeroplane.

'How long have you been waiting for me?'

The boy pulled a thinking face, calculating, 'Five weeks?'

He met D's surprised look with a cheerful, 'It's been great! I've had to keep her running, so I've got my flying hours way up on circuits and bumps! And I've been *paid* to do it! Result!'

D primed the engine, and turned the key. The little Cessna fired first time, and he taxied out onto the apron. There was a light wind, nothing too much to affect the controls. The sweet-natured little machine wouldn't let him down. Now, D could only hope his own body wouldn't. Red weals were rising on his exposed skin again, and his vision was blurring.

D rubbed his eyes, and went through his checks. Temperatures and pressures all showed normal, the altimeter had been set, and he checked his brakes. The radio was still useless, so he did a quick scan for incoming craft before moving out onto the runway.

The visual signal came from the tower, and D opened the throttle. The aircraft gathered speed and gently rose, with so little fuss that for the first few couple of seconds it was hard to tell she was airborne.

D turned hard left and climbed, joining the circuit, the invisible roundabout that was the organising principle over every airfield. The ground beneath was heating unevenly in the hazy sunshine, making the air bumpy. The propellers chopped efficiently through the turbulence, but it still felt as if he was driving along a road full of deep potholes. Still climbing, he turned ninety degrees left again, and just after gaining circuit height, peeled away.

Turning the little red craft's nose northwest, he headed out towards the city.

Despite Richard's advice that they should, 'dust the barrows,' this craft wasn't a crop-duster. Tim's pride and joy, the lovingly nurtured, 'Lynmouth,' was a cloud-buster, a rain-maker. She had been named after the settlement nearest to '*Operation Cumulus*,' a cloud-seeding experiment. Attempted by the RAF in 1952, it brought down a deluge that lasted a month, and was rumoured to be responsible for flooding the Devon town of Lynmouth.

D's Lynmouth carried the appropriate delivery system, and a tank full of the chemical used to seed clouds, and make rain - silver iodide.

Free floating micro particles continued to irritate D's skin and eyes. He had to do this quickly, before he succumbed to the poison.

Although he was flying low enough to avoid detection, D kept a constant vigil, scanning the skies, anxious for signs of other aircraft. Right now, getting shot down by the RAF was not part of his plan.

It took him just under ten minutes to reach his target and begin his first run. Busy, dragging Ruby away, the enemy didn't even see him coming. The first drop, at two and a half thousand feet, took just a couple of minutes to take effect. It wiped out a huge skein of metas that had stretched across the sky. Instantly liquefying, they dumped tons of water on the streets, and Sam's helicopter took a huge hit. It felt as if it had been swatted by a giant hand, and he had to fight to keep his craft airborne. He managed to regain control, and alighted upon the roof, just as Ruby broke free from the grasping metas. He pulled her onboard, and slammed the cockpit door.

Surrounded by a toxic cloud of silver, Thyllym howled. Rubbing his burning eyes, he hurled Gnat and Cayden away. Gnat fell headlong, his twin tumbling beside him. This was it. This was what he wanted.

As if in a dream, he reached out to touch his brother, as they hurtled towards the grass of Abingdon

Green.   Cayden grasped his outstretched hand.   Their outstretched fingers touched.

And they flew.

Skimming the earth, they shot skywards again.

Gnat burst out laughing, he looked across at Cayden. Covered in spots and splashes from the silver, they both looked like they had bad cases of the measles, but he was laughing too.

Leaving the bitter intensity of the conflict far behind, they flew down to Waterloo Bridge, landing lightly on a broad pavement. An abandoned classic red double-decker had been left, pointing diagonally across the road.

'This is an old-fashioned bus. You get a lot of them in London.' Gnat announced gravely. 'They take people from one place to another.'

Cayden smiled uncertainly, he had no idea what his brother was talking about. Gnat hopped lightly onboard, and led Cayden to the top deck. Together they sat at the front, to watch the rest of the battle unfold.

As D took his next run, Sam frantically signalled Jim and Violet to get onboard. Fighting off flying metas, they hurtled towards him, elf-shot cascading against their armour. Then Violet stopped dead, struggling with a meta that had settled on her, and was twisting her helmet back to front, and trying to strangle her. She stabbed blindly, and freed herself, but something else had happened in the encounter and Violet dropped like a stone. Jim caught her up in the fold of his cloak, before she even hit the ground, and carried her to the waiting helicopter.

Ruby jumped out and helped them onboard, then slammed the cargo-door shut, against the next volley of elf shot.

By now, D had begun his second run. Just as it lifted into the air, the helicopter was deluged again, with a crashing avalanche of falling water. The rotors shuddered, and the engines spluttered, as the craft began swinging crazily, out over the river.

Sam struggled to regain control, but they were falling out of the air.

'Heads down!' he barked, and Jim and Ruby huddled over Violet in the back. The tail rotor was spinning intermittently, and the main blades were slewing to a halt.

With great skill, Sam dragged the howling machine

back from the river, and attempted a controlled crash onto the terrace. The engines shrieked, and the rotors carved great slices out of the stone-work. They landed heavily, but relatively intact, at a crazy angle, leaning across the terrace wall, balanced on a single wrecked skid, hanging out over the open water.

Sam waited for the craft to settle, and cut the engines. Even as the whining shudder diminished, the growing metallic creaks and groans from the fuselage made him nervous. He had to get everyone off before the helicopter inevitably overbalanced and slid, over the edge, into the water.

'Anyone hurt?' He was unable to see what was happening in the back.

Jim had removed most of Violet's armour. Directed by him, Ruby had clamped a hand over a wound in Violet's neck, and was pressing down hard.

Jim answered Sam's query bluntly. 'Violet's in poor shape. Poison blade. Punctured carotid, rapidly bleeding out. We can't move her, and we can't deal with the poison yet.'

Another wrenching groan juddered through the

downed craft.

'We have to get out!' Sam insisted. 'That plane is circling for another run. A blast of water like the last one will send us over the edge.'

Mercifully, D's next run took him north of the building, on the opposite side to the terrace. It gave Jim precious moments to raid the Aranars med boxes.

He carefully bound Violet's neck with medical tape, and then applied sturdy electrical tape over the top, to make sure nothing moved. Plugging the hole in her neck was keeping the poison in her system, but he currently had no other option. The poison would kill her more slowly than loss of blood.

Either way, they had very little time to get her on foot to a functioning hospital - even if they could find one. Had the helicopter been serviceable, a short hop home meant he could have operated upon her there, as he had done with Gnat's dad, but that was no longer an option. Ruby gently insinuated herself out of the crippled craft, and turned back to help Jim ease Violet out of the helicopter. They slid her slowly out, and Ruby carefully lowered her to the tiled pavement. With a sudden bang, the doomed helicopter lurched alarmingly sending Jim tumbling backwards, against the opposite door.

Something heavy slid across the floor. It was Violet's precious Baby, but Jim had no time to waste retrieving her. Using the front seats for purchase, he clambered slowly back to landside, and waited for Sam to appear in the cockpit doorway. As the craft had begun to overbalance, belly-up, the exits had tilted, and were now over ten feet from the ground. In one movement, like a pair of divers, Sam and Jim kicked off, and jumped clear. Sam rolled as he hit the hard paving of the terrace, and he jumped up lithely, whilst Jim's long legs made less of an elegant escape.

With a final, shrieking metallic scrape of complaint upon the lower wall, the wreckage of the stricken helicopter slid from the terrace, and dipped beneath the boiling waters.

The river suddenly stopped thrashing about, and became calm, as the aquids fled from the potency of Baby's silvered blades.

Through bleary eyes, D gazed out through the Plexiglas windscreen. He was feeling nauseous, and on the edge of consciousness.

By an intense act of will, he talked himself through

surviving the next few minutes, then after that the next few minutes. Marking time by shorter and shorter intervals, until, by his fifth run, the skies were clear.

All the metas had dispersed. The combination of Baby and the silver laden run-off had seen to it that the Thames ran calm, and clouds had begun to gather above the city.

As the first enormous drops of natural rainwater began to fall, D pointed his craft south, and flew Lynmouth back to her hangar.

82

The army patrol found Gnat and Cayden wandering aimlessly through the streets. It was more than their uncle had done. Freed from hive mind, and fixated upon finding his Dad, Gnat had proved hard to locate. Cayden just wanted to be human.

The army had settled the boys in a, 'displaced person's centre,' a sports hall, telling them that their Dad would be traced, and they could go home soon. Gnat couldn't help but wonder if it would be that simple, but the army gave the boys food, and something to drink, and they had gratefully accepted.

This had sealed Cayden's fate, as it had done for so many humans taken into enchanted places by the metas. Eating and drinking in an alien realm always made for a long stay.

A thought struck Gnat. He carefully unlaced his battered shoes, and pulled a lumpy shape out of one sock - his mobile phone. He retrieved the precious battery from the other sock, and reunited the two.

Gnat held his breath as the screen slowly awoke.

There were seven messages, all sent today. All from his Dad.

Gnat sobbed.

'What's wrong?' Cayden was beginning to learn how to vocalise his speech, rather than think it into the receiver's mind, but his words were still strangely accented.

Even as the battery breathed its last, and the screen shut down before any of the messages could be opened and read, Gnat was grinning hugely through his tears.

'Nothing,' Gnat whispered, 'Nothing is wrong, we're going to have to find a charger.'

Cayden's sympathetic smile faltered, 'But Nathan, that will be difficult!'

Gnat regarded Cayden quizzically. Cayden patiently explained, 'There are no horses here.'

Mystified, Gnat nodded slowly, and gave his earnest twin a big hug.

83

Returning, defeated, to his home barrow, Thyllym felt the sudden snapping of the boys' detachment, and he knew he had lost them. For now.

There would be other times. There would always be plenty of time. His immediate concern was facing the wrath of the hive mind.

Thyllym knew there would be a reckoning.

84

The aide waited respectfully a few steps behind her on the lawn, whilst Queen Elizabeth the Second inspected the rose closely. The size of a large tea plate, it filled both her hands as she gently lifted the heavy flower-head for a closer look. The full skirted rose was deepest red, with a purple velvet bloom at the throat of each furled petal. Bearing its raindrops like jewels, it exuded an opulent, spiced perfume into the warm, damp air.

His monarch was playing a waiting game.

Finally she spoke. '*Ena Harkness*. A very beautiful rose, don't you think?'

He observed the flower and nodded, uncertain where she was going with this.

'Has a tendency to hang its head.'

She sniffed, adding, 'As I believe some of my ministers should!'

She turned abruptly, and he faltered under her keenly penetrating gaze.

'It would appear certain Treasury ministers have wilfully put our nation, and themselves, into grave danger with their short-sightedness.'

Elizabeth tutted. Her father had always spoken very highly of D, and she in turn, had come to regard him with genuine affection. She had assumed he was continuing his sterling work. Now she regretted not keeping a closer eye on him. The recently uncovered news of how D9 had been continually short-changed had grieved her.

Long ago, when she had been a child, D had shielded her little family after alerting them as to the true provenance of the predatory, insectlike creature that had called itself Wallis.

A breeze sprang up, and she folded her arms against the sudden chill. Turning back to regard the scattered creamy petals of *Peace* being carried away on the wind, she observed quietly, 'I cannot be seen to influence policy.'

'Ma'am.'

'However, if recent events alone have not already proven the urgent necessity for D9 to be fully funded, there is further evidence within the archives at Windsor.'

The aide nodded, he had an update, but he hesitated, the Queen had not finished. 'And if *that* is not enough, there is more at Glamis. *Compelling* arguments for the continuing support of D's organisation.'

She took another sniff of the red rose's deep perfume, and continued. 'Logic would dictate further funding should not be an issue, but ministers are not just short-sighted, they are apt to be short-*minded*. When this present fuss dies down, they will forget, and grow complacent again.'

'Ma'am. I am given to understand D9 is to be fully supported in all their future endeavours.'

'I am very glad to hear it, but I will be watching these matters far more closely from now on.'

85

Watkin was getting quite adept. He hopped along on his crutches, confidently weaving between the poles of scaffolding that had been a feature of the damaged Houses of Parliament for the last week or two.

All the bit-part players who had sought to make his life difficult, his ex-colleagues, his old boss Alice Reidy, his bossy sister Kate and her husband, the insufferable Rhodri, could all go and whistle. His employment problems had been abruptly resolved. Had he been able to put both feet down, there would have been a spring in his step.

Leaning against the terrace wall, he stared down into the dark green water; remembering the many scattered meta wings that had lapped at its margins, like a rainbow petrol spill, following the Battle of Westminster.

A local team of Watchers had been summoned and had taken to the water in canoes and inflatables, and in a night-long operation, every wing had been painstakingly collected. And destroyed.

Now Watkin watched intently as a heavy chain was pulled slowly from the depths. It snapped taught, and a few moments later the dripping carcass of Sam's wrecked helicopter broke the surface as it was hauled up from the cloying mud of the Thames.

The crane operator expertly swung the smashed

cockpit and fuselage clear of the water, and gently laid it down on the broad, steel deck of the crane boat. Another man in yellow waterproofs hopped across from the wheelhouse, and peered into the helicopter's interior. Then, whilst the crane operator held the craft steady, he crawled inside the mangled fuselage. For a full twenty minutes he searched, meticulously checking the interior.

Watkin gave him another five minutes before reaching inside his jacket for his mobile. By now the man had clambered back out of the wreck and was shaking his head at someone else in the wheelhouse. Watkin didn't have to call the salvage operator to know the search had been unsuccessful.

He made a call anyway; to Violet, to relay the unhappy news.

High above, from his vantage point behind a tall window in the Palace of Westminster, D scrutinised Watkin's body language. He finished his call, his drooping shoulders echoing his disappointment, and then momentarily struggled to put his phone away, hampered by the bouquet under his arm. Then he took to his crutches and left the scene. 'Give my regards to Violet,' D murmured under his breath.

'He will see you now,' the secretary announced. D cracked his neck loudly before following her into a book lined study.

The Gatekeeper greeted D with an air of forced bonhomie. D eyed him drily. This was a creature as treacherous as Jockey. More so if anything, at least poor lost Jockey had his motivations, his demons. The Gatekeeper was the kind of human who was capable of far worse acts, for far lesser reasons. He'd rip up any rule book, and commit any sin, if it only promised to further his career.

After their missed 'meeting without coffee,' - ministry-speak for his appointed dressing-down, D now sat through the Gatekeeper's non-apology. It was a cunningly worded exercise in cynicism, and he barely listened to it. Only one thing piqued his interest; the revised funding offer. D was not inclined to accept this either.

He rose to go.

He had never seen a suit melt so quickly. Within seconds a far more substantial proposal had been graciously offered for approval.

D eyed The Gatekeeper cooly. He had long overstepped the mark as far as D was concerned, but seeking to bargain with resources that had already been awarded to D9 was adding insult to injury. His lives-long familiarity with the ways of humans told D that the chances were that the Gatekeeper was still holding out, clinging to what little power he had left, but D knew there would be no more offered for now, and he had got as much out of the man as he could that day. There would be other days, and the money currently on offer would go a long way. Under careful stewardship.

Violet would accept the role of Quartermaster from her hospital bed. D's leverage would be the treasure he would rescue that night, under the cover of darkness, from the depths of the Thames.

He sighed at the thought of wild swimming in lightly silvered water, but with Baby down there at least he would be free from any aquid attention. He imagined her reaction. Eyes shining, cradling Baby once again; Violet would agree to anything.

The Gatekeeper misread the smile playing around D's lips as gratitude. He was mistaken. D took his leave, and rang Aled and Andrea, forewarning them that they were going to be extremely busy.

After all, he knew how seriously Violet could shop.

85

The disaster that had befallen London had been overshadowed by further economic woes for the entire country. The conspiracy theorists had so much grist for their rumour mills that their multiple contradictions quickly ground any grains of pure truth down into useless dust.

YouTube had been hit with a spate of spoof videos presented as fact, and some surrealist art installation, involving people falling to the ground and lying posed in public places, had been misreported as *actual events*.

With the eyes of the world temporarily turned away, it appeared the inhabitants of London had been displaying a variety of extreme behaviours.

American observers shook their heads with knowing smiles. They had long suspected that beneath their clenched hair and straight laced image, all Brits were just waiting for the opportunity to shed their repressions, and spring into some outrageous act worthy of a Monty Python routine.

Sketchy news reports about children camping out on the roof of The Houses of Parliament, were linked to earlier demonstrations, carried out by members of an unofficial organisation calling itself 'Fathers For Justice.' Eye witnesses had reported that a lot of the kids had been in fancy dress, like the fathers.

As all modern digital-image gathering equipment is now meta-dampened, no one could produce a single picture on camera, or mobile phone, so word of mouth was the only source material, and that was soon distorted by inaccurate repetition.

Whatever had happened, the gang of kids had dispersed following another insect attack, similar to the one that had happened at Charlecote. No children were recorded amongst the casualties, of which there had been fewer than half-a-dozen. Once again wasps became the focus of a hate campaign, and helpfully took the eyes of the world away from the suggestion of any other cause.

It was reported that a famous, if somewhat overweight and unfit, newsman had suffered a heart attack. Possibly when two peers of the realm had flung themselves to their deaths, in a double suicide, in front of him.

Although their motive was much speculated upon, under threat of legal action not a single word of the sordid stories that were being circulated ever made it to print, and 'dire financial circumstances' were promoted as the most obvious catalyst for this tragedy.

Other deaths in that place, and at that time, failed to make the news, including that of an ex-soldier who had got drunk and fallen into the river. Some three dozen bodies are pulled from the Thames every year and Jockey was recorded as just another one.

His funeral had been attended by his father and older brothers, and whilst they genuinely mourned him, they all knew the real Jockey had never come back from his near-drowning years ago. They had been simply marking time, waiting for him to self-destruct ever since.

London had braced itself for the aftershocks from the bizarre, 'once in a millennia,' seismic event that had cut the capital off from the rest of the world for several hours, toppled Underground trains, and even flooded part of the system - but none had come, yet.

The extraordinary weather event that had coincided with this other natural disaster, and had contributed to the Underground flood, had been followed by one of the wettest summers on record. The rain had fallen for weeks. Previously parched, London and the Home Counties had seen severe incidences of flooding that had sent insurance costs rocketing up again.

Now, for the first time in many days, the sun shone brilliantly on the recently rain-washed streets, steam rose from the pavements, and the new day felt fresh and full of possibilities. The core members of the revitalised department were having an alfresco breakfast meeting at one of the many unofficial D9 'offices.'

This one was a kerbside café. A small boy, riding past on a gleaming, silver bicycle, looked expectantly across at D and his party. D inclined his head a few degrees, and Beeny hopped his new bike expertly up onto the kerb. Staring into the middle distance, D apparently took no notice of the kid on the bike riding past his chair.

Anyone watching would not have detected the subtle exchange. Beeny discreetly pocketed the folded note, and raced off. Watkin watched him go.

'Is that the kid?'

'Who saved our lives? Yes.'

D9's newest recruit, Dylan Watkin was celebrating,

with a latte, the start of his first full day without a cast on his ankle.

D resumed sharing the message he'd received by more conventional means earlier that morning. He turned the brightly coloured postcard over, and read aloud.

Thanks for keeping him safe. Having yet another second honeymoon. Bit tipsy! Weather is here, wish you were lovely. Allegra.

'Class!' Violet grinned.

'Before we all get too self-congratulatory, it's business as usual. Recent, pressing events, have led to much else being neglected. There's an overwhelming amount of work still to be done.'

'We're facing multiple public enquiries. More activity has been reported around Clocaenog, the watchers updates need collating, and there's this ongoing case of the missing hikers...'

D stopped rattling off his list like scatter-fire, and took a quick gulp of coffee before continuing with the next items.

'You're off to Llangollen?'

Violet nodded and checked her watch, 'In just

under an hour.'

D turned to Watkin.

'I need your report on Rhys and Gnat's new location, and how Cayden's settling in.'

Watkin didn't answer.

'Watkin?'

Dylan Watkin was distracted, staring at something. A brightly decorated hippy campervan, much like Diamond's old one, was approaching.

They all followed his gaze. The campervan had been hooked up to a large chain, and was being towed away, nose in the air, by a breakdown-truck. There was something about it being dragged along, in such a comically undignified manner that made Violet giggle.

As it retreated from view, they all turned to read the legend that had been hand painted across the van's broad rump

'Powered by fairy dust.'

Even D laughed.

EPILOGUE

In the back yard of a terraced house in Acton, there had been a titanic struggle. Mr. Snuffles had fought hard when, what had been a simple opportunity for a tasty snack, had become a fight for his life.

The spindly, long-legged thing, with the body as big as a hare, had fought hard. It had hissed and spat at him, but Mr. Snuffles had given as good as he had got.

His thick fur had repelled the nasty chips of flint the thing had fired at him, and he'd grabbed it by one leg, and dragged the frenzied, furiously struggling creature backwards, through the cat flap.

Now he held it at bay, in a corner of the kitchen. Mr. Snuffles played with his victim for a while, enticing it to escape, before each time dragging it back with an accurate paw. But it was limping, fatally damaged in the encounter, and just not making the kind of half-decent effort Mr. Snuffles expected of his prey.

He sighed, and patted it, but it just crawled a few pitiful steps. Like its odd green blood, the fun was rapidly

F.R.MAHER

leaking out of this game. Mr. Snuffles regarded it, his head on one side, his huge yellow eyes taking in every detail.

Stretched out, it was almost three times as long as he was. Not a patient cat, Mr. Snuffles grew bored. He batted it, quite gently he thought, but the creature collapsed, and folded in on itself, like a crushed spider.

Mr. Snuffles wrinkled his nose, and bit into it.

Not bad. Hint of insect.

The creature that had moved as fast as a mouse tasted really quite spidery. It reminded him of the things he'd feasted upon in the farm fields when he'd been a younger cat, years before he'd been brought to the grey city.

Mr. Snuffles took another mouthful from the satisfyingly crunchy wing, his fur streaked with pinky-green dust.

Mrs. Caldicott bustled in to make her bedtime cocoa. She took one look at Mr. Snuffles, who was chewing on what appeared to be an enormous insect-wing, screamed, and fled her kitchen.

THE END

ABOUT THE AUTHOR

F.R.Maher began reading at the age of three and quickly outgrew childrens' books. At a village jumble sale as a discerning eight year old, the fortunate find of a collection of short stories by H.P Lovecraft was a turning point, and an early education in just how thrilling story-telling can be.

She grew up wanting to be an author, then got sidetracked by the tricky business of actually making a living.
Having been hijacked into being an artist, lecturer and film maker, she finally returned to her first love, writing.

The Last Changeling is an escape from the close confines of film budgets and her celebration of the kind of special effects no amount of money can buy - those created in the mind of the reader.

www.thelastchangeling.com

facebook.com/LastChangeling

Printed in Great Britain
by Amazon.co.uk, Ltd.,
Marston Gate.